THE
MAGYAR CIPHER MURDERS

EUGENE JAMES

Trafford
PUBLISHING

Disclaimer:

Lawyers make liars of every writer in the legalistic pro forma ritual about how stories are made…who and what is, or was, used or referred to or hinted at in their books. I suppose I'm obliged to take part in this exercise. I'll go this far -- This is a work of fiction. Save for a few well known public figures, the characters are purely creations of the writer. Some of the events and settings, however, are real enough.

THE BLACK FRIDAY GAMBIT

- Book 2 of the series - coming soon

About the Author

First he was a commercial fisherman, then a boat builder, tow boater (mate and engineer) and, later, worked as a naval architect and mechanical designer. He now writes full time from his home in Campbell River B.C. He draws from his own history and that of friends and 'people observed' for the stuff of his stories. If you want to know more, read his books. He's in there somewhere.

Acknowledgments and many thanks to:
Clint and Donna (who nagged it into existence)
Reagan and Kelly for patience and support
Jan DeGrass and her Gibson's workshop gang
Marcy and Pauline, my captive fan club
Joe Takacs for invaluable Hungarian stuff
Deb White for her careful reading and valuable insights
A certain Iron Butterfly who knows why she's here

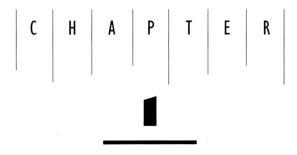

C H A P T E R

1

October 7th, 1957

He fell with a rush that ended with a chopped-off cry and the sickening sound of flesh impacting concrete. I staggered back against the masonry wall, stunned. He'd hit the pavement four feet from me. I waited for my heart to slow. And shivered with delayed fear. Seconds passed – they felt like minutes – before I could make myself lean over the dead man. He'd landed on his back, arms outflung. The face was a battered pulp.

My God. It was Sandy Kovacs.

I closed his eyes.

Fine rain misted up from the harbor, leaching his blood in a jagged trickle into the sidewalk gutter. *Blue Suede Shoes* echoed between buildings from a passing Olds hardtop.

The Marine Building's main doors were unlocked and I stepped inside. The night security guard wasn't at his desk. After several minutes, I pulled myself together and used his phone. I needed three attempts to dial the numbers.

I was staring at Kovacs' ruined body, trying to make sense of his death when the police and ambulance and fire-rescue trucks (with their sirens and flashing lights) converged on the scene.

The Marine Building has a shallow entrance arch two stories high, framed in carved granite. Above the doors, half a dozen art deco embossed geese fly a confused migration, each half going in opposite directions. Like my confused brain.

A uniformed cop pushed me into the archway, not quite out of the rain, and told me to wait. Wait for what? For someone to ask me about Sandy? I had no answers. Why had he died? Would he be dead if I'd been on time? What the hell had made him do it?

A detective went through the dead man's pockets, riffling through a wallet and calling out the amount of money and other contents while a uniformed officer recorded the items in a notebook. Twenty-three dollars. Driver's license. Business cards. Some photos. Other pockets were exhumed and their contents placed in plastic bags. A police photographer took a dozen flash pictures and a chalk line was drawn around the sprawled figure. Then somebody covered him with a piece of orange tarpaulin.

Soon after that a small crowd pushed at the police barriers. Reporters and photographers badgered me. *"Did you see him fall?"* *"Were you close when he hit?"* Their questions broke into my mental funk but did nothing to dispel it. I shook my head and they eventually gave up, but not before blinding me with their flash cameras.

Police, plain clothes and uniformed, moved in and out of the building measuring things, making notes, cracking wise and asking after each other's kids and who was going to win the hockey game. Their callous armor helped them deal with violent death. My lack of it was one reason I hadn't stayed in the cop business.

The police ignored me until, after half an hour, a rumpled cliché of a detective, straight out of a Philip Marlowe mystery, stopped in front of me and said, "You the witness?" He pointed at me with an unlit cigar.

"Yes."

"Sergeant McRae, Vancouver PD. You are?"

"Hank Sutter."

"That's Henry Sutter, I suppose?"

I nodded.

McRae wrote something in his notebook, then looked up at me. "Address?"

"I live aboard the tug *Solange Picard*. Down there." I pointed in the direction of Picard and Son's offices and dock, four blocks west along the waterfront road.

"You don't look like a tow boater."

"Because I'm wearing a suit? We don't all drag our knuckles."

"Forget it. What position you play?"

"Play?"

"Linebacker? Guard? You got the size and the look."

I've never understood rabid sports fans. "Mate and salvage master," I said.

"Lions coulda used you, the other night," he said. "Where were you when the guy hit the pavement?"

"Right under him. There." I pointed.

"Nearly bought it yourself, huh? You didn't look up before he hit? Maybe hear something?"

I shook my head. "I looked up after."

"What were you doing here?"

"Going to his office to meet him. On business."

"You knew the guy?"

I nodded. "Sandor Kovacs. I knew him slightly. He worked for my lawyer."

I would never get to know him now and I felt a twinge of regret at that. Sandy Kovacs had been young, with his life and future ahead of him.

McRae studied me in silence. Waiting.

"I met him last Friday," I said.

"That's Friday the fourth?"

"Yes."

McRae scribbled in his notebook. "Take your time and tell me about it," he said.

So I told him.

*

My boss, Henri Picard Jr., in one of his famous, rambling, incomprehensible memos, had dropped a bomb on us. The Federal Search and Rescue Standby Subsidy was ending, and therefore the *Solange Picard* would be sold for scrap at the year's end.

Sputnik and I went into orbit that same day, but I'd landed in Picard's office.

"Mr. Picard won't see anyone today," Jeanie had said. "He is in conference with the company lawyers."

"What's he doing? Going bankrupt?"

"Hank, I can't tell you anything. You know that." But her eyes said a great deal and we'd all heard the rumors.

Some firm of consulting bean counters had recommended scrapping the *Solange*. It mattered nothing to Junior that she was the flagship of his late father's fleet, that she carried his mother's name. Steam pots were inefficient and required larger crews than diesel boats. The *Solange* was far too powerful for log towing unless the logs were in Davis rafts, in fact too big for anything but a major salvage operation, trans-ocean towing or ice breaking, which is what she'd been designed for, just after the First World War. I loved that grand old ship.

But the world doesn't listen to lovers any more. It listens to bean counters.

And lawyers.

I knew that the only way to fight lawyers was with other lawyers. Beyond that I hadn't thought when I called Jake Feldman for an appointment. Feldman was married to my mother's cousin Ella, the wealthy fragment of my scattered tribe that rarely spoke to our fragment. Feldman's schedule was frantic, he said, but he would squeeze me in at the end of his working day.

The law offices of Feldman, Tauber, Slibowichs and Brown, on the nineteenth floor of the Marine Building, looked out on a view of Vancouver harbor and the North Shore mountains that must have added digits to the rent. Secretaries trained to speak in reverent, hushed tones herded me across carpets three inches thick and into his sanctum as if I were somebody important. Evidently there was money in marine law.

"I'm asking Sandy Kovacs to sit in on this, Hank," Feldman said, after the mandatory exchange of family news. "He'll be assisting with whatever your problem is. Just what is the problem, by the way?"

Kovacs and I exchanged nods. In sharp contrast to Jake Feldman's shiny baldness and expansive form, Kovacs was compact and athletic, with thick black hair and a matching moustache. I figured him for one of the city's horde of newly arrived Hungarian refugees and I wasn't long confirming that. Slave labor for my wealthy cousin-in-law.

I launched into my scheme for saving the *Solange Picard*. Voiced out loud, it sounded emotional and completely idiotic but nobody laughed. Feldman looked relieved that I hadn't murdered somebody.

"Form your own company. Then out-bid the scrap dealers," he said, over steepled fingers. "What you do with your new toy after that is your business." Did lawyers actually get money for advice like that? But I bit my tongue and said, "You think that could work?"

"Why not?"

"Because Junior, I mean Picard, would strip the ship of her outfit first. I'd get nothing but an empty shell."

"Ah. There's that. I take it Picard doesn't want you as competition with a ship he sold you."

"So he's said."

"There may be a way around that problem. Picard's is a public company?"

"Yes but sixty percent of the shares are held by the Picard family. I bought a few shares so I could go to the next stockholder's meeting. Whenever they call it."

"Good move. Your first step is to incorporate."

"So I should become Sutter Salvage and Navigation?"

"That the name you're going with?"

"Good as any, I guess."

"Sandy will start the process Monday morning. He'll get in touch when he needs you."

Kovacs looked up from his notebook. "You are a man of passion, Mr. Sutter," he said.

"You mean I'm a romantic?"

"Perhaps, but where would the world be without its romantics? You make this old ship sound worth the fight." He smiled. He seemed quietly competent. More so than my august relative.

The meeting had broken up, leaving me with the eerie feeling that I'd just spent a large bundle of money I didn't have.

*

McRae said, "Was it Kovacs that asked for the meeting this evening?"

I nodded.

"At what time?"

"Eight. He called me on the dockside phone at the tug this morning. He needed me for signatures. I was late. If I hadn't been--"

"How late?"

"Ten minutes."

"Time of his death was, what? Eight-ten?"

"That would be close. I didn't look at my watch."

"I take it you walked up from your ship?"

"That's right. You can see her stack from here." I pointed. Coal Harbor, a narrow arm of Vancouver's vast harbor, is tucked between Stanley Park and the West End. It was jammed with yachts and fishing boats. The *Solange* was by far the biggest ship there.

"What was Mr. Kovacs' state of mind on Friday?"

"He seemed fine. Confident and businesslike. Feldman did most of the talking."

"One of those refugees from last year's fracas in Budapest, was he?"

"So I believe. We didn't discuss it."

"Then he can't be a lawyer. They're making them do their law schooling over again to work here. Same with their doctors and all of their professionals."

"Poor buggers," I said. "I think he was just doing Jake's leg work."

"You on first-name terms with Feldman?"

"He's a relative," I explained.

"Did Kovacs have family here?"

"I'm not sure."

But I was sure. I'd seen the color photo of a lovely young woman on Kovacs' desk. The same sleek, blue-black hair in shoulder-length brackets framed a fine-boned version of Kovacs' features. The resemblance was unmistakable. "A sister, I think. Jake would know."

"One of my officers has gone to find Feldman. He's at some Conservative Party fund-raiser." McRae jerked a thumb in the direction of the Vancouver Hotel a few blocks up Burrard Street. "Meanwhile, I'd appreciate it if you could remain here for a while. We may need to talk to you after we find Feldman and get access to his office."

"Did he jump from there?"

"We aren't sure. There's a deck at the nineteenth floor with access from Feldman's office. It was either from there or the roof."

"I see. Who will tell his sister?"

"Probably best if Feldman does that."

I looked at the floodlit tarp covering what had been Sandy Kovacs. A trickle of blackish blood eluded the rain to collect in the little dimples in the concrete sidewalk. "This doesn't make sense," I said.

"Why not?"

"Why would he call me to a meeting and then jump? Surely a person intent on suicide would do it alone?"

"God knows. It isn't exactly a rational act."

"Will she have to make a formal identification?"

"Feldman can do that. Or you. Unless I'm mistaken, you've seen death before."

"Not since Korea. And never that close."

"A note from our switchboard says you called in the information. That right?"

"Yes. I couldn't find the building security guard. He's back now, I see."

"Probably in the crapper."

A plain-clothes officer parked a squad car facing the wrong way at the curb, got out and approached McRae.

"What is it, Jamie?" McRae said.

"Mr. Feldman telephoned the victim's sister from the hotel. I would have stopped him if I'd known who he was calling. Sorry, Mac."

"Shit! The man's an idiot. Not your fault, Jamie. Damned if I want her seeing her brother like this, though."

"Sergeant? Mr. Feldman is..." He nodded in the direction of the squad car. I made out Feldman's pasty round face in the darkened interior. He looked green.

"Good. He probably heard me," McRae muttered.

Feldman didn't seem anxious to join us.

A Black-Top Cab dropped a fare at the Hastings and Burrard corner and a moment later I was aware of a slight figure in a long raincoat standing beside me. "Someone please tell me what has happened?" she said in a soft contralto.

"Who are you, Miss?" McRae asked.

"I am Tatiana Kovacs."

"You are the sister of Sandor Kovacs?"

She nodded.

"I'm afraid there has been a terrible--"

"He is dead?" she interrupted, pointing at the obscene lump under the tarp.

"Yes, Miss," McRae said reluctantly. "I'm very sorry."

"I must see." She moved towards the tarp.

"I'd rather you didn't look, Miss."

"It is necessary."

"There's no need for you to make an identification. Other people can do that." McRae looked at me as if I might bail him out but all I could offer was a shrug.

"It is necessary for my anger. Against the men who killed my brother."

"You think he was murdered?" McRae said. He looked at me as if he was afraid the woman was about to have some kind of hysterics. He wrote something in his notebook, then said, "Come into the building lobby, out of the rain. Then tell me why you think he was murdered."

"First I will look." She planted herself, foursquare, in front of the tarp. She didn't seem to be crying, though her face was wet. It might have been just the rain.

McRae shrugged, then gestured to a uniformed officer. He stepped forward and lifted a corner of the orange death shroud.

Tatiana Kovacs stooped over her brother's body, her lips moving in silent prayer. She reached out and touched his hand, then stood and crossed herself. She nodded her thanks to the officer and turned away, one trembling hand over her eyes. I thought I saw a quivering shoulder but I could have been wrong. This subdued grieving wasn't what I'd have expected from a sister.

McRae seemed to be of the same opinion. "You spoke of men who killed him, Miss Kovacs. Who, exactly?"

"I don't know. He wouldn't talk about his work but I have been telling him he was being followed for weeks. In the last few days he admitted I was right."

"You feel this was connected with his work?"

"What else? He knew few people here. He had no enemies."

"About this following, did he notify police?"

"Why would he? You would do nothing."

"You don't know that, Miss."

"You want me to believe police are better here than in my homeland?"

McRae squirmed. "What was your brother's state of mind when you last spoke with him? Had he received any bad news? Some family tragedy, perhaps?"

"He and I are -- were -- all that is left of our family. He was full of fun and joking, as always. Why do you ask?" McRae raised a hand. "A moment, Miss. When were you last with him?"

"At dinner, a few hours ago. At the Devonshire."

"I see. And he was followed tonight?"

"Yes. They sat two tables away. They paid their bill early and then waited to leave until Sandy left."

"Two men?"

She nodded.

"Had you seen them before?"

"Not those two, but others."

"Could you identify them from photos?"

"I don't know. Probably."

"Could you describe them?"

"Yes."

"Go ahead, then."

"Well dressed, business suits, ties. The younger man was about thirty. The other, mm, forty-five.

"Heights?"

"The younger man was about one hundred seventy-five centimeters. What is that in your inches?" She turned to look at me, for some reason.

I didn't want her to look away. Or to find me lacking. I thanked the fates for my year in Germany and said, "Five nine, near enough."

She gave me a tiny nod and continued. "He was slim with blond curly hair. The other was ten centimeters taller and heavier. Darker with gray over the ears, and balding. He wore glasses. Neither were Europeans."

McRae finished his note-writing. "Not Europeans?"

"From their table manners. Very Canadian."

McRae looked up sharply, a question in his expression.

"It is the way Canadians, and Americans, use forks."

"I see," McRae said. "I must tell you, Miss Kovacs, there was a suicide note. It was addressed to `Tats.' I presume that is you?"

Her eyes went wide. "That is not possible," she said in a near-whisper. "Show me this note."

McRae opened a leather file case and produced a sheet of note paper enclosed in plastic. "You'll have to read it through the plastic, I'm afraid. We've gotta check it for prints."

She read slowly, then read it again. Her face seemed frozen. "No. No, no, no. This was not by Sandy," she said at last.

"Not his writing?"

"Like his writing. But not his words. And it is in English. Sandy would never say such things to me in English."

"I know this is difficult, Miss, but why not? Why not in English?"

"Sandy's English was not so good as mine. He did not study English in school, as I did, so he has been learning only for a year. I have been coaching him. There are words he didn't know…and words he would never write to me."

"Why not, Miss Kovacs?"

"Whoever wrote this assumed we were sweethearts. Lovers. He didn't know we were brother and sister. Where did you find this letter?"

"It was in his jacket pocket."

"Crumpled like this?"

"Yes. He seems to have dashed it off in a hurry."

She locked stares with McRae, disbelief and anger in her expression. McRae lifted open hands in a helpless shrug and turned away, scribbling again in his notebook.

She turned to me. "You are police?"

"No, Miss Kovacs. I was meeting your brother tonight on business."

"You are Mr. Sutter? My brother spoke of you."

"He did? We only met on Friday." We'd probably exchanged fifty words, at most. I glanced at McRae who was busy with his notes. I wasn't sure he'd caught the fact that Kovacs had spoken of our planned meeting to his sister only hours before his death.

"Sandy had good impression. What is your first name, Mr. Sutter?"

"Hank. Hank Sutter."

"Hank is, mm, nick-name for Henry, yes?"

I nodded.

"Then you call me Tats, not Miss. Sandy said you were tall but he didn't say you were a monster."

"Is that all he said? I was tall?"

"He thought I should meet you. Sandy was, mm, frustrated people-matcher?"

"Match-maker?"

"Yes. Always trying to marry me off. So now I have met you. Why did he think I should?"

"I'm sure I don't know, but I'd be happy if you'd allow me to see you home, Tats," I said.

She searched my face. Looking for what? Wide dark eyes too big for her face, both stoic and somehow starkly tragic. All planes and angles, and yet…beautiful. "I will not be good company," she said.

"We will provide a car for you, Miss Kovacs," McRae said.

"No," she said, flatly. "I need to talk to someone. Police are no good for that."

McRae said, "I'll need your address and phone number, Miss. We'll set up a picture ID session for you. Could you do that in the morning?"

She shrugged, then nodded.

"And I'll need to talk to you again, Sutter. Don't leave town."

I explained the facts of life to Sergeant McRae about our search and rescue standby contract. We compromised. I would notify his office at once if we were called out. He wouldn't beach me. Tatiana handed him a business card with her home address on the back.

"You will find me, one place or other," she said.

"A dance academy?" McRae's eyebrows climbed his forehead as he read.

"Why not? I am a dancer."

"Classical dance? You are a ballerina?"

"I *knew* you would figure out," she said with a tiny smile. McRae winced as she turned back to me.

I got my first glimpse of the woman under the raincoat. She was in dance practice gear; black leotards with fluffy purple knee warmers and a ragged, gray, turtleneck sweater. Somebody had loaned her a pair of men's galoshes which she'd put on over her ballet slippers. Slim, taut figure with long legs. "I was rehearsing," she explained, in response to my stare.

"Rehearsing what?" I asked.

"A bewitched swan princess."

"Oh?" But she didn't explain any more.

"The rain has stopped so we can walk. My place is not far. It is near the Stanley Park," she said.

CHAPTER

2

Burrard climbs gently for a few blocks south from the harbor and the Marine Building, up to Georgia Street. Georgia is the east-west spine of the peninsula that is Vancouver's downtown core.

I turned left on Georgia and Tats came to an abrupt stop. "Where are you taking me? I live that way." She pointed west, behind us.

"I think you need a drink. I know I do. The Cavalier is only a block." The Cavalier Grill, in the hotel Georgia, was one of about eight bars in the city established since the liquor laws were eased. More were promised soon but we no longer had to drink in bottle clubs.

"A bar?"

"It's nice. Not like a bar at all."

"Please. I do not want to drink. Just take me home."

So I took her two blocks farther south, to Robson, before turning west. We might find a coffee shop open at this hour on "Robson Strasse." I found myself stretching to keep up with Tats, a new experience for me.

"What is your work, Mr Sutter she asked, after a block of silence.

"Hank. Please. I'm mate and salvage master on a large tug."

"Not captain? Why not?"

"I have a master's ticket but you don't get to be skipper of a tug like the *Solange Picard* without company seniority." I was the de facto master of the *Solange* since O'Conner would be at least another three months drying out, this time. Junior Picard, cheapness being his credo, hadn't hired a replacement. But Mick O'Conner, with thirty years of service, was the master of record.

"You said salvage master. What is that?"

"I do the diving and underwater welding. Place collision mats, pump lines, stuff like that. Not very interesting. And I take a watch as mate." I was both relieved and alarmed that she didn't want to talk about her brother's death. Relieved because I'm not good at dealing with other people's grief. Alarmed because my instincts told me she was, somehow, containing her emotions out of some imagined obligation to seem "normal." And I knew she had to let go.

She was full of small talk and a vivacious, bantering manner that I knew was a façade and a shaky one at that. She seemed to have decided the subject of our conversation would be me.

"Ah! You are frog monster!"

"Frog? Oh you mean frogman? No. I do hard-suit diving. I can do scuba but we often have to go too deep for that."

"This makes much muscle. Yes?" She probed my bicep painfully. "Too much for dancer."

"I don't think you'd ever make a dancer out of me. Except maybe waltzes or whatever."

"So? Maybe a tango?"

"I'll try anything, if you teach."

"I teach. And what is your family? You are from Vancouver?"

"One brother, back east in the air force, and a sister here in Vancouver. Dad is a retired sea captain. He's over in the Gulf Islands with mother on the family farm. And yes, we were all born here."

"Wonderful! Everybody I meet so far seems to be born someplace else."

"The city has grown tremendously since the war. And the prairie snow-birds have discovered our climate."

"And then we Hungarians land on you."

"There's room."

"Ah, such room!" She was silent for a moment "Canada treated us very well," she said, seriously. "What they did for our refugees is, mm, how do you say it? Unprecedent?"

I had no answer. It was a matter of pride that Ottawa, for once, did the right thing at the right time. And then the people who'd done it lost the election to John Diefenbaker and his Tory penny-pinchers. Who had, among other things, killed the search and rescue subsidy that meant life to my ship.

"You gave Sergeant McRae a card from a dance academy. Are you a teacher? Or do you attend classes?"

"Both. All dancers need somebody to crack whip. Or we get lazy and technique suffers. I help with teaching the young ones."

"So you are a professional dancer?"

"You mean do I get paid? Sometimes, when the academy has money."

"What are you rehearsing? A new show?"

"A very old show. The academy does a recital next week. We do scenes from *Swan Lake*. I dance the enchanted swan princess and her rival."

"Will you be able to go on with it?"

She turned away for a moment, then back. "Yes. I must."

"I'd like to see that."

"This interests you? Swan Lake is old-fashioned fairy tale. But demanding of dancers. Our ballet master wants to show us off."

The Neapolitan Cafe, on the south side of Robson near Thurlow, was open, though it had few customers. I steered her inside. The night air was cold. She was lightly dressed and I didn't want to be responsible for a case of pneumonia. And I sensed, too, a gradual unbending of her stiffness, a crumbling of the façade. She made me think of a lost doe pretending to be a fearsome buck and, for some reason probably connected with biology, she mattered very much to me.

I ordered hot chocolate and donuts for both of us.

Tats gazed around in wide-eyed wonder. The walls and ceiling were a fresco of the Tuscany hills, complete with olive groves and peasants leading donkey carts, all in shades of brown and yellow. What it was doing on the ceiling of a place that called itself "Neapolitan," I was afraid to ask. The portly proprietor seemed so pleased that Tats had noticed the scene that I felt sure he'd painted the disaster himself.

She noted my bemused expression and said, "What?"

"I was thinking of Michelangelo, lying on his back painting the ceiling of the Sistine Chapel. His method, not the result."

"Oh dear. It is possible he did it that way?" She laughed, a sort of strangled giggle. The proprietor beamed in delight.

My God she was beautiful. Pale alabaster complexion contrasted sharply with blue-black, straight, shoulder-length hair. Black unplucked brows. High cheekbones and a straight nose. I didn't think she wore makeup. Her dark eyes were shadowed and uneasy. She wouldn't hold my gaze but looked away quickly, as if I might discover something best not found.

"You don't have to do this," she said, staring straight ahead.

"Do what?"

"Look after me this way."

"Yes I do."

"Why?" She turned to look at me.

I thought about her question. Why had I asked to walk her home? I wasn't sure I knew. I said "Because I want to."

"That is no answer."

"No. I suppose it isn't. Perhaps it's because you are alone. No one should have to grieve alone."

She searched my face, then looked away again. "That is a great kindness, to share a stranger's grief. I have met few men who would do that."

"But I don't grieve well."

"So? I think I understand why Sandy thought we should meet."

I said, "Tell me about your brother. You came here together?" I knew she would have to talk her tragedy through. I wasn't sure she was ready for that yet but I had to give her the opening.

After a moment, she nodded. "Last year, from Vienna."

"How did Sandy get started with Feldman?"

"My big brother was doing his law studies again. He was lawyer in Hungary but not here," she said.

"So I've heard. That sounds rough."

She shrugged. "You have different legal system and Sandy understood that. Mr Feldman talked to Law Society, to offer a position. Sandy was best candidate. Mr Feldman gave him work like legal secretary, only he did investigations, also, and filed court papers and helped with legal research. Pay was not much but that didn't matter. Sandy knew he would be lawyer again."

"He wasn't depressed over having to study again for his profession?"

"No. Sandy had much energy and much enthusiasm for our new country."

"So he studied part time and worked part time?"

"He did both full time. He worked too hard."

"And somebody was following him? Have you any idea why?"

"We make progress. You do not imply I am seeing things, like that policeman."

"Tatiana, this is Canada, not iron-curtain Europe. Who could be following him? You sure it wasn't you they were following?"

"You flatter me." She flashed me a brief smile. "But as I told that policeman, they paid their bill early and then one of them copied the amount down in a little notebook. Then they waited until Sandy left."

"Were there other times? Other people you saw?"

"Sometimes it was just a feeling of being watched. Twice before tonight I saw men who seemed to follow."

"But never the same men?"

"No."

Was it paranoia? Or was it real? I caught myself studying a young couple entering the restaurant. Harmless. A guy and his girlfriend on their way home from an early movie.

Or maybe not. They did seem to notice Tats.

Hell, everybody noticed her. Stop it, Sutter.

I said, "Did you and Sandy live together?"

"We did at first, when we came here. But he couldn't stand me, so after his first payday he found his own place."

"Did you fight?"

"Not fight, really. He is – was, too sweet for fighting with. But he hated my stereo and classical music. Sandy liked jazz." She gave a jazzy wriggle to demonstrate. "Also, I am lousy cook," she added. She washed down her donut with the last of her hot chocolate. "I am ready," she said.

The causeway leading to the Lion's Gate Bridge, and dividing Stanley Park, takes off from the end of Georgia Street about ten long blocks west of Burrard. Maybe far enough that I could learn a little about this enigmatic beauty if I could keep her talking. She'd said little about herself, not that I was concerned about her pedigree. She'd completely bewitched me.

I did learn a little about her, but only a little.

She'd been a principal dancer for the Hungarian National Ballet in Budapest. Not Prima Ballerina, she corrected me, but a soloist and not far off that. She had been on a provincial tour with a troupe of the company and out of the capital when the revolution broke out. Everyone was excited and most of the dancers, especially the men, wanted to be back in Budapest where all the action seemed to be. They'd cut their tour short and returned, arriving just in time to meet the Red Army and its tanks.

Nine dancers, Tats included, had made the trek west to the Austrian border and freedom, along with something like two hundred thousand defeated revolutionaries, their families and hangers-on. At first the Austrians put them up in public buildings, schools, even an old castle, and she'd searched frantically for her brother and an aunt, with no success. Only when the refugees were marshaled in Vienna, prior to leaving for new homelands, did she finally find Sandy. It had been her twenty-second birthday.

"You never found your aunt?"

"No. I searched everywhere in Budapest. Her apartment block had burned and she hadn't been seen since the fire."

She seemed on the point of saying more, but then stopped. My questions about her parents evoked some terrible sadness and I didn't press her.

She turned us left off Robson Street before we reached the park. Seven blocks south on Denman we came to Davie and English Bay Beach, now shrouded in darkness. Just beyond the Davie-Denman intersection was a tiny wedge-shaped park with a wooden band shell. Beside that, facing English Bay across the park and Beach Avenue, stood a fine old Victorian clapboard, one of the survivors fending off the developers running amok in the West End.

"We are home," she said.

"So soon? Well, I'd better say good night. I'm so sorry about your brother—"

"You are abandoning me?" She interrupted, turning to search my face with those wide, dark eyes.

God almighty, I was a goner.

"Pardon?" I gulped.

"You are going to tell me you must go back to your ship. Yes? Isn't that what sailors do?"

"Well, I should be aboard—"

"Should? This is not such strong word as must? Yes?"

"Um, yeah. What do you—"

"I frighten you off? I am too, mm, not conventional?"

"No Tatiana, you don't frighten me. Absolutely not."

"Absolutely? You are sure? Then come in and talk."

Inside, only a dim night-light and stray glimmers of neon from the streets illuminated what seemed to be a huge room. She made no move to turn on lights, taking my overcoat instead. Pointing to a couch she said, "Sit," and disappeared into the bathroom. Somewhat desperately, I said after her, "Shall I make coffee?"

"I will be only a moment. Just sit."

So I sat. One wall of the long room was a myriad of reflections, sometimes repeated. I puzzled over what seemed to be a huge broken mirror. And why she would need one.

Then she was back. She'd changed into a thin, flowered wrapper of, I thought, silk.

"Don't talk. Just sit with me. Hold me," she said.

I felt the quivering tension of her, and the fact that there was nothing under the silk. Tentatively, I put my arm around her shoulders and she snuggled against me as if she owned the space.

After a while she looked up at me, then reached to touch my face. "You have tears," she said. "Why is that?"

"Because you can't cry," I whispered. "You must."

"Oh God…yes."

We sat together for a long time. And eventually the dam broke and the grief poured out of her.

And some time not long before dawn we became lovers. It wasn't my intention – but then I was no longer in control of my life. She was.

*

I awoke to daylight flickering through billowing curtains and the noise of morning traffic. My new love seemed to be a fresh air fanatic. Surroundings I'd barely glimpsed last night both intrigued and puzzled me.

Tatiana's ground floor apartment was a single long room that I thought might have been a billiard room, fifty years ago in the mansion's heyday. A kitchen and a bathroom had been partitioned off at one end. Her furniture was a set of highboy drawers and a massive built-in oak wardrobe that almost reached the nine-foot ceiling. At the kitchen end the battered couch in green leatherette that I'd met last night faced a red and yellow drop-leaf table surrounded by four unmatched, tipsy chairs. A big Electrohome hi-fi system in an oiled teak cabinet and the king-sized bed where we'd spent the night were the only new items.

Between the bed end and the kitchen end, twenty feet of polished bare hardwood floor gave the place the look of a vacant warehouse, albeit a neat and tidy warehouse. On the wall, at the end of a long waist-high exercise bar, was a schoolroom-sized blackboard with a chalk ledge and brushes. Five-line staves, like a giant musical score had been painted onto the blackboard in white. Except that the "notes" weren't like any I'd ever seen.

Tats had been watching my puzzlement. "It is dance notation. The new Benesh system. I fool around with choreography," she explained.

I was still puzzled.

"You didn't imagine we improvised our dances, did you?"

"Uh, to be honest I never imagined anything about ballet. Except maybe what the girls looked like out of their tights."

Opposite the bar another of last night's puzzles was explained. A patchwork wall mirror pieced together from smaller mirrors of various shapes and shades created a fractured illusion of space.

Faint pangs of conscience assailed me. I was supposed to be living aboard the *Solange* and here I was, sleeping over without leaving word with Marty at the dispatch office. None of his bloody business but I thought I'd better call in before Marty had a heart attack.

Tatiana stretched beside me. "You are hungry?"

"Mm hmm," I said

"The restaurant is across the little park and around the corner on Davie Street," she said, smiling. "You will like their food better than my fried eggs."

"We're supposed to see McRae this morning," I reminded her. "He's setting up an ID session for you."

She made a face.

"Tats, you have to let the police do their job. If you feel Sandy was murdered, you owe it to him to convince McRae."

"You think he is good policeman, this McRae?"

"He is meticulous and thorough. I've never seen better."

"What do you know of police?"

"I was one once. Military police. During the Korean war."

She sat up in bed and turned towards me with a quizzical expression. "You did not tell me this?"

"It didn't seem important, last night. Why should it matter? The navy spent two years and a great deal of taxpayer money training me as a diver and in underwater demolitions. Then with wonderful logic, they shoved me into a military police unit. Probably because of my size."

"What kind of police is this? Intelligence?"

"No. We chased vanishing quartermaster's stores heading for the black market and we had some dope-running cases. And a triple murder.

She continued to stare, silently.

"Look, I haven't got the bloody bubonic plague! What is it with you?"

"It is nothing," she said, without much conviction.

She levitated off the bed in one effortless movement and stood, stretching a leg out to the bar. "Now you don't need to imagine any more," she said.

I watched my new love, fascinated, as she and her assorted reflections worked through her morning warm-up routine, naked. Black hair cascading over white shoulders and rippling down her back. Breasts not large but well formed and firm, with dark prominent nipples. She didn't seem to own a brassiere. At least there wasn't one in the heap where we'd dropped our clothes the night before.

I didn't think I'd ever seen a woman in such fine-drawn physical condition. Or with so little self-consciousness. My God, what did you have to do to earn calves like that?

And she walked like a well-rehearsed prowling panther, except that her toes pointed out at a forty-five degree angle which gave her the damndest mixture of fine grace and duck-like awkwardness.

"What?" she demanded.

"Nothing."

"You were watching me. I saw your eyebrows doing things. What?" She smiled.

"Your walk. It's, ah, weird." There. I'd gone and put my foot in it now.

But she still smiled. "It is the ballerina's waddle. We all walk like penguins, when we're not dancing. It is because of the turn-out we are taught."

"Mmm. Delicious penguin. Why do they teach you that?"

"It makes us more secure *en pointe*. See?" She shifted to a toe-point stance, barefoot, and held it, effortlessly. I couldn't see why the turn-out made much difference but I was impressed as hell anyway.

"I thought it was the special dancing shoes that let you do that."

"The slippers have some blocking but not much. I have good feet and don't really need it."

"What makes your feet so good?"

"They are square. See? And I have a low arch, but very strong."

And by God they were square, damned near. Her first three toes were almost exactly the same length. I would take her word for the arches.

At least we weren't talking about my stint as a military cop. I wondered why that had spooked her.

She ended her stretching with a series of quick, whipping pirouettes, barefoot, across the floor, finishing with one foot delicately perched on my shoulder. Then she leaned forward and kissed me. God almighty! Was she double jointed as well?"

"I am going to shower. There is room for two. Come along, monster."

*

Eventually I made it to the phone. Marty Haines was his usual charming self. "Where the hell have you been, Sutter? You know what our contract calls for. You're supposed to be aboard."

"Yeah, Marty. I know. How long does it take to steam the Solange, from cold?"

"What the hell has that got to do with anything?"

"How long?"

"Four hours. As you bloody well know. Listen, if you—"

"And since you are too cheap to keep her at stand-by pressure, I'm on four-hour call. Right?"

"I don't think Mister Picard would go along with—"

"What does the contract say about Picard using Cam to rebuild the engine of his precious antique speedboat?"

"Uh…"

"Sobering up Mick O'Conner? How long does that take?"

"What are you implying?"

"Oh, I think you can figure it out. I'll leave you a few numbers where you can reach me if something comes up. If I'm anyplace else, I'll let you know."

"Mister Picard's not gonna like this."

"Yeah, Marty, and you're going to tell him about it. Right?" There was a long silence. "That's what I thought," I said. I gave him the telephone numbers and cradled the phone.

"You are in trouble at your work?"

"No Tats. No trouble. I'm yours for the day."

"First we go out for breakfast. Unless you'd rather…?"

"We did that in the shower. Let's eat before anything…else…happens. Oh damn."

She giggled. It was the first real laughter I'd heard from her and a welcome sound.

We didn't eat first, after all.

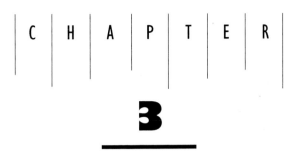

3

"Miss Tatiana very healthy," Blossom said with a huge grin. "Not diet all the time like crazy."

We were at breakfast in Blossom's Cafe on Davie Street when Blossom, sometimes known as Mr. Lee Tong, delivered this observation. Tats was embarrassed at being the object of his personal attention.

"It's not you, it's your appetite he's in love with."

"A dancer must eat," Tats said, indignantly.

"So it seems," I said, carefully neutral.

Blossom grinned with delight and piled more scrambled eggs on her plate. She made no protest.

Tats wore a thin, white, jersey turtleneck with, I knew, nothing under it. A navy blue skirt, low-heeled shoes and the long, gray, European-cut rain-coat that I'd seen last night completed the ensemble. She wore no jewelry and little makeup.

"Why do you stare at me?"

"Because I can't help myself. You're mesmerizing."

"I am just a girl."

"No, you're a revolution. You just turned my life upside down."

"This is a bad thing?"

"Not bad, Tats. Unless it stops."

"Mmm? Then maybe I will keep you for a while. Will you drive me to my rehearsal today?"

"With a taxi. I don't have a car."

"I thought all Canadian men have cars," she teased.

"No, we all fix cars. Mine is in a million pieces in a garage I rent from my sister, up in Mount Pleasant."

We left Blossom's to stroll across Alexandra Park enjoying the misty morning sun and, for once, the absence of rain. Tats steered me into a detour so she could inspect the chocolate box bandstand. I think we both felt that talk would ruin the mood.

Shyly, she took my hand. I felt more like an anchor than a lover, somehow, but the gesture gave me a wonderful possessive glow. A feeling that all was right in the world.

But across the park, in front of Tats' Victorian, a double-parked Vancouver PD squad car reminded me that all was not well in Tatiana Kovacs' world. McRae wasn't leaving us an option about the meeting in his office.

The police, most of them, worked out of a square, featureless, four-story concrete block called the Public Safety Building at 312 Main Street. Not an especially safe part of town. McRae led us to a room filled by a conference table and a dozen oak Works Department chairs. "This is Corporal Nunn," he said, introducing a stranger, sprawled across two chairs.

Nunn was a big man, nearly my size, with a pale complexion and "carrot top" red hair. He looked like what he was, a cop in a sports jacket. He stood and leaned across the table to shake hands, trying the "forceful personality" handshake on me. His mistake.

"I've set up some books of pictures for you, Miss Kovacs," McRae said. "Based on your descriptions, there aren't too many to look at."

Tats took her time going through the large-format picture albums. Nunn seemed impatient with the process. He massaged his knuckles and stared at Tats.

"They are not here," she said at last.

"We may have more pictures for you later," McRae said. "I'm sure this has been a terrible shock to you and shocks can do queer things to memory. Are you certain your brother never mentioned what he was working on? Never talked about the details?"

"No. Mr. Feldman must have this information."

"I'll be interviewing Feldman later today. He was upset about your brother's death and has closed his office for the week."

"He never got out of the police car to speak to me last night."

"Mr. Feldman explained that he becomes physically ill at the sight of blood," McRae said. "He asked me to convey his apologies for not speaking to you. He also asked me to tell you he will look after the, er, funeral arrangements. I understand an employee death benefit is payable to you. He didn't say how much that involved."

"I see. He sends me presents and asks you to speak for him?" she said. "Why could he not tell me?"

"Tell the truth, I don't know, Miss Kovacs," McRae said.

"Convey to him I said `thanks'," she said. "I also am ill from sight of blood."

"Oh now, Miss Kovacs--"

"Is this over?"

"I have a few more questions but they can wait," McRae said.

"Mine can't," Corporal Nunn said. "Miss Kovacs, what did you do in Leningrad, the three years you were there?"

Tats seemed to shrink into her chair. "I danced with the Kirov Ballet," she said, cautiously. "This is well known."

"That is all you did?"

"Yes." She turned to McRae. "Please, what has this to do with my brother's murder?"

"Nothing that I know of, Miss Kovacs. Corporal Nunn is not with the Vancouver Police Department. He is RCMP."

"This is federal police? Like FBI?"

"Yes. Except that they have jurisdiction everywhere, so when he asked to be present--"

"This is secret police? Yes?" She paled.

"Ah. You'll have to ask Corporal Nunn that one." McRae got a dirty look from Nunn.

"How did you arrive in Austria, Miss Kovacs?" Nunn demanded.

"On foot, wet and frozen, and badly in need of a tampon."

Nunn squirmed.

Tatiana smiled at his embarrassment. "With a lot of other people," she added.

"How did you become separated from your brother?"

"We didn't leave Budapest together. I was on tour with a troupe of the ballet company--" "In what city?" Nunn interrupted.

"In Pecs. When the revolution began we returned to Budapest. But Sandy had left his rooms. I couldn't find him for a long time."

"Did he participate in the revolt?"

"Yes."

"Did you?"

"Yes. They wouldn't give me a gun but I got one later. When the revolution was lost, we crossed into Austria--"

"Where, exactly?" Nunn interrupted again.

"Near Andau. It is a village on the Austrian side of the border. Sandy and I crossed the border separately. I found him nearly a month later, in Vienna."

"What camp did you stay in?"

"At first in an old castle."

"What was it called?"

"I don't know. No one told me." She turned to McRae again. "Detective McRae, you asked me here to look at pictures. Instead, I get third degree from secret police."

McRae returned her look with, I thought, sympathy, but gave no answer. But if Nunn had meant to rattle her, he'd failed miserably.

Nunn stood and leaned across the table, scowling. "Miss Kovacs, last night you gave the investigating officers at the scene of Sandor Kovacs' death the impression you did not know Mr. Sutter."

"So?" she said.

"Yet this morning we find he has spent the night with you. Would you explain this please?"

"Hey! Back off on that shit!" I said.

"No, Hank," Tats said. "I will answer. It is called biology. Do they not teach biology in police school?"

Nunn went all thin-lipped and nasty-cop-looking. I'd seen cops practice that look. "That's a smart-assed answer, Miss, and hardly appropriate."

"Neither was your question," I said.

He ignored me. "Miss Kovacs, you came to Canada on special ministerial warrants. You can go back the same way."

"For sleeping with one of your citizens? Oh, sorry, I forgot. In Canada you are not citizens, you are subjects."

She'd risen to her feet, facing away from Nunn and I caught her fleeting smile.

Nunn flushed, beet red. "We will continue this another time, Miss Kovacs." He left. Well, not exactly. He made an exit, as the theatrical people have it. Complete with slammed door. I could almost hear the jangle of his spurs.

"Asshole," McRae breathed.

"Amen," I said.

McRae looked startled. He'd voiced his thoughts without realizing it. He turned to Tatiana who was edging towards the door. "A moment, Miss Kovacs. I have to tell you that we do not have evidence that would support a murder investigation. If something turns up, that could change, of course."

"My brother's killers leave a phony note and you are helpless? What sort of police is this?"

"We are having a professional handwriting analysis done on the note as a result of your charges. That may tell us something. But can you explain how strangers would know your nickname is Tats?"

"Probably because they looked at my picture on his desk. That is how I signed it."

"Ah," McRae said, writing in his notebook.

"You did not search the building?"

"Why do you think we should have done that?"

"The killers could hide until morning and leave when they chose. The suicide note gave them time."

"Ma'am, searching a place the size of the Marine Building would have required more manpower than I had available last night," McRae said. "I didn't see any justification for calling in off-duty officers."

"I see," she said, obviously not seeing.

McRae went on, "And consider this. There are quieter ways to murder a man than by throwing him off a building. Why would killers do something so public?"

"Sandy would fight. He was very strong and they would have trouble to, mm…subdue him. Maybe he did not look like a suicide, after," Tats said.

McRae looked thoughtful. "I'll have the medical examiner look for signs of a beating. They might be hard to detect, considering his…fall. In the meantime, the case remains officially a suicide, unless the coroner's inquest tells us otherwise."

"Then call me when your police department wakes up."

McRae made an "ouch" face.

Tats was still quivering with anger from her exchange with Nunn. But I was beginning to think she was a better cop than either McRae or me.

"Is Nunn from the Security Service?" I asked.

"I'm not supposed to say but I suppose it's obvious. The branch is now called Security and Intelligence or S and I, for short. He's the resident Hungarian watcher. He may be a royal pain in the ass but he isn't stupid, and he is persistent."

"Gotcha. Thanks, sergeant."

"Think nothing of it, lieutenant."

I stared at him. McRae was a better cop than I'd imagined, to have fished out my naval and military police record so quickly. "It wasn't lieutenant," I said. "It was sub-lieutenant. I was pretty junior."

"Sure you were."

*

"Okay, where to, Tats?" I asked as we left the building. But I was talking to thin air as she stormed off down Main Street towards the Hastings corner. I trotted after her.

"Nunn frightened you." I said.

"No. He made me angry. Stupid cold-war questions when Sandy is dead and killers go free." She simmered.

"Look, Tats, Nunn's questions may have seemed stupid but his method wasn't. It was meant to upset you, and it has."

She glared, straight ahead. I was certain fear and a wary caution had been her first reaction to Nunn's questions. But either she was one hell of an actress or…or I had missed something. Nunn had made a complete ass of himself when he'd gone after her personal life. She'd ended the interview in charge and angry.

I hailed a cab. For a moment I thought she was going to ignore the open cab door and take off but she got in.

"Just drive around," I told the cabbie. "Tats, you're too upset to be rational. You'll see things differently when a little time has passed."

"Differently how? That it doesn't matter any more?"

I sensed that we were on the verge of an explosion and I bit down on my retort. Let her cool off. And God damn the Corporal Nunns of this world. Tatiana seemed to sense our imminent clash as well and she sat back, closing her eyes, rocking gently to the cab's motion. After a while, she put her hand on mine. "My poor monster," she said. "What a mess you have found, for your kindness."

"Are all penguins this messed up?" It sounded stupid but it seemed to snap her out of her funk and she smiled.

She sat forward and looked at her watch. "We have lunch," she said. "Then I must go to the academy."

But she only picked at her lunch.

The Western Academy of Classical Dance, located in a barn-like second floor rehearsal hall on Hastings Street, was run by a character named Donal Gowan. Tats vanished into the changing room after hurriedly introducing me to Gowan. Why he'd dropped the last "d" off his name escaped me but Donal was not your cliché powder-puff male dancer. He was a little under six feet with a slim, well-muscled frame and a hostile expression. He'd have fitted in well with the crew of the *Solange Picard*, especially his language.

"I suppose you are fucking my lead dancer? Gowan said, looking me up and down like a dog scouting a lamp post.

"I beg your--"

"Don't get her pregnant. Or I will personally kill you. Do we understand each other?"

"Listen, you little shit-head, what concern of yours is Tats' personal life?"

"It's very much my concern. Tatiana is a gift from the gods. She will be prima ballerina of our new company."

"Gowan, if you had a scrap of decency, you'd postpone this bloody recital out of respect for the woman's grief. She's lost her only brother, for God's sake."

Taken aback by my vehemence, he paused. He took a deep breath and said, "Certain people -- knowledgeable and wealthy people -- are coming to watch Tatiana dance, Saturday. They are possible backers and I cannot re-schedule their arrival."

"You ever hear of a telegram?"

He talked straight over me. "They'd also be most upset to hear that Tats had been dragged off by some local hayseed and bogged down in diapers."

"Listen, Donal, the only thing that keeps me from rearranging your ugly mug is the fact that you are dancing with Tats in that recital."

"Good! Oh very good. We understand each other." He grinned and punched me on the shoulder as if we'd been life-long buddies. But his broad grin was infectious and I found myself laughing with him. Damned if I knew why.

Tats, in black leotards and pink knee-warmers, launched into a warmup routine at the *barre*, as I was told to pronounce it. The routine became progressively more frenetic as she moved to mid-floor. I thought Nunn might have been on the end of some of those kicks.

Then Gowan joined her and they rehearsed a sequence in which he caught her in mid-leap, ending in a graceful posture that should have been impossible. My estimate of Donal Gowan went up a notch or three. I noticed dancers from the academy's classes had stopped to watch.

Late in the afternoon she gave me a few minutes attention. She'd hardly broken a sweat. "Tell me what you thought about Donal Gowan," she said.

"An obnoxious little shit but he does have some redeeming qualities and he seems to be a good dancer."

"I saw you laughing together."

"So you did. I guess that's the quality I meant. Oh, and not dropping you, that was the other one."

"He is strong. Dancers feel secure with him. He wants to make me his big star with his new company but he has no money to begin it."

"Like me and my salvage company."

"Yes. I do seem to collect dreamers. I will shower and change. Then we must find some dinner."

"Are you always hungry?"

"You want me to be like those poor things Blossom talks about? Girls who diet all the time and have no juice?"

"No, Tats. I couldn't imagine you without juice." But I was beginning to wonder if I could afford to feed the lady. Payday was a week off.

*

"Those men who watched Sandy watch me, now," she said as she slipped between the sheets and snuggled close, later.

"You've seen them?"

"No, but my nerves tell me they are there."

"You haven't seen anyone and you've no idea why anyone would follow you, yet you're sure someone's there?"

"Exactly so."

"I see," I said, skeptically.

"You don't believe?" She propped herself on an elbow to stare at the unbeliever.

"I don't know what to believe. I don't know what the hell is happening. But something is going on."

She seemed to accept that. After a pregnant silence, I said, "Tats?"

"Mmm?"

"How did you come to be in Leningrad?"

"The Kirov Ballet is the finest in the world. It was a great honor to be asked to dance with them."

"Not the Bolshoi?"

"The Bolshoi is more, mm, athletic. In Russia, dancers call it the circus. The Kirov is more lyrical."

"How long were you there?"

"Nearly three years. Why do you ask?"

"Just curious. Do you speak Russian?"

"Of course. And French because it is the language of ballet, and Hungarian and German and English and a little Czech." Then suddenly smiling and playful, "Anything else you would like to know? My blood type, maybe? I am type B."

"Hey! Relax, girl. It was only idle curiosity."

"In April 1955 I came home from Russia and rejoined the Budapest company. Now good night." She turned away from me and pulled the covers over her head.

Later, after Tats was asleep, I was restless. She'd tried to make fun of my questions and it hadn't quite worked. Something in her response troubled me. I decided I needed to take a walk.

English Bay has a block-long sidewalk promenade with benches where you can look down on the beach fun. Beneath it are changing rooms, public washrooms and a lifeguard's aid station, all locked for the winter. Two sets of stairs lead down to the rooms and the beach. A faint odor of sea salt and last summer's fish and chips clung to the place. I walked slowly down the stairs, stopping every few steps to listen.

Nothing.

Beyond the fringe of sand lit by street lights, the rushing sounds of a slow, gentle surf drifted out of the black. Lights of Kitsilano and Point Grey districts glittered a few miles to the south, across English Bay.

Then I heard a murmur of laughter.

Two people were making noisy love in a sleeping bag behind one of the beach's long row of edge logs.

I climbed to the promenade again and crossed Beach Avenue to Alexandra Park, checking out the little bandstand that had so intrigued Tats.

Was I mistaken or had the beach lovers fallen quiet the moment I'd returned to the street?

My intentions, making this damned-fool walkabout, had been to reassure her. Uneasily, I knew I couldn't do that. Yet I knew perfectly well that a proper surveillance would never be conducted from bathhouse stairs.

C H A P T E R

4

Funerals are not my cup of tea. In fact I rarely see the inside of a church unless a friend is getting married. But Catholic funerals, I have to admit, have a certain style, especially if the priest is good with his Latin. You can let the hypnotic, numbing rhythms of the language wash over you, not knowing or dwelling upon what is being intoned over the departed.

I don't grieve well. My sentimental nature is part of the reason I couldn't stay in the police business, despite tempting offers, after Korea. Too much death. I couldn't understand how a detective like McRae lived with the carnage as an element of his professional life, part of the scenery, and then came to the funerals of victims.

McRae sat at the rear of the church on what I had come to know as "the groom's side." Nunn sat in the same row on "the bride's side."

Holy Rosary Cathedral, at the corner of Dunsmuir and Richards streets, was packed that wet Thursday morning. The Hungarian community had turned out in force for Sandy.

Jake Feldman -- who was paying for this and who I knew was Jewish -- was there with most of his office staff. I recognized faces from the dance academy, though I didn't see Gowan.

Jake Feldman made truce and offered his condolences to Tatiana, enfolding her in a bear hug, both of them in tears. I'm not sure if he redeemed himself but if he did I gave the credit to his being a silver-tongued lawyer. Or maybe it was the hug. She didn't bite off his head.

Tatiana seemed like a lost little soul in the crowd.

I didn't think she was any more religious than I, so I was surprised when she stepped forward to the rail when communion was offered. She scurried back to me, afterwards. "Sandy would have done that," she whispered.

The crowd grew and changed when the ceremony moved to Ocean View Burial Park, several miles away in South Burnaby. Rain, driven by a blustering gale, flipped umbrellas inside-out and, I suspected, shortened the service.

I caught McRae's eye as the crowd dispersed. "Nothing new," he said.

"What's Nunn doing here?" I asked.

"Paying his respects, I suppose. You know he's Irish Catholic?"

"I wasn't even sure he was human."

"Human and fallible. Left a wife in Ottawa when they shipped him out here. Kids, too."

"How did you discover that?"

"It wasn't hard. Gets talkative when he's had a few. Probably the reason they booted him out of Ottawa, where the real spooks are."

Tats had asked Jake Feldman not to arrange a reception after the funeral. So instead the crowd was milling around her in a sea of umbrellas, offering condolences in Hungarian and English. I thought she was bearing up well. Better than me. My function was to hold a large umbrella over her and keep her from blowing away.

Across the grave site I spotted Nunn's carrot-top head. He was talking to someone with sense enough to wear a hat. But suddenly the wind caught the other man's hat and lifted it over the shrubbery. He scrambled after it but not before I'd seen his blond and curly hair. Suddenly it hit me that this guy was a match for one of the men she'd described following Sandy.

I moved to block Tats' view of him. She had enough on her plate. I looked for McRae but he'd vanished.

When I turned back to Tats, I was looking at the back of Donal Gowan's head. He hugged her and whispered something. It didn't sound like condolences to me and I moved in on him.

"Leave her alone, Gowan," I said.

"You think you're her keeper?"

"Tats, what did he say to you?"

"It is the black swan *pas de deux* in Saturday's recital," she said.

"What about it?"

"It needs work. He is right."

"For Christ's sake, Gowan, If you can't postpone your damned recital, at least give her a day to bury her brother. What difference could it make?"

"We had this discussion, I believe. Our performance must be completely professional."

"Screw your bloody backers. Leave her alone." My voice was rising and people were looking our way.

Gowan looked as if he'd like to disappear into the grass. Sheepishly, he said, "I'm sorry to have to ask, but could you come in tomorrow, Tatiana?"

"I will come. All day," she said.

I moved into Gowan's face and he retreated, hastily.

"No Hank, this is important," Tats said, grabbing my arm. "We must give a polished performance." She reined in her monster, but only just.

*

We returned to Tatiana's apartment at three in the afternoon, to the tune of an insistent telephone. Marty Haines. "Jesus Christ, Sutter, where the fuck've you been?" Haines imagined his language made him "one of the boys" but the cussing was a bad match for the "big shot" suit-and-tie office persona he also tried to project. Marty never could see the comedy of his posturing.

"Burying a friend. What's up?"

"Chief says we gotta bunker the *Solange* and top up her water. And Lee's got galley stores coming aboard. Mr. Picard would like you to look after it today." I could hear the cash register's jangle in Haines' voice. The price of Bunker C was set to go up two dollars a barrel, after the weekend.

"All right, I'll be there shortly."

" Couple of the guys are ashore. You want I should call them?"

"We got a full watch aboard?"

"Yeah. Except for you."

"We don't need everybody, then."

Haines was overjoyed at the nickels that saved.

But what was I going to do with Tats? I couldn't leave her alone. Not today.

Then I had an inspiration. I dialed my aunt Clara who lives on the North Shore. Clara was famous, in the Sutter clan, for pulling people through tough emotional situations.

"You want me to babysit your girlfriend? This doesn't sound like your kind of woman, Hank."

So I sketched Tats' situation, leaving out the part about her being followed. And the part about Sandy's death probably being a murder. I saved the clincher for the end of my pitch. "She's a dancer, Clara. From the Hungarian National Ballet."

A long silence ensued. "Oh my!" Clara said. "And she's going with *you*?"

"What's the matter? I'm not good enough for a ballerina?"

"I'm sure you are, Hank." She didn't sound especially contrite.

"Then you'll come over?"

"On my way." She hung up. Clara had been a dancer herself, twenty years ago, and I knew she'd never be able to resist.

*

Jeep Sawchuck, my senior deckhand, had already singled up the *Solange*'s lines and disconnected the shore electrical connections when I made it to the Picard dock. Dunc McAdams, our venerable chief engineer, was rocking his engines slowly back and forth, a half-revolution each way, working surplus condensation out of the cylinders.

I flipped the remaining lines free and stepped aboard over the after rail. "Take her out, Jeep," I yelled.

Jeep liked to play mate whenever he could and he waved from the bridge wing and vanished into the wheelhouse. The engine room telegraph clattered and the *Solange Picard* shuddered to life with the peculiar, hissing quiet of a steamship. The voyage up harbor to the Oil Dock would be short and the weather, though still blustery, was clear. I decided to let Jeep have his fun. He was long past being qualified to be mate of his own ship.

I found Cam Douglas, our second engineer, in the mess room, playing crib with Axel Oberg, the off-duty fireman. The *Solange* was one of only five tugs on the Pacific coast big enough to have a separate mess room, apart from the galley.

"Hear you got yourself a new bird," Cam said, carefully casual, not looking up from his hand. "Fifteen for two," he added, for Axel's benefit, laying down a five.

"Twenty for two," Axel gloated, laying another five on the table and pegging his points.

"You heard right," I said. Carefully noncommittal, pouring myself a coffee.

"What's she like?"

"You want an inventory?"

"Just wondering. Jeep was spreadin' rumors. Thirty," he said, turning back to Axel.

"Thirty-one for two, und I am out," Axel said, dropping his ace in triumph.

"Shit," Cam said, by way of congratulations. He seldom beat Axel.

Jeep was my cousin and his family information pipeline was sometimes a liability. "What rumors?" I asked.

"Said she was some sort of dancer. Tippy-toe kind."

"So?"

"You're goin' out with a no-shit ballerina?" Cam's incredulity was a little forced. And some faces had popped up, listening at the galley door. I'd been set up.

"No shit. You got that part right," I said. "What else did my obnoxious cousin have to say?"

"Said you're sleepin' over already. And you got Marty Haines' knackers in a knot on account of you not livin' aboard and the standby contract's crewing provisions."

"What else?"

"Must be serious. You ain't givin' us any answers. Guess she's not like June, huh?"

"Not like June," I agreed. June Striker was my last girl, a Jane Russell look-alike with, unfortunately, a roving eye. She'd have made two of Tats. "She makin' a dancer outa you? Jeep says you're gettin' fitted for tights and a tutu."

"He does, does he? There's about as much chance of that as for my mouthy cousin becoming the sugar plum fairy. But I will say I'm worried about her. She's got problems."

The card shuffling stopped. "What kind?"

"Tell you about it when we tie up. I want Jeep handy to answer for his big mouth."

The engine-room telegraph rattled "stand-by" and I dumped the dregs of my coffee and made my way up to the wheelhouse. Jeep eyed me nervously as he handed the wheel over. I kept a strictly business face. My long silence seemed to panic him.

"Jeez, Hank, I didn't say anythin' nasty about your girl," he babbled.

"I'm sure you didn't, Jasper," I said, smiling. "Since you've never met her."

His face fell about three decks. I had never, in living memory, addressed him by his proper given name. In fact I was probably the only person aboard who knew it and would dare to do so. He slunk out of the wheelhouse.

Topping up the *Solange*'s fuel and water took about two hours. Cam and Axel finished their coffee and left to move some filler hoses and sound tanks. So I had Jeep and Tooey, the other deckhand, and Jimmy Lee the cook, to myself for a while. Or maybe they had me.

"You gonna tell us about her?" Jeep agitated.

"Nope," I said.

"Jeez, Hank. I tell you about my birds."

"Yeah, you do. You got no couth at all, Jeep. What is it with you, you have to know all the nitty gritty about everybody's love life?"

"I'm makin' a study. To find out what I'm doin' wrong I keep losin' girlfriends. If you guys won't tell me nothin', how'm I gonna learn?"

Cam re-entered the mess room, wiping his hands on an oily rag. "Flapping your mouth, now that'd be high on the list of no-no's, with the feminine gender," he said. "Like you did about Hank's new girl."

"Aw, I didn't mean nothin' by it," Jeep protested. "Is she really a Hungarian ballerina, Hank?"

"Really," I said. "I'll bring her aboard some day when she's in a more cheerful mood. She just lost her brother."

"Yeah? That the Hungarian guy jumped off the Marine Building the other day? Was in the paper."

"Same guy. Whether he jumped or was pushed is a good question."

"No shit? It was murder?"

"Not for sure but it's possible. Anyhow, I'll need to spend some time with her. Can you guys cover for me?"

"No sweat. Marty's such an asshole, it'll be fun to run him around in circles a bit," Cam said.

"Okay. I'll touch base whenever I can."

"Anything we can do to help?" Cam asked.

"Could you let me use your car for a few days?"

Cam paused in the middle of shuffling for another crib game. "That heap of yours not running yet?" he asked with a note of caution. I'd just asked him to loan me his precious new baby.

"It's still in pieces up at Janet's place. I'm not sure when I'll get back to working on it." As transportation, my pre-war Alfa Romeo Gran Tourisimo made as much sense as Junior's fancy antique speedboat, or Cam's Chrysler 300 Hemi for that matter, but they were all pretty.

"You got it." He threw me the keys. "So long as you're the only guy drivin'. Just remember, you're handling 350 horsepower. Take it easy."

"You still working on Junior's pride and joy?" I asked.

Cam had been months rebuilding the converted aircraft engine that powered Junior's antique runabout *Miranda*.

Cam shrugged. "Just a little tuning, now."

"Your friend find you Tuesday night?" Jeep asked me.

"What friend?"

"Name was Mike, he said. Pock-marked face. Crew cut. Ears like jug handles. Said he was passin' through town and needed to look you up. Wanted your address. Said he knew you in the army, in Korea."

"Didn't have any army friends. We were all navy in my unit."

"That's what I figured. He looked a bit shifty, so I didn't tell him anything."

"Thanks, Jeep. If you see him again, keep it that way. Tell him nothing. Okay?"

"Not a friend, huh?"

"Not a friend."

"Better check out what Marty told him, then. He headed for the office after he left the ship."

With the Solange back at her berth I headed up the dock to Marty Haines' dispatch office on the chance he'd still be there. He was gone.

Down the hallway I could see a light in Jeanie Halford's office. Jeanie was Picard's overworked and underpaid bookkeeper-cum-office manager. She seemed to be working a lot of evenings lately.

"Jeanie? You know if Marty went home?"

She removed her half-glasses and dropped them in a pocket. Shot me a "look." "No. *Mister* Haines doesn't speak to the female hired help these days. Or hadn't you noticed?"

"Figures. You happen to see him talking to some guy, late Tuesday? Pock-marked face, ears and crew cut?"

"Ears? Yes, I did see somebody like that in his office," she nodded. "Creepy. Gave me the eye on his way out."

"I'm not surprised," I said. Jeanie was in her forties but still a looker, though she didn't seem to know it.

She blushed. "You know what I mean," she said.

"Yeah, I know. Damn."

"This guy is a problem?"

"I hope not. Thanks, Jeanie."

*

A burble of feminine laughter surprised me as I knocked on Tatiana's door. "Come in, monster," she shouted.

Something smelled delicious and I homed on it, meanwhile stealing a cautious look at Tats. She seemed relaxed and normal, yet in quiet moments her eyes were shadowed, as if her inner self was elsewhere.

A pot lid lifted and fell to the steam of something bubbling. Other things were cooking. Very domestic looking.

"We went shopping," Clara said. "The poor girl didn't have a crumb of food in the place. We even had to buy some pots. I can't imagine how she kept body and soul together."

"Ask me about that," I said.

"We are having shrimps with linguini and Clara's wonderful sauce," Tats announced proudly. "Hank, Clara has been teaching me all kinds of cooking things."

Clara had outdone herself and I smiled at her, tipping an imaginary hat. "And I thought you'd be talking dancing all afternoon."

"Oh we did that, too," Clara said. She pulled me aside and lowered her voice. "My goodness, you've got yourself a catch, Henry Sutter."

"I think so," I said smugly.

"I meant that a little more seriously, Hank. Tatiana is a first-rank artist with a marvelous future. I don't know how the two of you could have a home life, with you on the ship and her on tour half the time." She paused, watching me for a reaction. I waited her out and she continued. "That is, if you're serious about her. No. I don't want to hear about it if you aren't."

"I'm serious. I asked her to marry me."

"You asked her? Already?"

"Twice."

"And?"

"She said `no.' Twice."

"Well, it sounds as if she's got more sense than you have. One of you will have to give and I don't think it should be her."

Tats had been fussing over our dinner, pointedly ignoring us. She said, "When you two have finished talking about me, this is ready, I think."

*

That night I was restless, thinking about the curly-headed blond man I'd seen talking to Corporal Nunn at the grave-side that morning. Where in hell did Nunn fit in, if the guy was one of his spooks? And what about Jeep's "hard case" asking questions about me? He couldn't be one of

Nunn's boys, since Nunn knew where I was living. I would get it out of Marty Haines what questions this Mike joker had asked about me. And what he'd answered. In the morning.

"You are awake, still?" Tats asked in a sleepy voice.

"Yes."

She sat up in bed, letting the covers fall to her waist. "Will you do something for me?"

"Anything. You know that."

"Will you be policeman again, for me?"

I'd been afraid she would ask that, and I still didn't have a ready answer. "Tats, that's impossible. The police have the resources to do the job. I don't."

"`Anything,' you said."

I stared at her in mute frustration. Passing headlights and a distant neon flickered, lighting the room in fitful glimmers and making her expression hard to read. She turned away from me and, with a quiver in her voice, said, "Somebody must look for Sandy's killers. The police do nothing."

"We don't know that." I sat up beside her and touched her, gently, to turn her to me. Her cheek was wet. "Sergeant McRae isn't obliged to tell us everything he's doing," I said. The words seemed useless, dissolved in her tears.

"But I know, Hank. I am Magyar. I cannot rest if those men live." Her voice quivered.

"What? You want me to kill them?"

"You will not do that?"

"I'll do what I can but I won't kill, unless…"

"Unless what?"

"Unless somebody's life is threatened. Yours, for instance."

"You have a gun?"

"No, I don't have a gun. Just sticking my nose into this investigation will get me in enough trouble with McRae." But I knew it might also prod him into action.

"You must have a gun. These men are dangerous."

"Tats!"

"I knew you would be policeman for me." Her voice was muffled against my shoulder and I held her close. "Make love to me. It will relax," she said. "You're sure you want to?"

"Absolutely sure. I am cure for worrying."

"That you are, my love. But I wish I was sure of anything."

"Me, you are sure of. Everything else is maybe."

C H A P T E R

5

I dropped Tats off at the academy at eight-thirty Friday morning. I had in mind to whisper some truths in Donal Gowan's shell-like ear about the care and handling of my love, but she wouldn't let me come in.

"Dress rehearsals are chaos," she said. "Besides, it will spoil things for you when you come to watch tomorrow."

From the wary look that went with the kiss she gave me I think she might have been afraid for Gowan's life.

I found a parking spot near the Marine Building and spent an hour staring up at the east facade of the place through a pair of Zeiss seven-by-fifties.

One of my favorite buildings, the office tower is an elegant early Vancouver contribution to the *Art Deco movement*, having been built a few years after the *Parisian Exposition des Arts Decoratifs* of 1925 which gave the style its name. Terra cotta panels of a creamy off-white cap the curtain walls and surround the entry. They are molded in displays of west coast fauna, mixed with historical tableaux about the early *explorations* of the Pacific coast.

I tried to imagine the trajectory of Kovacs' body as it fell. A recessed panel in the central third of the buff-colored brick wall, above the fifteenth floor, left a ledge, suggesting that a body falling from the nineteenth floor deck would have to be given a damned good shove to fall clear.

Was Sandy dead before he fell? If Tatiana was right, the killers had to beat him senseless to subdue him. If they'd planned a quiet "suicide" and then been forced to throw him over the rail to cover the signs of the beating, his fall made a kind of sickening sense. I made a mental note to ask McRae to give me a look at the medical examiner's report. He might be reluctant to do that but Tatiana should be able to demand to see it. She had an arguable legal right. Meanwhile, I would try for a look at the nineteenth floor deck and the fifteenth floor ledge.

My God. I was already thinking like a cop. What had she done to me?

The elevators in the Marine Building go only to the eighteenth floor, a minor but healthy inconvenience for those who could afford floors nineteen through twenty one. I wasn't certain I'd find anyone in Feldman's office. McRae had said they were closed. If need be, I'd drive out to Feldman's house in West Van. Jake Feldman was going to talk to me, one way or another.

The reception desk of Feldman, Tauber, Slibowichs and Brown, Attorneys at Law, was functioning. For the first time I noticed a second company logo beneath the gold letters listing all of Jake's partners. "S M E, it said, with a wavy, thin, blue line running through the stylized black letters. Probably some little branch company tax dodge for the law firm.

The svelte blond behind the reception desk was attractive, in a business-like way. She was unaccountably glad to see me. "Mr. Sutter," she said. "I understand you nearly became a victim of the tragedy on Monday."

"It was near enough, thanks."

"What a terrible thing. Mr. Kovacs seemed so, well, buoyant. Not depressed or moody. I can't believe he would jump."

"Neither can I, Miss…" I leaned to look at her desk name-plate. "Miss Bradshaw. Is Jake in?"

"Mr. Feldman has cancelled all appointments this week and closed the office. But I'm sure he will see you."

Feldman appeared at his office door in stockinged feet and without his tie. "C'mon in, Hank. Sorry your business has been held up. I closed the shop for a few days. Couldn't work after what happened Monday."

"My business can wait. I wanted to talk to you about Sandy."

"Bloody shame. Fine young man. Smart as they come. Been pushing the Law Society to let him article before his citizenship comes, uh, came up."

Jake almost fell into his padded leather chair, then put his feet up on the Japanese oak desk. "Bloody shame," he said again, shaking his head.

No wonder the blond at the front desk had been glad to see me. Jake Feldman was loaded. The flushed face and slurred words bespoke at least a few good stiff ones. I seemed to remember that Jake liked martini doubles and I couldn't think of a faster way to get drunk. Sure enough, there was a shaker on a side table, beside a folding hidden bar.

He followed my gaze. "Get you a drink, Hank? Least we can do to pay our respects."

"No thanks. I wanted a look at your deck, and then I need to ask a few questions."

"Be my guest. You running in cop mode? Heard you were good at that stuff out in Korea. Got you a field commission, I'm told. Unusual for the navy."

"It was a cultural necessity. Some Koreans wouldn't answer questions from a non-commissioned officer."

"That was your story. I heard some others." Jake gestured towards the double doors leading to the open deck. "Police have been all over that deck with a microscope. Asked a helluva lot of questions, too. Nosey buggers."

I examined the concrete floor carefully. There'd been no sign of a struggle in Jake's office. If Tats was right and Sandy had fought for his life, he'd done it out here.

The floor of the deck might have been surgically cleaned, except for one patch of fresh seagull droppings. Then I saw the drains in the outer corners of the deck.

"Jake? You keep a bucket in your washroom? Or anything that would serve as one?"

"Bucket? What the hell would I use it for?"

"Is that a no?"

"Wait a minute. I had a plastic foot bath for soaking my bunions. Maybe it's still there."

It was. The few drops of moisture in the footbath were not something left over from Jake's bunions. If Sandy's death was murder, and I was beginning to suspect it was, I thought the killers might have used it to wash away the traces of a fight. The rain, that Monday, had lasted until about nine in the evening so the deck would have been wet in any case.

High on the parapet railing, beneath the concrete cap, I found a discolored smear. It might have been a rust stain. And it might have been made by a bloody hand clutching at life.

"Do you lock those doors at night?" I asked, pointing to the double glass doors leading to the deck.

"Just the snap latches. No point in heavy duty locks. Have to be a human fly to get up here."

"How about your inner office door?"

"Locked and dead-bolted."

"Do you have a safe?"

"It's in here." He pointed to a wall panel.

"Would Sandy have access?"

"No. Irene put his reports in the safe. 'S for documents, not money."

"What was he working on, Jake?"

"Not at liberty to say. Client confi-dent-shality, y'know." He was having trouble getting his mouth around big words. He'd had more than just a few.

"Did you give McRae that line?"

"'Course. He respects the position of an officer of the court."

"I'll bet he does. He's probably going after a court order for the information right now."

"Well...if he does, I'll have to comply, won't I? But I don't think it's going to happen real soon. I mean if the case was a murder, it might be different. But suicide?"

"You know what his sister says about that?"

"Tatiana? Sonofabitch, ain't she a looker?"

"She says Sandy was followed for weeks before his death. Including the Monday night he died. You know that?"

"Yeah, yeah, she bent my ear about it. Should stick to her dancing an' leave the police work to the police. High strung, that girl. Rumor is you and she are a number. True?"

"Who's been talking to you?" Jesus. The Sutter family grapevine moved at the speed of light these days.

"Was obvious, the day of the funeral. I checked with Clara, just to be sure."

"It's true. And so is her story about Sandy being followed."

"You're really gettin' into this thing, eh Hank? She got you jumping through the hoops?"

"Are you going to tell me what Sandy was working on?"

"No."

"At least tell me what *kind* of thing it was. Insurance fraud? Digging out dirt for a lawsuit?"

"None of the above, and no, I won't give you any more. There's more'n one reason." He paused, tugging at his lower lip, thoughtfully. "You think foul play was involved?"

"Jesus Christ, Jake, you are drunk. You know that? Pissed. Of course he was murdered. Right here in your own damned office. And you don't want to help find the killers? How does that square with your 'officer of the court' bullshit? You going to drown your responsibilities in booze?"

Jake slid down in his five-hundred-dollar padded leather chair. He seemed to wilt under my vehement endorsement of Tatiana's view that her brother had been murdered.

Miss Bradshaw tapped on the door and looked in, anxiously.

"'S all right, Irene. Everything's fine. My cousin gets carried away, sometimes. You got those boxes of Sandy's stuff?"

"Yes, Mr. Feldman."

"What stuff?" I demanded.

"Personal effects. Stuff from his desk, et cetera. The detective had a look but nobody can read Sandy's personal shorthand. If Irene can't do it, that means nobody, take my word. Those notebooks are no help to anybody."

"What shorthand?"

"Notebooks are crammed full of it. Damnedest note taker I ever met. Never missed a thing. I'll show you."

We waded the carpet to the outer office. Two small cardboard boxes stood beside Irene Bradshaw's desk. In one a solid mass of law textbooks greeted me, wedged in place by spiral-bound notebooks like overgrown steno pads stuffed down the sides. On top were a dozen large, color photographs featuring Tats dancing in some major ballet production. Or most likely it was several productions, since the costumes and scenery differed.

The second box had similar contents except that there was more personal stuff, including an album of black and white family snapshots that obviously went back a few years. One group of pictures that startled me showed Tats and Sandy, as youngsters, skinny dipping in a lake with four adults. Two were middle-aged, a man and woman. The second couple I judged to be in their late thirties. The family resemblance between Tats and the younger of the two women was unmistakable. Her mother?

A careful look at people in the background revealed that they were in some kind of nudist park. Maybe that explained Tatiana's unnerving lack of embarrassment about her body.

"McRae says Tatiana might as well have these. They're no use to the police," Feldman said.

"I'll see that she gets them," I said. "Sorry if I got a bit loud, Jake."

"'S all right. Ev'body's unner a strain. Me, you, ev'body. Sure you won't have a drink?"

"I'm sure. But I'll be back with the same question when you're sober. You might want to think about how you're going to answer me next time."

"Yeah. I'll do that."

*

I lugged Sandy's boxes to Cam's car and returned to the building. The manager for the firm of chartered accountants inhabiting the offices that overlooked the fifteenth floor ledge was reluctant to talk to me at first, until I mentioned that the tragedy of the previous Monday might be a murder. I didn't actually say I was a cop but I can't help it if I look the part.

McRae hadn't talked to him or looked at the ledge below the firm's windows. That surprised me. He should have done that. A brownish stain that could have been blood was visible on the top outer edge of a panel of terra cotta sea lions and whales.

The manager, volubly helpful now, said, "We noticed that stain Tuesday morning. We thought it was the remains of a meal for one of the peregrines. The falcons roost in the building's nooks and crannies and prey on passing pigeons. Once we found a rat and another time a half-eaten salmon. Building maintenance gets upset with them."

"Tell maintenance not to touch that one until the lab has a look."

"Yes, sir. Always happy to cooperate with the law."

*

Building security was handled by a sub-contractor. They had a desk in the main lobby. I knew it hadn't been manned at the time of Sandy's death, though the guard had reappeared shortly after I'd made my call to the police. I needed to know why.

The security man on duty that morning wasn't helpful. "We've got three buildings to look after and we're short-staffed," he said. "You heard there's a recession on?"

"You mean whoever is on duty here circulates between three buildings?"

"Jeez, I went over all this stuff with you guys on Tuesday."

"Humor me. I wasn't here Tuesday."

I leaned over to read the brass name tag on his jacket pocket; Herbert. "Herbert what?" I asked.

"Wayman," he said. His Adam's apple bobbed as I wrote his name in my notebook. But his nervousness loosened his tongue.

"There's usually a man in each building plus a relief man. Guards can call in backup or a relief if they need to," Herbie said.

"You said `usually.' What does that mean?"

"We were short a person on Monday night. The relief man called in sick."

"So there were gaps in the coverage here? Say around eight on Monday evening?"

"The desk was covered most of that time. Y'know? Just, like, if you asked about some particular time, like maybe twenty minutes, half hour, nobody might be there, sitting behind the desk. Guy gone to the can. Lunch. At some particular random time, if you take my meaning."

Herbert was sweating.

"Who covered for the sick guy?"

"I did, I guess. They asked me to double shift."

"You guess?"

"Like I said, there was gaps. Guy's gotta answer the call of nature, ya know. How come I'm gettin' all these questions again? You cops went over this about six times on Tuesday."

"We're forgetful. Who was on shift Tuesday morning?"

"I was. See, that's my regular shift. Mornings. Why is that important?"

"*All* morning?"

"Except for coffee break and at lunch time. Company fired the guy who didn't show Monday night, so we're still short a body."

"Herbert, I hope you gave Sergeant McRae the same answers when he interviewed you?"

"More or less. I'm not in trouble, am I?"

I grinned at him. "Somebody will let you know." I left him staring after me.

*

Sandy's rooms on Harwood Street, about six blocks from Tats' Victorian, were on the upper floor of a ramshackle old mansion that had been defaced by numerous fire escapes. It was about the same vintage as Tatiana's but it hadn't weathered the years so well.

Mrs. Thompson, the broad-beamed landlady, was in a vile temper when she came to the door. "You another of those damfool cops?"

"No ma'am. I was a friend of Sandy's. His sister asked me to look in on his rooms."

"Thought maybe you was going to try renting 'em. Can't even get in to paint the place, never mind show the rooms."

"Why not?"

"Police sealed 'em, along with damn near my whole top floor. How'n hell 'm I supposed to make a living when they do things like that to me? I'm gonna write the mayor." She scratched a wooden kitchen match on the door frame and lit a ragged home-rolled cigarette, blowing acrid smoke at me and picking shreds of tobacco from her lower lip.

I coughed and asked, "Why did they seal his rooms, ma'am?"

"It was just a simple break-in. We have 'em all the time. Well, two or three a year, since they made us add all those fool fire escapes. And they never locked us out of the rooms those other times. Hardly even looked around."

"When did this happen?"

"Monday night, late. Around midnight. You'd think a whole week 'd be enough, but I phoned that Sergeant McRae today and he said no, I couldn't get in. And no, the police weren't going to pay the rent on the place neither. You got any more questions, come back tomorrow. I'm watching my soaps."

She'd have slammed the door in my face, except that my size fourteen foot was in the way.

"That doesn't seem fair," I said. "Did you hear if anything was taken?"

"They weren't saying. There was a whole dumb herd of cops dusting powder on everything and prying things up, snapping flashbulbs. Take me a week to make it fit to live in. And where in hell is Kovacs? His rent's due, end of last month. He leave town?"

"Sandy Kovacs died Monday night."

"No! You don't tell me! Young fella like that? How'd it happen?"

"Probably murder."

Mrs. Thompson backed away from me, wide-eyed. She seemed to sag and, for a moment, I thought she was genuinely upset about Sandy's death. Then she said, "Oh my God. If that gets in the papers, I'll never rent those rooms."

"Could be, ma'am. So maybe you shouldn't write the mayor?"

"Oh my. No. I won't do that. Who's gonna pay his last month's rent?" she shouted after me as I left.

*

When I caught up with her at the academy, Tats said, "We are doing a final rehearsal with costumes and lighting after dinner. But I have two hours off now."

"That's generous of Gowan, to let you eat. Does he plan to have you sleep tonight as well?" I looked around for Gowan but he wasn't in sight.

"I think you are jealous, Hank."

"Jealous? Not bloody likely!"

"Maybe because he gets to hold me? Put his hands in certain places?"

"If it doesn't bother you, it doesn't bother me. But he should be a little more considerate of you. I'm sure he could have postponed his recital."

"No. It is not possible. We are wasting time. Where shall we eat tonight?"

"You ever try Chinese food?"

"I love it."

Why wasn't I surprised? We headed for the Lotus Gardens at Abbot and Pender streets, the western fringe of Chinatown and close to the academy. The district isn't a place you'd want to walk alone at night but the restaurant, down half a flight from street level, has a quiet oriental elegance that makes it a favorite with touring theatrical people.

Over the remains of dinner, we relaxed and I described my meeting with Feldman and the negative results.

The break-in at Sandy's rooms came as a shock to her. She said, "If they went to his rooms after Sandy died, that means they searched for something he had but…"

"But didn't find at his office. Logical. Probable, even. But not proven."

"What is it? You have doubts that he was murdered?" she demanded.

"No, Tats, I have no doubts any more. Coincidences like this don't happen in real life. But what could he have had that someone wants badly enough to kill for?"

"I don't know. Sandy was full of ethics. He wouldn't talk about what he did for Mr. Feldman."

"He told you about me."

"That is different. He wanted me to meet you but he told me nothing about your business with Mr. Feldman."

"And Feldman won't tell me what Sandy was doing either. Something queer about that. Aside from Jake being drunk as a skunk at ten in the morning."

"You will find it out," she said with finality. "And when I come home tonight, we will look at Sandy's boxes. Maybe I can read what he wrote."

I thought Tats' chances of reading her brother's notes were slim. Irene

Bradshaw was a shorthand expert, according to Jake. She knew five varieties of the stuff and it was none of those.

Maybe I'd find out what Sandy had been up to if McRae got his court order. If he thought the case warranted that. And if he then told us what he found out. If.

I had a brief inspiration that I might somehow get to Irene Bradshaw. Senior secretaries, in my experience, know all there is to know about a company's inner works. But she'd impressed me as being tough as nails, under the sleek exterior. Without her boss's agreement, I'd probably need the same court order to get her to open up.

*

The late rehearsal lasted until ten-thirty. I expected to collect a weary Tatiana but I was wrong. She was fired up to work on Sandy's papers and attacked the two boxes with a vengeance, when we got home.

I put the snapshots of Tats and her brother frolicking in the buff in front of her. She giggled. "This bothers you, Hank?"

"It looks like some kind of nudist resort. Was it?"

"Yes. It is on Lake Balaton. These are my aunt Elena Horvath and uncle Horvath. Sandy and I lived with them. And these are my parents." She pointed. "We were all…mm…strong nudists. Many Europeans believe in that."

"You still do, hussy."

"What is this hussy?"

"Cheeky and sexy."

"You want me in pajamas?"

"No. I want you just the way you are."

"Good. Hank! Pay attention to what we work on!" She removed my hand from where it had strayed.

"You didn't live with your parents?"

"No. It was a…problem caused by the war."

I waited for more explanations but she seemed to withdraw, and then changed the subject.

"After the recital, I will look for his shorthand. Sandy would not try to invent complete system. Maybe your new library has something? Or maybe the second-hand book sellers on Granville Street?"

"Okay, but let me see if Clara will make the rounds with you. I don't want you out on your own for a while."

"Clara will make it fun. What will you do?"

"Look at this. See where he's listed proper nouns, like names? And addresses? I guess you can't record the spelling of names in shorthand. I'll start tracking those people down and maybe discover Sandy's connection with them."

"There are dates here," she said.

"Right. We should concentrate on the most recent entries. I'll copy the names and addresses."

There were eleven names in Sandy's last notebook, and seven addresses, though these didn't relate directly to the names. Or not all of the names. A quick look through the telephone directory let us match two names to addresses. Both were international shipping agents. It was a start.

Sometime after midnight I managed to chase my nudist lover into bed and join her colony. We were in the middle of some particularly delicious love-making when the door shuddered to a violent thumping.

"Hank! The door!" she said, breathlessly, pushing me away.

"They can bloody well wait," I said. But Tats was frozen with fright.

"Open up, it's the police," McRae said.

"Shit. McRae at this hour?" I grunted. I reached for my shorts. Couldn't find them and gave up. The door thumping continued. "Yeah, yeah, okay for Christ's sake."

Anyone who interrupts lovers after midnight deserves whatever sights greet him, but I took shelter behind Tats. McRae was rather startled to be met by a pair of sweaty nudes at the door, one of them holding her favorite brass lamp base like a baseball bat.

"I need you downtown in my office, Sutter. Now. For Christ's sake, put some pants on. Both of you."

"Yeah? What's happened?"

"You'll find out soon enough."

Tats was gray. Police at her door at midnight was not something an eastern European woman looked forward to. "You are arresting him?" she demanded.

"No, ma'am. Not at this time. But I have some questions and Mr. Sutter has the answers, I believe."

I grabbed her by the shoulders. "Tats, just stay calm. Okay? I'll find out what's eating our friend here and be back as soon as I can."

"Okay," she said. But I wouldn't want to be on the receiving end of the look she gave McRae.

C H A P T E R

6

McRae took me to an unused third floor office in the Public Safety Building. The room had a frosted glass door and glass wall panels facing the interior hallways and a high, mesh-reinforced window on the Main Street side. Like the corridors, it was painted a hideous Department of Public Works green. Sounds, fragments of speech, assorted door slams, gurgles from the heating system and, once, a scream filtered through the glass.

A wall mirror overlooking the old wooden desk made me suspect one-way glass but the desk held no revealing papers for me to be caught looking at.

McRae left me there, shifting from cheek to cheek on the hard chair and breathing the fumes of his last cigar. For forty minutes, by my watch.

There are probably as many interrogation techniques as there are cops. I'd tried a few myself, some of them through interpreters -- which lends a certain color to the proceedings. McRae was an artist.

After my "softening up" period he conducted his questioning like a friendly chat, leaving the room from time to time, as if his questions were unimportant, some kind of spare-time affair. And then he'd return to ask the same questions, having "forgotten" or misconstrued my original answers, over and over -- until, and unless, I screwed up and said something inconsistent.

By three in the morning I was in screw-up territory.

"Let's go over this again," McRae said, talking around a fresh cigar which he proceeded to light with a large kitchen match. He dropped the bumbling, forgetful pose, put his face close to mine, and said, "Why, exactly, did you go to see Jake Feldman this morning?"

He held the stare for a moment, then turned away from me and paced up and down the narrow office while I sat, following him with smarting eyes. It was a new take on the third degree. Neck cramps, eye strain, and a gas attack.

"It was yesterday morning."

"Let's not be a wise-ass, shall we? Answer the question."

"Sorry. If you want proper answers you should ask your questions carefully. Strictly speaking, I didn't go to see Feldman at all, `this morning'."

My exposé of police interrogation techniques was having its intended effect -- throwing McRae off stride. But I thought I'd better not push my luck. "I went to see him to clear up some formalities for Tats. And to pick up Sandy's personal effects," I said.

"And you went after him to tell you what Kovacs was working on?" It wasn't a question.

"I asked him that, sure. He wasn't answering. He was drunk. Did he tell you what Sandy was doing?"

"I'll ask the questions. At ten in the morning, Feldman was drunk? Intoxicated? Not just feeling happy?" He seemed to have missed that, the first four times through.

"I told you that."

"You said he was drinking. Not drunk."

"He was drunk as a skunk. And still drinking."

"After you left Feldman's, where did you go?"

"To Sandy's apartment on Harwood Street. Nice of you to tell Tats about the break-in. The landlady was pretty steamed, too. Why have you got the place sealed?"

McRae was good at concealing his irritation but he was developing a twitch over his left eye. With exaggerated patience he said, "Look, Sutter, I'm the investigator. You're the witness being questioned. Got that? Now let's try again. Later that morning, immediately after leaving Feldman's office, you called on the offices of Peabody and Strange?"

"No. I went to the parking lot half a block west on Hastings and put

Sandy's boxes of stuff in the trunk of my car. Or the car I have borrowed, to be precise."

McRae looked ominous. He flipped a chair around and sat on it, backwards, in authentic third-degree style. Edward G. Robinson couldn't have produced a better glower. "Well, you did say `immediately after',," I said, piously.

"Peabody and Strange. When did you go there?"

"Who?"

"The chartered accountants on the fifteenth floor. You talked to their office manager. Yes or no?"

"Well, yeah. I was curious about how Sandy's body could clear the step in the outer wall at that level. There was what looked like a bloodstain on the ledge that I spotted from street level. I meant to tell you about it, soon as I saw you."

"And you told the office manager you were a policeman?"

"Oh, now, wait a minute, sergeant. I said nothing to suggest that. I merely cautioned him about disturbing any possible evidence."

"Sure you did. Then you put the downstairs security guy through a ten-minute grilling. What was that about?"

"It was about why the security desk wasn't manned at the time Sandy died. Anybody could have been in that building. And anybody could have gotten out of it."

"So you *are* conducting an investigation?"

"No. But Tatiana might be considering suing the building management for negligence."

"Oh sure she is. And I'm the tooth fairy." He leaned over me in his best intimidation style. It didn't quite come off, given the difference in our sizes. "Look, I'm going to give you one warning. You have no status as an investigator here. I don't give a shit what you did in Korea. Or any place else. You aren't going to do it here. Understood?"

"Did I interfere with your investigation?"

"You came squeaky close to that."

"So long as I don't interfere, I can ask anybody whatever I want to ask. Right? It's not my fault if my questions are ones you forgot to ask. Or I looked at stuff you forgot to look at."

"You can also spend a few months in the crowbar hotel, for your... What stuff?"

I just stared at him.

"What stuff did we forget to look at? Goddammit, quit jerking me around."

"The blood stain on Feldman's nineteenth floor deck."

"What d'ya mean, blood stain? There was no sign of a struggle."

"Unless that stain really is blood and not rust," I said. "It's high up on the rail, right under the cap-piece about halfway along."

"Huh. We'll have a look. But dammit all, that doesn't change anything. Interference with a police investigation is a matter of judgment. And the judges are for damned sure on my side. Do we understand each other?"

"Yes. This doesn't sound like a suicide investigation. Has Sandy's death been designated a murder?"

"I'll tell you when the status of the investigation changes."

"You don't work double shifts and pick people up in the middle of the night just to warn them off a case."

McRae stared at me for a long moment. "You got that right," he sighed.

"So what's happened?"

"Jake Feldman was shot dead in his office last night."

I felt like I'd been kicked in the gut. "Jake?" I croaked. "Oh my God." Jake Feldman was one of my family's very few pillars of rectitude. Family jokes about him were the price of his wealth and success but they weren't mean- spirited. We knew he was generous to a fault -- not the sort of man who gets shot.

I shook my head in denial.

McRae said, "You were the last person who talked to him, apart from Bradshaw and the killer. I couldn't establish where you were at the time he died. Until half an hour ago, that is. That's why I pulled you in."

"What time was he killed?"

"Around nine P.M., according to the MO," McRae said.

"And how did you -- Oh, I get it. One of Nunn's spooks was watching Tats and that means he was watching me. Right?"

McRae was impassive but he seemed to relax just a little. Or maybe it was resignation, or a change of tactics, because his interrogation sure as hell wasn't working. He shifted his cigar to the other side of his mouth. "You ever run into a case like this?"

"You mean a phony suicide?"

"Assuming it was phony," McRae said.

"No. The Koreans were pragmatic about how they killed people. They liked car bombs but mostly they just shot people." I said.

"Feldman's secretary left the office at five. He told her he was going to take a nap and go home later. He keeps a cot in his inner office. My guess is he didn't want to risk driving, if he was as blitzed as you say. His body was found by cleaners at around ten-thirty. Nobody heard a shot and we have no suspects."

"Do you know what he was shot with?"

"Nine millimeter full jacket slug behind the ear."

"So the weapon was an automatic. Probably silenced, if nobody heard it."

"Eh? Automatic for sure. I don't know about silenced."

"Was the slug deformed?"

"What's that got to do with anything?" McRae looked puzzled.

"People who use silencers, if they know their business, use twenty-two caliber. Nice and quiet, but not too certain. If they use larger calibers they reload their ammunition to cut the charge and keep the slug's muzzle velocity under nine-hundred feet per second, the speed of sound. The silencing works better. If the slug wasn't deformed, that would tend to suggest it was a reload. So was it?"

"Deformed? No." McRae stared at me. "You a ballistics expert?"

"No." I bit down on some smart remarks I could have made. McRae was talking to me like a human being and I didn't want the mood to change.

"Then where in hell did you run into that gem?"

"Pusan, Korea. Their bad guys have real experts."

"I'll run that by ballistics. Too bad we don't have an empty casing."

"Whoever these people are, they're very tidy," I said.

"Yeah. Too damned tidy. I guess you could use a coffee?"

I nodded.

McRae was looking thoughtful and much more friendly. I hoped that meant the questioning was over. His questioning, not mine.

He left to get the coffee and I puzzled over where he'd been going with this midnight inquisition. I was sure I hadn't been a suspect in Jake's murder so McRae had been trying to find out what, if anything, I knew.

But two could play the brains-picking game.

McRae returned. His tray held two black coffees in chipped "White Lunch" mugs and two stale, khaki-colored donuts. Ambrosia.

"Why is Nunn hounding Tatiana Kovacs?" I asked.

He studied me over his cup for a moment. "Not completely sure," he said. "He certainly is interested in her, though.

"Make a guess."

"This is off the record. Understood?"

"Of course."

"B section, counter-intelligence, is where Nunn came from. When they booted him out of Ottawa he was stuck in D section, counter-subversive, and he doesn't like it one damned bit."

"Why did they ship him out here?" I asked.

McRae sipped his coffee, then blew across the top of the cup. "Hot," he said. "He drinks. And he talks when he's drinking."

"Ah. And that's how you…?"

"Let's just say I'm a good listener." McRae smiled, faintly. He sprawled in a chair and I realized he must be at least as tired as I was. But he seemed to be well launched into his subject. "Anyway, B section has all the glamour and the budget. D section makes life miserable for left-wing trades unionists and anyone they think is a security risk, or might, some day, become one."

"Jesus Christ! They think Tats is a subversive?"

"I don't think Nunn believes that for a minute," McRae said. "He's stuck with his assignment, which is watching the local Communist party and the few bad apples we got with our influx of Hungarians. But he's desperate for brownie points that will get him back to Ottawa."

"The people following Sandy Kovacs, and now Tatiana, act as if they're being deliberately clumsy," I said.

"What gives you that idea?" McRae seemed surprised and skeptical.

"She spotted them, weeks ago, without even looking for them. I saw a guy who fitted her description of one of them at the funeral, talking to

Nunn. That takes some kind of prize for clumsiness and we both know the RCMP is much better than that. Unless Nunn is trying to shake her up."

"Um. See what you mean," McRae said. "How come you didn't tell me about this joker at the funeral?"

"You got away before I could."

"Well, it figures. I hear he's training his own surveillance crew. Ottawa won't give him a Watcher Service unit."

I knew something about the force's elite Watcher Service surveillance teams. They were expensive to run so they were usually reserved for high priority cases. "I'm worried sick about my poor girl's mental state and Nunn's class of `beginner spooks' is following her around? Grown men looking for subversive sugar plum fairies? Jesus suffering Christ!"

McRae made a placating, pushing-away gesture with his hands. He could probably hear my fuse sizzling. "Look, Sutter, don't underestimate Nunn," he said. "He works hard at giving the impression he's a dumb flat-foot but he's nothing of the kind. He's not stupid and he is persistent."

"Yeah. So are warts."

Then McRae dropped his bombshell. "Oh, by the way. The Kovacs case is now a murder investigation. Your pretty lady was right. The suicide note was a phony."

*

I got back to Tats' apartment some time after four that morning. Her door was double deadbolted, according to my instructions, and she wasn't answering to my knock. "C'mon, Tats, it's me. Hank," I said, wearily. "Open up."

"Prove who you are," she said in a tiny voice from behind the door. "What do you call me?"

"Huh? Oh, penguin. And you call me monster."

The locks clattered and the door opened a crack. Then wider. "They let you go free?" she said in a tone of awed disbelief. She still had the brass lamp base cocked over her shoulder, as if I might turn out to be somebody else.

"Of course. I did nothing wrong. McRae just had some questions."

She let me in. "At midnight? In my country you would not be free in less than two weeks, even if the police had made a complete mistake. Here they do not worry about saving face?"

"Not that way. But McRae was damned mad about my investigating. I'm not sure how long I can get away with it."

"You found out some things he did not know?"

"A few."

"He will let you continue. Was that all he wanted to talk about?"

"No." I took a deep breath and said, "Jake Feldman was shot dead last night, at his office. And your brother's case is officially a murder. You were right. The suicide note was forged."

She folded onto the edge of the bed, knees together and arms wrapped tightly across her breasts, rocking gently. Her eyes were closed and her mouth moved, though no sound came from her. I felt as though I'd kicked her.

I dropped my overcoat and sat beside her, holding her, expecting tears or worse. I felt her shiver through the thin wrapper she wore. After a long silence, she said, "So now it is both our families." She lifted one of my hands with both of hers, studying it. "So strong. They are like clubs. But you must have a gun."

"So you said. Several times."

"You disagree?"

"Not exactly. Buying a gun is a nightmare of permits and character checks that take weeks. And they won't issue a carry permit unless you're a target-shooter or transporting millions."

Tats chewed her lower lip, looking thoughtful. I should have noticed that.

Of course you could buy whatever you wanted on skid row, for a price but I didn't think I wanted anything they had for sale. You never knew where it might have been.

There were a hundred Browning Hi-Power automatics in the armory at HMCS Discovery, my reserve unit's barracks in Stanley Park. But I couldn't think of a way I could pry one loose from Chief Petty Officer Watson, in whose loving care all weapons resided.

The only other handgun I could get my hands on readily was my father's Colt .44 and that was forty miles away on Galiano Island. But I couldn't simply grab it and run. I'd have to spend a couple of days visiting. Dad would give me the gun for sure, but not without a lot of questions. And if I knew him he'd be up to his ears in this investigation before mother could stop him.

There was one other way. You could drive to Bellingham or Seattle and buy a gun without much hassle. The hassle came when you smuggled it back into Canada.

Maybe I'd have to borrow Cam's shotgun. A bit unwieldy but at least it was a gun. Tats was looking worn. "You've got to dance this afternoon. Better try for a few hours of shut-eye."

"I can't relax. Not after what you have told me."

"Got any sleeping pills?"

"You are my sleeping pill. Come to bed with me."

I made love to her, not well but effectively, I suppose. She was asleep and snoring inside half an hour.

But I was wide awake and trying to make sense of Jake Feldman's death. The faceless bastard leading the killers was either a clever tactician or damned lucky. That phony suicide note bought them exactly what they had to have. Time to get clear. They hadn't bothered with anything so elaborate when they'd killed Jake. Not necessary? More and more, I was convinced that Herbie, the security guard, knew something.

And who was the joker who'd been asking for my address?

Damn. I'd forgotten to call on Marty Haines to find out what he'd told the guy. It was Saturday. Haines would be handling dispatch calls for the Picard fleet from his home but it would be useless to call him. Marty considered himself one of the company big shots. On Saturdays and Sundays, he did what big shots were supposed to do. He vanished into one or another of the city's golf courses. I wouldn't catch up with him until Monday.

I dozed off, counting "what ifs" and "maybes." I'm not sure how much time had passed when I woke but the darkness was breaking up in a watery dawn. Tats moved restlessly beside me. I wondered if she wanted me to hold her, or make love to her again. But she wasn't awake.

She thrashed violently, then sat up with a moan, staring into the shadowed room with wide, terrified eyes. Distant neon splashed blue and red on the rain-streaked windows. Tats cursed in rapid-fire Hungarian. I was sure it was cursing, though I knew only a handful of words in her language. But I knew one that she repeated, over and over in a strangled cry of fear. Nem, nem, nem…No, no, no.

I grabbed her by the shoulders and pulled her to me.

She clawed at me like a trapped wild animal until I managed to pin her arms. Glistening with cold sweat, heart pounding, she gave a piercing shriek.

Then she stiffened, suddenly awake, breathing rapidly. "Mi…Wha… what?" she mumbled.

"It's all right, Tats. You're safe." I rocked her like a baby, crooning.

"Hank? That is you?" More coherent now.

"Yes, my love."

"I dreamed…something terrible."

"A nightmare. Do you have them often?"

"Not often. Did I say things? What did I say?"

"You said a lot but I'm damned if I know what. It was all in Hungarian."

"Ah," she nodded. "Oh! I have scratched you."

"It doesn't matter. What was the nightmare about?"

She shook her head in an exaggerated negative that was more than "no." A denial of her ghosts? "Please. I don't want to talk. Just hold me." So I held her. Her trembling fear was a long time leaving her but at last she slept.

And I lay awake again, wondering what horrors drove her psyche.

C H A P T E R

7

Blossom's Cafe was our first stop after we fell out of bed at noon. Tats didn't order her usual scrambled eggs and hotcakes and sausages. She settled for toast and five cups of coffee. Blossom worried aloud that she might be ill.

The restaurant seemed to have a lot of staff on hand and I suspected Blossom had brought in a few relatives to witness, first-hand, one of Tats' phenomenal meals. Too bad she'd let them all down. She was quiet and introspective.

I thought her dispirited mood might be the aftermath of her terrifying dream last night. "Do you want to talk about it?" I asked.

"About what?" She watched me from beneath lowered lashes.

"Your nightmares."

"No. Nothing can be done about them."

"Do you know what causes them?"

"Yes. They will go away." She paused, then said, "Hank, I want to meet your other woman."

"My *what*?" So much for Hank Sutter, psycho-therapist.

"My, mm, competition? This wonderful old ship you talk about so much. Can we do that after the recital?"

"Sure. Would you like to have dinner with the crew?"

"Oh! Could I? That would be fun."

"I'll phone Jimmy Lee and warn him you're coming."

"Why must you warn him?"

"So he'll be sure to have enough food aboard."

The look I got for that was normal Tats.

I delivered her to the academy early, resigned to be abandoned while she prepared. The Western Academy of Classical Dance was in the process of being converted into a theater for the day. Youngsters were setting up folding wooden chairs and an electrician was buried, head-first, in a stage-lighting console.

Two dozen musicians tuned up. The academy's practice hall had a stage but no proper orchestra pit so musicians were seated behind the backdrop. Obviously Donal Gowan was sparing no expense.

The noon edition of *The Sun* gave an account of Jake Feldman's murder but before I could open my copy Clara found me. "There's nothing new," she said, gesturing at the paper. "Have you talked to Ella Feldman?"

"Not yet."

"Poor thing. I called her this morning. She was upset, of course, but not as badly as I'd have expected. I gather things were a little strained between her and Jake."

"I didn't know."

"Are you investigating his murder too?"

"I'll try. So far the police haven't found a clear connection between Jake's death and Sandy's but at least they are admitting Sandy was murdered. The connection has to be there."

"Tatiana phoned me in the middle of the night. My goodness, she was in a dreadful state, in tears and nearly incoherent. She said you'd been arrested and taken away."

"They didn't arrest me but I spent the night at the cop shop being interviewed. Seems I was nearly the last person to talk to Jake."

"Who was last?"

"The killers, obviously."

"Oh. Of course. Tatiana says you need a gun. Are either of you in danger?"

"It's possible. I was hoping you could put in some time with her this week. She's going to look for Sandy's shorthand system in the library and used bookstores while I snoop elsewhere. I don't want to leave her on her own."

"I can do that. Besides, she needs to do some more shopping. That girl doesn't own enough underwear. Here, I brought you something." She pulled a brown-paper-wrapped package from her shopping bag and handed it to me. It was unexpectedly heavy and I nearly dropped it.

"What...?"

"Alf's Smith and Wesson. There's a box of shells with it."

"Clara! I can't--"

"Yes you can, Hank. If anything happened to Tatiana, or you, for that matter, I'd never forgive myself for not having given it to you. It shoots a little high and to the left, I remember he said."

Alf Sutter, my uncle, was Clara's late husband, killed in 1954 in a flying accident in the Yukon. Like most bush pilots, he believed in having a gun aboard in case of a forced landing. Why he'd left his magnum at home on that last trip, we'll never know.

"Oh, and don't feel guilty or anything," she said.

"Um? Guilty?"

"About not getting me invited to this recital. Never mind. Tatiana fixed that," she said. Miffed. No, pissed off.

"I'm sorry, Clara. I should have thought of that but I had things on my mind."

People were filing in, being greeted by Donal Gowan wearing a red velvet dressing gown over his costume. Much of the audience consisted of family and friends of the academy's students but a small group near the front of the hall were obviously Gowan's prospective backers.

I'm not sure what I'd expected of a ballet performance, but the occasional snippets I'd seen in movies or on television hadn't prepared me. The combination of mime and dance and music mesmerized me and I was swept up in the old fantasy in spite of myself. I had watched Tats dance and exercise at the academy and I knew, in an intellectual way, that she was very good indeed, but what I had seen were bits and pieces, fragments. The lyrical eloquence of her Odette, the bewitched swan princess, and the crisp precision of Odile, the sorcerer's daughter (and the lightning costume change Tats made to dance both of them) left me in stunned amazement. I scarcely needed Clara beside me to know what I was watching but Clara positively glowed.

Donal Gowan as Prince Siegfried was excellent, as were the swans and cygnets of the *corps de ballet*. Obviously Gowan had pulled together some able dancers, and no doubt all of them were hopeful for the advent of his new company. The final curtain broke the spell. Applause was long and generous with some "bravos" that I'd thought only happened in Italian opera houses. But while the dancers were still taking bows a slightly frantic catering outfit rushed in with platters of finger-food and punch bowls.

Dressing room space seemed to be at a premium so many of the dancers simply wandered out into the milling audience in costume, some to chat with family or friends, others to be introduced to "important people." I made my way in Tats' direction, arriving just as Gowan was introducing her to an austere, middle-aged woman wearing a dead fox for a collar and too much jewelry. "My God, Donal, where did you find her?" the woman asked. Her accent was light. Russian, I thought.

"She found me, Irina," Gowan crowed. "Budapest. The Hungarian National Ballet."

"Eh? Budapest? Really, my dear?"

"Yes ma'am," Tats said.

"Tell me, when did they start teaching the cabriole to danseuse in Budapest?"

"They haven't. But why should only men do it?"

"No reason, except that it requires fantastic elevation. And Lord, you certainly have that. I've never seen a *grande jette* like that. Tell me, can you do an *entrechat dix?*"

"I don't know, ma'am. I never counted."

"You are being modest. Donal, she dances like a Russian. Kirov, I should say, with that amazing turn-out. But then I hear the Hungarians all do that since Vianonen went there. Did you know him, Tatiana?"

"Yes, ma'am. Vasiley Vianonen was our choreographer and ballet master."

"Until you left Hungary?"

"Oh no, ma'am. He went back to Russia in 1952."

"Ah yes, of course. What did you dance for him?"

"Flames of Paris, and the Nutcracker. But I was only eighteen and not a principal." Tats seemed nervous.

"You are what? Twenty-three?"

"Yes ma'am."

Tats seemed intent, as if she was on trial. In a way, I suppose she was. The woman tossed her fur and looked at Gowan, who moved in, like a salesman about to pounce. Then she turned back to Tats. "Donal tells me you did the choreography to make this abbreviated production work."

"We didn't change much. Just dropped the grand ballroom and castle scenes and three characters," Tats said.

"And put it back together beautifully, I must say. Have you developed any full-length ballets?"

"Not yet, ma'am. But I'm working on one, when I have the time."

"You must come and have tea with me and tell me about it."

"Yes ma'am. I'd like that."

The woman nodded. "Donal, she is a jewel. Guard her with your life."

"For sure, Irina," Gowan said, grinning broadly.

"Kirov," she nodded, smiling slightly. I wasn't sure what was going on between the lines here, and Gowan had pointedly left me out of the introductions. But the inquisition seemed to be over and Tats relaxed as Gowan moved away with his guest. Tats turned to Clara. "Well?" she asked.

"Oh my dear, you don't need my opinion, do you? But I will give it anyway. You were simply superb."

"Adequate, anyway," Tats said. She turned to me. "Did you like me?" she asked.

"I wasn't the only one, judging from what I just heard."

"But you. Did you like me and the ballet?"

"I thought your swan princess was the most incredible piece of witchcraft I've ever seen. I mean, I know nothing about ballet but…"

"Oh my. And we hardly had any scenery."

"Yes you did. You were gorgeous."

"Hmm. Such flattery will go to my head. But don't stop."

"What's an entra- um, entrechat?"

"*Entrechat Dix?* That's when a dancer goes straight up, like this," she demonstrated. "And crosses her feet while she is in the air, mm, in a sort of beat. *Entrechat dix* is ten crossings. Very unusual. What I just did is *entrechat quatre*."

"Can you do it?"

"Ten? On my good days."

Clara sucked in a breath, her eyes round.

"And a cabriole?" I asked.

"I will show you at home. There isn't room here. Have you met my cygnets?"

"The little swans? No. Why are they yours?"

"I coached them for the quartet. Just a minute, here are some of them." She rounded up three bubbling youngsters who were probably twelve or thirteen, and introduced them. They giggled and whispered whatever girls whisper to each other. They seemed relieved when Tats turned them loose.

"Let's talk about dinner. What are they serving aboard your ship?" she asked.

"I've no idea."

"I'm starving."

"When are you ever not starving? Why did that woman -- Irina? -- say you danced like a Russian?"

"She is Russian, so she meant that as a nice compliment. She is Irina Ivanova. She was a famous Bolshoi dancer, before she married a rich American."

"But you didn't take it as a compliment?"

"I took it as it was meant. Ivanova never met Russian tanks in the street outside her theater."

"Why didn't you tell her you danced with the Kirov Ballet?"

"I did not want to talk about it. Tell me what you thought about Donal Gowan's dancing."

"Well, he didn't drop you."

"Donal is a professional."

"And a dreamer."

"Yes. Like you. I will shower and change. Then we will go to your ship."

Clara moved in as Tats left. "Hank, I hope you know what you have here, with this young lady," she said.

"I think so. Why?"

"I've never seen a dancer to compare with her. And when you consider the emotional strain the poor thing is under, her performance was even more remarkable."

"She seems able to put her grief away, somehow. Lock it away in another compartment. Underneath, there's a frightened girl. I wish I knew what that is about."

"Frightened? You don't mean heartbroken?"

"Maybe both. She has the damnedest nightmares."

"Well, you've certainly got her undivided attention when she's awake, Hank."

"Maybe I'm a substitute for what she's lost."

"That wasn't my impression, after spending a day with her, Don Juan Sutter," Clara said, impishly.

"Uh, yeah. Well, we do get along, uh, rather well," I mumbled, feeling my color rising. I thought it was about time to change the subject. "Gowan guards her like she was Fort Knox."

"I'm not surprised. Tats could be the making of his company."

"I've never known anyone like her, Clara. But…"

"She still says no?"

"Yeah. I keep asking."

Gowan drifted by at that moment, glass of punch in hand, eavesdropping. His face looked like a thundercloud. Then he brightened. "She turned you down?"

"Is this any of your business, Gowan?"

"Yes it is. If you asked her, and you're not crowing about it, she must have turned you down."

"Goddammit, get lost."

"Ah! She's an angel, that girl. Please keep doing whatever you are doing that pisses her off." And he drifted away to join another group.

I glared after him.

"That man is plain rude," Clara said. "But are you and Tats having problems?"

"None at all. I asked her if she wanted me to leave her but she didn't want that either."

"Give her some time."

"That's probably wise. But I don't think that's the problem."

"You are talking about me?" Tats pounced on us.

"Guilty. Is there anyone else to talk about here?"

"Sneaky flattery again. I will shower at home. There are too many waiting. Then we will see your old ship."

"Wear your shortest skirt. It'll keep the animals at bay."

"Very funny."

*

She didn't go for the short skirt. Instead she wore red toreadors that must have been sprayed on. Our arrival on the dock found most of the crew of the *Solange Picard* on deck to rubberneck the arrival of the skipper's new lady.

"Holy shit!" Jeep said, and walked straight into the towing winch spooling gear, nearly braining himself.

Tats blushed. Then she worried that he might have hurt himself.

"The winch'll be fine," Cam said. "And Jeep's okay. It was only his head."

I handed Tats over the rail, not that she needed any handing, and she was immediately surrounded. Jeep's reaction seemed to be the general consensus.

Tats wanted to see everything, including the engines and the boilers. Cam Douglas gave her the royal tour below decks, explaining such exotic stuff as the difference between Scotch marine boilers and the Solange's high pressure water-tube variety. Tats didn't yawn even once. She asked so many questions that Cam was about to launch into a discourse on the theory of triple expansion steam engines, until I got in the way.

"Everything is so clean and polished," Tats said. "And I didn't know engines could be three floors high."

"Decks high," I corrected. "The galley is even cleaner. Jimmy Lee has dinner ready for us." I knew food would get to her.

Jimmy had outdone himself with stuffed mushroom caps and baby oysters as appetizers, French onion soup and a filet mignon main course that would have made Junior's accountant weep. Ten of the crew were aboard for dinner and Tats held forth from the seat of honor at the head of the horseshoe-shaped table. It was one of the few meals I'd eaten aboard to be followed by polite after-dinner conversation. Jeep looked silly holding a cup with his pinky extended, said pinky being the size of anyone else's thumb. Cam and Axel seemed at home in the sudden upsurge of civilization. Cam had even found a tie and not one of them ripped loose with any of the cuss-words they normally used for punctuation. And nobody was prepared to let me have Tats to myself. They crowded around like party kids who'd trapped the Easter bunny.

She basked. I swear she did.

"You dance up on your toes, Miss Kovacs?" Jeep, the social butterfly ventured.

"En pointe. That is normal in classical ballet, though usually only women do it. And please, who is this Miss Kovacs? Call me Tats."

"How long's it take to learn?"

"They start preparing us at eight but they don't let us do much until we are ten. The bones are too soft. After that it takes two or three years, if you have good feet for it."

"What's a good foot like?" Jeep was getting into ballet? He would hear about it later, after the ragging he'd given me over when I was going to appear in a tutu.

"Like mine," Tats said, displaying a nylon-clad foot for inspection. But I think Jeep was distracted by the rest of a shapely leg.

"But why do they do all that toe stuff? I mean it seems so, uh, formalized." This was my cousin Jeep, from Vegreville, Alberta, talking? Sheesh!

"It is a hundred and thirty years tradition, like the rules of harmony in music or meter in poetry. Without form, composers and poets would be nothing but noise and wind. It is so with dance, as well. Dancing en pointe changes a dancer's, mm, shape? Her, mm, what is the word?" She made vague shapes in the air with her hands. "Hank, help me."

"What? It's bigger than a bread box? Square shaped?"

"Don't be silly. In Hungarian the word is mretek."

Axel spoke up. "Proportion, you mean?"

"Ah. Thank you, Axel. It is nice somebody here speaks this language." She gave me a wry look. "It changes her line and…proportions? as is not possible with feet flat on the stage."

"A hundred and thirty years ago they wore tutus?" Jeep asked. The tutu seemed to be Jeep's favorite feminine attire, after the "European cut" bikini.

"A French theater owner got the idea that if dancers did such clever steps, people would like to see them."

"I bet that was a sensation," Jeep said.

"A scandal. But as they say, scandal never stopped the French."

Jimmy Lee brought in dessert, then. Cherries jubilee, floating in a glass bowl of flaming brandy.

When talk resumed, Cam took up the inquisition. "So you've been dancing since you were eight?"

"Fifteen years, yes."

"But how did you go to school? Or just fool around like an ordinary kid?"

"I attended a dance academy which was also a school. So many hours dancing and so many hours of school work every day. We had to do our exams at regular schools, though. And there was plenty of fooling around. Our ballet master thought we were holy terrors."

Somehow I had no trouble believing that. My grin got me an elbow in the ribs.

"And then you went pro?" Jeep asked.

"I graduated at sixteen and they offered me a position in the *corps de ballet* at the National Ballet Theater."

"Wow! I guess that's like first draft pick," Jeep said.

"Pardon?" Tats looked puzzled.

"He means that was an honor," I said.

"Perhaps. I was excited at the time. I loved to dance and I didn't know how to do anything else, so it made sense I should have a career as a dancer."

"And now I get to show you my end of the ship," I said.

"Aw, Hank. You think she wants to see your crummy wheelhouse and the radar and all that? When she could stay and talk to us?"

"Yeah, I do, actually."

So I showed Tats around the navigation end of the *Solange Picard*. She was full of questions and I soon realized she wasn't asking them just to please me. She had a quick and curious mind and wanted to know how everything worked.

The wheelhouse was a modern anachronism, having dual radar sets, electronic sounders, gyro compass, LORAN and three kinds of radio telephone, all of which were fairly recent additions. A geared, steam steering engine, original equipment behind a polished brass rail, occupied the after half of the wheelhouse and forced the helmsman to stand in front of the wheel. Fortunately, Cam didn't have steam valved to it at the moment or the thing would have been hissing at us.

We stepped out onto the bridge wing. The night sky was ablaze with stars, the air crisp. Tats moved close. "You can find your position from the stars?" she asked.

"Yes. I'll show you some day, when we're at sea. We can't get a decent horizon, tied to the dock."

"Hank, I've had a wonderful time. Your crew has been most gallant."

"Yeah. Haven't they just? I couldn't believe that Jeep. He sounded nearly literate. Tooey and Jimmy are in love with you. Me too."

She kissed me, seriously and in detail. "Me too," she said. "Where is your room?"

"There, beside the skipper's day cabin," I pointed. "It's rather small."

"Show me, and we will see if there is room to do something about all this love."

There was room, just.

*

I tend to do my serious thinking when I'm half awake in the middle of the night. My berth was wider and longer than standard but it had never been intended for two. Tats was tangled up with my legs and arms, doing her best to make one body of us. She made delicate little cat snores.

I knew I had no way of pulling this case together without knowing what Sandy had been working on. As it was, I couldn't even guess. But maybe there was another route. Corporal Nunn seemed to be connected to the people tailing Sandy. If Tats was right and they'd switched their attention to her...

Hell, I knew she was right. McRae had virtually admitted that Nunn's surveillance had been my alibi, the night Jake Feldman was killed.

Was there a way to discover what else Nunn knew? Get him to talk? Or could McRae get him to talk?

The usual Canadian view of the RCMP varies between the Hollywood demi-god cop-hero rescuer-of-damsels icon who sings like Nelson Eddy, wears his dress red serge and stetson to work every day and performs in the musical ride -- and the jerk who just gave him a traffic ticket.

I didn't subscribe to either view. They were just hard- working cops cursed with a cumbersome, nineteenth-century, paramilitary command structure which wasn't remedied by an incredibly good public relations department. Many communities, and several provinces, contract with the force for their police work and in that kind of situation they are efficient and virtually incorruptible.

But they had no business·messing around in intelligence work. There were rumors out of Ottawa of an independent civilian intelligence agency being formed but nothing had happened yet.

Nunn's surveillance of Tats had something to be said for it. No self-respecting crook was going to make a move with Nunn's trainee spooks hanging around.

And what was I going to do with Clara's damned cannon? Tats was certainly responsible for that so I wouldn't be able to ditch the thing. A Smith and Wesson model nineteen isn't a weapon you stick in your belt, movie fashion. Not if you want your pants to stay up. I decided I would carry it in a zip-up brief case like school kids and insurance salesmen use.

Tats stirred. "How will you explain me to Jimmy at breakfast, Hank?" she asked, sleepily.

"No need to explain, my love. Just ask him to set another place. I hope you realize you've made my reputation for life."

"Mmm? That's nice," she said, and went back to her cat snores. My last coherent thought was that the one thing an investigator had to have was emotional distance, and mine was all shot to hell.

And I didn't give a damn.

8

"If you are captain, you can have bigger bed. Yes?" Tats said, sometime around dawn.

"You don't like to sleep close?" I teased.

"Yes, but you give off much heat and you have rug on your chest that tickles. A girl needs cold weather for sleeping with you."

"Is that a complaint?"

"No. It is easy to fix. Just shave off rug."

"Whaaaat!?"

"You don't like to shave?"

"Not that."

"Why not? I shave things for you."

"That's different. The rug wouldn't tickle if you slept closer."

"Closer than this?"

"Much closer," I said.

"Oh." Later, she said. "Is this too early for breakfast?"

"No. The rest of the crew will have finished. But I told Jimmy we might be down late."

"They eat so early?"

"At sea we change watches at six, so breakfast is between five-thirty and six-thirty. Seven o'clock to eight when we're in port."

"What is this `watches'?"

"Six hours on and six hours off."

"Twelve hours? This is as bad as ballet school!"

"We collect time off to make up for it."

"Ah. Where is the shower?"

"Main deck, aft of the galley. I'll show you. I'd better stand guard on the door."

"Why? I am not afraid of your crew."

"I know, nudist. I'll be guarding them from you."

The shower was uneventful, once Tats learned that "hot" meant what it said, aboard a steam ship. She consumed a large breakfast, to Jimmy's amazement and delight. I could have told him she was off her food and he hadn't seen anything yet.

"Mornin', Hank," Jeep said, poking his head through the mess-room doorway. "Mornin' Miss Kovacs. Hank, you still want us to chip and prime the aft bulwarks? I mean, what with the subsidy bein' cancelled and all, doesn't seem like much point."

"What's the subsidy got to do with anything? I'm buying the ship and I want it properly primed and painted."

"Thought that was all b.s. Where'n hell you gettin' a million bucks from?"

"That's my worry. Yours is stripping the rust off that piece of bulwark plating and making it real pretty."

"I suppose you want the deck stoned too?"

"Yep. Soon as you finish painting. Steam hose first, though. There's some grease on deck by the winch."

"Fuckin' yacht. Oh! Excuse me, Miss Kovacs."

"It is okay, Jeep. I have heard the word before. But my name is Tats, still."

Jeep grinned and withdrew. I figured his questions were an excuse for another look at Tats. The painting of the aft rails and holy-stoning the deck was work Jeep had known about all week.

What was I going to do with Tats for the day? Clara had volunteered to help with the hunt for Sandy's shorthand but that couldn't begin until tomorrow when stores were open. She'd left me with the impression I was supposed to bring Tats to her North Vancouver home today but I couldn't just turn Clara's life upside down, no matter how willing she was. I knew she did fund-raising for a hospital burn unit and volunteer work with mentally retarded children.

After coffee in the mess-room, I tackled the problem on the telephone. "What do you mean you aren't bringing her over? Of course you are," Clara insisted. She sounded outraged. I wavered.

"I don't like leaving her alone," I admitted.

"You can't. But I'm having second thoughts about giving that gun to such a lame-brain. What would your father say if you shot yourself in the foot or something?"

"Hey, take it easy, Clara. I know how to shoot a gun."

"That's what they all say. Anyway, Tats and I have hundreds of things to talk about. I can take her to the public library for a few hours. They're open this afternoon. We can start the search for Sandy's shorthand there. Oh, and tell her to bring her suit. It's nice and warm and we might get a swim in the pool." Tats had been hanging on my arm, listening. She made strenuous gestures which I divined were about a swim suit, or the lack thereof.

"She doesn't own a suit, Clara," I said. "Listen, I still feel like we're imposing."

"Well, you're not. Besides, Tats is the only dancer I ever met whose feet aren't a complete ruin. I want to find out how she does it. She doesn't swim?"

Tats nodded, vigorously, making swimming motions.

"Oh she swims, all right. Just not in a suit."

"Ye gods. Then take her somewhere and buy her one."

"It's Sunday, remember?"

"Oh that's right. I forgot. Well, she'll just have to swim in her panties and bra."

"Fine. I'll bring her over for the inquisition about ten."

"You are arranging things for me?" Tats asked, as I disconnected.

"You don't want to go to Clara's?"

"Clara is lots of fun."

"But?"

"No buts. I will go to Clara's for the day." She sounded a little miffed.

"I worry about you, Tats. You're addictive."

"So? But now you have a gun so I don't worry so much about you."

"Promise me you'll do what Clara says? If she brings you into town to the library, don't go wandering around on your own. Okay? And you watch what is happening around you. If anything looks weird, you run like hell. Got it?"

"Like hell. Yessir, captain." She saluted, sticking her tongue out at me.

"I will pick you up at around six, so save your appetite for then."

"Which appetite?"

"Uh, yeah. That one, too."

*

In Vancouver they say "if you don't like the weather, just wait ten minutes" -- which is especially true in October. One day it's raw and blustery with rain that's half sleet. The next, it's warm and sunny. Saturday the weather had done an Indian Summer flip-flop and Sunday was going to be warmer. This late in the year, the flip-flops were short-lived and you grabbed them while you could. The town's parks and beaches exploded with people out soaking up the last of the year's sunshine.

I didn't have much of a plan for my day's sleuthing. Vancouver on a Sunday, to quote Jeep, was "shut tighter'n a bull's arse in fly time." But I thought the university might have some clues to Sandy's activities and, Sunday or not, certain things functioned on the campus. The law library was open.

The University Endowment Lands are two thousand acres of lush evergreen forest on Vancouver's westernmost promontory, Point Grey. I'm not sure who Grey was but Captain Vancouver claimed the place for Britain in 1792. There are plaques commemorating his landing, and even some that mention his meetings with the Spaniards who had been here years ahead of him. The endowment lands are a natural buffer between the city's wealthy Point Grey district and the campus on the western tip.

Using a lot of time and shoe leather, I discovered that the law faculty was split between its original gray concrete building near the northeast edge of the campus and "The Huts," sometimes called Fort Camp, half a mile away. Its library had remained with the original building.

The lady on the front desk was fortyish and wore her blond hair in a schoolmarmish bun. She made helpful noises, without producing any help, when I asked her for Sandy's borrowing record.

"We don't normally give out that kind of information, sir," she said. The slight emphasis on "normally" seemed to invite more from me. She had lovely blue eyes and she kept them well swept with long fluttery lashes. That must have been hard to do while holding a deep breath intended to keep her other formidable assets in view.

"Not even for a murder investigation?"

"A murder?" Her eyes went round and she exhaled.

"Sandy Kovacs. On Monday of last week."

"Oh, no! The papers didn't say that was murder." She looked as if tears were imminent.

"You knew Sandy?" I pressed.

"Not well, but he was here often. He was nice."

"Yes he was. So, what about his borrowing record?" I did my best to thaw her with a smile but I felt like a lame version of Dragnet's Sergeant Friday.

"Well…I guess in a case like that, there'd be no harm." She disappeared into a back office and reappeared, several minutes later. "Twelve books in the past month." She said, handing me the list. "Oh, and four of them haven't been returned. Do you suppose you could…?"

"I'll make sure they get back here."

"How did it happen?" she asked.

I gave her a brief account of Sandy's supposed suicide that wasn't a suicide, making it sound like a police report.

She was dabbing at tears when I finished. The books Sandy had read didn't sound promising. Several were CCH Law Binders, records of provincial and federal criminal cases covering recent years. The four overdue volumes were "Summary Proceedings of the Nuremburg Trials." That gave me pause.

"Do you know who his law advisor was?" I asked.

"Hugh Dalls, I believe."

"Where would I find Professor Dalls on a Sunday?"

"Maybe in his office, in Fort Camp," she said. "But on a day like this, more than likely he's down on the beach."

"Do you know which one?" There were about five miles of beaches to choose from.

"Tower Beach," she said. "The trail goes down from beside the old gun emplacements. He sometimes takes papers down with him when he's marking. Hugh is a sun worshipper and I don't think he could resist soaking up a little more. But try his office first; the beach trail is steep."

Fort Camp was a run-down emergency classroom complex using old barracks blocks left over from the wartime days when Point Grey had a battery of coast defense guns and searchlights. Nobody wanted to spend money on the buildings since they were supposed to be torn down. It showed. Hugh Dalls had a corner office in hut sixteen. He wasn't in it.

I'd heard about the famous Wreck and Tower Beaches, miles of sand beneath the 200 foot high bluffs that fringe Point Grey. The University Detachment of the RCMP made occasional, embarrassed forays to arrest nude sunbathers but, mostly, they left them alone. I seemed to be running into nude people regularly, ever since I'd met Tats. The day was sunny but only fairly warm. Beach weather, if you stayed out of the wind. I hoped it wasn't police weather. I was congratulating myself on getting away from the librarian without being asked for my police credentials when she intercepted me on a path between huts. She'd reconsidered her schoolmarm look and shaken her hair out. There was a lot of it. "I'll show you the trail to Tower Beach, officer," she said. "That is, if you promise not to arrest any of the sunbathers. It's an unofficial nude beach."

"Not my concern at all," I said.

"Good. You might have trouble locating Hugh, since I couldn't tell you what he was wearing." She giggled.

"That's kind of you, miss, but I'm not--"

"No problem. Anything I can do to help with your investigation, detective…" She left me the space to fill in my name. I didn't.

*

Professor Dalls was about fifty, skinny, bespectacled and stark naked. He was seated on a blanket, propped against a large drift log, near the base of an abandoned concrete searchlight tower that had served the heavy guns on the bluffs above. Dalls held a briefcase between bony knees and, periodically, extracted a handful of papers.

"Ah, Mandy! Who have you brought me?" Dalls continued to study his papers, glancing only briefly at me. He had a cultured British accent. Mandy, somewhere behind me, seemed to be disrobing. A few dozen people were sunning themselves, scattered across the sandy part of Tower Beach. I seemed to be the only person wearing clothes. Mandy said, "This gentleman is investigating the death...murder of Sandy Kovacs, Hugh."

That got his attention. "And you are?" he demanded.

"Hank Sutter. I was a friend of Sandy's."

"Not police?"

"No."

"Then how is it you are investigating?"

"I'm acting for Sandy's sister, Tatiana."

"A private investigator? What is the police view of your involvement?"

"About the same as their view of your involvement on this beach. Not legal but tolerated."

"Touché, Mr. Sutter."

"I gather you were aware of Sandy's death," I said.

"A secretary from his office telephoned to tell me on Tuesday. I understood it was a suicide."

"It's a murder investigation, now. How well did you know Sandy?"

"Personally? Not especially well. I saw him here on the beach, from time to time last summer, with a young lady who I assume must have been his sister. He was my brightest student by a wide margin. I'm not happy to hear he was murdered but I couldn't believe he'd commit suicide."

"Had he mentioned anything he was working on for Jake Feldman's office?"

"Nothing I can remember. Oh...there was something. I'd been talking about pro bono work and client privilege and whether a client you didn't charge was entitled to the same confidentiality as any other."

"I'd have thought that was obvious," I said.

"Nothing is ever obvious in law. But as it happens you are right in this case. Paying and non-paying clients get the same treatment."

"No exceptions?"

"Sandy approached me after the lecture and asked that same question about exceptions."

"And you said?"

"Not unless there were unusual circumstances."

"Such as?"

"Say that a serious crime was about to be committed, and could be averted only by breaching confidentiality."

"Did you tell him that?"

"Yes. He did seem somewhat relieved. I asked him for more specifics but he declined discussing it."

"Sounds like Sandy was getting ready to blow the whistle on somebody or something," I said.

Mandy, now in the buff, seated herself beside Dalls and snuggled up to him, rump to rump, cadging blanket space. She began applying suntan oil to both of them.

"It does, rather, doesn't it?" Dalls said. He made space for Mandy and went back to his marking.

"Would you care to join us, Mr. Sutter?" Mandy asked. She was nicely browned in all the places that usually have ugly white marks. And forty or not, she had a fabulous figure. "This is probably the last warm and sunny weekend we'll get this year," she added.

"No thanks, ma'am. I've got other people to see."

"I brought some sandwiches and beer," she coaxed. She'd produced a picnic lunch from somewhere. "There's lots," she added. Indeed there was, and not just of food.

"Not this time, thanks. Just one other question, professor. Why would Sandy be researching the Nuremburg trials?"

Dalls looked startled. "I've no idea. We weren't dealing with them, this trimester."

"Thank you. You've both been helpful."

"I suppose I'll get these questions from the police, as well?" Dalls asked.

"I'm sure Sergeant McRae will be around to see you."

"Bloody marvelous."

*

Sandy's landlady wasn't answering her doorbell and I put my ear against the door. If she was watching soaps, she was doing it somewhere else. I didn't expect to learn much but Sandy's stuff needed to be picked up. Tats wasn't ready to deal with that sort of problem yet and I couldn't think of a place to store his things. The trunk of Cam's car would have to do for now.

"You back again?" The landlady leaned out of a top floor window, directly above me. She had a painter's cap jammed on top of a bun of unruly gray hair and there were yellow spots on her face.

"I came for Sandy Kovacs' stuff. Can you let me in?"

"No need. It's all in boxes, down in the alley."

"You threw his stuff out?"

"It's waitin' fer the welfare to pick it up. I got no space for storin' people's junk. Gotta keep my rooms rented."

"That's right kind of you, ma'am."

"So sue me!"

"Somebody should. I'll be sure to mention it to Sergeant McRae."

"Asshole."

Four large cardboard boxes were stacked beside a telephone pole in the alley. A derelict of uncertain sex and age said, "Get lost, Mac. I was here first." I think it was a "he."

"Friend of mine owns this," I said.

"Yeah? We take turns at pickins, 'roun' here."

"Not today, we don't." I extended a two-dollar bill. He snatched it from me and backed away, muttering. Somebody had already picked through Sandy's stuff, probably the night of the break-in, even if the landlady hadn't done it since. I loaded the boxes into Cam's car.

*

Anton Milloss lived in a two-room basement "suite" at the rear of an elderly, shingled bungalow off Kingsway on Victoria Drive. He was slow to answer his door but his dog wouldn't let him ignore me.

Milloss was slight and leathery with a tobacco-stained moustache and he needed a shave. He was seventy-eight and hard of hearing, he informed me. Deaf or not, he could hear the whining, growling cocker spaniel lurking between his legs. "Binker," was admonished to shut up several times. Binker didn't. Milloss neglected to invite me in so I asked my questions standing in his doorway. I noticed the lock had been splintered.

"I think you understand me, Mr. Milloss. But I'll write my questions for you, so there'll be no mistakes." I flipped my note pad open and wrote "Sandy Kovacs. Did you know him?" and held it up for him to read.

Milloss shrugged again. Then, giving me a sly look, he said "How did you find me?"

"Your name was in Sandy's notebooks," I wrote. And said aloud for good measure.

"Ah. Dead. Poor man."

"How did you know that?" I wrote.

"Newspaper," he said. Then, "Are you police?"

"No."

"What then?"

"A friend. I'm investigating his murder."

"Ach. So many police, now, after he is dead." Milloss' hearing problem seemed to have miraculously cleared up.

"Police were asking you questions about Sandy?"

"Police and not police. First came two men. Dangerous men. They did not give me names."

"Why do you say they were dangerous?"

"Binker knows." He reached down and scratched Binker's ears. The dog responded with an outburst of barking. "He does not bark when there is real danger," Milloss said. He smacked the noisy Binker, affectionately, with a rolled newspaper, with no noticeable effect.

"I see. What did they ask you?"

"Where did Sandor Kovacs work and where did he live."

"They used his full name? Not `Sandy'?"

"Just so."

"Why would they come to you for that information?"

"I am part of Hungarian Cultural Society we make here. They thought I have list of members and addresses."

"And did you tell them what they wanted to know?"

"I told them I did not know any Kovacs."

"But you did have the information?"

"Maybe," he said. Again that sly look.

"When did they call on you?"

He stared at me with his uncomprehending look. Didn't trust me, I thought. But then, why should he? "I'm looking into Sandy's death for his sister, Tatiana. Do you know her?"

"Maybe." There was a subtle change in his expression.

"Why maybe? She was a dancer with the Hungarian National Ballet and left Hungary with the rest of the revolutionaries. And she is my girl-friend."

"So? What is her nickname?"

"Tats?"

"Ah, yes. And where does she live?"

"Near English Bay. Bidwell Street."

That seemed to convince Milloss. He looked skyward, then scratched his ear. "I am old and memory does not work so good any more. They came…maybe three weeks ago?"

That would be two weeks before Sandy's murder. I had the vague feeling that I was getting close to something. "You said they came first. There were others?"

"Yes. But the police came long time after the robbery."

"You were robbed? After the two men came to your door?"

"Two days after. Ah. I remember date, now. It was September 11th. A Tuesday. I was just going out to a meeting when they came. The robbers broke in on Thursday when I was out again." He gestured at the splintered door jamb. "They took nothing, since I have nothing worth taking. I re-ported to the police. But different kind of police came to talk to me."

I made notes. September 11th was nearly a month before Sandy had died. Could that have been when people started tailing him? Tats would know.

"Different police? How were they different?"

"Like Hungarian AVO only you have different letters."

"RCMP?"

"They are secret police. Yes?"

"Among other things. Did they call on you before or after Sandy's death?"

"That I remember well. It was day after. Tuesday. But they had no interest in robbery or the first two men. They ask me about Sandor Kovacs and his politics."

"Did the officers give you their names?"

"One did. But I forget."

"What did you say about his politics?"

"He didn't have. Except maybe hating the reds like most of us."

"Did other people come and ask questions?"

"Sure. Regular police came yesterday. My robbery didn't matter so much, since nothing was stolen. Only my place was messed up. And now you. I never have so many visitors since I come to this country." He gave me a gap-toothed grin. It sounded as if the company was welcome.

"Could you describe the two who weren't police?"

"I wrote down description after they left. I gave to secret policeman and I will give to you a copy."

"You wrote it down? That's an odd thing to do," I said.

"When you live in a fascist country that turns into a communist country, with all kind of secret police, you learn to be careful, what you remember."

His written description was a faded carbon copy of a lined notebook page. It was in Hungarian. From the twinkle in his eye, Anton Milloss was having some fun with me. He seemed disappointed that his little joke hadn't worked.

And I was sure he had never for a minute lost track of the date the two "dangerous" men had called on him. "Sept. 11" was printed at the top of the page of descriptions.

I thanked him and made my way towards the front street and Cam's car, using the narrow, overgrown garden path beside the house.

A Vancouver PD squad car turned off Kingsway onto Victoria Drive and pulled to a stop in front of Milloss' house as I was about to open the front gate. I dropped to my hands and knees and scuttled, crabwise, to get behind a huge old japonica tree that nearly filled the postage-stamp front yard. I held my breath as I watched McRae walk right in front of Cam's Chrysler hardtop without, apparently, recognizing the car.

He entered the yard and headed for Anton Milloss' back door entry. Binker sounded off again, nicely covering my racket as I vaulted the fence and dove into Cam's car. I tried not to peel rubber as I left.

*

The drive through south Vancouver and across the harbor to North Vancouver and Clara's felt like a week-day rush hour, only worse. Everybody in the city seemed to be out for a Sunday drive. And the damned Second Narrows lift span was open again. A tanker waddled from inner to outer harbor, shepherded by berthing tugs, taking her time. The new Second Narrows Bridge was supposed to be ready next year, along with the Upper Levels Highway. For a mile west of the old bridge, the harbor's north foreshore was a vast heavy construction site, with unfinished bridge piers and massive unconnected pieces of span cantilevered over thin air or propped up on too-thin temporary struts. Concrete trucks, piles of steelwork and construction cranes were everywhere.

We Vancouverites were conditioned to the chronic rush-hour jam on Cassiar Street and the old railway-cum-auto lift-bridge that snaked across the Second Narrows. Some of us wouldn't miss it a damned bit, when the new bridge was finished. My head felt like the bridge construction site. I had a bunch of pieces of the puzzle and no clue about how it went together. Or even what kind of a puzzle it was.

The pair of "bad men," as defined by Binker, who'd called on Milloss looking for Sandy must be important. Were they the killers? Had they broken into old Milloss' place to get Sandy's address? Or was that connected at all? And what about an old geezer who made detailed notes about people who came to his door asking questions? And had photocopies to hand out? Damned careful, Mr. Milloss.

Clara's place was a lovely old mock Tudor on a huge grassy lot on Osborne Street, east of upper Lonsdale, North Van's main drag. She was probably over a thousand feet above the harbor, right against the base of Grouse Mountain, and she had a view any real estate developer would kill for.

"You are looking puzzled," Tats said, greeting me at the door. "This means progress?"

"Christ, I hope so," I said. We kissed, thoroughly, so that Clara had to clear her throat to get our attention. "When you two come up for air, I'd like to hear what happened today," she said.

"Not much, I'm afraid. But I picked up the trail of the guys following Sandy, I think." I handed Milloss' description copy to Tats. "Translation, please," I said.

She scanned Milloss' sheet. "Two men who refused to give names. The first man was in middle twenties, muscular with face like craters of the moon. Not smiling and swearing a lot. Short brown hair. Big ears. The second man was older and more polite. He was tall and, mm, wide? He wore glasses and a blue suit with stripes and, mm, two breasts?" She wrinkled her brow in puzzlement.

"Pin stripes and double breasted, you mean?"

"Ah. Yes. But I have never seen these men."

"You're sure?"

"Yes. But look, here on the back Milloss has written `Corporal Nunn.' Did he visit Milloss?"

"I think so. Yes, he must have."

"You make good progress."

"Progress? I'm working my way deeper and deeper into a hole and it feels like it's going to fall in on me. If that's progress, then yeah, we made some. But Sergeant McRae is working on this case, too. He nearly caught me at Milloss's."

"That's wonderful, Hank," Tats said.

But if Corporal Nunn wanted to know about Sandy's politics, why hadn't he asked Sandy? Instead he had asked old Milloss. And then had people following Sandy around. I would never understand the spook business.

C H A P T E R

9

"I will come with you today. You need to be cheered up."

"Pardon?" I came out of my mental haze with a jolt. Over breakfast, I'd been worrying at the fragmented pieces of the puzzle and not paying enough attention to Tats.

"I said I will come with you, while you do your detecting. Unless you don't want me."

Tread carefully, Sutter. That last bit sounded ominous. "Tats, I thought—"

"Never mind. I will stay home and lock my doors."

"You and Clara were going to hunt for Sandy's shorthand system today. Wasn't that--"

"Clara called me this morning. You were sleeping. She said she had a talk last night with Ella Feldman. Ella needs someone to help her through the funeral."

Damn! Of course she was right.

I'd intended to call on Ella after Jake's funeral, which was to be tomorrow at three. I wasn't planning to attend but it should have been no surprise that Clara would be lending moral support to her widowed cousin. Clara and I had both been intent on raising Tats' spirits Sunday at dinner and neither of us had mentioned Jake Feldman's funeral.

I hadn't planned on dragging Tats around the waterfront. I suspected she had some romantic notion about detective work gathered from watching her favorite Cagney gangster movies. She was in for a big let-down. Romantic it is not. But without Clara my choice was leave her on her own or take her with me, which was no choice at all.

"Okay, Tats, you're my girl Friday for the day, and maybe tomorrow. Bring a good book or you'll be bored to tears."

"What is this Friday girl? It is only Monday."

"Just an expression, my love. It means you're my helper."

"Ah! I am `Girl Monday'? That will be exciting."

"Yeah. About like watching paint dry. But first I have to check in at the dock."

*

Henri Picard Jr. awaited me on the dock. Short and pudgy, with thinning hair plastered across his bald spot and wearing a pencil moustache that should have been erased, Junior harbored fond illusions of being a lady's man. Nobody shared them. Junior's eyeballs nearly popped out of his head at the sight of Tats, and his prepared tirade seemed to have evaporated. "Introduce me to the charming young lady, Hank," he oozed. Junior had recovered his long-lost Quebec French accent from somewhere, symptomatic of "lady's man" mode. And never in his life had he addressed me as Hank.

I mumbled an introduction, meanwhile watching Tats with growing incredulity. Her royal highness was giving Junior the gears! At five- foot-six, Tats was already two inches taller than Junior and for the first time since I'd met her, she was wearing three- inch heels. Those canceled the two-inch lifts in Junior's shoes. She looked down a regal nose, then extended a hand to be kissed!

Junior wasn't sure what to do about the proffered hand. At last he bowed over it, breathing heavily, and made a low pass with his lips in a fumbling attempt at continental courtesy.

Meanwhile, Jeep, at the rail amidships, was taking this in with his mouth open. So were Cam Douglas and Axel Oberg.

"I wanted to speak to you about your time off, Hank," Junior said. "But it can wait." He was smiling at Tats and ignoring me. Hard to be a lady's man in the middle of an argument.

"I've got four months in my time bank," I said. "What's the problem?"

He turned to me, reluctantly. "If you aren't living aboard, I'll have to log you as being ashore on time off."

"I told Marty I could be here before you could raise steam for any callout. What's changed since then?"

"We've had an inspection by the DOT."

"On a Sunday?" My God, somebody at DOT had it in for Junior if civil servants were doing Sunday inspections.

He nodded. "We're required to maintain the ship on stand-by pressure with a full crew aboard at all times. That means thirty minutes notice to leave the dock."

Damnation. I'd half expected a snap inspection. Even Junior knew he couldn't get away with his cold-ship scam forever. And with Mick O'Conner hung out to dry in Valley Sanitorium, I was the only Picard employee with the foreign- going skipper's ticket the *Solange* required. "Who are you going to get in my place?"

"That's not your problem."

"Oh? You've got somebody with foreign-going master's papers willing to take on offshore salvage or rescue jobs? For mate's pay? I'd like to meet that guy."

"Er, yes, well, if a job turns up requiring your unique talents, we'll recall you. In the meanwhile, take some of your accumulated leave."

The *Solange* should be carrying a skipper and two mates, for a start. The cheap bastard wasn't even going to hire a replacement for me, no more than he'd hired a skipper to cover for O'Conner. For that, Junior should squirm a little. "I'll do it if you raise Jeep to mate and me to skipper," I said. "Otherwise you'll have to get Mick back from his sanitorium to comply."

"Er, I'll think about that."

"When you've thought about it, I'll let you know about the time off."

"Tomorrow!" Junior croaked. "I'll have to know by tomorrow." He looked as if he'd like to chew me out but, instead, he said, "It's been a pleasure meeting you, Miss Kovacs."

"Charmed, I'm sure," Tats said, sounding like Hungary's answer to Marlene Dietrich. Junior, of course, didn't know his leg was being pulled.

He never did. Confused, he backed out of the royal presence, then scuttled up the dock.

"Tats!" Jeep waved for her attention.

She waved back, smiling. Jeep was one of her favorites.

"Couldn't you've made the evil dwarf grovel a bit longer? I was enjoyin' that." He grabbed Axel's hand and mimicked Junior's hand-kissing scene. Axel recovered his hand with an indignant look and wiped it vigorously with an engine rag.

"I was not rude to Mr. Picard," Tats said, suppressing a giggle.

"No you weren't. And I almost had it figured out how you did that to him," Jeep said.

"Why do you call him `evil dwarf'?" she asked.

"Ask Hank about that. It's well deserved."

Over coffee in the mess room, I negotiated an extension of my loan of Cam's car. Surprisingly, Cam was willing but I caught an exchange of looks between him and Jeep. "What are you two cooking?" I asked.

"Nothing." Jeep looked nervously at Tats.

Tats felt the undercurrents, just as I had. "You would like me to go for a walk?" She asked, looking at me.

"No Tats. I want you right here. What the hell are you two up to?" I glared at Cam.

"We've decided to get involved in your investigation," Cam said. "You know, provide some muscle and just help out generally."

"Muscle? What in hell do I need muscle for?"

Cam seemed to lose his tongue and Jeep jumped in. "We figure it this way," he said. "Tats is in danger, same as her brother was. And his boss. We can look after her when you gotta be away."

"Why do you think she's in danger?"

The pair exchanged looks again. Cam shrugged, passing the ball to Jeep, who continued. "Like he usually does, Cam took a walk up the dock before he turned in, Saturday night. The night you and Tats stayed over. Tell him, Cam."

"I saw this joker sitting in a car in the company parking lot. Didn't look like anybody who works here, so I went up to him. The son of a bitch took off and damn near ran me over, gettin' outa the lot."

"Saturday night?"

"Right."

"Why didn't you say something then?"

"It was late and we didn't want to worry Miss Kovacs," Cam said. "And we couldn't be sure he had anything to do with your investigation. But it sure seemed queer, what with her brother being followed before he was killed."

"What did he look like?"

"Hard to tell much in the dark and him sitting in a car. Must've been there a while. His windshield was all fogged up. Big guy, judging by his shoulders. Damn near your size, I'd say."

"What kind of car?"

"Brand new Buick Century sedan. Dark blue or black. B.C. plates, DGH-4…something. There was mud on the plate."

"You sure it wasn't one of Jeep's creditors?" I watched Tats who seemed concerned and didn't think I was funny.

Jeep didn't think I was funny, either. "So we figured maybe the Department of Motor Vehicles over on Georgia Street could run that partial number for us. We pay our two bits a shot for every number from DGH 400 to DGH 499. Then we go through what they give us for all the new Buick sedans. Can't be that many."

"Sounds great, Jeep. But you'd be tying up DMV's whole operation for hours. I don't think they'll do that, unless it's for the police. And if they did, they'd spread it out over a couple of days." I said.

"You think?" Jeep looked deflated.

"Uh huh. So apart from screwing up the DMV, how do you figure to get involved?" I asked.

"Well…, since you're using Cam's car, we figure he gets a say about who rides in it," Jeep said. He grinned and nudged Tats. She grinned back but there was a shadow of worry in her eyes. Damn. I didn't need that.

"This is blackmail," I said.

"Yup," said Jeep.

"You figure Junior is going to let you guys just bugger off ashore? You heard him go after me about using my time off?"

"Yeah, we heard. What he don't know won't hurt him. And even if he finds out, what's he gonna do? Fire us all?"

"With Junior, you never know," I said.

But like it or not, I was going to have a car full of her majesty's idiot bodyguards and my investigation was going to look like a three-ring circus. But it was just possible they could be useful, keeping Tats amused. And of course it was Cam's car.

"What you got on your hand, Tats?" Jeep asked, breaking the slightly hostile silence.

"Pardon?" She looked confused, holding up the hand in question for inspection. A dark, thin smudge crossed her knuckles.

"It looks like…By God it is! It's mascara!"

"I don't use mascara," Tats protested, retrieving her hand and staring at it.

"Didn't think so," Jeep said. "So if it ain't yours, it's gotta be Junior's."

"I don't understand," she said.

"Junior uses mascara on his itsy bitsy moustache! It rubbed off when he kissed your hand. Hank, he ain't gonna fire anybody. He does an' we tell the Board of Trade guys and that political party he sucks around with and he'll never be able to show his face again."

We had a good laugh over that. And Jeep's threat might actually work.

*

Atlantis Shipping Ltd., in the Rogers Building on Granville, was my first stop. Alfred Lipinski was the manager. Both he and his company were names on Sandy's list. But Mr. Lipinski insisted he had never heard of Sandy Kovacs and could think of no reason his company's name would be in the dead man's notebook. Atlantis handled mainly bulk wheat shipments to the Soviet Union and the far east. I thought Lipinski seemed open and straightforward, if a little puzzled. I pressed my new business card into his hand.

"Why on earth would I need your tugs?" he asked, staring at the freshly printed card.

"Good question," I said. "You haven't considered towing bulk carrier barges? They could be a coming thing."

"Our clients provide their own ships, Mr. Sutter. If you want to convince them to hire your tugs and barges, you'll have to go to Moscow and Singapore to do it."

"Uh, yeah, I guess. But we also do ocean salvage work. If you need someone to take a Lloyd's Open Form contract on a breakdown, we're ready to sail on short notice."

"I see. You have such a tug?"

"We do. I'll send you some literature and cost studies, just in case."

"You do that. In the meanwhile, good day."

I returned to a carload of giggling idiots. Tats was attempting to coach Jeep in basic Hungarian. The results were hysterically funny, Jeep sounding like he'd been fitted with a mouthful of hot marbles.

"I think you'd better teach him English first, Tats."

"Oh, Hank, you are unkind. Jeep is doing marvelously."

"Yeah. I bet."

Tats had been having a ball but I think she realized she had a hopeless student and was happy that I'd bailed her out. "Where to next, skipper?" Jeep asked. He'd moved into the driver's seat to my great surprise. I looked a question at Cam but got only a shrug for a reply. What blackmail had Jeep pulled off to persuade Cam to let him drive his new baby?

"We do it alphabetically, I guess. Beyer and Son is next. Powell Street, opposite Ballantyne Pier," I said.

We made our way across Chinatown to the East Vancouver waterfront in slow fits and starts. The elder generation of Chinese living around Powell and Main had never absorbed the concept of pedestrian crosswalks and orderly traffic. Jeep was patient, fortunately.

I was in the back seat, beside Cam, while Tats occupied the front passenger seat. Cam sat sideways, more interested in where we'd been than in where we were going. I was just about to ask him how he'd come to let Jeep drive when he said "You see him, Jeep?"

Jeep adjusted the rear-view mirror. "The Buick? Yeah. I got him. Sneaky bastard is layin' back a couple of cars."

"Are we being followed?" Tats asked.

"Yeah. I think we oughta do somethin' about him," Jeep said.

"Like what?" I asked. I didn't like the sound of Jeep.

"If we park you two someplace safe," he said. "Cam an' me can lead our friend back there on a wild goose chase. Long as he don't see you get out, he ain't gonna know the difference."

"How are you going to make sure he doesn't see us leave the car?" I asked.

"Leave that to me. When I stop the car and say `go', you skedaddle. Just walk right in the front door of some business."

"Okay, but get us as close to Beyer and Son as you can." I didn't like having somebody following us and Jeep's scheme seemed as good a way as any to get rid of the tail without Jeep and Cam taking any risks. Or so I thought.

Jeep made a sharp right onto Hawks, without signaling, earning a blast from an air horn. He gunned the big Chrysler to the alley corner, then slammed the car into the alley in a sliding turn that made Cam wince. He goosed it up to fifty or so, fishtailing between unloading trucks, heading for the other end of the block and Heatley Avenue. The Buick must have missed the turn. If he did, he'd have a four block circuit via Raymur and Cordova to get back to us. That Jeep was smarter than he looked, sometimes. But had we lost the Buick?

Jeep didn't think so. He peeled around the exit corner onto Heatley and slammed to a stop. "Go!" he shouted. Tats and I slid out of the car. Cam dove into the front seat.

Jeep squealed off, doors still open, leaving a year's worth of tread wear on the pavement. He was back onto Powell Street, driving sedately in our original direction, before Cam got the rear door shut.

"In here," I said, steering Tats by the arm. We stepped into a Chinese grocery store, ringing the bell above the door. The place reeked of curry, incense and a clutch of mysterious oriental smells I couldn't identify. A portly Chinese gentleman with gold-rimmed glasses smiled at us from behind the counter.

Two minutes later, Tats and I watched from behind his cluttered window display as the Buick screamed past on Heatley, flat out in second gear.

"That was fun!" Tats said.

"Damned dangerous, if you ask me."

"But Jeep is such a wonderful driver. I'm sure we were in no danger."

"If you say so, my love. But get him to tell you about his driving record, sometime. His fines support the whole damned police traffic division."

"So what should we do now?"

"First, we buy something from our host here."

"Buy what?"

"Something to eat, I guess. Then we find Beyer and Son. I think it's just down the block."

"I am not hungry."

"Oh?"

"You are making fun of me?" She slugged me on the shoulder for that. Then she bought a purse full of candy bars.

Beyer and Son, Shipping Agents, was lettered in gold on the door glass of a small building fifty yards away, around the corner from our grocery.

"What is it you wish?" the slim, blond man asked, in halting English. His receding hairline gave him a high forehead and he squinted at me through wire-framed glasses. He was the only occupant of the office.

"I am looking into the death of Sandor Kovacs. He listed your firm's name in his notebooks and I'm wondering what the connection was."

"Bitte? Death? My English iss...poor. My secretary is...gone." He gestured, helplessly, at an empty desk. Whatever the quality of his English, he'd gone pasty white at the mention of Kovacs' name.

"Sandor Kovacs," I repeated. "He was pushed off a building on Monday evening. His notebooks say he called on you."

"Please? I do not understand. You are police?"

"No, not police."

"Please come back when I have a new secretary." He waved at the empty desk again. "She was translating for me."

I was wondering how this guy managed a business in Canada with such poor English. And how his accent could be so good, yet he couldn't understand me. I was about to offer that opinion when Tats touched my arm and stepped forward. "Verstehen Sie mich?" she said.

"Ah! Gott sei dank! Ich verstehe nicht seine Fragen." He gestured at me.

She spoke at length in German, translating my earlier question. The man was obviously badly frightened and not very coherent. Tats turned to me and said in a quiet voice, "Hank, you scared him out from his skin. He thinks we are, mmm, criminals come to rob him."

"Does he know anything about Sandy?"

"He says not."

"Did you ask him why his company was listed in Sandy's notebooks?"

"That is what scared him. He thinks we are crooks, come to shake him up."

"Shake him down?" I corrected. Tats had seen more Cagney movies than I thought. "Oh hell," I said. "This is going nowhere. Ask him if anyone else has been around with questions. Then we'd better go."

Nothing about this investigation was going the way it was supposed to. Instead of a quiet, methodical inquiry, I was leading a three-ring circus that played at car chases, while scaring the bejeezus out of anybody who might help.

I wasn't paying attention to their rapid-fire German but Tats' translation seemed overlong for the simple question I'd asked. She turned back to me. "He has spoken to no one and promises to say nothing about our visit. He offered me a job. He says my German is better than his secretary's."

"Let's get out of here. We're getting nowhere."

She thanked Beyer and we left.

Outside on the street, I said, "That isn't all he said, Tats. Even I know the German for `pretty'."

"Yes he said I was pretty. You disagree?"

"Not at all. You think he just wants a secretary?"

"Maybe not. He offered a lot of money."

"Tats!"

"I said I'd think about it," she teased.

"I'm sure he reacted to your brother's name. Did you see the way he went pale?"

"Yes. I too think something mmm, smells of fish?"

*

We taxied uptown on the way back to Tats' apartment, making a stopover for lunch in Chinatown. Tats discovered the Mandarin Gardens and took two hours exploring their menu.

"Why does everyone dislike Mr. Picard so much?" she asked, over Chinese green tea. "Jeep called him the evil dwarf."

"He'd be a comedy turn if he wasn't so damned dangerous. He takes shortcuts with the ship's safety gear. And last spring, Gus, our dayman, came down with a burst appendix when we were out on the west coast of the Queen Charlottes. Luckily, we were able to buy some cracked ice from a fish packer and we packed Gus in that and took him to hospital in Prince Rupert."

"He is well again?"

"Yes, but no thanks to Junior. It was far too rough to get a seaplane alongside and that meant we had to leave our tow and take him in with the ship. Junior threw a fit. Tried to order us to wait until a plane could fly Gus out. Then he tried to fire everybody, claiming the insurance company was going to raise his rates if he didn't."

"What were you towing? And what happened to it?"

"It was a Davis raft. A big cigar-shaped raft of logs made up especially for towing in the open sea. We tied it to the cliffside in a sheltered cove before we left but it broke loose. We found it eventually. All the company lost was some time. And it turned out Junior hadn't reported the incident to the insurance company."

"He changed his mind about firing you?"

"No. The union and the guild did that."

"I think he is a selfish man."

"You got it. The evil dwarf."

"Your crew all seem to like you. I think that is a good sign."

"They're a good bunch. We get the job done in spite of Junior."

*

We arrived home at four in the afternoon, stuffed to the gills and having accomplished virtually nothing. Cam's black Chrysler hardtop was cooling in Tats' parking space. It had turned brown, being covered in mud and dust. A fender had been dinged.

Cam and Jeep were seated at Tats' kitchen table. Between them was a bedraggled, glowering Corporal Nunn, locked in his own handcuffs.

Ye Gods! What had they done? "Look what we found," Jeep said, sheepishly.

I let the silence build for a minute while I scrambled frantically to think of something to save our collective asses. "I think you'd better let me do the talking, Jeep," I said.

"Right, skipper." He sounded relieved. I hoped to hell his confidence in me was justified because I certainly didn't feel any.

"I take it you were in the car tailing us this afternoon?" I addressed Nunn. He glowered back at me.

"A dark blue Buick sedan. Right? The same car that nearly ran over Cam Douglas in Picard's parking lot, late Saturday night?"

"Fuck you, Sutter. You'll pay for this."

"Maybe. If we do, you'll pay too."

"What do you mean by that?"

"Look at it from the point of view of your boss. Or maybe the editor of the *Sun*. Bad and good."

"Bad and good? What the fuck is this?"

"Tch. There's a lady present and I'll thank you to keep that in mind. Now what is your boss going to say? Who is it, by the way? Inspector MacIntyre?"

Bingo. I could tell I'd hit the jackpot by the change of Nunn's color.

"He'll throw the book at you," Nunn growled.

"And you. Two unarmed amateurs lead you on a merry chase, take your gun away and lock you in your own cuffs. Impressive police work, corporal. They'll bust you right back to constable and ship you to Tuktoyaktuk with the next dog team."

"Go fuck yourself, Sutter. The force will be on your ass for life. We take care of our own."

"You figure they'll circle the wagons, huh?"

Nunn nodded, glowering at me.

"After the story gets written up on page one of the *Vancouver Sun* and the *Province*? Maybe in a few national magazines, too? You may be one of theirs, as you put it, but I'm not sure the force will want to admit it. I've got the press connections and I'll make sure that angle is covered before I turn you loose."

"We can muzzle editors. National security is involved here." He looked, sidelong, at Tats. She was keeping very still, watching me.

"What national security? Why are you hounding Tatiana Kovacs? Why were you following her brother?"

I watched Nunn carefully. He'd have been a lousy poker player. Suddenly I knew I had the winning hand and Nunn was bluffing. "You were following a notion of your own, without authorization. There isn't any national security involved. Right?"

Nunn's glare didn't waver. He wasn't going to answer my question. Nevertheless, I was sure I'd rattled him with a lucky guess. Time to raise the stakes before he folded. "Okay, corporal, this is what we'll do. We will release you and give you back your gun. We'll even bring your car in from wherever it is."

"Surrey," Jeep mumbled.

"And we will say nothing to anyone about today's happenings. In return, you will also say and do nothing about today's incident. In addition, you will leave this lady strictly alone." I gathered Tats to me. She was trembling. "Do we have a deal?" He stared at me, unblinking, as if memorizing every pore. Then, almost imperceptibly, he nodded.

"Speak up for the record, corporal," I said.

"All right. We have a fucking deal. Get me out of these cuffs and I'll go get my own car."

*

Nunn's departure was like a thundercloud lifting. Everyone seemed to breathe easier. I had a few sweet nothings to whisper in Cam's and Jeep's ears. I just wasn't sure I wanted to say them with a lady present.

Tats moved in on me and kissed me in detail. "That was wonderful, Hank," she said. "I'm so proud of you."

"Holy shit!" Jeep said. "You were fantastic, skipper."

"No. I was lucky," I said. "And so were you. About this muscle business--"

"Aw hell, we didn't know who he was. We led him into one of those dead-end loops, you know? A cul-de-something?"

"A cul-de-sac?"

"Right. We sacked him, anyway. Blocked his way out with the Chrysler. He shoulda stayed in his car."

"Why was getting out of his car a mistake?" I demanded. I was afraid of the answer, knowing Jeep.

"You'n me've worked out at the judo-ka. Go figure."

"I know you can throw a Swede boom-chain thirty feet. What did you do to him?"

"Nothin'. He made the first move. Went to grab me by the arm. That was kinda dumb."

"And?"

"And he ended up on his face in a flower bed. Sure was pissed about it. That's when I found the gun and took it off him. He was yelling the whole time that he was a cop but he never showed us a badge or anything. Then we found the handcuffs and figured maybe we were in trouble. We decided to bring him back here and let you sort it out."

"Thanks a lot."

"Good thing you got those press connections or we'd sure as hell be in the shit."

"What press connections?" I said.

CHAPTER
10

On Tuesday the muscle contingent was down to Jeep, and he had strict orders from me not to beat on any policemen. Cam had discovered the *Solange*'s standby generator needed an overhaul. Cam wouldn't have bothered if he didn't have faith in my plans to somehow acquire the *Solange Picard* from a reluctant Junior.

How in hell was I going to pull that off? I had a Thursday morning meeting scheduled with Peter Levi, the Howe Street financial wizard. Levi knew, and I knew, that the meeting was on only because Jake Feldman had set it up. It would be a hard sell. I should be working on my pitch to convince Levi of the future of ocean towing in the North Pacific. Instead, here I was, playing amateur cop for a revolutionary beauty bent on vengeance. If I had any sense I'd...

But what did sense have to do with it?

I picked up my paycheck and mail at the office. Apart from a larger-than-average collection of bills, the only thing of importance was a notice of an extraordinary meeting of Picard's stockholders, called for November 5.

I continued chasing the remaining names from Sandy's list, leaving Tats in the car in Jeep's care, or maybe it was the other way around. Jeep's Hungarian was sounding better than it should, considering his English.

Two of my calls turned out to be minor functionaries in the Vancouver Harbor Master's office and neither admitted to knowing Sandy Kovacs. They were either telling the truth or they were academy award actors.

Harry Reimer was a business agent for the International Longshore-men's and Warehouseman's Union. He gave me five impatient minutes between bargaining sessions with his major employer. "Kovacs? Yeah, I remember him. He asked for a meeting. Tuesday, last week. Said it was important but he didn't give me any details. Couldn't have been too important. He didn't show."

"He was killed the Monday before that."

"Killed? You mean murdered?"

"That's what I mean."

"Holy Jesus."

Eric Toombs and David Hutchinson were captains working for the pilot-age authority, based in Victoria. I contacted Toombs by telephone, with no result. Hutchinson was taking a ship through the inside passage to Prince Rupert and would not return until he had a southbound vessel. With Al-fred Lipinski and Heinrich Beyer, the managers of the shipping agencies we'd already called on, the people I'd interviewed numbered seven. No one had any idea why their names had turned up in Sandy's notebook. The hell of it was that I believed them -- with the possible exception of Beyer.

The only tenuous clue was that every name on the list, so far, had con-nections with marine cargo handling or shipping.

Wednesday morning, I attacked the two latin-sounding names on San-dy's list in the public library with the help of an earnest young librarian who took pity on me. But neither Figuero Sanchez nor Dolores Olivera could be found.

The plain language list of names in Sandy's notebooks that had been such an exciting find was proving a bust. Sandy had contacted few of the people on it. I was rapidly running out of ideas.

Tats and Jeep, on another floor, searched for Sandy's shorthand but the reference material mostly dealt with English and French language systems. Tats thought Sandy had used a German system but didn't know who the author was or what he'd called his shorthand. With no car chase to keep Tats and Jeep amused, their enthusiasm was fading fast. Neither had the mind-set for the numbing boredom of police leg-work.

I decided a break was needed.It was time I called on Ella Feldman.

Clara was again available and I delegated Jeep to be chauffeur and watchdog while Tats and Clara searched the used book stores for Sandy's shorthand system. My plan was for Jeep to drop me at the Feldman estate high in West Vancouver's British Properties, then go on to collect Clara.

So much for my plan.

Tats did her usual and reorganized everything, insisting on visiting Ella with me.

"Jeep will take us both to Mrs. Feldman's, Hank," Tats said. "Then we will go to Clara's place and back to the city. That way, you won't have to take a bus to get home and Jeep could visit Mrs. Feldman with us."

"Thanks but I'll wait for you in the car, if you don't mind. Grieving widows…" Jeep shuddered.

"Aren't you related to Mrs. Feldman?"

"About sixth cousins, I think. I'll let Hank do the visiting."

I'd had a vague notion that I might be able to ask Ella Feldman a few questions in the process of offering my condolences but, truth to tell, I hadn't the slightest idea what Jake Feldman's home life had been like. Had Jake discussed his work with Ella? I didn't think that would have been his style.

The Feldman place was a sprawling, ultra-modern rancher on Eyremont, near the top of the "Properties." The exclusive residential enclave, clawed out of the rain forest, had now spread two thousand feet up the side of Hollyburn Mountain, high above West Vancouver's posh "martini belt."

A yellow Volkswagen beetle was parked in the Feldman driveway. Jeep pulled in behind it and slumped down, out of sight, to await our return.

I had only now realized that putting Tats together with Ella might not be good for either of them. Most of the time Tats kept up a cheerful front but there were moments when I sensed that she was holding herself together by a thread.

"You going to be all right?" I asked her, at the front door.

"No. But I will do my best for Mrs. Feldman," she said.

I scooped her up and kissed her. It seemed like the right thing to do and I guess she agreed because the kiss lasted a long time. Then she squirmed free, flustered.

"Well, Hank," Ella Feldman said from the doorway. "Clara told me you'd found yourself a rare beauty. I must say she was right, but the neighbors will talk if you make love to her on my doorstep. Do come in and introduce us."

Ella led the way to a spacious, high-ceilinged room with folded bronze glass panels forming the south wall. Too large for a living room but not quite a ballroom, the place was obviously intended for entertaining.

The property was terraced, with the next level below the windows consisting of a vast swimming pool and sun deck. Beyond that, the view over Lion's Gate Bridge and the harbor was stunning and, for a moment, I didn't notice the third woman in the room. Then the shock of recognition derailed my memory. Ella saved me. "You've met Irene Bradshaw, I believe?"

Of course. Jake Feldman's secretary. I hadn't realized that Tats knew Bradshaw but it seemed they'd talked a number of times when Tats had been meeting her brother at the office. She hadn't met Ella Feldman but she and Ella seemed to become instant friends. I felt like an outsider as the three women chatted.

At last, Irene Bradshaw said, "I've got to get back to the office. I am so sorry about your brother, Tatiana."

"Thank you. Mr. Feldman was kind to Sandy. I am sorry for him also."

An awkward moment followed as we stood in a group near the entry. Bradshaw took my hand as if to shake it, then dropped it. As she exchanged goodbyes at the door, I realized she'd slipped a business card into my palm. Without thinking, I put the card in my jacket pocket.

Ella Feldman proved to be of stronger stuff than I'd expected. She wasn't tearful, but then maybe Clara had helped her through that. She seemed more angry than grief-stricken when she turned to me. "I understand Tatiana has persuaded you to investigate Sandy's death, Hank."

"Yes. I'm not making much progress, though."

"I'm sure you will. Jake told me about your famous triple murder case in Seoul."

"Pusan, not Seoul. Hardly famous. I was lucky."

"To solve a complicated case in which everybody spoke a language you didn't know?"

"I know some Korean," I protested.

"The record speaks for itself. I won't argue," she said, like a judge pronouncing sentence. "But I would be pleased if you would also look into Jake's death."

"Of course. It's likely that his and Sandy's murders are connected."

"You knew Jake and I were not getting along?"

"I didn't know, Ella. Mother didn't say anything to me. Not that she would gossip, mind you." Mary Sutter was second only to Clara in the gossip stakes. But telling Ella that the whole family, except for me, knew about her marital problems wouldn't help.

"Well, it's true," she said. "The police were around Friday, of course, asking questions and being very polite. They knew I'd had Jake served with divorce papers the day before and I told them we'd had a row about the settlement Thursday night. I was packing my things when they came."

"I see," I said. Maybe that explained why Jake was roaring drunk at ten in the morning of a working day.

"Do you? Do you realize that I will do much better as a surviving widow than I'd have done in any settlement?"

"Did you have him killed?" The words tumbled out before I could shape the question in more diplomatic form. Tats recoiled from me, aghast at my blunt question. But sometimes you just have to ask. Ella didn't even flinch. "No, of course not. I was divorcing Jake Feldman but I felt no animosity towards him. I had...other reasons for leaving him."

"Another man?"

"Yes. Silly, at my age, I suppose."

"Not at all." Ella Feldman was a handsome woman at forty-five. In her twenties she had been a great beauty. I couldn't imagine her sleeping with Jake at any age.

"Whatever our relationship had become, I still had feelings for Jake. Those grow on you, after twenty years of marriage. He didn't deserve to die like that, shot by some sneak thief."

"Why do you think it was a thief?"

"Wasn't it?"

"No. At least we...I think it was much more complicated than that. The killers were probably the same in both cases."

"Then you have another complicated murder to solve."

"Solve?"

I was beginning to think the solution was vanishing over the horizon, getting farther away with every turtle-like move I made.

"You will have expenses, of course."

"Nothing I can't--"

"And you are losing wages. Both of you," she interrupted.

"Oh, now, look. I'm only an amateur detective. I don't want your--"

"Enough! I won't hear of you working for nothing. Jake told me about your plans to form a company and buy that old tug from Junior Picard. You won't go far in business, turning away money."

"You know Junior?"

She gave me a long-suffering look that was answer enough. "See that Hank cashes this, Tatiana," she said, handing her an envelope. Tats promptly squirreled it away in her purse. Obviously, Ella had planned this scene right after I'd telephoned to say we were coming. But she'd given me the lead I wanted. "Did Jake ever discuss his work with you?" I asked.

"Rarely. He only talked about you because you were family."

"I was hoping he might have said something about what Sandy was working on."

"I'm afraid not. Sorry. Oh, I did hear him grumble a bit about having Sandy working pro bono. But he did a lot of unpaid work and always had a good-natured grumble about it."

"I see."

"Poor Hank," she said. "You came expecting to console a tearful widow and found an angry shrew instead."

"Hardly a shrew, Ella."

"Not dutifully tearful, anyway. But I want you to know this. I really liked Jake Feldman. Otherwise I couldn't have lived with him for twenty years. I just didn't love him."

*

It was after two PM when we exited Ella's mansion. To discover Jeep and Irene Bradshaw standing beside their cars in animated conversation.

"Oh my!" Tats said.

"You think?"

"Mmm. Definitely. Something happens there."

"Better not say anything. Jeep blushes easily, unless it's somebody else's love life he's talking about."

In the city, Tats discovered she'd missed lunch. With Clara along, that meant an inevitable two-hour lunch while they explored a trendy Robson Street restaurant, Italian but much more expensive than the Neapolitan. Much time was frittered away but it was worth it to see the look on Jeep's face as he watched Tats stow away a huge platter of spaghetti and meat balls. "You're going to send that cheque back to Ella, aren't you Tats," I said, as sternly as I could manage.

She looked right through me and said, "Clara and I will talk to people who teach shorthand. Somebody must know about the European sys-tems."

"Good plan. Now about Ella's --."

"She thought of it," the two of them said in unison, pointing at each other. They broke up. I might have been talking to a wall. A stubborn Hungarian wall.

I said, "Jeep, drop me at Tats' place so I can change. I need to find a guy who lives under Burrard Bridge, or somewhere along the creek. No place for a good suit."

"This guy lives under the bridge? What kind of character is that?" Jeep said.

"Clay Harper. He's my source of last resort," I said.

Burrard Bridge was a high steel and concrete span -- one of three city bridges -- over False Creek. The "creek" was not a creek, despite its name, but a shallow tidal inlet, partly dredged, that meandered inland all the way to Main Street. False Creek was home to several noisy, smoky sawmills and other assorted evil-smelling industrial plants. Log booms, fishing boats, tumbledown houseboats, shacks, float wharves and live-aboard craft of every description cluttered the muddy foreshore and clung to bridge piers. Finding Harper wasn't going to be easy. He was mobile and he usually had good reasons not to be found.

I changed into jeans and a turtleneck and walked the few blocks from Tats' apartment to a small boat-building shop under the north end of the bridge. They had no rowboats to rent and I was about to turn away and go elsewhere when I spied a well-worn twelve-footer that looked serviceable. At least it was afloat.

"How much?" I asked the proprietor.

"Not for rent," he said.

"How much to buy it?"

"That's different." He eyed me, doubtfully. "Le'me see, now. There's a life jacket and a bailing can and a good pair of oars--"

The life jacket was a soggy-looking lump and the oars had been taped where they'd been splintered. "How much?" I asked.

"Seventy bucks?"

"Fifty."

"Done." Sutter Towing and Salvage had acquired the first of its fleet. It leaked.

I headed for the Imperial gas barge, moored against the south bridge pier. Harper's Achilles' heel was that he lived on a gas boat and there were limited places to buy fuel.

"Harper? Whatcha want with that ol' goat?" the keeper of the gas barge said.

"He's an old friend. I need to talk to him."

"Sure you ain't from the sheriff's office, servin' papers?"

"Do I look like a cop?"

"Yeah, you do, matter of fact."

"Be worth his while if I get to talk to him."

"How about my while?"

"Ten bucks do it?"

"I guess. Last time he filled up, he was stayin' up by the Cambie Bridge. Just t'other side. Can't guarantee he's still there. Had a net on his drum, when he was in here."

"He's still running that old gillnetter?"

"Yeah. The *Hellusay*. He put a new fifteen-eighteen Easthope in that old crock. Coat a paint onna hull. Said he was goin' fishin', if you can believe it. So he coulda drowned or blowed hisself up."

"Thanks."

I was looking at a mile and a half of hard rowing against an ebb tide that was running about as fast as I could persuade my new craft to move. A prudent oarsman would have waited the tide out but I needed the exercise, so I didn't wait.

The headsaws of Rat Portage Sawmill screamed metallic agony, slicing cedar logs into planks, just east of the CPR railway trestle. The mill was supposed to close down this year to make way for a fisherman's wharf. But meanwhile, their untidy log boom straggled out into mid-channel. Granville Island loomed behind its pallisade of creosoted pilings. A barge was loading logging trucks and a bulldozer at the Arrow Transfer Dock while, nearby, National Machinery crowded the western tip of the man-made island. At mid-island, under Granville Bridge, a chain forging mill and a plant stamping out nails and spikes crashed and thumped at my unwary eardrums. North, across the creek, Sweeny Cooperage and a tannery added their pungent effluvium to the late afternoon air.

It took me three hours to reach the Cambie Bridge. Harper wasn't there.

But, leaning against the barnacled beams of a tidal haul-out grid, I found the *Ibedamned*. The craft belonged to Rob Alsop, a crony of Harper's. Alsop's chief claim to fame was his service as a World War I fighter pilot, a war he was still fighting for anyone who would listen. He and Clay Harper were feuding friends, one about as deaf as the other.

"Afternoon, Rob. You seen Clay Harper?"

Alsop, bearded and grizzled, squinted at me from his deck. "Watcha want with that ol' fart?" He spat for punctuation.

"Talk. Just talk."

"You're one of Dan Sutter's boys. Right? Captain Sutter, ain't it? Last time I saw you, you had a steamboat under your butt. Come down a piece, ain't ya?"

"Couldn't get a steamboat in here with a shoe horn, Rob. You seen Clay?"

Alsop nodded. "Bugger's taken on airs since he got that engine. He's tellin' everybody he's going fishin' again."

"Where is he?"

"Over t'wards the viaduct. Got himself a cheap tie-up." He jerked a thumb over his shoulder towards a particularly malodorous, narrow branch of the creek that ran north into Chinatown, beside the old gasworks. "Guess his nose ain't no better'n his ears," Alsop shouted, as I leaned into my oars again. The old man watched my departure, seeming disappointed that I couldn't stay to hear any of his dogfight stories but I needed to find Harper before dark or risk wasting another day.

The *Hellusay* was well hidden, tucked between a gravel barge and a houseboat in the shadow of the Georgia Viaduct. The Creek, at this backwater end, smelled like somebody had forgotten to flush. Somehow the stink was a fitting reminder of scandals past. The crumbling viaduct, scarcely thirty years old, was scheduled to be knocked down and replaced. Before it fell on somebody, I hoped.

I tied my rowboat alongside *Hellusay* and stepped aboard. The gill-netter heeled to my weight and I heard Harper muttering curses inside. The business end of a double-barreled shotgun protruded from the open wheelhouse door. "Who's out there?" Harper growled.

"It's me, Clay. Hank Sutter," I bellowed.

"Can't hear you. Step out an' show yourself, 'fore I send a load o' buck-shot your way."

I edged around the rear corner of the low pilot house, holding my hands up like a suspect in a police raid, and grinning. "God damn, you look like a Sutter," he said. His beard had gone snow white since I'd last seen him.

"Hank Sutter," I yelled, nodding vigorously.

Harper stood the shotgun inside the pilot house. "Better come inside, 'fore some of them bleedin' bill collectors see us," he said. "How's your old man?"

"Fine. Retirement suits him."

"Retired, ain't he?" I shrugged. Harper's hearing hadn't improved in the two years since I'd seen him last.

The *Hellusay* was a typical canoe-sterned gillnetter of about thirty-five feet, one of thousands seized from Japanese fishermen -- most of them Canadian citizens -- by the government and re-sold to non-Japanese fishermen when the ethnic Japanese had been uprooted and "relocated" off the coast during the war. The boat's interior wasn't intended for people of my stature. Nor of Clay Harper's, but Harper had the advantage of a chronic stoop.

I perched on the step that led from the pilot house to the diminutive forward sleeping cabin, beside the shiny new, bright green, two-cylinder Easthope's exposed flywheel. Harper arranged himself on the end of the triangular shaped bunk that filled the craft's bow. "What can I do for you?" he said. I had brief illusions of escaping with my information in a reasonable time. It was not to be. Before I could say anything, Harper had turned away, rummaging in a locker. More than half of Harper's "hearing" was actually lip reading, so I waited until he emerged from the depths of the forward storage locker. "Got some great Newfie Screech," he said.

Oh God.

"You gonna give it a try?" It wasn't a question. Anyone who wanted to talk to Clay Harper had to survive the ritual of drinking with him. His tastes in liquor varied. It had to be my foul luck that the infamous Newfoundland Screech was his liquor of the month. "Great Screech" was an oxymoron of nuclear proportions.

He filled two grubby-looking water glasses to within a quarter inch of the top. I accepted my glass, gingerly, as you might hold a glass of battery acid.

"Down the hatch!" Harper roared, and upended his glass.

I sipped. Not battery acid. It was a cross between Jamaica overproof rum and battery acid. With the emphasis on overproof.

"Howd'ja find me?" he asked.

"Rob Alsop told me you were here," I said. Damn. That was a mistake.

"Alsop? That old bastard. D'ja have to listen to any of his bullshit stories?"

"No."

"Air war. Prissy bastards, never got to see the mud an' blood from his Sopwith Camel airy plane. Vimy Ridge, now there was a fight."

"You were there?" It was a ritual question.

"'Course I was there. How'd you think I lost my hearing? We was right in front of a division of the Lahore Heavy Artillery. Got my butt shot off, too." He squirmed and lowered his pants to show me the livid red scar crossing his buttocks. I'd seen it half a dozen times. I swear he wore oversize trousers just so he could display that scar easily.

Several hours passed and Harper's stories skipped around in time from the First World War to the "dirty thirties" to fishing the Fraser River under sail at the turn of the century to sailing the North Atlantic convoy route in World War II. Just my luck that Harper had made several crossings on freighters skippered by my father. Harper's prize story was a lurid version of father's famous deck-gun duel with a surfaced U-boat. The only place his and father's yarns agreed was at the end. The freighter's gun crew put a four-inch shell right through the hull of the U-boat and sunk it.

But Harper was a walking encyclopedia of marine history and happenings. Which is why I'd hunted him down.

It was near one in the morning before I got my chance. "I've got the names of some people I need to find. `Dolores Olivera' and `Figuero Sanchez'," I said. I passed the names to him, written on an envelope. I didn't trust him to lip-read Spanish names.

"Whatcha need 'em for?" Harper's speech was slurred. It was now or never.

"I'm investigating a friend's murder."

"Murder? Holy Jesus. Don't want nothin' to do with that."

"But do you know the names?"

"Sure I know 'em. You should, too, bein' in the steamboat business."

"Why should I know them?"

"'Cause they're ships, not people." He sniggered. "Reefers, runnin' outa South America with fruit and the like."

He'd fallen asleep before I could ask him which shipping agent handled them.

*

I left Clay Harper the rowboat for his trouble and made my way to Pender Street and Chinatown on foot. I'd kept my drinking to the bare minimum, resisting Harper's frequent urgings to "drink up." Even so, I was light headed. I walked uptown in a mist of rain, hoping the cool night air would sober me up.

Halfway home I realized my appointment with Peter Levi, the money man was for nine that morning. Barely seven hours away. Jesus. I was in no shape for that, and no more a businessman than I was a detective. Around two in the morning I reached Tats' place.

"You smell like a distillery," she said, at the door.

"You going to let me in?"

"If I have to. What disgusting things have you been drinking?"

"Newfie Screech. If you want information out of Clay Harper, you have to drink with him and listen to his stories. Tonight, I got the last two names on Sandy's list. You aren't really angry, are you?"

"Yes I am. You could have telephoned to say where you were."

"Tats, I couldn't. Part of the time I was in a rowboat on False Creek hunting for the guy and after that I was aboard his smelly fishboat. No telephones."

"Well, my telephone is working. Your office called. You are wanted aboard your ship at once."

"Oh, shit. Did you tell them I was on time off?"

"I told them. They said it is an emergency. The ship is at some place called the oil dock."

"The oil dock? We just topped up her tanks last week."

"They said you must be...mmm...aboard? by three in the morning. Sit down. I will make you some coffee. Did you eat?"

"Not since lunch. Did you have any luck with the shorthand?"

"We found his system. Clara and I have been working on the notebooks all evening. I will make you a ham sandwich. You look awful."

"That's great, Tats. I feel as if we are making real progress for the first time."

"It will do no good if you are at sea. Or out all night drinking with crazy men. How long will you be away?"

"Hard to say. Did they say what we'd be doing?"

"Something about towing a broken-down ship off the west coast. I thought this is the west coast."

"They mean the west coast of Vancouver Island. It shouldn't be too long, then."

I loaded myself and a duffle bag of laundry into a cab at two-thirty in the morning. Tats wouldn't let me kiss her good bye.

C H A P T E R

11

I dropped the cab at the corner of Dunlevy and Powell streets to walk the last two blocks and clear my head. I heaved the bag of laundry up on my shoulder. God I was going to have a hangover. Harper must have gotten a bad batch of screech, if there was such a thing as a good batch, screech being uniformly horrible. The coffee and sandwich Tats made for me had done wonders but I still felt fuzzy.

I was puzzled about many things. Why had dispatch sent the *Solange* back to the oil dock only a few days after bunkering? Of course there could be a reason. We sometimes carried supplies, including drums of lube oil on deck, for log-towing tugs in the Picard fleet. At this time of year they were often weathered-in up the coast and unable to leave their tows. If Marty had a chance to use the *Solange* to re-supply his log towers, never mind that we were supposed to be rescuing somebody, he'd grab it.

I felt uneasy about leaving Tats. Deep down she was frightened and there seemed to be more to it than Sandy's and Feldman's murders. Trying to get her to unload that fear by talking it through had resulted only in her becoming angry with me. I was treating her like a child or an incompetent, she said. She made jokes when I pressed her to take the most elementary precautions but that, too, was a facade. I was no closer to understanding her than I'd been the first day I met her.

With her landlord's agreement, and Tats' amusement, I'd spent three hundred and fifty dollars having a two-inch-thick solid oak door installed in place of the original apartment door, a flimsy, paneled affair that wouldn't have survived one good kick. Two deadbolt locks completed the improvements. Her windows, except the bathroom window, had ornamental iron bars that would stop anything short of a cutting torch. The bathroom had the same bars but on a hinged, lockable frame which, the fire department had agreed, constituted a fire escape.

"You are locking me up like a prison," she complained.

"Just remember to shoot those locks when I'm not here," I said.

Now I wondered if it was enough. My cab driver gave me a questioning look when I ordered him to do a slow circuit of the block, before leaving her place.

But there'd been no obvious problems. I decided I would call Virg Hogan on the radio-phone in the morning and organize some kind of security baby-sitting for her. Virg was a husky young car nut who hung around my garage whenever I was working on the Alfa. He was out of work and would probably jump at the chance.

Those last two names on Sandy's list turning out to be ships put a new light on my investigation. I'd have to go back to Beyer and Atlantis and find out if either of them handled those ships. Just proved an old adage. If you want a wrong answer, ask the wrong question. I'd been doing that all week.

Another thing that gnawed away in the back of my mind was that both Professor Dalls and Ella Feldman had mentioned pro bono work Jake had done. Feldman, Tauber, Slibowichs and Brown seemed an unlikely outfit to be approached by indigent clients in need of legal help. Their specialty was marine law and tax law, at the corporate level. Jake's clients were big bucks people.

I was mulling this over as I made my way down the cobbled slope of Dunlevy to the harbor and the oil dock's tank farm, paying no attention to my surroundings. Two shadows materialized out of an alley and moved into my path. "Excuse me," I said, moving to pass them. But I'd already caught the glint of steel.

"Naw, don't think so, Mac. Ya gotta pay toll on this road. Ya know?" He held a longshoreman's sack hook, twisting it to catch the reflections from a street light. He reached with the other hand, as if to relieve me of a wallet.

His partner moved sideways, trying to get behind me. They'd both been drinking some evil-smelling stuff though neither were seriously drunk.

"I think you better get lost before you get hurt," I said. I didn't feel as brave as I sounded but my head was suddenly marvelously clear.

"Hey man! Hook inna ribs'll make ya sing a different tune." He sniggered, making a pass at me with the hook. I sidestepped and backed away, into the middle of the street. I needed room.

A sack hook is a vicious, close-in weapon. Forged and tempered, the hooks are bent like the old fashioned claw once worn by men who'd lost a hand, but sharp-pointed and with a cross-handle at the top end. They are used to heave heavy objects around, like packing cases or three hundred-pound sacks of raw sugar. This pair looked far too seedy to be longshoremen and I had no intention of letting their hooks get anywhere near my ribs.

The punk who'd done the talking gestured at his chum to get behind me. I turned to block that and we did a clumsy dance in the road. Then I dropped my shoulder and heaved the duffle bag straight into the talker's knees. Sixty pounds of laundry took him down.

His head made a resounding crack on the brick cobbles. The other thug stared at his mate. "Fuck," he said.

That's when I hit him.

I put my whole weight behind it. My fist caught him flush on the temple. I felt bones crunch. From the agony in my hand, I couldn't tell if they were mine or his. He went down and bounced.

I stuck the sack hooks in the top of my bag and sprinted for the dock just beyond the oil tanks. The *Solange Picard* wasn't there.

"Ain't seen her tonight," the dock watchman said.

"I need your phone," I said.

"Oh well, I don't know about-- Hey!"

I dialed, cursing myself for an idiot. Tats didn't answer her phone. After fifteen rings, I dialed again. She wasn't a heavy sleeper, at least not most of the time. I hung up and called the *Solange*'s dock number. I got Axel Oberg. "Axel, get Jeep and Cam up and tell them to get over to Tatiana's place, pronto. Something's wrong there."

"Wrong? Ya, Hank, I do that. I go myself if George will finish my watch."

George Farnham was Axel's opposite number on the other watch. With the ship on stand-by pressure, both firemen's watches were working. "Do that, Axel. And hurry. I'll get there as soon as I can. Tell Jeep to call and ask for me at the police station as soon as he knows anything."

I dialed the police. There followed one of those aggravating, tragi-comic exchanges with officialdom that you don't believe when people tell stories about them at parties. No one seemed to grasp that I had subdued two would-be muggers and wanted to hand them over. Valuable time was wasted while my name, address and purpose in the area were duly recorded. After telling my story for the third time, I lost my temper. I called the cop-clerk on the other end of the phone a jerk and told him to get a squad car and an ambulance over to Dunlevy Street, six short blocks from the Main Street station, and I'd meet them. Otherwise the felons would be long gone.

I was half right. Only the thug that I'd hit was still there.

He was so still that I felt a prickle of alarm. I bent over him, listening for a heart beat. It was there, irregular and ragged. His breathing rattled like marbles in a bucket. Heavy smoker. He carried no wallet and aside from a greasy half-full package of Export cigarettes, his pockets were empty. No, not quite. I felt the crackle of paper in a hip pocket and fished out a Welfare Department voucher for forty dollars, made out to "Joe Warren." Going through the man's pockets left me with a strong urge to wash my hands.

The squad car and ambulance arrived, sirens growling.

"You'll have to come over to the station and file a report, Mr. Sutter," the patrol cop said. He was a good deal brighter than his buddy on the phone had been.

The ambulance crew gathered up Mr. Warren and departed, after a hurried, whispered conference with the police constable. The next few hours was one of the horrors of my life. It began when I demanded the use of a phone.

"Calling your lawyer?" the desk sergeant asked, pointing to a bank of pay phones in the lobby.

"My girlfriend."

"Hope she's got a law degree," he said.

The phone rang for several minutes. Then I remembered reading somewhere that you couldn't actually hear the phone ring at the other end of a call. The ringing sound is called a "pacifier" and is inserted at the exchange, presumably to keep waiting callers from going berserk and bombing the phone company. I dialed the operator and asked her to check the number.

"Sorry, sir," the operator said. "That line is out of order."

"Then why the hell did it ring?"

"Outages sometimes respond that way, sir. You can speak to one of our technicians during business hours."

Shit. What a time for her phone to go out. I felt a brief surge of relief. Maybe my panic was unwarranted and she was just fine, with a broken-down phone.

Cam and Jeep should be there by now. Why hadn't they called the cop shop for me? I returned to the desk sergeant. "Nobody called for me? Left a message?"

"Nope." He didn't even look at his stack of phone message forms.

"Can we do this report in the morning? I've got to get out of here. My girl could be in trouble."

He gave me a knowing smirk. "Mister, I don't think you're going anywhere. Write a description of the incident." He handed me a lined foolscap pad and a ballpoint.

My right hand felt like a collection of broken bones. Slowly and painfully I scribbled a report of the mugging attempt. No one could read it. After describing the same event three more times, verbally, to a progression of uniformed officers it was decreed that my fingerprints should be taken. Getting them down on paper, unsmudged, was a painful process. I think they enjoyed it. Then they left me.

The office where we'd done my prints was a replica of the one McRae had used to grill me last week. I was told to wait. Did I have a choice?

Half an hour later the door opened to admit a jaded- looking detective. Sergeant Kidson was tall, with the remains of a faded English accent, a many-times-broken nose, and a decrepit brown fedora with the brim drooping, all around, which he apparently never removed. He began affably enough. Or maybe I just wasn't registering the subtleties by then. "What did you hit him with, Mr. Sutter?"

"I beg pardon?"

"I said, what sort of weapon did you hit Warren with?"

"No weapon. I hit him with my fist." I held up my bruised right hand for his inspection. Even Jeep admits I have large hands. "How many times did you hit him?"

"Once. Look, what is this--?" I stood. What was happening to Tats while these idiots jawed?

"Sit down, Sutter," he interrupted.

I sat.

"Once, eh? That's hard to believe. I'm informed by Vancouver General's emergency admitting surgeon that Mr. Warren has a severe depressed skull fracture. He may not survive the night. So I'd advise you to get your story straight. Where did you hide the weapon?"

"There was no weapon. Look, I weigh two hundred and forty-five pounds and I'm in good shape. I work with wire rope cables and boom chains and my hands are like rocks. I'll show you." I made a fist. Then winced and wished I hadn't done that.

Kidson backed away from me. "Are you a professional pugilist, Mr. Sutter?"

"No. Look, call--"

"Because I once was, and I've never seen anyone done so much damage by a single blow. How many times did you hit him? Or did you kick him?"

"Once. I damned near broke my hand on the bastard. Call Sergeant McRae. He knows me."

"Had dealings with the department before, have you?"

"What? No. I mean yes but not the kind you mean. McRae is investigating the murder of two business associates of mine."

"I see. And who might those persons have been?"

I gave him a condensed summary of the two murder cases, though I had the feeling he knew all about them.

He shuffled through a stack of papers, some of them my hand-written report. At last he said, "I note that you gave us an address on Bidwell Street. Do you keep an apartment there?"

"My girlfriend's place--"

"And she is?"

"Tatiana Kovacs. I normally live aboard my ship but I'm on time off from my job. Somebody claiming to be from my office called her tonight and left a message that there was some kind of emergency and I should meet my ship at the oil dock. The call was a phony. The ship wasn't there. Now I can't get an answer at my girl's place and I'm afraid she's in danger."

"Why would she be in danger?"

"Her brother was Sandor Kovacs, one of the people murdered at the Marine Building. He'd been followed for weeks before that. Can I get out of here now?"

"No."

"Jesus Christ, what do you want from me? I give you a sleazy thug on a platter and all you can do is ask questions as if I was the criminal."

"Yes, well, since the other party is unable to talk at the moment, we have a certain responsibility to determine who did what to whom."

"Jesus." I stood again. "This is impossible."

He gave me the cop's evil eye and said, "Sit down, Sutter." Nastier this time.

I sat.

"Fortunately for you, we found two sets of prints on those sack hooks, besides yours, that is. And Mr. Joe Warren is known to us. Otherwise I'd find it hard to believe your story and I'm not sure I believe it yet. I'm going to release you with the caution that you remain in the greater Vancouver area until this matter is cleared up. There's a chance you will face an assault charge, or possibly manslaughter if Warren doesn't make it, though I'll tell you frankly, the department won't miss him. But I warn you, if we find a weapon with your prints on it, I'll order your arrest."

"Can you contact Sergeant McRae? He has to know about what's happened tonight."

"Sergeant McRae has taken Friday off with his weekend. I believe he's promised his wife a holiday out of town."

"You must have a number for him."

"Yes. But you haven't convinced me I should break up his holiday. Detectives have the highest divorce rates of any occupation, after union business agents. Did you know that?"

I couldn't blame their long-suffering wives. "Can I get out of here now?"

"Yes. I believe there are two people downstairs looking for you." I was halfway down the stairs before he finished saying that.

Cam and Jeep were perched on chairs in the lobby. Their expressions stopped me cold. My heart sank.

"What happened?"

"She wasn't there, Hank," Jeep said. "The place has been wrecked. It's an unbelievable mess. The bastards smashed the door right off its hinges, like with a sledge hammer."

"Holy Jesus."

"It's worse than that. Tats must have put up a hell of a fight. There was blood on the floor and on that brass lamp base. I don't think it was hers."

"Did you call the police?"

"Phone was dead so it was quicker to just make a report when we got here," Jeep said. "We did that, while we were waiting for you. They said they'd come and look at it."

"Not good enough," I said. "I need McRae on this."

"Axel is watching the place. Jesus, what happened that you got stuck in here?"

"I'll tell you on the way. Let's move."

*

Jeep's description of the mess was an understatement. Every container, drawer and cupboard, even the refrigerator, had been dumped into the middle of the floor. Tats' oak wardrobe, a "built-in," had proven too big for them to move but they'd dumped its contents on top of the pile. The bed stood, upended, with mattress ripped open, stuffing on the floor mixed with melting, frozen soup stock that Aunt Clara had left. It looked as if they'd used their feet to sort through it.

Sandy's two cardboard boxes of papers and books were gone and so were his notebooks.

"So what do you think?" Cam asked.

"Jeep is right," I said. "She fought like a wildcat. How long do you think this took?"

"Dunno. Depends how many guys did it, I guess. They'd need one to sit on Tats, after they subdued her. I'd say three guys, minimum. Maybe four. It wouldn't take long."

"Why didn't somebody upstairs phone the police?" I said.

"That's easy. They cut all the phone lines before they went in. Everything in the building."

"Bastards cover their asses, whoever they are," I said.

"Lady in the apartment upstairs is hysterical an' her dog's been goin' nuts. Yappy little fucker. She heard everything but she won't even come to her door," Jeep said.

I'd been pacing in the small clear patch of floor they'd left. I turned and grabbed the phone, only to stare at it dumbly. No dial tone. Idiot!

I found a pay phone in working order a block away on Beach Avenue. Twenty minutes of futility finally produced Sergeant Kidson on the line. "I think you'd better call Sergeant McRae," I said. "Tatiana Kovacs has been kidnapped and her place has been totally wrecked."

"Are you sure she hasn't simply gone somewhere safe for the night? It could be a simple smash and grab," Kidson said.

"There's blood on the floor and Sandy Kovacs' personal stuff is all that's been taken. That's the guy that was pushed off the Marine Building last week. If you tell McRae that, he'll come."

"I'll come around myself, first. Then, if it seems necessary, I can call Sergeant McRae."

Detective Sergeant Kidson arrived in less than ten minutes without using his siren. He made us wait outside while he examined the apartment. Half of police work is simply a matter of using your eyes and ears. Looking carefully and critically at the crime scene -- in a way most people rarely learn to look -- is sometimes all that's needed to break a case. I watched from the doorway. Kidson was a master of the art. "Four men," he said, when he emerged.

He examined the broken door closely, kneeling beside it.

I said "They didn't expect a solid hardwood door. The sledge hammer they brought was too light. Took them thirty or forty blows to break in."

Kidson looked at me with patient annoyance but he nodded. He thumped a fist into his hand in a measured count, timing the blows of the hammer. "Four or five minutes," he said. "Your girlfriend might have gotten away through the bathroom window in that much time."

"But the blood…?"

"Exactly. She didn't try to get away. You said she's a dancer?"

"A ballerina," I said.

"Then she'd be athletic and agile, I expect."

"Very agile." He had no idea.

"So she had a chance to escape. And yet for some reason, Miss Kovacs decided to stay and greet her attackers with a brass lamp stand."

"You saw the blood on the lamp stand?"

"Yes. Looks like she bent it over somebody's head. I also found two broken teeth on the floor near the door."

"Way to go, Tats!" Jeep said, grinning.

"She's not very big but take my word for it, you wouldn't want to tangle with her, angry," I said.

"Yes? Well, she does seem to have done a lot of damage to the four of them. Subduing her must have delayed them. Possibly it explains why they simply dumped everything on the floor."

"Obviously they were looking for something," I said.

"Not necessarily. Tossing everything is a standard technique of B and E artists. Can you tell us what she was wearing?"

"I left at two-thirty. By three in the morning she could have been asleep but she was so angry with me for being out so late she was probably still awake. My guess is she heard those guys coming. She slept nude."

"Why do you think she'd gone to bed?" I pointed at the flowered silk wrapper she'd been wearing when I left. "That's why," I said. The wrapper was on top of the heap of clothing on the floor.

"Then we'll assume she'd turned in," Kidson said. "She would take time to dress when they started on her door, I imagine?"

"No," I said. "She wouldn't. Tats has no inhibitions about her body. The shock value of unexpected nudity might give her a few seconds and she'd use that. They'd have made her dress, later. Hard to explain why you're carrying a nude woman to a car at three in the morning."

Kidson looked at me as if I'd been reading his lines. "Probably," he said. "So have another look at that pile on the floor and tell me what she's wearing now."

Poor Tats. Virtually nothing she owned would be fit to wear again. Not that she owned much of a wardrobe but what she did have was as expensive as it was unconventional. I sorted through the sad pile, looking for something that I knew she liked to wear. But it was a black two-piece leotard that she'd worn at her dancing classes that was missing. So was a short wrap-around tartan skirt and a light windbreaker. An old pair of sneakers rounded out the list.

Jeep, Cam and I retired to Blossom's Cafe while a crew of police technicians went over the apartment and took photographs. Axel went back to the ship to finish his traded hours for George Farnham. From Blossom's corner window we saw a yellow and white B.C. Tel line truck pull up in front of the Victorian.

I had an idea.

"Blossom, you're up early to start your grill, aren't you?" Blossom's living quarters were upstairs above the restaurant and his windows overlooked Alexandra Park.

"Oh yes. Working people come for breakfast early. We open six o'clock sharp."

"I don't suppose you were awake around three?"

He nodded vigorously. "I old man. Old man sleep too little and pee too much."

"Did you see a car and maybe some men across the park at Tatiana's place?

He nodded. "Little black truck park in front. Chevrolet 1952."

"Yeah? How do you know it was a '52 Chevy at that distance?"

"Truck exactly same as nephew's. He run wholesale vegetable business. I think he come to borrow money again. Wait for me to open. But not him."

"Did you see who was driving it?"

"Only see two fella, too big for Chinese. So I know it not nephew."

"Thanks. That might help."

"So sorry to hear about Missy."

"Thanks, Blossom. We'll get her back."

*

They let us back into Tats' place around two that afternoon. Kidson said, "I'll pass this on to Sergeant McRae. He'll be the best judge of his need to be here."

"Can we clean the place?"

"Of course. Your telephone should be working again."

I picked up the handset and heard a dial tone. "Thanks for getting it fixed so--" But Kidson was gone.

We stared at the mess for a long time. Jeep went out and bought some garbage bags and started on the cleaning chore. Two hours later the place was looking reasonable, except for the broken door. Jeep washed windows and scrubbed the kitchen. It sparkled. He moved to clean Tats' blackboard with her dance step notations. I was asleep on my feet by then and only caught him at the last moment. "No Jeep! Leave that. She's got hundreds of hours of work in that stuff."

"What the hell is it?"

"Dance notation. She's been building a ballet."

"Jeez. I thought they just made the steps up as they went along. They write it all down like music?"

"That's what they--"

The phone rang. I picked it up.

"Sutter? You better lay off or your cute little piece of ass is gonna get her fuckin' head beat in. Understand?"

"Is she okay--?"

"Shut up. We'll do the talkin', see. I'm gonna call you random, like. All sorts of times. You better be there if you want the bitch in one piece. We'll put her on the line just so you know this is straight. Got it?"

"Yes." Somebody shouted to somebody else and I could hear industrial machinery or maybe a motorcycle somewhere nearby. Then Tats' voice, "Hank?"

"Hang in there, penguin."

"Oh God, I'm so sorry--"

Somebody pulled the phone out of her hands. "Remember, random calls," the voice said and disconnected.

C H A P T E R

12

"They're gonna nail your foot to the floor. Keep you outa action. You must've been getting close to somethin'," Jeep said.

"Yeah. But what?" I said.

"Had to be one of those jokers you talked to. Nobody's been followin' us since we grabbed Nunn. Leastways I don't think."

True, Nunn's keystone cops had given up shadowing us, but I'd seen "Special O," the RCMP's Watcher Service teams and Jeep had no idea how professional surveillance worked. I just didn't think we warranted that kind of attention.

I said, "Sandy must have been onto something. If I could just find out what he knew…"

"How you gonna find out anythin' you gotta be here sittin' on the phone?"

"I was just thinking about that. Which of you can do the best imitation of my voice?"

"You mean one of us answers this guy's calls? You think that'd work?"

"It should work if Tats doesn't give us away. She's too sharp to do that."

"But our voices are different," Jeep protested.

"I'm still hoarse from drinking Harper's booze and being up all night. And I only said about six words. These bastards haven't met me, face to face. I say they don't really know what I sound like."

"So who do you think?" Jeep said.

"Cam is closest. At least we both speak English."

"Hey. Watcha think I speak?"

"You speak Jeep. It's a dialect of English."

Cam said, "All I need is a quart of screech and I'll be perfect. But she'll for sure know it's not you."

"Sure she'll know. And if I'm not answering the phone, I'm out doing something about her. That should give her spirits a lift. I hope to Christ it's justified."

"Give her an even bigger lift, we get her back and I get my hands on the pricks," Jeep said.

"Cam, you'll need my nickname for her and her's for me."

"So what does she call you? Lover boy?" Jeep asked.

"Monster."

"Monster! Is that because of your size? Or the size of it?" Jeep snickered, pointing at "it."

"You'll never know, Jeep."

"Yeah, I know. I seen you in the shower."

"I call her penguin."

"Okay, you gotta explain that."

"Why?"

"How we gonna be believable, we don't know the background?"

"We? This isn't a committee. Cam is doing this. By himself."

"So whisper it to Cam and he can tell me later, if you're embarrassed."

"It's because of the way she walks. The way most ballet dancers walk because of the turn-out they're taught. Toes out, sort of duck-like," I said.

"Why don't you call her ducky?"

"Because I value my life, smart ass. Where are you going with those garbage bags?"

"To find a Dumpster."

"What about my suit? I think maybe the cleaner can save that. It cost me a fortune," I said.

"You got a hell of a cleaner, then. I'll pull it out." He rummaged in a bag, extracting my crumpled blue serge suit jacket. Then the pants. Both were dripping with Clara's soup stock. I hoped she didn't use much tomato in it or they were ruined.

"While you're out, get Blossom to make us some take-out breakfast and send it over," I said.

"What you wanna eat?" Jeep, the attentive waiter.

"A steak and eggs breakfast. Eggs over easy. Hash browns."

"Cam?"

"Sounds good to me," Cam said.

"Okay, and I'll get a big thermos of -- Oh oh. We got company."

Sergeant McRae sauntered in, staring at the wrecked door as he entered. "Kidson thought I should come in for this," he said. "He gave me a rundown on the break-in. Has anything else happened?"

"They called half an hour ago. Threatened her life if I didn't back off. Said they'd make random calls to be sure I stayed here. They put Tats on the line for a few seconds. She sounded scared."

"You don't keep your nose out of this investigation, I'm going to threaten your life, Sutter. But since you've been such a nosy bastard, tell me what you've found out."

"Hey, sarge, you want it both ways? Warn me off the case and pick my brains too?"

McRae gave me a disgusted look, then looked at his watch. "We'll argue this later." He dialed a number. Then said, "Give me the chief of security...I don't care if he's on his way out...this is police business and I need him now. Not some time next week."

The conversation was brief and testy on McRae's side. A "nuisance hold" circuit was to be installed immediately on Tats' phone line at the exchange. A second phone was to be installed at the apartment. Tonight. "Don't worry about the overtime," McRae said. "The complainants will pay for it, I'm sure." He replaced the phone and gave me a smirk.

"Okay, now, pay attention while I explain how this works. The nuisance hold circuit is state of the art. It will hold the connection open after anybody calls here. After they hang up, I mean. A technician at the exchange will call you on a second line and ask if the call he's holding is to be traced. You tell him `yes' or `no' and hang up. Got it?"

"Yes."

"You're going to have a nice bill for double-time at IBEW union rates.

I told them to keep somebody on that switching bank twenty-four hours a day. Now tell me what you've found out."

I summarized my run-in with Joe Warren and friend, and the phony message that had decoyed me away from Tats' place. I didn't tell him about the two names on Sandy's list being ships because I hadn't told him about the list in the first place, although it was obvious now that he was working from a copy of the same list. Nor did I mention Ella Feldman's story of her impending divorce. He'd already heard about that.

"Why do you suppose these guys trashed this place? They didn't have to do that to kidnap her," McRae asked.

"I'd be speculating."

"So speculate. That's what we're all doing until we catch these bastards."

"Looking for something," I said. "Same reason they broke into Sandy's rooms. Probably the same reason they were in Feldman's office the night he got shot."

McRae sat on the edge of the kitchen table. It creaked ominously. He fished out a cigar and pruned the end of it. "Speculate some more," he said. "Why do you suppose they didn't kill her? They didn't hesitate to kill two other people."

I felt the cold chill of McRae's logic. I said, "Maybe the mugging was supposed to take me out. If the guy I knocked down first, that got away, called and reported their screwup, they might have changed plans."

"More likely he's still running," McRae said. "Assuming Joe Warren and friend had anything to do with the killers."

"Did you get any answers from him?"

"Not yet. Bugger is stupid enough it's believable he doesn't know anything. Look at it this way. Tatiana Kovacs isn't a threat to them. You are. Probably they figured they could sweat some information out of her, find out what you know, and maybe have some fun, before they killed her."

"Christ!" I shuddered. I resumed pacing the floor, using up nervous energy I didn't have to spare. I couldn't imagine what I'd do if Tats was raped. But I knew I was capable of killing somebody with my bare hands. It wasn't something I was proud of.

McRae watched me, impassively, while he fired up his cigar. "You have to face reality," he said. "She's a very beautiful young woman. It happens all the time."

"It's hard to even think about things like that."

"So think of something else. Speculate about what, exactly, these people are searching for."

"I have no idea. Obviously it's something Sandy had, or controlled, or had stashed, that they badly want. Or did not want him to have."

"Why do I have the feeling you know more than you're telling me?"

"If I do, it sure as hell isn't much. Talking to his law professor, I got the feeling Sandy was getting ready to blow the whistle on somebody. He didn't have a clue what Sandy was working on, beyond the possibility it was something Feldman's office was doing for free."

"That's odd. How did he come to that conclusion?"

"Sandy asked him a question about confidentiality in a pro bono case."

McRae scowled. Puffed a blue cloud of pungent air pollution, courtesy of Havana. He seemed to be flipping a mental coin. He said, "Feldman called the office on Friday, the day he was killed, asking for me. He left a message asking to meet with me last Monday. He said he had information that might bear on the investigation."

"He didn't say what it was?"

"Just that client privilege was no longer an appropriate reason for withholding it. Guess you rattled him with your questions. Of course I'd threatened him with a court order to access Kovacs' files and that might have done it. No help to us now."

"I got nowhere on the subject," I said.

"How did you find Kovacs' professor?"

"A librarian at the UBC law library put me onto him. Name is Dalls."

"What the hell were you doing there?"

"Looking at Sandy's borrowing list for the last month. Aside from about a thousand pages of case law in CCH binders, the only thing unusual was that he'd taken out a four-volume set on the Nuremburg trials." Which were overdue and still in the trunk of Cam's car, I remembered.

"What the hell, the Nuremburg trials?"

I shrugged. "It could have been just a passing interest," I said.

"They took those two boxes of Kovacs' stuff," he said. "Could this, whatever-they're-after have been in those boxes and we just missed it?"

"If it was there, they wouldn't have wasted the time turning her place upside down. Tossing is a standard B and E search technique," I said. "According to Kidson," I added, hastily. I was getting fuzzy-headed from lack of sleep. I'd come close to lecturing McRae on police work. Not a good idea.

"Miss Kovacs complained about her brother being followed. Any sign of that sort of thing now?"

"No. At least not since...No."

"Not since what?"

"Nothing."

"Not since your boys trapped Nunn and threw him in a flower bed?"

"Oh, now, look..." That bastard Nunn had talked! Jeep stood, frozen, against the wall.

"Way I figure it, you and Nunn came to some agreement. Right? Otherwise, you'd be counting bars and waiting for an arraignment."

"If we did, he hasn't lived up to his part."

"Relax, Sutter. He hasn't talked."

"Then how did you...?"

"Buddy of mine, retired from the force a few years ago, lives on that cul-de-sac. I knew it was you and Nunn when he told me about the blue Buick and the black Chrysler and gave me the plate numbers. He knew Nunn by sight. But he's a heart case so he couldn't go to Nunn's aid."

"No comment."

"That's what I figured you'd say. Maybe you're half-assed bright after all but you better pray Nunn doesn't skinny out of whatever lock you got on him or Canada won't be a big enough country to hide in. Now I am going back to Harrison Hot Springs and my wife, if she hasn't left me already."

"What if we get a number from the trace?"

"You won't. B.C. Tel will pass that to Kidson and he'll run it down. Do try and keep out of trouble until I get back on Monday."

A long silence followed McRae's departure. Then Jeep said, "Phew! I thought we'd had it."

"No fear, Jeep."

"Why not? That guy could chuck us in the slammer and throw the key away."

"He won't."

"How the hell can you be so sure of that?"

"Because he wants us on this case. He ordered a second phone for us. Right?"

"Yeah. So what?"

"A second line isn't necessary for the phone company technician to call us back, when he's using the nuisance hold circuit. McRae knows that and he knows I know it. The second phone is to let us keep working without blocking incoming calls from the kidnappers. Sort of a professional courtesy."

"Well I'll be a ringtailed sonofabitch," Jeep said.

*

I stretched out on the ruined bed in a half-hearted attempt to get some rest. Sleep wouldn't come. I tried to visualize what Tats would have done from the moment her kidnappers started smashing at her door. She wouldn't panic. Tatiana Kovacs wouldn't know how to be hysterical. My love was bright. If she didn't run from her attackers, it was for a reason. But what?

Then it came to me. She'd be trying to leave me a clue they wouldn't find. But a clue to what? If they hadn't yet broken down the door, it had to be something other than who they were.

Something she'd found out?

"Oh Christ! Jeep!" I sat bolt upright. I was suddenly wide awake.

Jeep, dozing on the couch, said, "Give a guy a heart attack, why doncha? What's eatin' you?"

Cam had been sleeping, sitting at the kitchen table, using the phone like a Japanese wooden block pillow. "Unhuh?" he said.

"We're going at this all wrong. We've got to think about this place the way it was when they left here."

"A bloody mess. Why?"

"She left us a clue to something. We just have to find it."

"How do you know?"

"Figure it out. They got Sandy's boxes. Right?"

"Yeah."

"But they still trashed the place, risking the extra time it took to do that. Why?"

"Didn't find what they wanted?" Cam said. "You and McRae went over all that, didn't you?"

"Yes, but neither of us was paying attention to the implications. Whatever they were after *wasn't in those boxes*."

"So where does that get us?" Jeep said. "You already went through the boxes and so did the cops. And didn't find nothin'."

"No. We found eight notebooks of Sandy's shorthand. McRae's boys just saw the unreadable shorthand and gave up. But they copied the same names in plain English that I found in the last book. Must have, because McRae's been calling on the same people I have."

"Last? You mean Sandy dated the books?"

"Right. Tats and Clara found his system and she'd been working on it all yesterday afternoon and evening."

"What did she find out?" Cam asked.

"She didn't tell me. She was so damned pissed off with me for coming home at two in the morning and not phoning her about where I was--"

"And drunk?" Cam asked.

"No. But I smelled bad, I guess. Anyway, she wasn't in a mood to talk to me about anything. Think of places she could hide something that they wouldn't find."

"Fat chance. They ripped the place up real good."

"Has to be something. C'mon, guys. Look!"

"Behind the blackboard, maybe? They didn't pull that off the wall."

"You could have something...Wait a minute."

"What?" Cam and Jeep said together.

"That notation. There's something wrong with it."

"You can read that stuff?"

"The figures represent positions for the dancer's body, arms and feet. She told me that much."

"So what's wrong with it?"

"That arrow shouldn't be there. See? It runs right across two of the staves." A ragged, chalked arrow ran through the notation symbols Tats had been working on. I stared at it, willing my brain cells to work, to produce the answer.   .

Jeep shook me loose. "Where does it point?" he asked.

Of course! It would point at whatever she wanted me to look at. "It's the wardrobe," I said. "Let's go over it."

We attacked the massive cabinet as if our lives depended on it. Double folding doors with a scroll-cut pattern for ventilation, and brass piano hinges. A pair of deep drawers in the bottom for shoes and small stuff, sweaters and such. Empty and nothing behind them. The shelf near the top would be for hats, if Tats owned any hats. A round bar of hardwood, now stripped of hangers and clothes, spanned the six-foot wide cabinet.

The wardrobe held a faint, sharp smell of oiled white oak and a whiff of camphor, and not a damned thing else.

Then I saw the gap or, rather, the lack of it. Whoever had built the wardrobe had cheated on the "built-in" part. He'd stopped an inch short of the nine-foot rough-plastered ceiling and covered the gap with a pair of decorative, carved oak fascia pieces on the two exposed sides. Both had been removed, apparently when the ceiling had last been painted. I remembered them standing in a corner of the bathroom, nails still poking through the wood, waiting to stab me.

Now they were back in place. Tats would have had to stand on a chair to reach that height. My God, she must have been flying, to get those facings up before they broke in. Tatiana Kovacs was not only bright, she was incredibly cool and collected. "I need something long and skinny," I said.

"Curtain rod do it?" Jeep asked.

"Maybe." I tugged the front fascia board free. It was held by a single finishing nail that had been pushed back into its original nail hole. Then I raked the thin brass rod across the top of the cabinet. Something stopped me at the inner corner of the space, bending the rod. We wasted an hour trying to poke, pull and persuade whatever it was free. In the end, a better curtain rod with a bent drapery hook lashed to its far end did the trick.

A dusty, spiral-bound notebook fell at our feet.

"Way to go, Tats!" Jeep said.

"Amen," I said. The notebook was Sandy's last, judging by the September 1 date. Jammed between its pages was a thin, soft-cover booklet in German entitled *Unterricht die Staedler Kurzschrift*.

"Bingo!" I yelled, grinning.

"What the hell is it?" Jeep asked.

"It's his shorthand system," I said. But I knew making this find pay off was going to be a lot of work.

CHAPTER

13

"How'n hell do you know what that says?" Jeep demanded.

"If you hadn't dropped out in kindergarten, you might have learned a language or two in school, Jeep. I did some German in school and then I was stationed in Kiel for a year. Remember?"

"Kiel? That's in Germany. Right? See? I ain't stupid."

"Unlearned, not stupid. There's a difference."

"Yeah?" Jeep looked pleased with my definition. "So if this stuff is a breeze for you, how come you needed Tats to translate with Beyer?"

"Haven't used it in ten years. I'm rusty and I couldn't afford a mistake, questioning a guy who was playing games with me. But it's Tats' handwriting that's giving me fits. She's made notes in the margins of nearly every page of the notebook and her writing is so bad I can't be sure what language she used. She told me Sandy kept his working notes in English as part of his effort to master the language. She might have done the same. Or she might not."

"So how many languages does Tats know?" Jeep wondered.

"I dunno for sure. She's fluent in German and Russian, that I know. French is used a lot in ballet so she did that in school at the academy. Plus English and Hungarian, of course."

"Sheeesh! So how come such a smart and pretty lady writes so ugly?"

"I'll tell her you said that. But you're right. Look at this." A line of shorthand squiggles was encircled in red ink and an excited, underlined note in Tats' scribble was followed by half a dozen exclamation points. And I couldn't read it!

Jesus. My love had been kidnapped and here I was condemning her for her handwriting! Talking about her as if she were in the next room. Jeep did it, too, so maybe we were all doing some kind of weird psychological dance of non-acceptance. The shrinks would have a name for it. I didn't.

I said, "Jeep, go find us some writing materials. Get lots because we're going to attack this systematically. There must be a drug store open that carries school supplies. Try the place on Denman near Comox."

"You got it." He left at a jog.

I stared at the notes for a long half hour. I managed to unravel "and" and "to" but I couldn't sort out "it" and "at." Anything longer was hopeless. But the longer I looked the more I realized that her handwriting wasn't the scrawl I'd first thought. It was consistent and not so much bad as different. I'd seen writing like that in Germany.

I called the *Solange*'s dockside number and got Jimmy Lee. "Wake up Axel, Jimmy. Tell him I need him at Tats' place."

"Okay skipper. You found Miss Tatiana?"

"Not yet. Soon, I hope."

"You need me, I'll be there. She's such a nice lady," he said, wistfully.

"Thanks, Jimmy. Maybe later." I hung up the phone and stared at it for a minute, wondering what to do next. Obviously Tats had got a long way into deciphering Sandy's notes. Re-inventing the wheel didn't seem to make sense.

"What do you need Axel for?" Cam asked.

"Huh? Oh, because he speaks the best German around and he also knows some Hungarian. I think he might be able to help with her handwriting."

Cam nodded, then gestured towards the broken door. Donal Gowan was staring through it, into the room. "What's going on, Sutter? Where's Tatiana?"

"Come in and sit down, Donal, and I'll bring you up to speed."

"Up to-- Something has happened to her?"

"She's been kidnapped. By the same people who killed her brother." I gestured at the doorway. The meaning of the smashed door seemed to register on Gowan. He went pasty white. "Oh my God. Oh dear God, no."

"The police are on it. So are we."

"It's your meddling that has gotten her in trouble, Sutter. Oh God, I'm ruined. Our company is ruined. You do realize that, I hope? You realize how many people are depending upon her? Without a ballerina of her stature, we can do nothing. Our backers will withdraw…Oh God, oh God…"

I stared at him, silently, until he ran out of complaints. "Then there's the little matter of the danger to her life." The acid in my voice brought him up short.

"I didn't mean…Oh I'm sorry. Of course her safety is of primary importance. Is there anything I can do to help? I mean anything at all."

"Not unless you can read her handwriting," I said.

"Of course, but I don't understand…"

"You don't have to understand, Donal. What does this say?" I held up the red-circled passage and her unreadable note.

"I'm afraid…Oh. Just a moment. Yes, this is the way she makes a `t' and this is an `l'. She never closes the loops on her `o's but always does on her `a's. Her `e's look like little `l's and she dots her `i's but sometimes not over the letter. I've never been able to tell her `g's from her `y's. And `j's are anybody's guess."

"How did you get that far with it?"

"When she first came to the academy, she used to make up the junior class schedules by hand. After a few months I gave up and bought a typewriter for her. I still can't read her writing. I'm sorry. I'm not much help, I guess."

"You've been more help than you know, Donal. Now go home and stay off this phone line. If you must call, use this number." I gave him the number of our new line.

"What is going on? Has there been some kind of ransom demand? Why aren't the police here?"

"You could call it ransom, I guess. The police have been all over the place. I'll keep you posted if there are any developments."

"I only came by to see if she'd be coming back to work tomorrow."

"And obviously she won't."

"You make that sound so…so…"

"Final? Christ, I hope not. Look, Donal, we're busting our asses to unravel some of this, to find her, so…"

"And I'm not helping, standing here talking. Right. Call me if there's anything I can do."

But he was wrong. He'd helped a lot.

Jeep arrived as Gowan was leaving. He dumped an armload of school exercise books and assorted pencils, pens and erasers on the table. "Who was that character?" he asked, staring after Gowan.

"Donal Gowan. Tats' ballet master at the academy."

"He's her boss?"

"Sort of. She teaches junior students and takes classes from him herself."

"Jeez, yeah? I thought she was already a pro."

"All dancers take classes. For life. It comes with the turf."

"He does that tippy-toe stuff too?"

"No. Male dancers rarely go *en pointe*."

"Yeah? Then how come she promised to teach me how to do that?"

"Did you ask her?"

"Well...yeah, I guess I did."

"Then that's why. Better stick to learning Hungarian, Jeep. You've got a brighter future there."

"You think she was makin' fun of me?"

"No, Jeep. For some strange reason, Tats likes you. Don't ask me why."

"You know she can stretch her leg straight up? Like doin' the splits, only standing up?"

"I know. How did you find out?"

"We were waiting in the car for you and she said she needed to stretch. I thought she meant go for a walk or something. But she did all these twists and bends and then she put a leg straight up the side of the building, and then changed to the other leg. I never seen nothin' like that, 'cept maybe in a circus."

"I suppose you asked her to teach you that, too?"

"No. Well, not exactly. I sort of asked her what kinda training a guy'd have to do, to learn it. She said I should take up yoga for a couple of years. Then come back and see her."

I grinned.

"What's funny?" he demanded.

"My mental picture of you doing yoga in work boots," I said. Jeep is shorter than me, about five-ten, but he's just as thick-limbed. The Sawchuck fireplug, he's called, in family circles.

*

Axel arrived around seven that evening and after that we began to make progress. He added a few letters to the Tatiana version of copper-plate handwriting and soon words popped out of the mess. I was surprised to discover that she had indeed written her notes in English. More or less.

"Is Junior around on the dock this weekend?" I asked, when Axel took a break to reload his pipe.

"Ach ya. He is a suspicious little shrimper. He vas aboard asking everybody ver is Cam unt Jeep unt vat iss going on."

"Maybe I should put in an appearance, aboard," Jeep said. "Junior's still there?"

"Ya, ya. He is polishing his toy boat for the big show at the yacht club."

"What d'ya think, Hank?" Jeep asked.

"That's maybe a good idea. Nothing much you can do here tonight."

"How come Hercule Poirot don't have some freaky little boss breathin' down his neck when he's solving all those neat English murders?"

"Because Agatha Christie never met Junior, that's why. If she had, she'd have killed the bugger off in an early chapter. Since when did you give up comics and start reading mysteries?"

"Since last week. See ya in the morning."

But Jeep had barely reached the front sidewalk before he turned back. He poked his head in the broken door, face grim. "There's a dark blue Buick parked out front," he said. "Guess who?"

"Okay, Jeep. Go on back to the ship. I'll deal with him. Axel, put all this paper away. I don't want him seeing it, if he comes in." I'm not sure why I felt that way about sharing evidence with Nunn. It just seemed safer that way.

"Him who?" Axel asked.

"Corporal Nunn of the Mounted," I said.

I walked out to greet Nunn. He stepped out of his car. "Well, Sutter, what sort of mess have you gotten the woman in now?" He watched the departing Jeep, warily.

"You've heard about the kidnapping?"

"McRae called me. So they suckered you away to make the snatch, eh?"

"Did he tell you about their phone call?"

"Uh huh. You going to stay home and take their calls, like they told you?"

"The calls will be answered. Did you have anybody watching her place last night?"

"Nope. We've got an agreement. Remember? Hasn't been any surveillance on either of you since Tuesday."

"Either of us? You watching me, too?"

"Sure. You too can be a star. I had only a loose surveillance on your lady friend, using trainee operatives. Frankly, they weren't very good."

"But why? I don't get it."

"Just call it a training exercise."

"Or a fishing expedition?"

"Or that."

"And you pulled them off because of our agreement? Or because there's a Russian trade delegation in town, plus a couple of their grain ships in harbor and you've got real spooks to watch?"

"One or the other. Mind if I have a look?" He gestured at the broken door and the apartment. It was obvious I wasn't going to get a serious answer out of Nunn.

"Been all cleaned up. But be my guest."

Nunn wandered the length of the apartment, hands in his pockets, staring at everything. He drifted into the bathroom, then back into the main room.

"I see why they didn't break in through a window," he said. The apartment's windows were six feet above the sidewalks to their sills and had close-spaced steel bars permanently fixed, except for the bathroom where they were hinged to comply with the fire marshal's rules. "Why didn't she make a run for it?"

"No idea," I lied. "Maybe they had somebody watching the bathroom window."

"Yeah, maybe." He didn't sound convinced. "I assume McRae's got a trace on her line?" He gestured at the phone.

"Yes."

"Hope it works. Come outside and take a walk with me," he said. Was he going to open up and give me some information? What could he have to say that he didn't want Cam and Axel to hear?

"I can't. They might call."

"One of your buddies can handle it. We won't go far."

We walked across the grass of Alexandra Park in a gentle rain, barely more than a mist. He stopped, then climbed the steps to the floor of the little wooden band shell and leaned with his elbows on the rail to stare out over English Bay. Kitsilano lights along the south shore were haloed in rain mist and the sharp, iodine tang of low tide drifted to us. One of Picard's smaller tugs hustled into False Creek, making a huge wash.

I kept silent, waiting for Nunn to get to whatever he had to say.

"Great country, this west coast," he said at last.

"I guess the winters are a little warmer than Ottawa's," I said.

He snorted. "Words are inadequate for the comparison. So you know I was moved here from Ottawa?"

"Rumor has it."

"Nasty things, rumors. They can get you into all sorts of shitty situations. Like mine."

He was silent for a long minute. "Like yours?" I prompted. I suspected Nunn had been drinking, though I couldn't smell it on his breath.

"Maybe you also heard that I had a wife and two kids back there?" I shrugged, doing my best to be neutral.

"Wife was hell-bent on having a career. Got a law degree and a job… oops, sorry, a position that pays twice what mine does. She's in criminal law. Never considered that we might wind up on opposite sides of the same case, some day. Whatever happened to wives that stayed home and raised kids? Looked after their husbands?"

I shook my head. I knew men who thought the way Nunn did. I wasn't one of them.

"Bitch threw me out. Gave me the boot when I asked her to move here when my transfer came through. Guess you know how that makes me feel?"

"Mmm," I said.

"But do you know what it does to my career, losing a wife that way? The force is a paramilitary outfit. Senior ranks have traditional ideas about what family relations should be. Goes towards your promotability."

"I can imagine," I said. I could understand his situation but not his blame-laying.

"Well, I got dumped out here in the boondocks. Not my fault but it doesn't matter why. If somebody important wants you out, you are out. In terms of Security Service work, and scope for promotion, the beautiful banana belt west coast is strictly hicksville. People's brains grow mold out here in the rain forest.

"There's a little activity whenever there's a few Russky grain bulkers in port but I don't even get to deal with whatever the KGB does send our way. That's `B' Section turf. I get to watch labor organizers. Oh, there's a little overlap, sometimes, because of the dock worker's and seamen's unions. And they throw me a bone once in a while. Like when 20,000 Hungarians landed here and they needed a body to watch out for intelligence plants. Big fucking deal."

Now I was sure he'd been tippling. It was a matter of emphasis, rather than any slurring of words. Most likely he was talking to me because that was safer than talking to a fellow member of the force. I was too sleep-deprived to think of another reason.

"Slim pickings, I imagine," I said.

"Damned near a total waste of time. Those Hungarians hate the Ruskies worse than I do. And I am never going to get back to Ottawa unless I pick up on something important out here."

"You want to go back?"

"I want my kids back!"

The bitter vehemence of his answer startled me. I did my best not to show it. I said, "I understand." And bit down on my need to ask questions.

"Kids are teens, now. Boy's fifteen. Girl's seventeen. She's got them in private schools, way over my salary." Let him talk, no matter where he rambled. I'd get more that way. And I sensed that he had some inner need to apologize, no matter how convoluted a form that apology took. "So you see how it looked to me when your lady's brother started making contacts in shipping companies that I'd been watching?" Nunn said.

"No I don't, to be frank," I said.

He gave me a resigned look, as if I were a brain-moldered rain forest dweller. "Damned country's like a sieve for anybody wants to get in. KGB runs agents in through Vancouver all the time. We watch them. Russian ships are the preferred means but we've picked off a few of their people, blown some expensive operations. They've been getting nervous about using their own ships, lately."

"They are using non-Russian ships?"

"Now you've got it. So when young Sandy Kovacs, ten months out of red Hungary, starts doing the rounds of shipping companies and talking to ILWU business agents, what am I supposed to believe?"

"That maybe you can get back in the spook business? But why were you watching Tatiana?"

"Pretty lady. Easy to watch. But the other side often sends agents in pairs. Usually a husband and wife team but we've seen brother and sister pairs. Between them, they'll have a mix of skills. Miss Kovacs was a believable partner for her brother."

"Was? You mean she's no longer a suspect?"

"Don't mean that at all. Everybody's a suspect. You, me, even McRae. It's involvement that counts. Let's just say I am somewhat less persuaded of her involvement since Kovacs' death. Otherwise, I'd never have made that agreement with you."

"Why are you telling me all this?"

"I'm coming to that. I figured Tatiana for the linguistic whiz of the pair. She speaks damned near everything. Fluently. Her brother wasn't so hot with languages but he probably was good at something they needed. Maybe radio operating or something. Between them, they could handle a large ring of informants of several different ethnic origins."

"Give me a break," I said, wearily.

"So to answer your question, why am I telling you all this? I checked out your military record. Very impressive. And your family connections. Not a chance that you're involved with anything red."

"Yeah? I signed all the petitions during last summer's anti-nuclear protest."

"Uh huh. I saw your signature."

"You did?"

"Sure. Where do you think those things end up after you send 'em to Ottawa? But don't sweat it. Several thousand other bleeding hearts signed the bloody things, for all the good it'll do."

"I'm pro-union. Doesn't that make me a suspect?"

"Yeah, but you're an idealist, not an ideologue."

"There's more behind this than just that you checked me out," I said. My alarm bells were trying desperately to wake me.

Nunn nodded, then said, "Ask Tatiana Kovacs where the hell she got advanced schooling in English and German and French in Hungary. She could have started on them in school but the reds pulled all those languages out of the schools after 1949. When she was fifteen. After that, Hungarian school kids got Russian and Hungarian. Period."

"I have the uneasy feeling I'm being scuppered," I said.

"Yeah, in a way, you are." Nunn stood and moved towards the stairs. "If your lady friend is clean, everything'll be rosy and you'll both live happily ever after. But if she's not…"

"If she's not, then what?" My temper was getting dangerous and it was coming through in my voice.

"If she's not, there's no way Captain Dan Sutter's eldest son can avoid blowing the whistle on her. And that's as good as having one of my members living with her."

"Nunn, you are a rotten prick!"

"Glad to see your faith in me is restored. G'night, Sutter."

After returning from my chat with Nunn, Cam and Axel practically wrestled me onto the bed and under a quilt. My anger over Nunn's remarks was one more mental hurdle that I couldn't handle in my befuddled state. I'd lost track of how many hours I'd been on my feet. Once Cam and Axel had me down, I was asleep in seconds. Nothing short of an atom bomb would have waked me. But at two A.M. a ringing telephone did.

I jerked awake and had my ear against the back of the phone as soon as Cam picked it up. "Sutter here," Cam said. He held the handset clear of his ear to let me hear.

"Just wanted to be sure you were having a good night's sleep, Sutter. Here's your lady friend. Only she ain't no goddamn lady."

Tats came on then. "Hank?" Her voice was tentative and frightened. My heart skipped at the sound of her.

"I love you, Penguin. Hang in there. We're on it," Cam said. God, he sounded like me.

A tiny pause told me she knew it wasn't me. "I love you too, Monster. I have to g--" The line went dead and a dial tone gnawed at the silence. Cam dropped the receiver and gave me a tired, worried look, eyebrows raised in query.

"You ever think of taking up an acting career, I'll write you a glowing testimonial," I said.

"Think I got away with it?"

"Jesus, I hope so. But you didn't fool her. That was a good wrinkle, telling her we were on it. She'll know what that means."

The phone rang again. "Was that a call to be traced?" the B.C. Tel technician asked.

"Yes it was. How long will the trace take?"

"Maybe a few minutes, maybe hours. Depends where it came from," the technician said and disconnected.

"I didn't hear the same background noise as on the first call, Cam. Did you hear anything?"

"Sounded sort of hollow, like somebody was listening on an extension, maybe. I was too nervous to notice anything else."

"You did real good. Thanks."

"Get some more sleep. You've only been snoring for a couple of hours. Axel was onto something with the notebook last night. He wants to talk to you about it in the morning but he had to go back aboard the *Solange* to do his watch. And he isn't getting any more sleep than we are. Damned stand-by pressure rule is screwing us up."

"Let me see the notes."

"Sleep first. There's nothing you can do about them before morning."

"I guess you're right." But I couldn't sleep. The frightened quiver in Tats' voice haunted me. And Nunn's vicious little scheme to co-opt me as a Security Service snitch still had me boiling. His insidious attempt to drive a wedge between Tatiana and me, to isolate her even more than she was, put a dangerous spin on my feelings about Corporal Nunn and intelligence officers of whatever ilk. And I was having second thoughts about Nunn's "trainee" surveillance team. Could they have been hamming it up, intending to be noticed? Just another move to rattle Tats? Nunn was certainly capable of that.

I'd come perilously close to exploding and doing something stupid about Nunn. Or to him. My roiled-up emotions were getting me nowhere. If I knew anything about police work it was that a rational, cool head was the first essential.

Around four A.M., I roused myself and tiptoed to the bathroom for an unnecessary pee, hoping to sneak a look at Axel's notes.

Cam was asleep on the couch. He'd set up a night light and he was using the phone like a Japanese neck pillow, padded with a folded blanket, so as not to risk missing a call. I didn't envy him the crick in the neck he'd have in the morning.

Damn. He'd put Axel's notes under the phone.

I went back to bed muttering imprecations about clever engineers. I dreamed, fitfully, of dozens of blood-red mounted policemen galloping in circles around some helpless prey, prodding it with lances in a silent, macabre musical ride. I was the prey.

*

Saturday morning dawned, wet and miserable with a raw south-easter blowing up a scud of whitecaps across English Bay. The air had an edge of winter. I went for a morning walk in the rain, then jogged along the beach to get my blood flowing. A couple of miles of that and I was ready to eat something large and not necessarily dead.

Axel arrived at eight-thirty, carrying a big Thermos container of coffee that I recognized as belonging to the *Solange*'s galley, and a shopping bag full of bagels from The Bayside Bakery. Axel loved bagels.

The phone rang and everybody froze. But it was Blossom wanting to know how many breakfasts to send over and what did we want to eat? Slowly, the day began. While not exactly rested, I felt functional again.

Axel was at the kitchen table. He spoke from under a low ceiling of poisonous pipe smoke. "Ziss fellow, Heinrich Beyer you spoke to…" He left that dangling.

"What about him?" I asked.

"He iss how old?"

"Thirty-eight or forty. Why?"

"He iss from Hamburg?"

"His shipping company is based there, so…" I shrugged.

"Vat does he look like?"

"Blond. Slim. Prematurely balding with a slightly receding chin. Scared shitless of us," I said.

"Hah. Scared? Ya, that is like him. He vas scared of hiss shadow. Except around women."

"You knew this guy?"

"I don't sail with him but ve had a Heinrich Beyer in the Kriegsmarine. In submarines. He vas famous for chasing the women. It saves his life."

"Wouldn't some angry husband be gunning for him?"

"Ya, but ziss one time he iss squeezing ze wrong girl. Her daddy iss Oberst of SS Panzer Grenadiers mit lots of, mm, big shot friends. Beyer spends the last two years of the war in military prison. His boat, U-174, is lost two weeks after zey lock him up."

Axel usually avoided discussing the war. This was the first time I'd heard him say he'd been·in submarines.

"He has no good English?"

"That's right. His English was poor so Tats translated for him. He took a shine to her. Offered her a job."

"Everybody shines for that lady. Unt Beyer vas itchy for women. Ve used to say if the allied airforce didn't get him, somebody's husband does." Axel punctuated with his pipe stem, for emphasis. "He vas not wanting to talk to Sandy."

"How do you know that?"

"It iss in Sandy's notes and in Tatiana's. Sandy was thinking Beyer knows something but Sandy has poor German. Unt Beyer pretends he has no good English. Sandy writes here he will ask Tatiana to help with his questions. She has perfect German."

"Pretends? Beyer knows English?"

"Unless he forgets since the war."

"He told Tats he thought we were part of a waterfront gang, come to shake him down."

"Ya? He tells Sandy Kovacs the same. Maybe I go talk to Beyer alone. Maybe talk about the good days in the Hitler time. Heinrich Beyer vas very strong a Nazi."

"You had good times under Hitler?" I asked.

"Nein! Not me. But I pretend."

"Will he recognize you? Did you speak with him when you were in the navy?"

"A few times. Submarine people drink allways in ze same places. Beyer brags all the time about the women he catches. Everybody knows him."

"What did you do in the navy, Axel?"

"I vas a radio operator. Beyer vas a torpedo man."

"You want to shout 'Heil Hitler' and watch him twitch?"

"Ya, but more quiet. Vat is the word?"

"With finesse?"

"Ya. Mit der finesse."

"Okay, Axel, Beyer might be there today. He didn't seem like the type to give himself Saturday off. Jeep will drive you over there after we eat. Tell him to park the car away from Beyer's office. He might have seen it."

*

"Get the fuck off this phone," Cam said. "Call back on this number." He gave the caller our second number and hung up, swearing under his breath.

"Who?" I asked.

"Marty. He's a little upset."

"I guess," I said. The other line rang. I picked it up. "Sutter? Where the hell do you get off telling me to get off your line? Mr. Picard wants to see you aboard the *Solange* right away."

"Yeah, okay, Marty. Don't get your knackers in a knot. What does he want me for? He told me to take days off, so he can hardly order me around on my own time."

"Just get your ass down here, pronto." Haines hung up.

I'd made his day. He loved to order people around. And Marty had made my day. Cam had fooled him into thinking he'd talked to me both times.

Breakfast arrived from Blossom's, followed by Jeep. I took my time eating, listening to Jeep's tale of woe. Junior had been aboard the *Solange* all morning, demanding to know where people were. Jeep seemed to have upset him by walking off in the middle of his tirade.

Jeep was right. Hercule Poirot never had to contend with this sort of insanity. But what could I do about Junior?

I bundled up my ruined suit and the best-looking survivors from Tats' wardrobe and wandered out to find a trolley bus on Davie Street. First stop, my dry cleaner. Nothing Picard had to say to me on my own time was worth a cab fare.

Zeke Zybryski, my dry cleaner, stared at the wreckage of my best blue serge suit, spread out on his counter. "I dunno, Hank," he said, running his fingers over the damp stains and then sniffing at them, giving me his undertaker's face. "I dunno. Must've been some party."

"Just see if you can save it. Okay? And it wasn't a party, it was a break-in. Here's some of Tatiana's stuff." Two skirts, a blouse, a couple of sweaters and a long overcoat seemed to be the sole survivors from her wardrobe disaster.

"I'll do what I can. Have to charge you extra."

"Whatever it takes."

"You want the stuff in the pockets?"

"What stuff?"

He handed me a business card taken from my side jacket pocket. It was Irene Bradshaw's. On the back she had written "call me" and her home phone number.

*

Junior Picard and Marty were lying in wait for me aboard the *Solange.* They'd taken over the mess room, to the disgust of everybody aboard. The crew had been obliged to take morning coffee break sheltering from the rain in the engine room. Which annoyed Dunc McAdams, our chief, who threatened dire consequences if anyone dropped coffee, crumbs or cigarette ashes on his gleaming machinery.

The huge, old, horseshoe-shaped, teak mess-room table had been built to fit the fore end of the main deckhouse and seat eighteen people at once. We normally carried a crew of twelve doing coastwise work but if we were diving, on a salvage job, we carried a tenderman and, sometimes, a second diver. On ocean-going jobs we carried a second mate and a third engineer as well. And Jimmy Lee was entitled to a mess boy for galley help so the crew sometimes went to seventeen.

A semi-circular cut-out on the galley side of the table allowed Jimmy to serve easily. At current hardwood prices, that table was worth five thousand dollars.

Junior occupied the captain's seat, front and center. Marty the lap-dog frisked at his side. I grabbed a stool from the galley and parked in the serving cut-out. The prisoner's dock.

"About time you got here," Marty Haines said.

"Depends on whose time it is, doesn't it? You're making so much noise, Marty, I assume you are paying."

"Don't get smart, Sutter. You're on thin ice. Mr. Picard has some serious matters to raise with you."

"First I need to know what you told that joker who came asking about me last week. The guy with the pock-marks and the ears."

Marty paled. "He said he was a friend from Korea."

"What did you tell him?"

"I, uh, gave him your shore address. I thought--"

"You do anything like that again and I'll wring your chicken neck. Got it?"

"Now look here--!"

"That bastard was probably one of the people who murdered Tatiana Kovacs' brother."

"Uh, I didn't--"

"So get lost, Marty. You have nothing to say that I want to hear." I stared him down.

Haines looked to his boss for support. But Picard was busy studying the view from the forward portlight. Haines sputtered his way out of the mess room.

I poured myself a fresh coffee, taking my time.

Junior cleared his throat. "Now then, Sutter, what is going on? Half this ship's crew seems to be away at any given time -- in violation of our government contract conditions -- and they all seem to be doing something involving you."

"Three people, not half. Half would be eight people."

"Let's not split hairs. You have no right to co-opt crew members who are on company payroll. I warn you, Sutter, this is a firing matter."

"While we are avoiding the splitting of hairs, let's not forget that some of those same people have been used to repair Picard automobiles and rebuild the engine of the Picard speedboat, not to mention feeding two hundred guests at Seraphin Picard's wedding reception using ship's supplies and the ship's cook. Revenue Canada might be interested in that."

"This is insufferable!"

"I thought so at the time, Junior. And while we are on the subject, let's get my cousin Jeep in here."

"Why?"

"He's the union steward for the Picard fleet."

Junior turned two shades paler at the mention of the union. "What does the union have to do with this?" he demanded.

"There are nineteen major grievances outstanding."

"See here, those matters are subject to due process."

"Two years of process? Then there's the safety infractions."

"Safety? What infractions?"

"The fire system has never been brought up to DOT standards. Not to mention the starboard life raft which should be replaced. But the item I want to discuss is Gus's burst appendix, last spring. You've been avoiding me for six months on that."

"We had no idea his condition was so serious."

"Is that the royal `we' or just you and Marty? Because both of you knew. I told you. Yet Marty ordered us not to take him into Prince Rupert, to hospital. That was at your orders--"

"See here! I didn't--"

"--because Marty hasn't got the balls to go out on a limb like that."

"Two hundred miles out of your way--"

"Fuck `out of our way,' godammit!"

"You abandoned your tow and took him in anyway."

"Damn right. And saved his life. And then you tried to bullshit us about the insurance company being involved. You never told them about it."

"I thought this was resolved. I rescinded your firing and had O'Conner amend his log." Yes, Junior had pushed some paper around. I don't know if my expression showed my contempt for him but it must have come close. He wilted. His tongue darted out to wet his lips and he said, "Er, well, can we discuss this situation?"

"What situation?"

"I want to know what you are up to."

No matter what I thought of Junior Picard, he had a certain logic on his side. I *was* using the *Solange*'s crew and we were in violation of the government contract. Not that Junior had ever been anything else but in violation. Maybe I could neutralize the little viper.

"Fair enough. You remember Miss Tatiana Kovacs?"

He smiled. "Of course. A delightful young lady. But--"

"And you are aware that her brother, Sandy Kovacs, was murdered two weeks ago?"

"I read about the death. I didn't connect--"

"She has now been kidnapped by the same people who killed her brother."

"Oh my God. How? Why?"

"Somebody telephoned her apartment around midnight, Wednesday pretending to be Marty and left a message for me to meet the *Solange* at the oil dock. When I got there, two punks attacked me. They didn't quite pull it off but the result was that I was tied up with police questions for hours. In the meanwhile, four men smashed their way into her apartment and kidnapped her."

"The police are investigating, of course?"

"Men who got her address from the ever helpful Marty."

"I...see. This is why you are using Sawchuck and Douglas and Oberg? To help with an unofficial investigation?"

"Yes."

"I am of course appalled at what has happened. Simply appalled." He paused to lend proper dignity to his concern. "However, I cannot permit this...this moonlighting to continue. The kidnapping is properly the business of the police. Not yours. And not this company's. You will see to it that crew members of the *Solange Picard* presently involved on your business report for work aboard at once."

"Except for me?"

"Eh?"

"You don't have a skipper to see to it, since you didn't hire a replacement for me and you sent me ashore with orders to use some of my time bank."

"I can designate one of our other captains."

"Only two of us in the company have the class of ticket required for this ship, Junior. Me and O'Conner."

"Yes, well…I've decided to make you temporary master of the *Solange Picard*, effective today."

"And Jeep?"

"As you suggested, he will be acting mate."

"With pay to match?"

"Er…Yes."

"Fine. Now that we have a proper crew we can sort out this time-off business. You are aware, of course, that the rest of the crew have weeks, even months, of accumulated time in their banks?"

"See here, you can't all just arbitrarily walk off. I'll replace every one of you. Permanently."

"Yeah. You might do that. If you could persuade your new hires to cross our picket line."

"Picket line?" he squeaked.

"The one closing down your operation. All twenty boats. And the shore staff."

"You couldn't! You wouldn't dare!" he shrieked. "I'd get a court injunction, the police--"

"And I would blow the whistle on you at the DOT and Revenue Canada. If you thought last Sunday's inspection was rough, you ain't seen nothin' yet."

Junior stared at me with growing comprehension. His mouth worked, guppy-like, but no words came. His color shifted like a winter sunset, from ash-gray to red to mottled purple. For a moment I thought he might have a stroke.

I caught sight of Jimmy Lee peering through the doorway to the galley. Obviously he'd been taking it all in. I made pouring-coffee motions and he ducked his head, returning a moment later with two mugs of black coffee and an inscrutable grin.

Junior clutched his coffee mug in both hands, knuckles white. The coffee rippled with his shaking. He sipped. And sputtered, "So…so…what do you…?"

"What do I want? I want you to keep out of our way. We will guarantee a full crew on an hour's notice if there's a call-out. And we'll hold her at stand-by pressure. I'm sure you can continue to bullshit the DOT on everything else."

"Bullshit the...? Oh. Yes of course." He pulled out a monogrammed hankie and mopped his forehead. His little mascara moustache had drooped on one side. "You're playing hardball, Sutter. Don't make a mistake."

Quietly, I said, "Yes, Junior, I'm playing hardball. I want my girl back and I want the bastards that killed her brother and did this to her and I'll go straight through anybody who gets in my way."

"Well, I didn't mean--"

"I'm sure you didn't," I said.

"Well...perhaps we can bend the rules a little? Quid pro quo, eh? After all, we are both reasonable men."

"Glad to hear it," I said.

*

I taxied back to Tats' place, arriving just as Jeep and Axel drove up. Both of them were grinning like monkeys and neither would say anything until we were seated in Tats' kitchen.

"This Beyer vas also my Heinrich Beyer," Axel said. "Unt he iss no better a liar than ever he vas. His English iss better than mine. He remembered me from the Kriegsmarine but he isn't sure vat is my politics."

"So he couldn't get away with his phony bad English?"

"No, but we talked in German."

"So what did you learn?"

"Something queer iss going on. We had a long talk about old times. I said I missed the good Hitler times und it was sad everything iss lost und Germany ruined with Russians in half the country und Americans und British und French in the rest. At first he stares at me with the sad face. But we drink some more schnapps, und I vas nearly in tears, und he iss reassuring me."

"Axel, you're an old ham. How did he reassure you?" I said.

"Not everything iss lost, he iss saying. Something important is saved. I ask him how is this? He makes his voice quiet und says somebody here knows about. He says you und the pretty lady with the black hair und the nice figure tried to question him about certain things. There vas a man, two weeks ago, who asks questions, also. Then you have the same questions! Zo!" Axel punched the air with his pipe stem. "He is sure you make the shakedown. I ask him how this is possible? He stops talking and does this." Axel put a finger beside his nose.

"You couldn't get any more out of him?"

"No, but I have the chance to try him again."

"That's terrific, Axel. I think you've hit on something important. Are you back on watch at six?" It was two PM.

"Ya."   •

"When do you ever sleep?"

"I take the little naps. I have the alarm watch so I can check the gauges." He tapped a wrist-watch that seemed too big for his bony wrist. "So far I don't blow up the ship." He grinned.

"How much schnapps did you drink?"

"Ach, not so much for a navy man. I am okay."

"Jeep will drive you back to the ship. Get some proper sleep before you go on watch."

I thought about my session with Heinrich Beyer. There wasn't much doubt he was up to no good but whether or not that related to Sandy's death was problematical. There was plenty of skullduggery on the Vancouver waterfront, heroin smuggling being the biggest single racket, but there were others. Yet something I had asked, and that Sandy had also asked, had set off Beyer's alarms.

I buried myself in Sandy's partially translated notes and Axel's and Tats' additions. Then I remembered Irene Bradshaw's card. I dialed her number.

"I thought you were never going to call," she said.

"There've been a few things happening. What's your pleasure?"

"I need to talk to you. Some place where we won't be observed."

"Okay. You name it."

"Second Beach pool at three o'clock? I hope that's not too soon."

"Three o'clock will be fine."

"I'll be on the outer pool wall."

If she wanted a cloak and dagger meeting, there could hardly be a better place not to be overheard. But observed? She'd be visible for miles.

Something nagged at me as I left for our meeting. Maybe it was just the feeling that we were getting close to something. Or maybe not. But for the first time since I'd acquired it, I picked up the leather zip case with Clara's Smith and Wesson. I could easily walk the mile or so to Second Beach pool. Instead, I decided to take Cam's car and get there the long way around.

CHAPTER

15

Second Beach and its saltwater swimming pool lies in a corner of Stanley Park adjacent to English Bay Beach, a mile or so north of Tats' apartment. The thousand-acre park is an almost-island of evergreen that pokes out from the tip of the West End like a hitch-hiker's fist. The causeway to Lion's Gate Bridge, Lost Lagoon and a broad grassy flat with trees, tennis courts and meandering walkways complete the connection.

I had a lurking suspicion Nunn might not be living up to his agreement with me. There was also the nebulous "Mike" who had inquired about me at Picard's. With Tats' life at risk, I needed to be certain I wasn't watched. The park road is one-way counter-clockwise so driving meant going the long way around, six and a half miles, but it gave me a chance to do some elementary counter-surveillance.

Traffic was light. I made a couple of loops around the tennis courts near Lost Lagoon and dove into the North-Van bound traffic on the bridge causeway. Changing lanes at the last possible minute, to the tune of some irate horns, I turned off the causeway onto the park road and slowed to a stop under the concrete pedestrian overpass leading to the zoo. Then I inched my way past the Rowing Club.

Nobody was following.

A mile east, along the Coal Harbor side of the park, Deadman's Island houses the local naval reserve shore establishment, HMCS Discovery. I turned onto the access bridge and flashed my ID card at the gate sentry. A quick tour around the admin building, through the parking lot and out the other side and I was waving goodbye to a puzzled sentry.

Nobody was waiting for me as I eased back onto the park road. Brockton Point, on the Burrard Inlet side of the park, was another chance to shed would-be tails but by that time I was feeling like a paranoid. I relaxed for the remaining five miles of forested road without further cloak and dagger excursions.

Second Beach is popular in summer as a family swimming and picnicking area with a large saltwater pool facing English Bay. Changing rooms and concession stands flank the pool and, beside these, the south side of the grassy flat has been manicured into picnic grounds and playing fields, bisected by the park roadway. The grass extends to Lost Lagoon and the tennis courts, where I'd begun all this foolishness.

Save for two people walking a bedraggled spaniel, and an equally bedraggled jogger, all was deserted. Bradshaw's yellow VW Beetle stood out among the half-dozen cars in the picnic-ground parking lot.

I parked well away from it and waited. Nobody pulled in off the park road to join me. Five minutes to three.

Bradshaw sat hunched in a shapeless rain parka on the wall of the now empty pool. I'd borrowed Jeep's rain parka, mine being aboard the *Solange*, but that didn't stop the wind-whipped rain from stinging my face as I made my way around the pool edge towards her.

She spotted me and gestured me to a halt, walking towards me. "Let's sit in my car," she said. "I'm frozen."

I nodded. That was a better idea than being perched on the pool wall like seagulls in the rain, for all the world to see.

Volkswagen Beetles aren't meant for creatures of my size. I shoe-horned myself into the passenger seat, doing some major squirming. Then got out and removed my rain parka and tried again. The VW sagged, alarmingly, on my side. My ears popped when I shut the door. Watertight.

That seemed to describe our fit in the tiny car. Bradshaw was well built, dammit, and we were "in close touch," as the diplomats put it. Matters weren't helped by her perfume.

She fidgeted with the ash tray and the steering wheel, and then the gearshift, then willed her hands to be quiet. "God," she said. "To think I used to read spy thrillers." She shuddered.

"Why all the cloak and dagger stuff, Irene? Somebody threatening you?"

"Not threatening. Following. At least I think so. After Mr. Feldman's murder, and Sandy's, I'm pretty jumpy. No, change that. I'm scared out of my wits."

"Have you seen somebody?"

"Yes. Once. He was more careful after that but I'm sure he's still there."

"He? It's always one man?"

"I...don't really know. I've only seen one."

"Why would anyone follow you?"

"You don't know much about law offices, do you?" She turned to look at me, her breast making a warm impression on my left bicep.

"I suppose not," I said.

"Senior secretaries know all about what's going on in a law firm. They have to know, to be able to function."

"I've never thought about it but it makes sense. Do you think something you know is the reason you're being watched?"

"And the reason Sandy and Mr. Feldman were watched. And, ultimately, killed."

My natural instincts were to discount Bradshaw's fears but I knew I couldn't do that. No more than I could ignore the tremor of fear in her voice. I'd paid less attention than I should have when Tats talked about being followed, when I'd first met her. Fears that were all too realistic.

"You think they were killed because somebody was afraid they'd pass on...whatever it was they knew?"

"Exactly. At first they thought they'd covered all the bases when they killed Sandy and Mr. Feldman."

"And now they aren't sure? Okay, then, the safest thing for you is to make sure as many people as possible know. So what is this fatal piece of information?"

The warm pressure eased as she turned away, thoughtfully. "I don't know everything but there's this. Late last summer, Mr. Feldman undertook an investigation for the Simon Wiesenthal organization. Sandy was doing the leg work."

"Wiesenthal? You mean the Jewish group that hunts down Nazi war criminals?"

"The same. You know, of course, that Jake Feldman was Jewish?"

"Yes. Had Sandy located someone? Is that what this is about?"

"I'm not sure. But on the Friday you met him, Sandy was excited about something he'd found out. He worked on it all through the weekend before his death."

"He must have filed progress reports with Jake."

"He did but he wouldn't have been able to do that during the weekend."

"Why not?"

"Neither Mr. Feldman nor I were there to open the safe. Anything Sandy wrote up that weekend went with his killers."

"Sandy started this work when? In August?"

"Yes."

"Wouldn't there be a stack of ongoing reports already in the safe. Stuff he'd filed prior to Friday night?"

"Yes, there were reports but the safe in Mr. Feldman's office was opened the night of his murder."

"They blew the safe?"

"No, nothing like that, but it was opened."

"How do you know?"

"That safe has a security counter that records the number of times it is accessed. I record the count at the end of each working day. I did that at five P.M., when I left the office, the night Mr. Feldman was killed."

"I see. And the count didn't tally on Monday?"

"It didn't tally Saturday morning. I was asked by the police to attend at the office that morning."

"Did you report that to Sergeant McRae?"

"He seemed to think my memory was suspect."

"And it isn't?"

"Mr. Sutter, I do know my job."

"And you'd remember details like that."

"Better believe it." She gave an abrupt nod.

The Beetle's windows were steamed and I rolled mine down an inch.

The chill, wet air was less distracting than her perfume. "Does anyone else have the combination?"

"The senior partners each have a similar office safe and each has access, but I am the only person with access to all of them, other than Mr. Feldman, of course. Ordinarily, Sandy would come to me when he needed to place a report in the safe."

"He typed them himself?"

"Yes."

"And now his reports are missing?"

"The only things missing."

"So we have to assume Jake was forced to open the safe at gunpoint. Then they killed him."

I stared out over the deserted playing fields. Bradshaw did the same, though I'm sure neither of us saw them. The cold-blooded style of our faceless killers was numbing in its implications. I said, "Would Jake have been in touch with anyone in the Wiesenthal organization about Sandy's work?"

"If he was, it didn't go through the office. No letters were sent and no phone calls logged. I would know about any contacts he'd made."

"But somebody from Wiesenthal must have contacted him to initiate the investigation in the first place?"

"Yes. But I don't know who. Wiesenthal doesn't have an office in Canada. My guess is that it began with a personal meeting. Possibly at a social event."

We were silent for a moment. I wrestled with the implications which seemed to be gaining on me like an incoming tide. The only thing Tatiana had going for her was the fact that she didn't know anything.

And if Irene was followed and her tail spotted me, nothing would protect her. Irene Bradshaw shifted in her seat and turned towards me again. She said, "Mr. Feldman was terribly upset that the work Sandy was doing for him might have gotten him killed. He felt responsible. Then when you came and asked questions, he was alarmed that you were getting involved and might also be in danger. He told me Friday that he intended to tell the police everything he knew or suspected. But he didn't get the chance."

"Why was he drinking on Friday morning?"

"That was unlike him. I think it was because of the divorce papers Ella Feldman served him with on Thursday."

"Irene, you've been a great help. I think we are getting somewhere."

"Anything I can do, I'll be glad to. Poor Tatiana, such a lovely girl. What a shame to lose her brother like that. Please give her my regards."

"I wish I could do that, Irene. She was kidnapped early Thursday morning. By the same people, I think."

"Oh! Dear God, no!" Her lip quivered and she stared at me in horror, her face ashen.

"They are using her as a hostage to keep me out of action and as long as they think that's working…"

"I'm glad it isn't, but my God, you've got to be careful."

"I know it. I think of nothing else."

"There was nothing in the papers."

"The police feel we should keep it out of the press for as long as possible. I'm not sure of their logic but…" I wanted to scream the loss of my love from the rooftops but I didn't think that would be any more help than the news blackout.

"The police don't seem terribly effective," she said. "I assume they are searching too?"

"They are doing their best, in their bureaucratic, methodical way. But I think her life depends on us finding her quickly. Anything occurs to you that might help, no matter how trivial, please call, any time, day or night. There's a new phone number." I handed her my company card with the new number on the back. "Don't be surprised if somebody else answers. Several of us are working on this."

"People from your new company?" She looked at my card.

"No. Some of my crew from the *Solange Picard*. That reminds me. Who are S M E ?" I made the wavy blue line with my hand. "I saw their logo on your office door."

"That's Mrs. Feldman's company. Seaford Maritime Enterprises. We take their calls and direct visitors but their offices are the twentieth floor."

"The whole floor? I thought it would just be some tax shelter deal."

She smiled. "No indeed. Seaford is big enough to swallow Jake Feldman's outfit whole. Mrs. Feldman is the real money behind Jake, though she likes to keep a low profile. But the law firm does well. She wasn't subsidizing him."

She certainly did keep a low profile. I was family and didn't know her company existed. "Thanks, Irene. Are you going back to the office?"

She shook her head. "No. Home. I've had enough for the day."

"Are you in the phone book?"

"What? Oh, no. I'm unlisted. I'm so scared I didn't even think of that."

"Maybe you should stay with a friend for a few days."

"I have a...friend staying with me." She colored, slightly. "And I intend to defend myself," she added. She flashed a nickel-plated snub-nosed twenty-five caliber hammerless. My God, she'd be safer with Tatiana's lamp stand to defend herself! That gun was good for driving tacks. But I kept my mouth shut. Maybe she could actually hit something with it. I knew I couldn't.

"I'm sorry if you were uncomfortable in my little car," she said, taking my hand. I gently put her hand back in her own lap. "It's okay. I'll live," I said. "Next time, though, we meet in my car."

She gave me a teary smile at that. I unwound myself from the VW, feeling as if I might capsize the thing if I sneezed.

The Beetle started with a tinny roar and she maneuvered it neatly out of the lot. I'd just reached the Chrysler when I noticed a slight haze of exhaust behind a late model gray Ford sedan parked fifty yards away at the far end of the lot. The Ford's windows were steamed.

That car had been empty when I pulled into the lot. I was sure of it. I avoided looking directly at the Ford as I seated myself behind the wheel of the Chrysler.

The Ford's wipers flicked to life now, but I couldn't see the driver's face. The car backed out and turned to follow Bradshaw's Volkswagen at a leisurely pace.

I waited a tense three minutes until the Ford was around the bend at the park exit and I wouldn't be seen in its rear view mirrors. Then I gunned the Chrysler out of the lot.

I'd driven Cam's car before but not on wet streets. And never in a hurry. I quickly learned not to be anxious with the gas pedal. A blip of the throttle would make the car fishtail at fifty, on wet pavement.

Cam Douglas was a car fanatic. He was mechanic for a racing team that built its cars from the ground up and most of his wages went into his cars. His precious '56 Chrysler "300 B Hemi" left the factory with three hundred and fifty horsepower and he'd added a few that Chrysler's engineers missed. He'd done much more serious things to the suspension.

Irene Bradshaw drove with that rarest of qualities, patience. I was three cars behind the Ford and six behind Bradshaw's Beetle before we hit the early southbound rush on Burrard Bridge. The bridge's six lanes can be scary in heavy traffic, with people jockeying for position.

Bradshaw hadn't seen her tail, or so I thought, until she did an abrupt double lane-change just before reaching the Cornwall Street exit at the south end. It was a near-accident but effective. The Ford followed, causing a major uproar of horns and curses. No doubt now. She knew.

With the advantage of six car-lengths and premeditation, I muscled my way across the lanes and onto Cornwall.

Bradshaw cruised west on Cornwall, staring at the rain-swept sands and deserted tennis courts and concession stands of Kitsilano Beach as if she were sight-seeing, holding to a serene twenty miles per hour. Cars began passing her, not a bright idea on that tightly parked, narrow road. I drifted back a few more car-lengths, relying on the canary yellow of her Beetle to let me track her and her tail.

Why would they follow her? I wondered. Assuming she was right and it was her knowledge they wanted, what could be the point of a tail?

Then it dawned on me. They wanted to silence her.

The guy driving the Ford planned to kill Irene Bradshaw. Yet she wasn't worth the risks of another killing at the law office, risks they'd thought necessary with Sandy and Jake. For a nice quiet murder with no witnesses, he'd need only to pull alongside her on an empty street.

I fished the magnum in its imitation leather zip case from beneath the front seat and laid it beside me on the seat. I closed the gap between me and the Ford. Cornwall runs west past the beach front and connects to south-going MacDonald after a mile or so. A few blocks on, the Ford and I were caught behind a traffic light at Fourth and MacDonald. Bradshaw could have lost the both of us there by diving into the maze of residential side streets but she seemed oblivious to the possibility.

Or maybe she wasn't oblivious at all. Bradshaw was staying on well-traveled main streets. Driving in the middle of clusters of moving cars. Smart girl. Both the Ford and I caught up with her four blocks up MacDonald, as she neared Broadway.

Four miles later, our convoy was southbound on Dunbar, crossing Sixteenth Avenue and I was getting worried. Surely to God she wasn't going to lead this guy to her home? Did she think she could barricade herself inside and defend herself with that ridiculous popgun?

I knew nothing of Bradshaw's personal life. She'd said a friend was staying with her. And blushed in the telling. A male friend? That seemed likely, considering her looks and the lack of a ring. But did he know he might have to defend her?

My speculations nearly got me in trouble. Bradshaw did an abrupt left off Dunbar onto King Edward Avenue, which used to be Twenty-fifth Avenue until somebody dubbed it with Mrs. Simpson's husband's name. Five blocks later, King Edward swerved right and connected with Puget Drive in the well-to-do Quilchena Heights district and I knew I had to do something drastic. The killer would find the streets empty enough for his purposes here.

The Ford shifted down a gear and burned rubber, pulling away from me. But I didn't think he gave a damn about me. He was trying to pull up beside Bradshaw's VW. Maybe cut her off at the curb. She zig-zagged, blocking him, and the Ford braked to avoid a parked car. Bradshaw gained a little. Not much.

The Ford's passenger-side window was cranked down. He could shoot at her from either side of the Beetle.

Then I saw my chance. I moved up tight to the Ford, getting nervous looks from its driver. He waved me to back off. I didn't. The Ford sped up. I gunned the Chrysler. Bumper to bumper, we screamed around the curve of Puget Drive and onto Eddington.

A red five-ton Mack flat deck with "Evans Coleman and Evans" on the doors was parked at the curb in the middle of the second block. The driver was making a delivery of sacked furnace coal and his truck was more than half loaded. I floored the gas pedal, ramming the Ford's back end, and kept pushing. The Ford's brakes were no match for Cam's Chrysler Hemi and I shoved it, tires screaming, straight into the rear deck of the coal truck. The truck merely shuddered but the Ford crumpled.

I backed away a few yards.

Bradshaw's Beetle hesitated, then disappeared around the curve of Eddington Drive. I hoped she didn't live here, or if she did that she kept her car in a garage or somehow out of sight. But she could give Jeep car chase lessons.

"What the fuck do ya think you're doin'?" A black leather apron and coal-black face identified the truck driver. He'd just emerged from a basement door with two empty coal sacks over his arm.

I stepped out of the Chrysler. "Give me a hand," I said. "I think this guy hurt himself." A groan emanated from the wrecked Ford.

"Followin' awful close, weren't ya?" The trucker asked.

Ah. He wasn't sure I'd caused this. Probably hadn't seen the actual crash. A quick look at the front end of Cam's car told me I'd lucked out. Cam had welded a massive chrome-steel "nerfing" bar with hard rubber inserts to his front bumper, for push-starting his race cars. Or push-stopping murdering bastards. There wasn't a mark on the Chrysler.

"Guess so," I said. "Nearly tail-ended this joker when he ran into you."

The truck driver peered into the Ford. "You all right, buddy?" The rear deck-edge of the truck had peeled back the first three feet of the Ford's top like a sardine can, just above the bottom of its windshield. The driver lay twisted sideways on the front seat where he'd ducked. "Fuck off," the driver snarled.

"S'pose ya got yerself a headache for that but it ain't no reason to go badmouthin' me. It's my truck ya hit."

"Go for the asshole in the Chrysler. He caused it."

"Looks like you caused the whole mess y'self, mister. You wanna get your ass out here and show me some insurance and license stuff?"

The door -- half a door now -- of the Ford was jammed and the driver kicked at it with both feet. With a shriek of rending metal it swung open, hard, knocking the truck driver off balance. "I said fuck off," the driver said, getting out. Crew cut with a pock-marked face. Jug ears. Tight, white tee-shirt covered in blood from his broken nose. He wanted the world to know about his muscles.

The butt of a Walther PPK hung over the waistband of his jeans.

The coal driver backed away. I edged towards my car. The magnum was ten feet away on the front seat. Pock marks pulled his gun and racked the action, giving me the evil eye. "Give me your keys, asshole."

"They're in the car," I lied. I backed away from him, edging towards the Chrysler.

"Nah ye don't. I'll get 'em," he said, moving to go past me.

I swung at him.

He slipped the punch and I missed. He braced and aimed.

I bobbed and weaved like a demented boxer, trying for a clinch.

The Walther went off with a flat pop. At the same moment the trucker hit the thug from behind at the knees with a hundred pound sack of stoker mix. Pock marks staggered, firing wildly. Ricochets whined off the pavement. I felt a burning sting across my left shoulder. Not a ricochet.

And I got angry.

For the second time in my life I hit somebody with lethal intent. Pock marks went down, hard. His gun skittered under the wrecked Ford. Blood oozed from his mangled nose.

He spat a gob of blood. "She's dead, Sutter. You don't take directions worth a shit. One phone call from me and she's a fucking dead woman," he snarled through a mouthful of blood. And spat out teeth.

And tried to rise.

A bitter acid of rage swept through me and something inside me broke. I straddled him, intending to strangle him. Or break his neck. Instead, I grabbed an ear in each hand. I twisted. "Where is she, you snivelling shit pile."

He screamed. Mouthed, "Fuck you," in bubbles of blood.

I twisted harder, feeling cartilage tear. "Where is Tatiana Kovacs?" I demanded, shouting down his shrieks. Shaking him. Rapping his skull on the pavement.

I felt a hand on my shoulder and shrugged it off. I shook uncontrollably, bent over the thug. Suddenly his eyes rolled up into his head and his body went slack. The screaming died with a gurgle.

Passed out. I hoped it was from the pain.

"Where is she?" I demanded, staring into the slack, bloody mess of a face.

I forced myself to relax my terrible grip, let go of his ears. What had been ears. I dropped him, like dead meat. Some frightful killing thing, not part of me, retreated. The tremors abated.

"Shit, ya tryin' ta kill the fucker?" the truck driver said.

"He's still breathing. See the bubbles?" I heard myself say. Jesus. What was I doing?

"Holy shit! Yer a fuckin' maniac!"

"I didn't do it. Couldn't." I got to my feet.

"You was gonna. Jesus, I saw it in your face."

"Yeah, I was. The punk is a killer."

"Not the only one, by God."

"Bastard clipped me with a round," I said.

Warm wetness seeped down my back from the dull ache in my shoulder. I leaned against the Chrysler, my knees wobbly. "Thanks," I said. "That sack of coal saved my life."

But I hadn't been able to make the punk talk. Tell me where Tats was. "God, if you're up there, find her for me," I said. I hoped he'd know it was a prayer, not an order.

"Jesus. I don' want nothin' ta do with this." The trucker's eyes were bloodshot white rings in the coal black of his face. "Hey. You gonna pass out? You went all gray."

Gray. The color of my second thoughts. I wasn't proud of what I'd done. But I was beginning to understand things like Magyar revenge.

"I'm okay," I said, not at all sure of that. "Let's see who this jerk is." I collected myself and stooped, patting the punk's pockets. Save for two spare magazines for the Walther, and a hundred dollars in small bills, his pockets were empty. No identification. No driver's license.

"The Ford's stolen," the coal driver said, peering at the car's dash. "Hot wired. It's a write-off." He gestured at the mangled sheet-metal of hood and roof.

If you want the police in a hurry in Vancouver the best way is to fire off a gun in a wealthy neighborhood. That is if it's more than a few weeks from Halloween and somebody figures out he's not hearing firecrackers and makes the "man with a gun" call. The police get real antsy about those.

Somebody had figured it out. I could hear the sirens.

I didn't want to be here. For the first time in this case, I had something to work on and I was damned if I'd waste a second not working on it. "Tell the police to check this guy's gun against the slug from the Feldman murder," I told the coal driver.

"What murder? Where ya goin'? Who's gonna be witness for what happened to my truck?"

"To the hospital. I feel sick." I sagged onto the driver's seat of the Chrysler, getting blood on Cam's top grain leather upholstery. I shoved the magnum and its zip-bag back under the seat. The coal driver leaned in through the driver's side window as I fumbled with the key. "Thought you was all right. Where'd he hit ya?"

"Remember. Tell them the Feldman murder. They'll know all about it." I started the Chrysler.

But I was too late. Squad cars converged from both ends of Eddington Drive. Four nervous looking constables advanced on us with drawn guns. And Tatiana's life hung in the balance.

C H A P T E R

16

"At times like these, I wonder what society did to deserve you," McRae said. I was in the same cubby-hole office McRae had used for my previous all-night interrogation. This time, I'd been at the police station for something like six hours, since the fracas with Pock Marks, and I was frustrated that time was being wasted.

Mostly, they'd left me to stew on my own, though I'd managed a phone call to let Cam and Jeep know where I was between filling out endless "accident reports" and writing a statement. Then McRae went into a re-run of his long-suffering-cop act. I demanded to be let go. McRae countered by threatening to lock me up. He wasn't buying my story. Not all of it.

Not that he could do much about it. Irene Bradshaw had confirmed that she had indeed been tailed by a gray Ford, and that I had followed both herself and the tail. She'd also reminded him of the missing reports and the opened safe, as we'd agreed she should.

McRae was only mildly pissed off that he was a week late absorbing that information. Chauvinism is a trap and McRae had fallen right into it.

Smart girl, Irene Bradshaw. She hadn't gone into the Wiesenthal connection and while I didn't want to make a habit of holding things back from the police, I was sure McRae had little tolerance for "melodramatic plots," to use Kidson's expression. Cops generally go for the simplest answer, usually with good reason. Irene seemed to have sensed this, or maybe it came with the territory when you worked in a law office. The simplified outline she'd given McRae fitted well enough with my story. It was the crashed Ford that was McRae's sticking point. And the punk's ears.

"You still claim you never pushed him into the coal truck, eh?"

"Scout's honor." I'd never been a scout.

"You're a lying bastard, Sutter. We found gray paint flecks on those weird chrome bumper bars. How do you suppose they got there?"

"How would I know? It's a borrowed car. Cam push-starts race cars with it. Maybe one of them is gray." Mention of the Chrysler made me sweat. The magnum was still under the front seat. I hoped.

"Sure it is. But you hit him?"

"Not with the car. I hit him with this. After he pulled a gun on me." I held up a fist.

"Oh yeah. The wrecking ball. The other guy you belted, this Joe Warren, is off the critical list, by the way. So your manslaughter charge gets reduced to assault. If we charge you. 'Course we might give you a medal."

"You get anything out of him?"

"Lot of abuse. He's not admitting anything and he's trying to talk some shyster lawyer into going after you with a lawsuit."

"For what?"

"Excessive use of force. If you can believe it. We're charging him with assault with a weapon. When his lawyer tells him he could get ten years for that, his tongue might loosen up a bit."

I shook my head in disbelief. Some lawyers would try anything, on a chance of a share of the proceeds.

"Anyway, this latest victim of yours," McRae grinned. "He can't talk yet but he gave us a written statement. Says you hit him first and he pulled the gun because he thought he was going to be killed."

"You get an ID on him?"

"Not yet. But he'll be after a lawyer, soon as he's out of surgery. He'll have to stop playing games about his name then. Were you trying to kill him?"

"No, but I didn't hit him hard enough," I said.

"Don't get smart, Sutter. What the hell did you do to his ears, for God's sake?"

"If I was smart, I'd have been gone before your guys arrived. Ask the coal truck driver what happened. He belted the guy with a sack of coal. Probably saved my life."

"Then you knocked him down and chewed both his ears damn near off?"

"He was shooting. I walloped him right after he creased me with that nine millimeter."

"Didn't think you'd hit a guy when he was down."

Oh yes I would. "He wasn't down when I hit him. How many times do I have to say it?"

"What'd you do to his ears, goddammit?"

"He hit the dash with them," I said. McRae snorted, not without amusement. "Hey, you ruined his nose, broke his jaw, knocked out six front teeth and did whatever the hell you did to his ears. The guy's in surgery as we speak. Then he's gonna need bridgework at the least."

"Before or after you hang him? Cheaper after. The undertaker could do it, cut rate."

McRae grinned.

"Did you do a ballistics check on the Walther?" I asked.

"Uh huh. It was the Feldman murder weapon. And Beyer's."

"Who?" I'm no good at "innocent surprise," even when I am surprised. If there'd been a spitoon handy McRae would have spat, to show what he thought of my "who?" He nearly did, anyway.

"Heinrich Beyer. Manager of Beyer and Son Shipping. Shot dead this morning as he opened his office. Shooter was in a car, pulled up to the curb behind him. One shot to the head at ten feet."

"Gray Ford? Our guy with the Walther?"

"It was the same gun."

"This guy is a one-man slaughterhouse," I said.

"You got that right. What do you know about Heinrich Beyer. Don't jerk me around on this, Sutter. I know you called on him."

"How do you know that?"

He reached into his briefcase and pulled out a plastic envelope with my new business card inside. "He had this in his pocket. Ink's hardly dry on it."

So I told McRae about my visit to Beyer with Tats and her translating my questions for him, and that I had since learned he spoke perfectly good English. I kept Axel's visit to myself. No use putting Axel through several hours of this. Besides, too much information was going to overwhelm McRae. Or steer him off in a wrong direction. Or cause him to throw up his hands and drop important leads because of the sheer volume of them. He wanted the simple approach? Keep it simple.

"Where did you get Beyer's name from?" McRae asked.

I knew I'd have to face that question sooner or later and I wasn't about to give up Sandy's notebook. Not yet. So I lied. "One of my waterfront contacts saw Sandy calling on Beyer, couple of days before he was killed. I thought it was worth a look."

"What contact? How did he know Kovacs?"

I was ready for that. "Clay Harper. He knows everybody and everything around the waterfront."

"And where do I find Mr. Harper?"

"God knows. He's a water rat, lives on his gillnetter. I found him in False Creek, under the viaduct by the gas works, but he's probably in Johnstone Straits by now. Or Knights Inlet. Or you could try Kingcome Inlet. He had a brand new six and a quarter mesh nylon net on his drum and he was talking about fishing winter springs, last time I saw him."

McRae gave me a long hard look. Couldn't find the spitoon again, I guess. He shrugged and said, "One other thing you had right. The silencer. The barrel of the Walther had the last quarter inch of the bore internally threaded. Only one possible reason for that. But we didn't find the silencer."

"No witnesses, I suppose?"

"Nope. As usual, in the east side, nobody saw or heard a damned thing. No matter it was broad daylight on a street full of rush hour traffic." Tatiana's chances of surviving depended on what happened next. And whatever that was, it would be my fault. "Do something for Tats, will you?"

"Like what?"

I was going to pay for Kingcome Inlet, but not now, I prayed. "Don't let that son of a bitch get near a telephone. The only thing keeping her alive is her hostage value."

"Um. That's a tough one. They're probably missing their boyo already. Be worse when he doesn't come home tonight."

"But they won't know I was involved. Not if you don't let them know," I said.

"The punk is going up on weapons and car theft charges but that's just to hold him. I could drop one murder charge on him. That should hold him without bail if we don't have any legal screw-ups. Case is full of circumstantial pitfalls. Possession of the murder weapon is persuasive but it isn't proof he was the perp. So the strongest single piece of evidence connecting him to the murders is your testimony."

"Mine?"

"When he shouted your name and talked about Tatiana being a dead woman. Did the coal driver hear that, too?"

"I'm not sure. He was badly spooked when the guy started shooting."

McRae said. "Okay. The punk has been sending me notes about his legal rights."

"Notes?"

"He thinks he's entitled to a phone call. Lota good that'll do him, seein' as he can't talk. What he is entitled to is a lawyer and a preliminary hearing. But his lawyer can make all the phone calls he wants. I can stall him about the lawyer but only until he gives me his name."

"What about the press? And what if he gets a visitor in hospital?"

"Technically, we don't have a suspect under arrest in that ward. What we have is a John Doe. Visitor wants to see him, he better know who he is. And if they do, I want to talk to them." McRae made a quick grabbing motion with his right hand. Gotcha. "Okay. I'll push it as far as I can to protect her. Be a damned shame, anything happened to that little lady."

"And the press?"

"Being fitted for a muzzle. I had them kill their story about gunshots and a fistfight between irate motorists, some little old lady on Eddington gave 'em."

"Thanks. Can you get away with that? Legally?"

"No, but the editors will usually cooperate if they know somebody's life is at stake."

"What happened with the phone trace?" I asked.

"No luck. The call came from someplace the other side of one of the main trunk lines. They can't trace through those unless they know in advance which exchange the call's coming from."

"They were calling me long distance?"

"Not necessarily," McRae said. "I'm no technician but the way I get it, phone lines are tied in directly only to the exchanges grouped in their area. More distant ones go through a trunk, and sometimes a toll switch, to make connections. Like if they cross water, say to North Van or West Van. There's sixty lines in the trunk from North Vancouver, for instance, but it's not long distance. You make a call over there and all sixty are in use, you get a busy signal. You need any more explanation, you'll have to talk to the techs yourself."

"Damn. I had hopes for that trace," I said.

"Me too. There's another way. We'll have B.C. Tel pull their billing tapes for all the exchanges in the region and look for a match. Your number and the time of the calls. Takes a court order and manpower, and maybe two, three days to go through. And it will only work if the call was long distance."

"Not much help for Tatiana."

"We could get lucky and find a match early but, basically, no. Not much help. I'm sorry."

I stared at the fermented piss yellow-green, Public Works Department paint job on McRae's office wall. It was a good color match for my mood, bleaker than I've felt in my life. Tatiana Kovacs could be dead. Or if she was alive, how much time did she have? How much did I have to find her? I couldn't imagine what I would feel, what I would do, if I would live, or care to, if she were to die. In the brief few days we'd been lovers something quite wonderful had grown between us. It would break, with my heart, if I were to lose her.

McRae was impassive but I sensed he was watching me, weighing options. I just didn't know what the hell they were.

"Why do I get the feeling you got more out of this interview than I did, Sutter?"

"I'm just a good listener, I guess."

"Yeah? And a goddamn inventor, too. Kingcome Inlet, eh?"

"Hey, I'm not Clay Harper's keeper. I gave you the best information I had on him." I was too glum to make a decent job of protesting my innocence.

"Sure you did," he said. "Okay. I'm going to turn you loose. I would like you to go back to that apartment and stay there. Get somebody to put some sulfa and a couple of stitches in that shoulder before it goes septic."

The shoulder was making sure I didn't forget it with no help from McRae. The first-aid patch, courtesy of the ambulance crew that took the punk to hospital, was oozing and the top left quarter of me throbbed at every move. But I was damned if I had time for stitches.

"*I would like you to...*" McRae had said. A tiny stress on "like." A gentle admonition, indeed, compared to his ranting last week about doing my own investigating.

"One other thing," McRae added as I rose to leave. "Stay away from Vancouver General. We know your sister Janet works up there as a senior nurse. You try to get near that John Doe, I'll bust you and Janet Sutter both. Got it?"

"I'd never dream of it, sergeant."

"Oh yeah?"

My God. I hadn't even thought of that. McRae had a more devious mind than I did.

*

I got back to Tatiana's place about eleven that night with much on my mind. The magnum was still under the seat when I retrieved the Chrysler from the police lot. Only the zippered leatherette case had been placed zipper to the rear. Which was not the way I'd put it there. McRae moved in strange ways but I was beginning to like him.

Aunt Clara's Austin was parked in front of Tats' Victorian when I arrived. Did I want to deal with Clara right now? Did I have a choice?

"Hank Sutter you are an inconsiderate lout!"

I was barely in the door. "I'm sorry, Clara. I've been so wound up in this thing, I didn't think to call you. You're right. I was thoughtless."

Jeep turned his face away so I wouldn't see his pained smirk. Axel arrived almost on my heels and took shelter under a fog of pipe smoke.

Clara fanned at the blue haze with a newspaper, coughing pointedly. "Contrition doesn't suit you, Hank," she said. "But I'm glad you at least admit you were wrong. Cam has been telling me what happened in the wee hours of Thursday morning. The break-in and the kidnapping and the muggers that came after you. Aren't you glad I gave you that gun now?"

"Yes, Clara. It was comforting to know it was handy."

"You didn't use it?"

"It was in my duffle bag when I tangled with the muggers. And on the seat of the Chrysler this afternoon."

"This afternoon? What happened this afternoon?"

I described my meeting with Irene Bradshaw and the cross-town car chase and run-in with Pock Marks. Cam leaped up to check out his precious Chrysler. I waved him back to his seat at the phone, giving him a "thumbs up," which he didn't seem to believe.

"You were shot?" Clara almost shouted. "Where? Let me look at that." She pushed me into a chair and pulled my shirt down, clucking, reproachfully. "Oh my God," she said. "Didn't you go to a hospital? Hank, you're bleeding all over everything," she said.

"I'll get it looked at in the morning, Clara. I don't have time now."

But she attacked my shirt with scissors anyway.

"Oh dear. This is bad," she said.

"If it's bleeding, it's clean. Leave it be."

"No way. I'm going to clean this up. Tatiana has some antiseptic so I'll make a new dressing. But it needs stiches." She vanished into the bathroom to reappear, moments later, with first aid supplies. "Axel, put that infernal pipe out, at least until I leave," she said. Axel glowered back at her.

"Ow! Jesus, Clara!"

"Hold still, Hank. That's hydrogen peroxide. It's bubbling like crazy so that wound wasn't clean."

"Okay, Clara." I didn't have the energy to do anything but hold still. I tried to figure out how long I'd been on my feet and lost count. "We find out what Sandy was working on yet?" Jeep asked.

"Jake Feldman took on some work for the Wiesenthal organization," I said. "Something about war criminals, I assume. But Wiesenthal doesn't have an office in Canada. Nobody we can ask." Jeep was looking nervously in Axel's direction, a point not lost on Axel.

"I find zem, I turn zem in myself," Axel said, with a vicious swipe of his pipe stem. "Zose Nazi filth…" He shook his head. "Zey shame my country."

"So how does Nunn fit in? Was it his guys that were shadowing Sandy?" Cam steered the conversation away from Axel, to my relief.

"Apparently they were a bunch of trainee operatives. Nunn hasn't got a unit of the Watcher Service to call on."

"What the hell is the Watcher Service?" Jeep asked.

"The real surveillance pros. Officially they're called "Special O." The RCMP has some units of them here but their teams are costly to run so they save them for high priority cases. Nunn told me he was using his own boys in what he calls a loose surveilance on Sandy. And they might not have been the only people watching him."

Jeep said, "So if there was somebody else watching him, Nunn's guys might have missed them. Too busy tryin' not to trip over their spurs."

"Something like that. He did say they weren't very good. One more thing I learned at the cop shop. Beyer was shot this morning--"

"Ach! Beyer too?" Axel said.

"Yeah. He was standing in front of his office, looking for his keys. Shooter was in a car pulled up at the curb. Same gun that killed Feldman and that this mug was carrying this afternoon."

"Jesus. I figured Beyer for one of theirs," Cam said.

"Most likely was," I said. "But Sandy talked to him more than once, I think, and then I called on Beyer, and after me, along comes Axel. Beyer must have reported each visit to his boss, like a loyal stooge.

"I think his calls and the questions he asked Beyer tipped these guys that Sandy was dangerous to them. They visited old Milloss, the Hungarian Social Club guy, looking for Sandy's address and didn't get it. But after he made another call on Beyer they tracked him back to his office. They must have discovered he often worked late and that gave them a chance to go in and find out how much he knew, and who else knew it. It was risky but they were well prepared and they'd had a few days to set it up, forge a phony suicide note and so on."

"They got Sandy's…what do they call it? His work log?" Cam asked. "I know lawyers keep those."

"Only what he'd written up during the weekend. Sandy couldn't open Feldman's office safe for them. And at the time, they didn't know about his notebooks. They probably intended to shoot him and leave a throw-away gun with the suicide note. Most likely, Sandy fought hard and they had to beat him to subdue him. He wouldn't have looked like a suicide after that. So they threw him off the nineteenth floor deck. Friday, they came back when Feldman was there."

"And cleaned out the safe?"

I nodded. "Forced Jake to open it at gunpoint. Then killed him," I said.

"Brutal bastards," Jeep said.

"Yes, but thorough. Whoever is running their show, he isn't an amateur."

"So what about Beyer? And this thing with Irene Bradshaw today?" Cam asked.

"Beyer was a loose cannon, in their view. He knew too much for their safety and he'd been the target of Sandy's and my investigation. Then Axel showed up. Axel, you fooled Beyer but I don't think you fooled his boss."

Axel shook his head. "It seems so," he said.

"You did real well, anyway. So they must have figured it was only a matter of time before McRae pulled Beyer in for a good sweaty questioning. As you said, Axel, he was afraid of his own shadow. They couldn't trust him to keep his mouth shut."

"And Irene Bradshaw?"

"A few days after they shot Jake Feldman, somebody on their side realized that a senior secretary in a law office was a very knowledgeable person. Maybe that isn't so true, wherever they come from. But they thought she might know enough about Sandy's work to be dangerous. The punk following her today was their cleanup hit man. Got Beyer and was going for Bradshaw. Until I got in the way."

"Jesus. Tats is in real bad trouble, eh?" Jeep looked gloomy and agitated at the same time.

"We have to move fast. Trouble is, I don't know which way to move."

I resigned myself to Clara's ministrations, thinking about Beyer's murder. His usefulness to his boss had obviously come to an end. And he knew something they considered vital to their operation. Whatever the hell their operation was.

Clara had kept out of our discussion as she finished taping a new dressing on my shoulder. Now, with my silence, she saw her chance. She cleared her throat. "How long has the poor thing been a prisoner?"

"Since early Thursday morning. Why?"

"I know you are going to get her back. Oh don't make that long face at me, Hank Sutter. I just know it. You were the most infernally *stubborn* little boy, ever was born, Mary used to say. Still says. And your father, too, only he swore about it, being a sailor. You've got your teeth into the problem, I can see."

"Nice that you've got confidence in me, Clara, but what's your point?"

"I'm no help at this detective business. Beyond reading *Ellery Queen*, I'm out of my depth. But that poor girl has been in the same clothes for three days. Probably doesn't dare take a thing off, so she can't even wash her undies."

"So?"

"What do you mean, so? Isn't it obvious? Her wardrobe is a ruin so I'm going to shop for her, first thing in the morning. You can take some fresh clothes with you when you go to pick her up."

"Thanks, Clara. She'll appreciate that."

"I'll be here early tomorrow. Good night."

"G'night, Clara."

Axel fired up his pipe with a sigh of relief as Clara's Austin roared off.

"Axel, did you get any further with the notebook?" I asked.

"A liddle bit. Some words I haf only ze guess. Und Sandy's English iss not better as mine. Some things don't make sense."

"Like what? Give me some examples."

"Look at zis. I at first sink she says `insane house.' Like ze asylum?" He pushed the notebook across the table to me, a stubby finger marking the passage where Tats' had written beneath Sandy's shorthand and encircled her note in red and added half a dozen exclamation points.

Insane house? Axel was right. It didn't make sense. I pulled over the sheet of paper that Donal Gowan had left us with his translations of Tats' script. Insane house? Insale house?...Oh shit. "In safe house!" I yelled. "Axel, that's an `f', not an `n' and it's three words, not two."

"Ya? Excuse please but vat iss safe house?"

"You don't read spy novels? Sandy was searching for a safe house. A place where they could hole up. Hide without attracting notice. He must have been getting close."

"Ya? Und who is Hilda?" Axel pointed to a plain English word sandwiched between shorthand squiggles, in Sandy's handwriting, two lines below "in safe house." Hilda?

I hadn't a bloody clue.

C H A P T E R

17

Cam and Axel dozed, unable to sleep properly but completely bushed. Jeep paced, seeming to have a bottomless supply of energy. Periodically he startled us with a cuss word or two and, once, he pounded the wall with a fist. I couldn't remember seeing him so upset.

Not as upset as me. My anger and frustration kept me awake and mulling over details of the case. Looking for what? A missing clue? Whatever it was I needed to break out of this nightmare, it stubbornly remained missing.

McRae's forensics crew had checked the blood stains I'd spotted on the Marine Building's fifteenth floor ledge and found them to be the remains of one hapless pigeon, lunch for a Peregrine falcon.

On taking a second look at Sandy's body, the medical examiner hadn't found anything to indicate Sandy had been severely beaten. Given the devastation wreaked on a body hitting a concrete sidewalk at something over 100 miles per hour, he couldn't say there hadn't been a beating, either.

But the small red smear under the rail cap on the nineteenth floor deck had been human blood. Sandy's blood type. McRae now admitted Tats' notion that the killers must have beaten Sandy senseless to subdue him was probably correct.

How Jake's killers, or Sandy's, had gotten into the building, and out again, remained a mystery.

Fragments of ideas floated in the foggy mush of my sleep-starved brain.

I had to rest or risk burning out completely. Yet I had to pursue those fleeting thoughts for fear of missing something. The physical result was a thumping headache.

Who was Hilda? And why had she turned up in Sandy's notes, in plain English, right beneath the shorthand entry about safe houses?

And then realization brought me fully awake, my heart racing.

"Axel? You awake?"

"Ya, ya. Who sleeps?"

"Did Beyer say anything about his secretary when you talked to him?"

"Only he vas unhappy he had to fire her after two years she works."

"Did he say why?"

"She vas not, mmm, reliable?"

"Did he mention her name?"

"Fräulein Brunning. Zis is important?"

"No first name? Could she be the Hilda in Sandy's notes?" Axel shrugged. "Zey are both German names."

Jeep said, "How in hell we gonna find that out?"

"I don't know. Let me think about it." I paced the length of the apartment and back, aware that I might be onto something. Not sure of what. How in hell did we find out if Hilda was Hilda Brunning? Or Hilda Smith? Or if she mattered at all?

I picked up the phone. Five minutes and two wrong locals later, Detective Sergeant Kidson came on the line.

"Sergeant, did a Hilda Brunning work for Heinrich Beyer until a few days ago?"

An edgy silence came at me down the phone line. Kidson said, "That's an interesting question, Mr. Sutter. Why do you ask?"

"She might be important to the case. Did she work there?"

"What would make her important?"

"I think she knew something damaging about Beyer. He fired her after two years on the job and then was upset about having to do it." In the middle of that sentence it struck me that if Beyer had been *ordered* to get rid of his secretary, his unhappiness at firing her made more sense.

Kidson said, "I see. How did you come by this information?"

"Beyer offered Tatiana Kovacs a job when we called on him last week. I wasn't sure of the fired woman's name and if he said anything about her, he said it to Tats, in rapid German. But he was agitated about losing her."

"You've just remembered this now?"

"It sort of came back to me. I take it the answer is yes, she worked for him?"

Silence was my answer. "Thanks, sergeant." I said and disconnected. I guess my face gave me away because suddenly everybody in the apartment was wide awake, watching me, expecting a revelation.

Halfway through dialing Irene Bradshaw I realized, that with a Hemlock telephone exchange, she lived in Burnaby. Miles away from Quilchena Heights. She'd been leading her tail into some of the most winding and complicated crescents in the city. Shaughnessy.

On the fifth ring a man's voice answered. "Who the hell is this? For God's sakes it's two-thirty in the morning?"

"Sorry but this is terribly important. Is Irene there?"

"Important enough to wake her out of a sound sleep? I don't think--"

A muffled argument broke out with somebody holding a hand over the mouthpiece. Then Irene Bradshaw came on the line. "Hank? Is that you?"

"Irene? Can you--"

"Oh thank God you're all right. I heard a crash and then some sirens. I didn't dare call, after you told me about the phone calls from the kidnappers. What happened?"

"The guy following you knew about Tats and their phone calls to me."

"Oh God. He was sent to kill me, wasn't he?"

"I won't lie to you, Irene. You're right. Heinrich Beyer was killed this morning by the same guy. Or at least with his gun. But he won't bother you now."

"Does that mean he's in jail? Or...or dead?"

"Secure ward at VGH. The police are keeping him isolated and they've got a news blackout on what happened this afternoon to protect Tatiana. But there's a limit to what they can do. We have to move fast."

"A limit to protecting her? I don't understand."

"McRae can't keep the punk from contacting a lawyer indefinitely and once he does that, his bosses will know I took him out. But I'm afraid they might not wait for confirmation."

"Oh my God. It's like a nightmare, isn't it?"

"Do you know anything about a Hilda Brunning? There's a Hilda in Sandy's notes and I discovered Hilda Brunning worked for Beyer and Son until a few days ago."

"No…, I don't think so…Oh, Brunning? I think I did see that name in his phone log."

"Did the log go when they cleaned out Jake's safe?"

"No. I keep the phone logs."

"You remember any details? Phone number or address?"

"No. Sorry. Not much help, I guess."

"Maybe more than you think. Could you get access to your office to-night?"

"Not a chance. The building is locked up after the cleaners finish and there's a guard on all night. Security has been tightened up since the murders. I couldn't get in before seven."

"Is there a fire emergency number?"

"You want me to try that?"

"Yes please. We're running out of time."

"Okay. I'll call you back."

"Meanwhile, I'll try all the Brunnings in the phone book. Maybe we'll get lucky. Thanks, Irene."

Tatiana's tattered telephone directory covered the metropolitan Van-couver area, Burnaby and New Westminster. It didn't have numbers in the outer circle of bedroom suburbs surrounding the city.

But the directory listed only three Brunnings.

I dialed the most distant, in South Burnaby. After a dozen rings a grumpy elderly man answered. "Who in hell is callin'at three inna mornin', fer Chrissakes?"

"Sorry but this is an emergency. Do you have a daughter or relative named Hilda Brunning?"

"Never heard of her." And he slammed the reciever down.

My second try was a number in Kerrisdale. A tremulous female voice answered. "Yes? Who is it?"

"Sorry to disturb you, ma'am but this is an emergency. Do you have a daughter or a female relative named Hilda?"

"Oh my God. What's happened to her? Has she been in an accident?"

"No ma'am. As far as I know, she's fine. But I have to talk to her tonight."

"Mister, you gave me a terrible fright. What on earth could be so important that you'd call a person at this hour?"

"It's a matter of life and death, ma'am. I'm investigating a murder and kidnapping. A woman's life is at risk and your daughter--"

"Niece," she interrupted.

"Your niece may have vital information that will help."

"I don't know what's going on but Hilda asked me not to give out her new address. Especially not on the telephone. Somebody has been frightening her out of her wits and for all I know you're the one doing it. Good night, sir." And she hung up.

Somebody was frightening Hilda Brunning?

Irene called at ten minutes to three. "Hank, I can't get an answer on the emergency number. I'm afraid you'll have to wait until I can open the office."

"At seven?"

"Yes."

I stared at the phone, blankly. Four hours to get an address for Hilda? Or maybe not. Maybe just a phone number? "Where do you keep those phone logs, Irene?"

"In a filing cabinet behind my desk. Why? What are you thinking of?"

"Don't ask, Irene. The security guard is on all night?"

"Yes. Hank! You can't be thinking of doing something criminal?"

"And the guard has master keys for the office suites in the building?"

"I believe so.

"Which drawer, Irene?"

"Top. And the cabinet is locked. I don't want to hear about this."

"Just one more question. The doors to Jake's suite of offices are alarmed. Right?"

"Yes."

"The alarm goes where? To the security desk in the lobby? Or to an outside alarm company?"

"The lobby, I think. Hank, don't do this."

"I can't waste four hours with Tatiana's life hanging on it, Irene."

"...Oh God."

I put the receiver down gently. "Jeep? Are you up for a little criminal activity?"

"You gotta ask?"

*

A slow drive past the Marine Building's main entrance established that Herbie, the security guard I'd interviewed a few days ago, was on duty. He had his feet up on his desk, working on his racing forms. A watchman's punch clock occupied one corner of the desk.

"You gonna knock on the door, or what?" Jeep wondered.

"He'd holler for the police as soon as he recognized me. We go in the back way."

"Won't holler if you stick that Smith and Wesson under his nose. Is there a back way?"

"Has to be." I felt like some kind of desperado with the magnum stuffed in my belt. No doubt the police would have the same notion, if they caught me with it. But if that happened it was game over for everyone, including Tats.

We approached the building from the lane. The service entrance side was bathed in glaring orange light from a pair of floodlights mounted high on the wall. A large, metal, roll-up door, firmly locked down, opened onto a small shipping dock. No doubt furniture and supplies were delivered here. A man-sized door beside the truck door was metal-clad and had outsized locks.

Jeep hopped up on the concrete loading dock and prodded the smaller door. "Need blasting powder for this one," he said.

"Keep it down, Jeep. They can hear you on Hastings Street."

"Yeah? Maybe our friend at the desk needs to hear us and come lookin'?"

He was right. I said, "It's Halloween in a couple of weeks. If we had some firecrackers, maybe..."

Jeep looked at me, nervously. He'd dropped from the loading dock to the lane and was now stooped over, searching in a ditch. "Collecting some rocks," he explained.

"Let's try these firecrackers," I said and drew the magnum.

"Holy Jesus," Jeep said.

"Sound'll be muffled by the time it gets to Herbie," I said. "He won't be sure what it is."

"It might work, I guess. If it doesn't we'll have to make a run for it."

I leaned against the building and steadied my aim with both hands. Ten yards. I was no pistol expert but surely I could hit anything that close.

The magnum's report was stunning.

The floodlight flared and spewed sparks. Then went out.

I decided to leave the second light. Pitch blackness wasn't what I needed to deal with Herbie. A haze of blue powder smoke drifted under the remaining floodlight.

Minutes passed.

Then I heard footsteps within the building. "The fuck's goin' on out there?" Herbie's querulous voice.

Jeep, crouched at the end of the dock, leaned out and heaved one of his rocks. It clattered off the slatted rolling freight door.

The man-door opened a crack and a sliver of light spilled out onto the concrete loading dock. "Get away from this building with your damned fireworks or you'll have the police to answer to," Herbie said. Jeep threw another rock, bouncing it off the metal-clad man-door. Herbie stepped out onto the dock, shining his flashlight into the shadows below the edge of the concrete dock.

Jeep grabbed him by the ankles, quick as a cat.

"Hey! What the hell--?" Herbie landed heavily on his rump in the lane.

"Shut your trap, Herbie," Jeep said.

"Oh shit. It's you," Herbie said, dismayed at the sight of me emerging from the shadows. "I told ya everything I know. Wadaya want with me?"

"Just behave yourself and do as you're told, Herbie and you won't come to any harm. Now, inside the building."

*

Finding Sandy's phone log was simple, once I broke the lock on Irene Bradshaw's filing cabinet.

The log consisted of eight sheets of numbered calls with time and date, single-spaced. Many entries had only initials to indicate the person or firm called. Cryptic coding in the margins seemed to have something to do with charges for the calls.

I riffled through the log quickly and found "Hilda B." at the bottom of the last sheet. She had a Fairview telephone number but there was no address. I dialed directory assistance but B.C. Tel had no new listing for any Brunnings which meant either her number was unlisted or she was living with a friend. Jeep watched me from across the Feldman office entry foyer where he had Herbie pinned down in a deep armchair. Herbie was close to tears.

"What's the problem?" Jeep asked.

"No address. If I call the woman, she for sure isn't going to talk to me. Her aunt said somebody had frightened Hilda out of her wits."

"Don't they print some kinda reverse directory?"

Sometimes Jeep was inspired. And maybe I'd have thought of it if I hadn't been dead on my feet. "Criss-Cross, it's called," I said, giving Jeep a thumbs-up. "Now where in hell would Irene keep hers?"

I found it in the office library. Hilda Brunning's phone number belonged to one David Henderson who lived at 1960-B, West third avenue. Kitsilano district.

"Okay, Jeep. We're out of here," I said.

"Fingerprints first," Jeep said. Jeep watched more detective movies than Tats did. Thank God. He wiped everything we'd touched and a lot of things we hadn't, just to be sure. At last he asked, "What do we do with Herbie, here?"

"I think he knows more about the killings than he's told us. Bring him along."

Herbie protested his innocence down nineteen flights of stairs. At the car, Jeep said, "Herbie, you'll live longer if you shut up. Okay?"

Herbie fell silent.

18

Hilda Brunning lived in Kitsilano, Kits to the locals, a long established working-class neighborhood that happens to be close to the city's finest beach -- and under the eyes of the city's rabid pack of developers. City council squabbles broke out regularly as people determined to preserve Kits "single family" residential status ran head first into the shortage of housing and the push to rezone for upscale apartments. Ranks of tall, narrow, nineteenth century clapboards, crammed with illegal suites, stood side by side with new apartment blocks. Few suites displayed addresses out front, apart from that of the main house, and finding Hilda's was taking time.

I left the gun with Jeep who stayed in the car to watch Herbie. The guard had gone into a snivelling funk, sure he was being "taken for a ride." Jeep wasn't helping with his Cagney act.

Stumbling around looking for house numbers and apartment entrances, I managed to wake most of the neighborhood's dogs before I found 1960-B West Third, where she presumably lived. The building was a clapboard built some time in the last century when twenty-five foot lots had been legal. The houses had grown upwards when they couldn't spread out. If Hilda's apartment was on an upper floor I would be out of luck, trying to get to her at this hour.

But I found a rear basement-level door with a large "B" inscribed on it. That looked promising.

No one answered my knock for several minutes and I was about to give up when a male voice within snarled, "Get fucking lost."

"Is Hilda Brunning there? I have to talk to her."

"Who the hell are you? It's four in the morning, for Chrissakes."

"I'm investigating the murder of Heinrich Beyer, her ex boss."

"Yeah? Well good riddance to the prick. Hilda quit that dump last week. She don't know anything. Bugger off and let us get some sleep. Come back in the morning if you got to."

"A woman's life is in danger. I haven't got time to be polite."

"Shit. This better be legit or you're toast." The door creaked open and I was looking at a slim, bespectacled youth holding a baseball bat.

"Baseball season's about over, isn't it?"

"Not until I see a badge, it ain't. Who in hell are you?"

"I don't have a badge. I'm a private investigator looking into the deaths of Heinrich Beyer, Sandor Kovacs and Jake Feldman. Kovacs' sister has been kidnapped by the killers."

A feminine murmur distracted the baseball player. "What is it, David?" she asked. David half-turned to a barefooted young woman in a long flannel nightie behind him. "Go back to bed, Hilda. I'll look after this."

I grabbed the bat from David who didn't seem unhappy to let go of it. I threw it into the yard, behind me, and stepped into the entry. "David" lost his nerve and staggered back, though I hadn't touched him.

"Sorry, David. There's no time for games." He sagged against the wall with a groan. I turned to the small, pretty blond behind him. She was pale and trembling. "No need to be afraid, ma'am. Are you Hilda Brunning?"

"Y-yes. What is it you want?"

"You worked for Heinrich Beyer?"

She nodded. "I didn't quit, as David said. He fired me. For no good reason."

"He gave you no reason at all?"

"No. Well, he said he couldn't rely on me anymore. I asked him what I'd done to justify that. He said I shouldn't discuss company business with strangers."

"What strangers?"

"I don't know. He didn't name anyone and I couldn't think what he was talking about."

I noticed her quick glance at her boyfriend. And then I knew. She said, "David, why don't you go make some coffee?"

David snorted. "Just like that? Guy invites himself in, the middle of the fuckin' night, an' I'm s'pposed to make him coffee?"

"Go, David," she said, with a meaningful look.

David exchanged glares with her, then trudged off towards the kitchen. "Find out if there's a reward," he said.

"Your aunt said someone or something had frightened you. Can you tell me what that was about?"

"Oh. The day before I was fired, in the morning, a man came to the office. He and Mr. Beyer argued violently but they were in Mr. Beyer's private office with the door shut and they kept their voices low, so I don't know what it was about. But as he left, that ugly man kept looking at me. It made my flesh creep. I had the impression the argument was something about me."

"Pock marked face? Ears like jug handles?"

"That sounds like him. Do you know him?"

"He was probably Beyer's killer. The police have him in custody."

"Oh my." She shuddered.

I said, "Hilda, let me guess. You met Sandy Kovacs. Right?"

"That's right. I was terribly upset when I read that he'd killed himself. But now the paper says it was a murder."

Her eyes brimmed with tears.

"Tell me about your meeting with him," I said.

"He came to the office twice, to see Mr. Beyer, the last time on the Wednesday before he died. Mr. Beyer was rude to him for some reason. After Sandy left, Mr. Beyer left the office early and I closed up at five. Sandy must have been waiting for me because he was at my bus stop and…"

"And what?"

She looked in David's direction, then lowered her voice. "I don't think it was an accident. He asked me to dinner that evening and, to be honest, I couldn't think of a single reason to say no. He was nice and…I guess you know he was very handsome." She colored, then smiled weakly.

"And you talked?"

"Yes. I didn't discuss company business with him. At least not shipping business."

"But you did talk about something. Tell me what."

"Just small talk. You know, funny things that happen to you at work or wherever. We both liked to ski and he asked me about different ski runs. I got the impression he really couldn't afford to go skiing but hoped to, some day. We were just, like, you know…getting to know each other. He told wonderful stories about his coming to Canada. And he talked about his sister, a ballerina, and how they were close but couldn't live together."

"It's his sister who's life is in danger. What did he say about her?"

"Just that she's such a fabulous dancer and such a dreadful cook."

"Anything else? What stories did you tell him?"

"A few about my boss. Mr. Beyer is…was a terrible womanizer. A girl needs armored panties to work around him."

I raised an eyebrow.

"He likes to pinch bottoms and…and things. Liked to, I mean."

"But he didn't get anywhere with you?"

"No. I was quite firm with him when I first came to work there. I don't think that had anything to do with why I was fired. He'd given up chasing me long ago."

"What else did you tell Sandy?"

She looked, furtively, in David's direction. Then in a near whisper, "He asked me if I would go out with him and I said I would. We were going to have our first real date the Friday after he was killed." She brushed away an escaped tear with the sleeve of her nightie.

"You don't remember any more stories? Anything connected to Beyer's office?"

"No…Oh, there was the Chinese potato farmer."

"Who?"

"His name is Chung Chuck."

I grinned. Everyone in Vancouver had heard of Chung Chuck. He was famous for fighting the quota and price-fixing potato marketing boards in court, and winning. Without a lawyer. "What about him?"

"Mr. Beyer rented a houseboat from Chung Chuck about a month ago," she said. "I had to deal with him on the telephone several times. Mr. Chuck isn't an easy man to deal with but conversations can be hysterically funny."

"A houseboat? I don't get it. I thought Chung was just a farmer."

"He is but I gather he's built a marina alongside the dike in Ladner, where his farm is. He advertised moorage and houseboat rentals."

"What did Beyer want with a houseboat?"

"I have no idea. But he wanted two parking places at the dock. Mr. Chuck only wanted to give him one. `Chung Chuck rules,' he said."

"Did Beyer say why he wanted two spaces?"

"No but Mr. Beyer doesn't own a car. Didn't, I mean. He hated driving."

"Did Sandy know about Chung Chuck before you mentioned him that evening over dinner?"

"I don't believe so," she said. "He seemed excited about the houseboat and the parking spaces. I didn't think the story was *that* funny."

"Did he say why he'd originally called on Beyer?"

"Just that he was checking out agents that handle freezer ships. Which the firm does."

"Coffee's ready," David announced.

I downed the near scalding coffee gratefully, my pulse quickening with anticipation. "So it happened like this -- Sandy called on Beyer twice, the last time on the Wednesday before he was killed. That same evening he took you to dinner. Where did you go?"

"Wait a minute. You went to dinner with some guy?" David demanded. "What in hell is goin' on, Hilda?"

"David, shut up. We'll talk about it later." She turned back to me. "We went to a big place in Chinatown. The Mandarin Gardens."

"You didn't recognize anyone else who was there?"

"No. But the place was full."

"And you told him about Chung Chuck. Then the next day, Thursday? this ugly joker called on Beyer and had an argument with him. Gave you the evil eye on his way out? Right?" She nodded.

"And the day after that Beyer fired you?"

"Yes. You don't think it was because I told Sandy about Chung Chuck, do you?"

"I think your dinner date was observed by someone. Sandy must have asked Beyer some questions that made him nervous and Beyer, or his bosses, had Sandy followed. They must have figured Sandy was going around Beyer, questioning you."

"Surely that wasn't something worth killing him for?"

"Depends on what they're hiding. I think you were in danger, too, until you moved. My guess is they couldn't find you."

"Oh my God."

"I don't think you're in danger now. Their hit man is out of circulation." I hoped that was true.

Was it a quirk of romantic luck or an instinctive hunch on Sandy's part that had attracted him to the one woman who could tell him about Beyer's dealings with Chung Chuck? The potato farmer was my first real break on the case. "Hilda, you've been a great help. Thank you."

David said, "Ain't it, y'know, usual there'd be a reward if somebody helps out with a murder investigation?"

"Oh David," Hilda said, embarrassed.

"No, that's a fair question. I'll look into it for you," I said.

"Hey, you do that, huh? Hilda's outa work and there's a recession on, ya know? Give us a call, you find out."

"I'll do that," I said, backing towards the door.

*

I fell into the car, parked in front of Hilda's place, my head buzzing. Was this houseboat Sandy's "safe house"? I had to find out before charging off to Ladner on what could be a wild goose chase.

Ladner Village is on the south bank of the main Fraser River channel, near the seaward end of the river's broad, diked delta. It was thirty miles from downtown Vancouver in a straight line and a lot farther by bridge and road. Awkward to reach.

Five AM. I was running on pure adrenaline but anxious to get moving.

Jeep, in the driver's seat, faced Herbie who huddled as far away as possible in the back seat. "Herbie here's been tellin' me a story," Jeep said. Herbie whined.

"Please, I didn't know I was gettin' in a mess like this or I wouldn't have done it." I looked hard at Jeep.

"I don't have time for this, Jeep. What the hell is coming down?" My diplomatic cousin had done something to Herbie, though I couldn't see any visible marks. The man was nearly wetting himself.

Jeep shrugged, all innocence, and said, "Just give it a listen, Hank. Herbert thinks he's goin' for his last ride. Told me a whole lot of stuff, tryin' to buy his way out. Tell the boss, Herbie. Maybe save your crab-apple ass." Jeep does a good Cagney imitation.

"What did you do, Herbie?" I demanded.

"Like I told your guy, here," Herbie quivered. "These two jokers busted into my room Monday afternoon--"

"That would be Monday the seventh? The day Kovacs died?"

"That's right. See, I got this crummy room over on Powell Street and I got no idea how they found out where I live. Anyway, they come bustin' in like the FBI. Like they never learned to knock and for Chrissakes yanked my girl-friend right off me an' kicked her outa bed an' into the hall, without even lettin' her get dressed. Boy, she ain't never gonna talk to me again."

"Herbie," Jeep said, ominously.

"Yeah, yeah. I'm comin' to it. Anyway, they showed me money. Looked like maybe a thousand dollars, all in twenties. All I had to do for it was come in late for my shift and get another guy to phone in sick. Just so the security desk had nobody on it 'til after eight-thirty that night."

"That's not the yarn you gave me last week, Herbie. Did they say anything else?"

"Said they'd pay half now. Then, I mean. And half after, if I kept my mouth shut. I asked 'em, `After what?' They said did I want the fuckin' money or not?"

"And of course you did?"

"Jeez, mister, you know what they pay us, doin' security?"

"Too much, by the sound of it. You realize you could be charged as accessory to a murder?"

"Oh shit. I knew I shouldn'a done it. Whatcha gonna do?"

"Turn you over to Sergeant McRae."

"Oh, shit."

"Maybe not. You got more to tell me?"

"Like what?"

"Descriptions, for starters."

"Sort of ordinary. One was medium height with black hair and a mous-tache like young Kovacs had. Some kinda foreigner. He did the talkin'. T'other was fair and big. Big as you, but older. Maybe fifty. Not much hair. He never said nothing. The third guy was different. No accent--"

"Third guy? You said there were two."

"Monday I only saw two of them, moustache and the big guy. But the Friday you was here, askin' questions, this other joker comes 'round at the end of my late shift. See, I was workin' split shift 'til they hired another guy. Schedule's all screwed up an' we're still short handed. Anyway, some time before I locked up the front this joker shows up. Waltzes right in the front door and sits on the end of my desk. Says if I want the rest of my money I gotta leave the rear service door loose and take a walk. Forget I ever seen him."

"The day Feldman was shot? What time Friday?"

"Maybe eight-thirty."

"And you knew why they'd bought you off the previous Monday? The night Sandy Kovacs was killed?"

"Yeah, I knew. But this joker wasn't the kinda guy you say `no' to. Know what I mean? He'd as soon off me as pay me, I figured."

"What did he look like?"

"Not so big but sort of musclebound with a crew cut. Face all chewed up. Big ears. Real nasty temper. I was back at my desk by nine. You gonna let me go?"

"No."

"Aw shit! I give you what you wanted!"

"Yeah, I know. Life's a bitch, ain't it, Herbie? Jeep, you'd better drive. I'm out on my feet."

"Where ya takin' me?"

"Damned if I know. I'll think of some place," I said.

Herbie looked sick.

Jeep started the Chrysler and eased into gear. I pointed in the direction of the West End and fell asleep.

*

"What in hell am I going to do with this mug?" Cam asked.

"Park him somewhere until McRae shows up. He'll be interested in what Herbie has to say."

"Yeah? And what happens if we get one of those calls and they hear numb-nuts here belly-achin' in the background?"

"Good point, Cam." My too-brief nap on the drive from Hilda's place back to Tats' apartment had done wonders for me, physically, but the benefits hadn't extended to my brain. "I'll think of something to do with him," I said.

Herbie emitted a mewling sound and sank deeper into the couch.

Time. What we didn't have. It was six-forty-five AM. "I wonder what time Chinese potato farmers get up," I said as I dialed Chung Chuck's number.

After fifteen rings, Chung answered. In Cantonese. I said, "Chung, you remember me? Hank Sutter? We met aboard Clay Harper's boat?"

A long silence followed. "Clay Harper all time drunk. You drunk too. Go way and let me work." He hung up.

I sat, staring at the phone. I dialed his number again. "Don't hang up, Chung," I said. "I'm not drunk and this is important. Life and death. You understand?"

"Be you life, you don't leave me alone."

"You talked to Sandy Kovacs, a young Hungarian man. Remember?"

"Sure remember. He dead. Jump off building."

"Murdered," I shouted, anticipating another hang-up. "He didn't jump. Do you remember what he talked to you about?"

"Murder, huh? Remember you now. Hank? You big guy? Seven feet high? Four hundred pound?"

"Not quite, but big. We met aboard Harper's boat in Steveston, two years ago." Steveston is a few miles north, across the river from Ladner.

"Okay, you not drunk like Harper. What you want?"

"What did Sandy Kovacs say? What was he asking?"

"Ask about houseboat."

"The houseboat you rented out?"

"You know everything, why you ask me? I make new business alongside dike, beside farm. Marina. Make lotsa space for fishboat tie-up. And houseboat."

"What did you tell him?"

"Tell him sure, fella from town rent houseboat from me. Give me lotsa trouble."

"Why trouble?"

"Want extra parking. Everybody only get one space. Parking lot too small. Also, houseboat not have phone. B.C. Tel don't put in quick so new guys want to move houseboat next to phone on wharf. I say no. Stay where is. They make lotsa argument."

"You said one guy rented the houseboat. Was it Heinrich Beyer?"

"Aha. You know about."

"And Sandy Kovacs phoned you about it?"

"He call me, lesee, maybe week ago Thursday. Before he die. I tell him I buy houseboat for fix up and sell. This fella ask if I rent for lot of money, don't care about fix up. I say okay. Then four men come and now is lady there."

"A woman? Young? Old? What's she look like?"

"Very pretty. Not old. Got black hair like Chinese. She not happy."

I stood, abruptly, staring at the phone, my heart racing. Jeep looked at me, an eyebrow raised. Suddenly Cam and Jeep closed in on me, trying to hear both sides of the conversation. I drew a slow breath. "Chung, listen carefully, please. Those men are extremely dangerous. They are killers. Understand?"

"Sure understand. You want me evict?"

"I want you to do nothing at all. The lady is in terrible danger."

"She kidnap? I already think."

"Right. Don't do anything, but stay near your phone. We'll be there real soon."

"Okay. You evict."

"Something like that. Thanks, Chung."

"You found her?" Jeep and Cam asked together. It was more of a whoop than a question.

"God. They're holding her in Ladner. I've got to get out there."

My watch said seven AM when our extra phone rang. I picked it up. McRae said, "Tell you this once, so listen up. John Doe's got some sleazy ambulance chaser to represent him and the schmuck's goin' after Judge

Leo Feinstein for a writ. Feinstein's a bleeding heart civil rights lawyer turned judge so if they meet, his writ is in the bag."

"How in hell did he get a lawyer?"

"Don't know. I find out which VGH staffer he bought, the sonofabitch is fired. Feinstein's a health freak. Jogs around Stanley Park every morning. I don't think John Doe's schmuck lawyer can talk him out of making his run."

"What does that mean in time?"

"His wife says he left his apartment on Beach Avenue twenty minutes ago, doin' his warmup walk up to Second Beach where he starts his run. She says he does the six and a half miles in fifty minutes flat. Give him fifteen minutes to get home, shower and change, you got maybe an hour and ten minutes, tops."

"Won't the lawyer just drive after him and catch up?"

"Feinstein goes wrong way around the park, against the one way traffic. You onto something, Sutter? I got the feelin' you're way ahead of me."

"I think I know where she is."

"Then you'd better tell me."

"Ladner. On a houseboat. It's out of your jurisdiction and if the local cops go charging in it could turn into a blood bath."

"Ladner, huh? Okay, I'll send 'em a wake-up and give Nunn a call. By the way, somebody broke into the Marine Building last night and hit Feldman's office. Kidnapped the security guard. I don't suppose you know anything about that?"

"Not a thing."

"That's what I thought. Okay, I'm not going to tell you what you gotta do, Sutter. Can you get there before the crud's lawyer makes a phone call for him?"

"Jesus, I hope so."

I disconnected and turned to Jeep and Cam. "How do we get to Ladner in an hour?"

"Take you an hour and thirty, forty minutes, even at Jeep speed. And that's if you don't get a ticket," Cam said. Jeep gave him a "who me?" look.

"Be two hours if we took the *Solange*, and we'd have to do the last few miles with the workboat. Ladner Reach is way too shallow for the tug."

"And Junior would have fits," Jeep said, with a smirk.

"Junior?"

"If you stole his tug, I mean." Jeep said.

Then it came to me. Junior's ultimate insult was the answer. I said, "Not the tug. The *Miranda*, his fancy speedboat. Cam? Is that thing running?"

"Like clockwork. Sixty gallons an hour clockwork, I mean."

"And you've got the keys?"

Cam nodded and tossed me a keyring with about a pound of keys on it. "The pretty brass set with their own ring," he said. "Leave me the rest."

I peeled the boat's keys off the larger ring. "Jeep, you've got five minutes to get me to --" But Jeep was already at the curb starting Cam's car. I dove into the passenger side front seat.

"Hey! What do I do with Herbie?" Cam wailed.

"You'll think of something," I shouted as Jeep burned rubber pulling away.

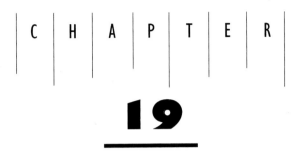

C H A P T E R

19

"**D**ammit, who'd have guessed Junior'd be workin' on his pride 'n joy this early on a Sunday mornin'?" Jeep grumbled. It was twenty minutes past seven.

"I think today's the big antique boat show over at the yacht club," I said. "Guess he's giving her a final touch-up."

From the company parking lot Jeep and I stared at the open doors of Junior's floating boathouse wherein lay our gleaming mahogany prey. We could see Junior Picard polishing the chromed windshield frame of the *Miranda*.

Two of Junior's log-towing tugs, the *Serafin Picard* and the *Chantel Picard* lay alongside, across from the boathouse, their crews busy loading galley supplies. A delivery van was parked in the middle of the floating dock beside the tugs. Nobody on the dock could see into the open end of Junior's boat garage. Nobody except us.

Across the far end of the dock, where there was depth for her, the *Solange Picard* lay. Nobody was in view on deck but a wisp of steam at the base of the whistle, high on her stack, told of life in the engine room.

"Got any ideas, Jeep?" I asked.

"Maybe he'll need to pee, or there'll be a phone call for him. Or somethin'," Jeep said.

I looked at my watch. Ten minutes since McRae's call.

"We don't have time for his bladder to work," I said. "Give me the magnum."

"Jesus, Hank, don't do somethin' stupid!"

"Give me the God damned gun!"

Reluctantly, he passed me the gun, butt first. I stuck it in my belt. "I'll do whatever it takes," I said, opening the door of the Chrysler.

Jeep tumbled out after me.

I turned on him. "Look, Jeep, you don't have to get into this. Tats is my concern. The only thing in this world I give a damn about, in fact. But I'd be selfish to drag you into the mess."

"Yeah? Well you did say she kinda liked me. I wouldn't want her to lose her good opinion."

"Thanks, cousin."

"We need a diversion," he said, a little frantically. "Maybe we could phone him from a pay phone, get the office to call him."

"We don't have any time left," I said.

"Shit. There has to be *somethin'* we can do," Jeep groaned. Short of shooting Junior, he meant. I think at that moment I might have actually done it, if I'd thought it would get us to Tats any faster. All I could think of was the haunting image of Tatiana Kovacs, staring down at her dead brother. And the images merged.

"Come on," I said. I headed down the ramp at a jog. Jeep trotted after me, alarmed but keeping his mouth shut.

Picard looked up, startled, as we entered the boathouse.

"Morning, Junior," I said.

"Mr. Picard, to you, Sutter. What do you want? Can you not see I'm busy?"

"I want you to take a walk. We need to use your boat and I don't have time to explain."

"Walk? What do you mean?"

"Jeep? Start her up. Junior, you can take a nice slow walk down the dock, or you can swim. Your choice."

The *Miranda* thundered to life as Jeep turned the ignition key. He stepped out of the cockpit and let go the boat's lines.

"Now see here, Sutter, this is piracy. I'll have the police on you. Furthermore, you are both fired." He moved between me and the aft cockpit of the *Miranda* in an effort to block me.

"Tatiana's life is at stake," I said. "Get out of my goddamn way, Junior."
I picked him up by the shirt-front, held him out over the water at arm's
length, and put him down gently on the other side of me. That seemed to
take the starch out of him.

Junior sputtered, "Whose life? Miss Kovacs? Then call the police." As
I stepped into the Miranda's aft cockpit, Junior shouted, "You're a luna-
tic! You've gone completely mad! You do realize you'll lose your master's
license and get a jail sentence for this?"

"Right. Swim it is. Help Junior into the water, Jeep."

But Junior wasn't going to swim today. He skittered out of the boathouse and broke into a run, short legs pumping furiously, heading for the
Solange's dock phone.

We paddled the Miranda out into the channel between Picard's and the
Canadian Pacific train-barge dock before easing her into gear. The water-
cooled exhaust burbled like some gigantic purring cat. The tanks were full,
according to the gauges.

I advanced the throttle gingerly.

The Miranda was a product of the prohibition era, one of a series of
fast, expensive runabouts originally designed to bring booze in from rum-
running ships lying outside the three-mile limit. The original 1933 Hacker-
Craft sales brochure talked of "Elegant High Speed Commuting for the
Gentleman of Distinction." A likely story.

The design race between the U.S. Coast Guard and the rum runners
produced some remarkably fast boats, if you didn't care about the fuel bill.
The Miranda's V-12 aircraft engine gave her more than enough horsepower
to fly, if she'd had wings. I didn't want to risk doing anything sudden.

As we gathered speed heading for Brockton Point and the Lion's Gate, I
looked back towards the Picard dock. Junior was standing on the Solange's
stern grating, shaking his fist and shouting imprecations after us. I looked at
my watch. Seven twenty-five. Fifteen minutes had passed since McRae's call.

*

Ten more minutes and we'd just passed the Spanish Banks can buoy and
turned south, running at something over fifty knots, when we hit the fog

bank. The Fraser River's numerous sawmill "beehive" burners belched enough fly-ash into the atmosphere to cause some dreadful pea-soup fogs, especially in October and November when the first light frosts arrived.

The fog swallowed the two hundred foot sand bluffs of Point Grey leaving only the tops of the highest towers of the UBC campus in sight. It lay on Spanish Banks and Sturgeon Bank, off the river delta, in a thick, gray blanket. Jeep was steering and he reached to pull the throttle back. I put my hand over his and pushed it forward again.

"Jesus! We can't keep goin' flat out in this shit!" Jeep said.

"I'm not going to any more funerals," I shouted over the engine's roar. "Tats is all I care about in the world."

He stared at me for a moment. "Hey. Take it easy, man. I've never seen you crazy like this."

"Steer one sixty-four degrees and pray," I said.

"You ain't sure of the course?"

"The course is fine. Just pray Junior's compass is a serious instrument. One sixty-four should get us somewhere near the light ship. With any luck, we'll hear their horn before we run into something."

"Over this racket?" Jeep said, hooking a thumb at our thundering power plant.

I looked at my watch. Seven thirty-five A.M. Point Grey abeam. Eleven nautical miles as the crow flies. I did the arithmetic in my head. Thirteen minutes at this insane speed to the Sand Heads Lightship.

To our left, we could wander into eleven miles of tidal mud flat. To our right lay the open Gulf of Georgia and lots of shipping traffic. Ships complacently depending on radar which wouldn't see our small wooden craft before they ran us down.

Our safest bet was to steer as close to the edge of Sturgeon Bank as possible. Larger ships would keep clear of that.

"We're gonna run smack into the jetty," Jeep opined. Optimistic bugger. But he'd read my mind. The main river channel between Sturgeon and Roberts banks is marked by a four-mile-long, curved, rock breakwater called the Steveston Jetty. Talk about hitting a brick wall.

The *Miranda*'s speedometer hovered around fifty knots. I didn't trust speedometers for navigation purposes but the gale of mist blasting our faces and condensing in streams on the windshield felt like fifty knots. My gut fear made that feel slow.

Thirteen minutes to the lightship. I stared at my watch again. That would put us thirty-nine minutes after McRae's phone call. Twenty-one minutes short of the best he thought he could do for Tats and we weren't into the main channel yet. The sea was glass calm, coffee brown. I was bleak gray and anything but calm.

"Sheeeeit!" Jeep swerved violently to starboard.

Deadhead! We barely cleared it.

Forty feet of hemlock log, escaped from some sawmill's boom. The log had absorbed water until it floated vertically with only a foot or so of its small end above water. A small end two feet in diameter. A deadhead that size could rip the propeller off a ship. Or flip us over in an instant.

"Christ, Hank, slow down! We keep on like this you'll need to walk on water."

I don't think I'd ever seen Jeep so frightened. I was as frightened but for my love's life, not for mine. "I'll put you ashore if you want, Jeep," I said.

"No fuckin' way."

At twelve minutes from Point Grey I yanked the throttle back to its stop and killed the engine. *Miranda* slowed with a lurch, like a jet hitting a haystack, still planing for a brief moment, then settling in the water, wallowing heavily as her stern wave caught up with her. The silence was numbing.

Then it shattered as the Sand Heads Lightship fog horn practically blew us out of the water.

The red-painted, rust-streaked hull materialized out of the murk. White letters as high as a man, painted on the hull, said "*Sand Heads No. 16.*" Junior's compass wasn't bad at all.

I re-started the engine. We rounded the light and followed the dredged channel towards Steveston, keeping the jetty close on our port side. I dropped our speed to twenty knots. It was all I dared in the channel. Any ship coming down river had right-of-way and it was our problem to stay clear. But we wouldn't hear a ship coming over our own engine noise.

The fog shifted from dull gray to muddy near-white, now that the invisible sun was well above the horizon. The effect made the fog seem even thicker. Sometimes we couldn't make out the jagged rockpile of the jetty, twenty feet away.

Ten minutes later we hit the bend of the jetty and the tricky part of our navigation began. I took the wheel from Jeep and headed at a slant across channel to the south side. I hadn't been here for a few years and things did change along the river. Dredging went on constantly and channel buoys and markers proliferated. Or disappeared. The main river was well marked but the lacework of side channels and byways, where we were going, was something else. Jeep crawled forward over the fog-slick, crowned engine hatch and slid into the forward cockpit, the one advertising art departments love to fill with bathing beauties. Plug ugly Jeep stood on the seat, peering ahead.

"Pilings!" Jeep yelled, pointing to a shadow just off our starboard bow. I adjusted our course slightly.

"See the dyke yet?"

"Nope. But it's gotta be there...Okay, there it is." He pointed again.

Like blind men in a strange room, we fumbled our way along the Albion Dyke and into Sea Reach. Moments later the low bulk of Westham Island was to starboard. An occasional tree along the muddy beach, or a group of pilings, loomed up to scare us. And enliven the bleak scene.

Canoe Pass opened suddenly beside us. I yanked the throttle back and steered hard to port, narrowly missing putting us ashore on the bulge of marshy beach east of the entrance to the pass. It would be tragic to run aground here, so close to our destination.

I peered at my watch again. The thing seemed to be galloping. We were fifty-eight minutes past McRae's call. Damned near out of time. Get hold of yourself, Sutter.

The loom of V-shaped wooden net rollers and the fat stern of a moored gillnetter, and then the tall poles and flared bow of a bigger salmon troller, told us we'd arrived in Ladner Reach. *Miranda* grumbled up the street-wide channel at her slowest speed.

Now to find Chung Chuck's establishment.

Newly built float-wharves and new pilings had to be his. The tide was high. Chung's boxy house should be visible, over the dyke.

There it was.

The fog cleared momentarily and we could read the black-on-white hand painted letters, four feet high, across the front of his house: "CHUNG CHUCK -- POTATO GROWER."

A dozen fishing boats and twenty houseboats, some of them two-story, were tied along the dock. Belatedly, I pulled the hood of my rain jacket up. We were passing close under the windows of the houseboats as we wended our way up the channel and I had no idea which was Chung Chuck's. I didn't know if the kidnappers knew me by sight but I'd be a fool to assume they didn't.

We drifted past the houseboats making maybe three knots. Nobody seemed interested in us. Beyond the far end of the marina, I stopped *Miranda*'s engine and let her drift, steering around a slight bend, out of direct view of the dock.

Junior's pride had an HF radio telephone and a VHF radio, both modern additions to her equipment. I erected the long HF whip antenna and called up the Vancouver marine operator. I placed a call to Chung Chuck's house. At Junior's expense.

"Sorry to bother you again, Chung."

"No bother. I study law book for new court case."

"We're in Ladner Reach, just east of your dock. Which houseboat did you rent to these guys?"

"You come quick. What you do? Fly?"

"No. We've got a speedboat. How do we find the right houseboat?"

"I come on dock and point for you."

"Chung, these guys are killers. It's dangerous."

"How many fella you bring?"

"Just two of us."

"You got gun?"

"Yes."

"They four fellas. Too many for you beat up. I catch some to come my office. Got lotsa paper for them sign."

"Be careful, Chung. They've killed three people already."

"You be careful. They used to me, all time yell at them. They break Chung Chuck rules. Lousy tenants."

Two minutes later, Chung Chuck's ghostly figure appeared at the head of the wharf ramp, then vanished into the murk again. I drifted *Miranda* along, trying to stay close to him but all I had to go by was the sound of his footsteps.

I'd thought, briefly, of getting Chung Chuck to disable the dock's pay phone but then I realized Pock Marks might already have made his call. If that was the case, and Tats was hurt, we might need that phone badly.

Then I heard Chung pounding on a door of the houseboat just ahead of us. Lights came on and it heeled slightly as people moved inside. Jeep and I paddled *Miranda* along until we were opposite the argument breaking out on the dock, on the other side of the craft.

"Damn. What do you want now?" somebody said.

"Got liability waiver to sign. Ladner council say. You come office, sign paper or they make big trouble, bring police," Chung said.

He was winging it. The Ladner Council had never made the slightest impression on Chung Chuck. Nor had the Delta Police, for that matter.

"We signed everything you wanted last week."

"Is new paper they send. They say take away my license, I no get all tenant sign. Give twenty-four hour."

"Max? Take Joadie and go see what he wants. I don't like the smell of this." The speaker had a faint European accent. I couldn't tell from where.

"Ja Hans. We take our guns. Ya?" A muffled voice from the interior queried. Two sets of footsteps clattered up the wooden dock, the sound becoming hollow as they climbed the angled ramp to the parking lot beyond the dyke.

I waved Jeep back into the after cockpit to take the wheel. Then pushed *Miranda* by hand along the side of the houseboat, holding her clear so the hull wouldn't scrape or bump. At the downstream end of the houseboat, a big aluminum outboard was tethered by a single bow line. A shallow porch or sundeck with a wooden railing gave access to the large main room by a door with a glass panel. I handed Jeep the magnum. "I can't go in shooting, not knowing where she is. Follow me as backup. Okay?"

"Better I should take out the other guy."

"How do you propose to do that?"

"I'll go bang on their dockside door. Soon as you hear 'em answer the door, you go in over the sundeck rail."

It was risky but it could split the opposition. "Okay," I said. "But for God's sake be careful."

Standing on Miranda's engine hatch, my chin was just above the sundeck railing. I waited while Jeep eased onto the dock, over Miranada's bow. He thumped hard on the door with, I thought, the butt of the magnum.

Muffled voices inside were followed by a shift of trim as the houseboat heeled slightly. Somebody moved to the door.

"Ya, who is it?"

"Open up. It's Joadie." Jeep's voice. Not a bad imitation.

Somebody opened the dockside door. At the same moment I chinned myself. Pain from my shoulder made me slower than I should have been but I got one leg over the rail, then the other. The houseboat trimmed down by the end from my weight.

I heard footsteps and a scuffle out of sight on the dock. Suddenly the door to the sundeck opened and a round face stared at me. Hans. "What the--?"

I lunged for him.

We crashed to the deck in a tangle of arms and legs. The sundeck was narrow and I couldn't get room to swing.

He grabbed my throat and clawed at my eyes. I did the same for him but he was on top and had an arm free. He tried to knee me and missed. Then he pulled away and yanked a gun from his belt and slammed me with the butt.

A jolt of pain and my vision wavered. Then suddenly Tatiana was there, right behind Hans. Her hands were taped together but not her feet.

He took aim. I had no place to go. An animal roar spoiled Hans' aim as Jeep swarmed over the sundeck rail from the dock side, magnum in hand. "Jeep! Don't shoot!" I screamed. "Tats, get away from him!" I motioned her away. She wasn't having any.

Hans braced in the doorway, facing his new target, feet apart to steady himself as the houseboat rocked to Jeep's weight. I grabbed an ankle and tried to pull him down. He kicked me and missed but I spoiled his aim. Tats, behind the thug, was a blur.

"Get away from him!" I shouted again.

Instead, she did one of her graceful, long-legged high-kicks, catching

Hans square in the nuts with a sound like the wet smack of a bursting watermelon. With a gasping shriek, Hans hurtled over me, crashing head first through the sundeck railing, smashing out a big chunk of plywood.

At the instant of Tats' kick, Jeep launched a classic flying tackle. He went right over the sprawling Hans and landed on me instead. I yelped with the pain exploding in my shoulder. Jeep untangled himself and took aim at Hans with the magnum.

Hans must have seen his number coming up because he slithered forward over the deck-edge with a whimper and a splash.

Tats stood in the doorway, chest heaving, her hands bound behind her. She stared down at the tangle of bodies, Jeep's and mine, choking back an hysterical little giggle. "What took you so long?" she said.

"Excuse me, Tats, but what the fuck just happened?" Jeep asked. He'd been airborne with his head tucked in like any good linebacker, so he'd missed the whole performance. He regained his feet and stooped to help me up.

"I could have kicked him much harder if my hands had been free," she said.

"Kicked him?" Jeep said.

"Like this," she said, and demonstrated.

Jeep cut the tape binding her wrists and Tats leaned on me, shaking, all the sass gone out of her. I held her but she wriggled free and reached out to pull Jeep into our huddle. She planted a large wet kiss on him.

Jeep withdrew in confusion and moved to drag his first victim into the houseboat's living room. The thug was out cold. One side of his face was a massive purple bruise. "What happened to him?" I asked.

"Jerk ran into the butt of my Smith and Wesson. Gonna need a lotta aspirins when he comes around." Jeep said. He bent to duct-tape the guy's hands and feet. Tats and I held each other, watching Hans swimming for the muddy island opposite the wharf. He wasn't making good progress, one handed. Probably still holding his nuts.

"He might drown," Tats said. She didn't sound worried about it.

"He might," I said.

"I had no time left," she said, with a quiver in her voice. "They were going to rape me. This morning. That is why they untaped my feet."

"*Big* mistake. You kicked him any harder, he'd be dead," I said, regretfully.

She threw me a tiny smile. "They were waiting to find out what happened to one of their men. But this morning they started arguing about who would have me first. Then Mr Chuck banged on the door."

Outside, the pay phone on the dock rang, stridently. Before I could stop him, Jeep trotted up the dock to answer it.

The conversation was short.

"Figure it was your John Doe from the hospital," Jeep said, when he returned.

"What did he say?"

"Kinda garbled. Like he didn't have no teeth or somethin'. Near's I could make out, he said, `tell the boss Sutter ain't playing our game. And save me a piece of the dame,'. I said `get yourself stuffed and mounted 'cause you're a prize asshole.' Funny, he hung up on me."

"Sounds as if they weren't going to wait for his call."

"Who is John Doe?" Tats asked.

Two shotgun blasts erupted from the direction of Chung Chuck's house.

"Jesus! That came from the Chinese guy's place. We gotta get up there 'fore he gets killed," Jeep yelled.

"Or somebody does," I said.

C H A P T E R

20

"**P**ut me down!" Tats complained in a vehement stage whisper as I grabbed her around the middle.

"Dammit, woman, stay behind me. Jeep? Hang onto her, will you? I don't want her getting shot now."

Tats said, "Can't you hurry? That nice old Chinese man needs help."

Red and blue flashers blinked, coloring the fog and a radio sputtered out cryptic directions that nobody seemed to be answering. Two one-man squad cars with their headlights on high beam faced Chung Chuck's house. The two officers crouched beside their cars, guns drawn. The house was quiet now and the two cops seemed to be waiting for backup.

Chung Chuck's house cast eerie shadows. Though it was daytime the thick murk created a night of its own. Shafts of light blazed into the gloom from the open front door and the windows.

I sprinted for the door. Tats twisted loose from Jeep and followed me. I waved her back with no visible effect.

"Keep clear of the house!" A police bullhorn brayed. "You are in the line of fire."

What line of fire? If the police had been shooting, Chung Chuck wouldn't need our help.

Then the cop fired a warning shot, making a liar of me. It sounded like the pop of a firecracker.

I reached the door, flat on my stomach, staying clear of its shaft of light.

Tats preferred to be upright. I dragged her down beside me.

In Chung's kitchen, broken chairs and an upside-down kitchen table told of a fight, though I couldn't imagine one elderly Chinese gentleman causing much trouble for two armed men. A guy I'd never seen before stood in the wreckage, waving a large automatic around as if he was directing traffic. Beside him, a leg protruded from beneath the inverted table. It bent in the wrong direction at the knee.

The standing gunman shouted at Chung Chuck, hidden somewhere in the debris. "Call a fucking ambulance, godammit."

Chung didn't answer. I spotted him, squatting behind an old-fashioned cast iron kitchen range, aiming the largest double-barreled shotgun I'd ever laid eyes upon. The gun's muzzle followed the thug's movements exactly.

"You drop gun, I call ambulance," Chung Chuck said.

"Just dial the fuckin' operator," the thug said. He raised his gun.

I moved in and Chung spotted me. The thug turned to follow Chung's surprised gaze.

I lunged, missing him with my right but hitting him in the midsection with my bad shoulder. He went down. His gun went off and his partner on the floor screamed.

The thug tried for an arm lock on me but didn't have the strength to make it work. Then he tried to pistol whip me. I grabbed a handful of scrotum and squeezed.

He howled.

Tats, dancing around us with an iron poker waiting for a chance to slug somebody, bent the poker over his wrist causing him to drop the automatic. She picked it up and drew a bead on him. I was on the floor wrestling with the guy. I thought I'd better finish this before she shot one of us. I got my knees under me and picked him up, then slammed him, face first, into the floor.

The fight seemed to go out of him then and I got to my feet. I wanted to give Tats hell for risking her life, and mine. Instead I told the thug, "Keep your head down. It's duck season."

"Fuck you, wise ass."

Tats cocked the thug's Mauser like a pro, holding it two-handed.

I said "This lady will shoot you dead as a doornail if you so much as twitch."

The thug saw Tats' wicked smile and froze.

"Chung? You okay?"

"Ah! Good morning, Mr. Hank," he waved the shotgun in my direction. I ducked. "I am okay. Believe other fellas not so good. They call me bad names. I point shotgun and shoot two barrel. This fella fall over chair and break leg." Chung pointed. "Second fella trip over him. Then he get up and point gun at me and you come in and knock him down again and he shoot friend in foot."

"You didn't do any of this?" I gestured at the wrecked kitchen.

"Oh no. Only make big noise with salt and pepper load. But now is buck-shot number three-o." He held up a fist full of red and brass shotgun shells.

"I think the massacre is over, Chung."

But it wasn't. Sirens growled to a stop as more police arrived in Chung's yard. Moments later, two snarling police dogs charged through the door.

The man on the floor who'd been shot in the foot kicked out at a dog. "Ow! Shit. Not my good leg," he howled, as the dog retaliated.

Suddenly police were everywhere.

A grizzled sergeant bent over me, aiming a large revolver at my head. "Flat on the floor, you," he said.

"Thank God you guys got here," I said.

"Yeah?" He turned to Tats. "Drop the gun, lady."

She dropped it.

"Turn over and put your hands behind your back so I can cuff you, mister," the sergeant said.

"No no. Is okay. Mr. Hank save my life. Knock down this fella with gun point at me. His lady take gun away from him," Chung Chuck said. "She kidnap by them. Keep in houseboat at my dock. No good."

"Worst piece of damn foolishness I ever saw. Charging in like that. You could've got yer fool heads blown off," the sergeant said. "Good thing we were right behind you."

"You were? Looks to me as if Chung did them more damage than any of us." From the several police glares directed at me I knew I shouldn't have said that.

The sergeant took charge again. "Okay, outside, you. We'll take a look at this houseboat."

I scrambled to my feet.

An ambulance had pulled into the yard and attendants were loading the thug with the broken leg onto a gurney. His partner was handcuffed and marched out to a squad car.

"I stay and clean up my house," Chung Chuck said. "These fellas make terrible mess."

"Okay, Chung, but you'll have to give us that shotgun and come in to the station and make a statement later."

Chung Chuck had lost none of his dignity, or calm, despite having a police constable on each side. I wasn't sure who was escorting who back to the house. One cop carried Chung's shotgun like a porter on a safari.

The sergeant turned back to me. "Your name Sutter?"

"Yes."

"We got this phone call from Ian McRae of the Vancouver PD detective squad this morning. He was sort of hazy on details but he said somethin' about a kidnapping and we should be on our toes, give you a hand if you called. Said you were a military cop."

His rising inflection made that a question. I let it slide by. "We've both been investigating the same murders. Turned out I had a way to get here first."

"Murders? I don't know what in hell this is all about but when Chung called us he said something about a kidnapping and I realized this had to be what McRae was talking about. You the person kidnapped, Miss...?"

"Kovacs. Tatiana Kovacs."

"Very well, Miss Kovacs. Tell me what happened." Tats stepped forward. "These men broke the door of my apartment. They taped my hands and feet with this, mm, duck tape? and put it over my mouth. They roll me up in a blanket and bring me here. This morning they talked about raping me and who should have me first and how should they get rid of my body."

"They said that? In front of you?"

"In German. They didn't know I understood."

"I see. The kidnap was to rape you?"

"No. Two weeks ago they killed my brother and…oh…It is complicated." Tats had been doing well but reaction was setting in. She was shaking and near tears. I gathered her to me.

Patiently, the sergeant said, "This kidnap happened when?"

"About three o'clock Thursday morning," I said. "Her apartment is in Vancouver, in the West End."

"I see. And your friends here came to your rescue?" He addressed Tats, gesturing at Jeep and me.

"Yes," Tats said.

"Okay, save the rest until we see this houseboat." We moved down the ramp to the dock. I said, "Sergeant, do you think I could make a phone call? Some people who were helping us will want to know what happened here."

"Well, make it short," he said, grudgingly.

I tried to pass Tats on to Jeep while I made the call but she wouldn't let me go. I got Cam at the apartment.

"What's happening, Hank?"

"We got her, Cam."

"You got Tatiana? She's okay?"

"I am fine, Cam. And thank you, I love you," Tats said.

"She's just…well you can hear," I said. "Nobody hurt on our side."

"And the killers?"

"Got them too."

"Hey! Way to go, Hank!" He shouted the news to somebody in the room. By the uproar it sounded like Clara and maybe Gowan and half my crew were there.

"We'll probably be bringing the *Miranda* home, whenever the police turn us loose. Are we going to have trouble there?"

"Yeah, I think so. Marty and Junior have both been bending my ear all morning. Junior claims the police boats are both out lookin' for you. To hear him tell it, you're gonna be keelhauled."

"Make sure you call Irene Bradshaw and Ella Feldman. Oh and Gowan at the ballet academy. And don't forget McRae."

"Gowan's here. McRae was here earlier. Took Herbie with him. Said he's real interested in havin' a long talk with you. What are you gonna do?"

"Don't know yet. Can you handle the tug if we need you?"

"No sweat. Dunc is ashore someplace so I'll let Axel play engineer. We can leave the dock on five minutes notice."

"Great. I'll call you on VHF when we're on our way."

"Channel sixteen?"

"No. Use ten. Nobody listens to that."

"You got it, skipper."

*

The houseboat was a treasure trove of incriminating evidence. A closet contained several Browning automatics, three Stirling submachine guns and half a dozen FN C-2 automatic rifles, suggesting somebody had raided a Canadian Forces base armory. Possession of the hardware alone was enough to send the four of them up for years. We found several suitcases of new clothing, all with Canadian labels. One case contained a complete document forging outfit with blank passport books, driver's licenses, birth certificate forms and an array of official stamps and seals.

"You broke in here to rescue the lady?" the sergeant asked.

"Right. Chung got two of them to come to his office to sign some papers. Jeep and I dealt with the other two."

"Dealt with, huh? Tell me about that."

I described our inglorious assault on the houseboat, leaving out the comedy. But giving Tats full credit for saving the day.

"So you subdued both of them?"

"We were lucky."

"No kidding. There's only one guy tied up here."

"Yeah, well, the other one had an accident."

"Wait a minute. You set this up with Chung Chuck? Had him decoy those people away from here?"

"It didn't go as planned. The idea was to call you as soon as Tatiana was safe. Getting them to sign papers was Chung Chuck's idea. But I guess he made the call himself."

"I see. I think. And the missing perpetrator?"

"He suffered an, ah, accident," I said. I pulled Tats close.

"You said that. What kind of accident?"

"He was trying to shoot Jeep when Tats kicked him in the nuts. From behind. He sort of went through the railing, as you can see."

"Jesus. That must have been some kick, Miss Kovacs."

"Why not? I am a dancer." She turned a radiant smile on him and demonstrated with one of her incredible leg extensions.

"Er...I see. So we've got three people, counting the two in Chung Chuck's kitchen. Did the other guy drown?"

"No. He was swimming for the islands, last time we saw him," I said.

"One handed," Jeep added, with a smirk.

"Was he armed?"

"He might have hung onto his gun. I'm not sure."

"Damn. We'll have to go and get him. Jack? Pete? Come with me. Bring the dogs. We'll take that outboard they've got tied alongside. Sutter, I want you and your people to wait here. George, you will keep them company."

*

George, our watchdog, introduced himself as Constable George Pyncher. He seemed friendly, an impression aided by his strong east London accent. "Don't look like this lot was up to any good," he said, once we were seated in the houseboat's living room. Jeep made coffee in the "galley."

"I can tell you what they were doing," Tats said. "They spoke openly in front of me – at first in German, as I explained--"

"Save it for the sergeant, Tats," I said. "You don't have to do this now. You've been through a terrible strain and--"

"No, Hank. I need you to understand. These men were helping to bring terrible people to Canada. Mass murderers. They will come by ship, to-night."

"Mass murderers? For God's sake, who?"

"Five men. They are war criminals, three from Germany, one from Latvia and one from Hungary."

"So now the police can do their job and pick them up," I said. "They'll be deported back to wherever they came from and brought before the--"

"No. I want you to stop them, Hank," she interrupted.

"My God, woman, do you realize how much trouble I'm in already? McRae is primed to throw the book at me. Jeep and Cam, too. No, Tats, it's time to let the police do their job."

"The police in your wonderful country are too careless, Hank. They did not even think Sandy was murdered, at first."

"But we found Sandy's killers and got you back. My God, what do you want of me?"

"This thing more. You must stop these men or they will disappear into this huge country. They were ready to do that." She gestured at the forgery kit.

"Why? What is it that makes these guys so important to you? Tell me that, first."

She gave me a long, inscrutable look. Then her gaze dropped and she said, "Do you love me?"

"You know I do."

"Say it."

"Tatiana Kovacs, I love you. More than anything in my life."

"If you love me, you will do this thing." We locked gazes. Dark, Magyar eyes that swallowed me up and dissolved my willpower.

Then she said, "But I will tell you why it is important to me, and to Sandy's memory. When the war came to Hungary in 1940, my parents sent Sandy and me to live with my aunt, Elena Horvath and her husband. They had an estate outside Budapest."

"But why...?"

She held up a restraining hand. "Our parents printed a newspaper for one of the socialist parties. They knew they were in danger after the Budapest government joined the war on German side. The paper was closed and presses were smashed. My parents were on a list for arrest but they hid with different friends, moving every few days.

"They came to see us when they could. Visits were always at night and mysterious. Sandy and I didn't understand what is happening -- why we had to live with the Horvaths. But we knew our parents loved us and Aunt Elena and Colonel Horvath were wonderful. They treated us like the children they never had."

Tats had begun her story sitting with me but she rose now and paced, growing more agitated. "In 1942 I began ballet lessons. The teachers said I had talent and asked my aunt to let me attend the academy's, mm, residential school. I loved dancing but hated being separated from Sandy and I saw even less of my parents. But we had short summer holidays together in 1942 and 1943."

"Is that when those, uh, pictures were taken?"

"At the nudist camp on Lake Balaton. Yes. Then in 1944, everything changed. The Horthy government, mm, collapsed? The Germans occupied our country in March of that year. The Nyilask Kereszt Part -- in English, the Arrow Cross Party -- took over. These were Hungarian fascists and they had death squads. Under German orders, they rounded up Jews, Gypsies and other `undesirables.'

"Our parents stopped visiting. In September, we learned they'd been arrested crossing to Yugoslavia. Aunt Elena asked her husband to speak for them. Colonel Horvath had been an important man in Hungary but he was retired from the army because of his health. Politics had changed. He could do nothing for them.

"Then in November, 1944, we learned that our parents were taken from prison by an Arrow Cross death squad and shot."

"Tats, that's terrible. I had no idea you'd lost your family like that, but…"

"What is my point?"

"Well…yes."

Jeep was remarkably quiet, for Jeep. Constable Pyncher stared intently, listening to Tats. Both seemed annoyed at my interruption.

"I come to that," she said. "The man in charge of the Arrow Cross killers was Lajos Kun. He ordered my parent's murders and turned down Colonel Horvath's appeal. He is one of the men coming here tonight."

"My God."

She continued. "The man with the broken leg at Mr. Chuck's house was Gestapo. So was the man you fought with, Hank. Who I kicked. He was the leader. The Gestapo men talked about what is happening in front of me. When I heard Kun's name I was so shocked I almost gave away that I knew German."

"Do you have names for the rest of these birds that are coming?" Constable Pyncher asked.

"Yes. Victor Liepa is the Latvian. The Germans are Jurgen Hauser, Dieter Shintz and Kurt Faber. Lajos Kun was responsible for ten thousand murders and shipping more than a hundred thousand Jewish Hungarians to their deaths."

"So these punks who kidnapped you are the support group for a Nazi smuggling ring? Two real Nazis and two local criminals?" Pyncher asked.

"There were three Canadians. One is missing," Tats said.

"He's in hospital," I said. Pyncher gave me a look. Then said, "Why were these people interested in you and your brother, miss?"

"Sandy discovered what they were doing. Bringing these men here from Argentina."

"Your brother was investigating? For who?"

"For his law office," she said. "His boss was doing this for Mr. Wiesenthal, the Nazi hunter. Sandy at first had only the names of two ships Mr. Wiesenthal believed they might use. Sandy found out the shipping agent."

"The late Heinrich Beyer," I said.

"Late? That word means he is dead?" Tats asked.

I nodded. "Shot dead in front of his office."

Tats shuddered and sat, silent, for a long moment. "They didn't trust Beyer. I heard them say it. My God, these are terrible people."

I said, "So Wiesenthal's people found out about this operation but didn't have anybody here of their own. They asked Jake Feldman to look into it?"

Tats nodded. "And Sandy was good, mm, investigator. They have Sandy's papers from Mr Feldman's office and they talked about what he knew."

"Excuse me, Miss. Did you say somebody called Shintz was among the men coming?" Constable Pyncher asked.

"Yes."

"SS Sturmbanfuhrer Shintz? From Saxony?"

Tats closed her eyes for a moment. "I heard them say Faber and Liepa worked at Auswich-Birkenaeu. I don't remember anything about Shintz so I don't know his rank or where he came from. Do you know about him?"

"Maybe. It could be the same guy, though I'm not sure of his first name," Pyncher said. "Do I understand these people here killed your brother?" He jerked a thumb after the departed ambulances.

"And my brother's boss. Yes."

"S'truth. Well I've a story you might be interested in. See, I was a sapper in a Royal Engineers unit attached to Eighth Division, Second Army, under Monty in Germany at the end of the war. Nothing glorious. I was a bulldozer driver. But my unit opened the camp at Bergen-Belsen, near Celle in Lower Saxony. April 15th, it was. Three weeks before the jerrys called it quits. We weren't prepared for what we found, I'll tell you. It was bloody awful."

"It was a death camp?" I asked.

"Not the usual sort. They didn't have gas and ovens. Didn't need 'em. They had typhus instead. Sixty thousand poor buggers were jammed into a place made for four thousand. Most had no roof over themselves, never mind sanitation or food. Some had been force-marched across country from other camps, ahead of the Russians. Most were living skeletons. Fifteen thousand died within a few days of us gettin' there. We had emergency rations and medicine flown in but we couldn't save 'em. Another fifteen thousand died in the next month. I know because my dozer was on the burial detail.

"Second Army didn't wait for any bloody Nuremburg trials. We held our own. Eleven of the camp brass were convicted and hanged that December. Six of the bastards that should've swung got away. Including Sturmbanfuhrer Shintz."

We were silent for a long moment, then. Tats came back to me and sat close. I put an arm around her, feeling her quivering emotional charge. "It's over, Tats," I said.

"It is *not* over," she said, bitterly.

"We can call Nunn now. He can have an RCMP cutter stop the ship and arrest them," I said.

"On what evidence?" she demanded. "My word?"

Oh Christ. She was right. Nunn couldn't stop a foreign vessel without a warrant. That meant having a judge listen to the evidence in support of the request and agreeing that "reasonable grounds" existed. It also assumed a judge could be found who would risk an international incident based solely on one person's evidence.

And cold-blooded killers, war criminals, were arriving in Canada to-night.

"You must do this for me, Hank."

Stop a ship and grab the Nazis aboard? How in bloody hell was I going to do that? I knew I should make one more plea to let the police do their jobs. And I couldn't. Not after hearing her story.

"Rescuing you was simple compared to what you're asking," I said. I guess I sounded weary.

"You are sorry you did it?"

"No, of course not. But…"

The silence between us was pregnant.

"Excuse me, Mr. Sutter," Pyncher said. "But I understand you are a tug captain? Do you have a way to stop a ship? Make it impossible for these bastards to land?"

"Christ, I don't know. Maybe." Did I have a way? It was a hell of a risk. "If I don't, we'll all be in the slammer for years, once they add up the counts against us."

"I gather you took some shortcuts in the interests of saving this young lady's life?" Pyncher said.

"We did."

Another long silence followed.

Then Pyncher said, "You know, since my experience opening that bloody butcher's nightmare of a camp, my bladder ain't been quite right. I think I need to go see a man." Pyncher rose and walked to the door. "Don't waste any sweat over the legalities," he said, and walked out.

We heard his footsteps receding up the dock.

Tats looked at me. "Well?" she said.

"I think we've just been given a ticket out of here," I said. "Let's move it."

"That means you will do it?"

"It means I'm an idiot. And hopelessly in love."

Jeep was already pulling the *Miranda* alongside at the sundeck rail. I handed Tats down to him and boarded myself.

Across the narrow gut of Ladner Reach we heard a police bull-horn, weirdly garbled in the fog. Then the barking of tracking dogs as the sergeant and his men searched through the scrub for the missing Gestapo man. Then we could hear nothing but *Miranda*'s engine.

Usually, a fog like this burned off around midday, once the sun was high, but it was early afternoon and the sun was an insipid pale patch overhead with no heat for the job. We crept out of Ladner Reach and back into the main river channel.

Tats shivered with the cold and I wrapped my parka around her, holding her tightly. "Why are we going so slowly?" she asked.

"No point in drowning ourselves now," I said. "If we hit a log or anything, we'd be in big trouble, going fast."

"How can you see where to steer?" she asked.

Jeep, at the wheel, said, "Can't. You steer by time and compass. And cross your fingers."

"You know when to turn to go into the harbor?"

"That's Hank's job. He's the skipper. But maybe this crud'll clear off before we get there. It mostly hangs around the river mouth."

"And then we can go fast?"

"That's what's bugging you? We aren't going fast enough?" I said.

"Tats, don't encourage him. He scared the b'jeezuz out of me, coming out here," Jeep said.

"But what if the police come looking for us? They have boats, too, don't they?"

"They do and they might. Then we go fast," I said. From her contented smile she seemed to be looking forward to a police chase. Or maybe my body heat was getting to her. No complaints about that, this time.

"What are you thinking?" I whispered to her. I'm not sure what I expected but she said, "Mm? About a big plate of macaroni with cheese. I'm starving."

What else! "Didn't those bastards feed you?"

"Some. The food was awful. I think I lost weight."

"We'll do something about that as soon as we get you aboard the *Solange*."

"And a shower, and some clean clothes. I thought about those, too."

That reminded me of Clara's shopping expedition for clothes. Clothes I couldn't bring with me.

We could hear the lightship's fog horn now. At a guess we were maybe two miles from it when the *Miranda* seemed to shift. "You feel somethin'?" Jeep wondered.

"Yeah, I did. Maybe something's loose in the for'd locker? Or else we ran over a piece of junk."

"I didn't see nothin'."

Tats' fingers dug into my arm like a steel claw as a shape rose in the forward cockpit ahead of us. "You will all please keep your hands in sight and no one will be hurt," Hans said. He was holding a Browning High-Power automatic on us.

C H A P T E R

21

"Scrunch down, Tats," I said. She couldn't have heard me but she read my lips and slid off the seat and onto the cockpit floor grating. Jeep, at the wheel, seemed frozen. We were rumbling along at a sedate fifteen knots, scant feet from the jagged boulders of the jetty.

"Tell the little ball kicker to sit up straight," Hans said.

"Why? What do you want with her?" I said.

"A little retribution, perhaps? I did not enjoy what she did to me. Or what the rest of you did, for that matter. But you have not ruined our operation, as you imagine," he said.

He spoke precise English, as if from a textbook, so correct that it was an accent of sorts. More important to me, he seemed to enjoy talking. He was a big man. My brief wrestling match with him on the sundeck of the houseboat left me with only a quick image of his power. I now realized he was as tall as I and at least ten pounds heavier. I thought he was in his late forties but my age advantage would be cancelled by my gunshot-lamed shoulder, still sore as hell after our earlier tussle.

"Your scheme sure looks screwed to me," I said.

"Yes. That would be the perception of an amateur, I suppose. But careful planning is the essence of any military operation. An officer must always have an alternative plan."

"You Germans are famous for good staff work." I said it with a resigned sigh. It was a poor try but he went for it.

"Ah? You are a military man? From what service?"

"Navy. This is a military operation?"

"Of course. Since you persist in persecuting the officers and leaders of the Reich, despite our surrender, we have no alternative but to continue on a wartime basis."

"So Sandy Kovacs sniffed out your operation and you threw him off the nineteenth floor of the Marine Building. That was a military operation?"

"Yes of course. Young Kovacs was too clever for his own good. But my tactical solution was also well conceived, don't you think? Fortunately the man accompanying me that night was Claus, our document expert. His suicide note provided us with time. Timing is, of course, the essence of any successful operation and ours was excellent."

Jesus. The prick was proud of himself! "But not so good tonight," I said, doing my best to make my delivery flat and unemotional. As if he'd disappointed me.

"What do you mean?" The automatic had been sagging but it twitched erect again with his question.

"Your ship isn't coming in tonight."

"Why not?"

"Look around you. This pea soup is going to last all night. Maybe for days. The River Pilot's Office will order the *Dolores Olivera* to stand off. They'll divert her to an anchorage."

"How do you know this?" For the first time he seemed uncertain. And I knew he was no seaman.

"Because that is my profession. I am a sea captain."

I caught the roll of Jeep's eye. Just sit still, Jeep, I prayed.

"Oh yes, the tugboat captain. Sutter, I believe?"

"That's right."

"You are the only person I require. These two...," he gestured at Tats and Jeep, "can be dispensed with." He cocked the automatic.

"If you kill them, I will kill you. And that will ruin your scheme, whatever it is."

"With your bare hands? I think not."

"Take a fraction of a second to steer us straight into that rock pile. Wreck the boat and drown you. It doesn't matter what you do to me, if you kill her." We locked stares. His eyes made me think of boiled grapes, not that I'd ever seen a boiled grape. I didn't blink first.

"I see. A lover's suicide pact in the old-fashioned romantic tradition," he said.

"Whatever. You will need me to find out where your ship's been sent. And then to find the ship. If you shoot Jeep or Tatiana, I promise you, you'll do neither." This was the trickiest part of my hair-brained notion. Would he buy it?

He paused, wrinkling his brow. "You can find out where the ship will be sent? How will you do this?"

"The pilot boat will be standing by in Steveston. I can call them on the VHF. The pilots will know."

"Very well. Do this, but be careful of what you say." Jeep handed me the mike and switched the set on. I prayed Cam was monitoring.

"Calling the pilot vessel *Cameron Douglas*," I said. "This is the berthing tug *Penguin*."

I heard Cam's carrier click on, and go off again. After a long silence while I held my breath it came on again and he answered, cool and professional sounding. "This is the *Cameron Douglas*. Go ahead, the *Penguin*."

God bless him! He didn't think I was making a joke. Or he was playing it straight until he figured out what in hell I was up to.

"We are standing by for the *Dolores Olivera*, off Sand Heads Lightship. Has she been delayed due to the fog? Or diverted?"

Cam's pauses were nerve-wracking. "Roger, *Penguin*. The *Dolores Olivera* is diverted to the anchorage off Spanish Banks until the visibility improves. She'll take anchorage twelve north."

"What the hell did Cam mean by that? Did he know something I needed to know? Not that I'd given him much of a clue about what I wanted to hear. And then I realized what he'd done. He'd given me some time. Clever bugger, that Cam.

"Thank you, the *Cameron Douglas*. We'll expect to see you here soon. *Penguin* over and out."

"*Cameron Douglas* is clear." But even as he said that, I heard Cam crank the *Solange's* engine room telegraph to "stand-by." Jeep had heard it, too, and he stared at me with something akin to awe. I sensed that Tats was itching to ask questions, and biting her tongue. Clammy sweat trickled down my back.

"Very well, then, Mr. Sutter. Where is this Spanish Banks?" Hans demanded.

Either he was a complete stranger to the coast, or he was trying me on. But I thought the truth could be stretched a bit without much danger. "About thirty miles that way," I gestured vaguely to the north. "There'll be a number of ships anchored there, most likely."

"You can find this anchorage place in the fog?"

"Yes." That was the biggest stretch of all.

"And we will come to this place before the *Dolores Olivera?*"

"I don't know. What time is she coming?"

"She was to have arrived off the lightship by eight this evening."

I made a show of looking at my watch. It was four-fifty P.M. and we were just about to round the lightship. Time flies when you're having fun, as Jeep would say. Spanish Banks was less than half an hour away on a direct course, even slowed down as we were. "Yes, we will be there ahead of her," I said.

"Very well, proceed to this anchorage. And I warn you, no tricks or someone will die."

"Steer two-ninety, Jeep," I said.

"Aye, two-ninety degrees," Jeep echoed back, big ship fashion. Jeep didn't blink but he caught my eye and his silent question was obvious. "Where the fuck are we goin'?"

I answered him with a shrug. He put the wheel over and Miranda banked into her turn as the lightship's foghorn belched out its oompah tune.

Keep him talking, at all costs, I thought. Maybe he'd let something slip, bragging bastard that he was. I said, "I don't see how your plan can still work. The police have got your men and your outboard. The ship will simply go up river and dock at New Westminster. Customs will go aboard and it'll be game over."

"Oh yes? I suppose it matters little what you know. We have an alternative drop point some miles up the river. We do not need the outboard, since we have your elegant runabout instead. It is true my navigator is in custody, but I have you to perform that service."

"Very clever," I said, tongue firmly in cheek. But he didn't recognize my sarcasm.

"I thought you would appreciate it," he said.

Hans faced aft, watching us, on his knees on the slippery, water-proofed, leather upholstery of the forward cockpit seat. His balance seemed uncertain and he braced himself with both hands while still managing to keep the gun aimed our way. I realized the man must be exhausted. How far had he swum to get back aboard the Miranda? I notched the throttle up to thirty knots. No use burning any more of Junior's gas than we had to.

A glassy ground swell ran under the fog, foretelling a westerly. Miranda skipped off the crests of the bigger swells, every so often, going completely airborne and landing with a smack and a cloud of spray. Great fun in bright sunny weather. Damned frightening in a fog bank. But it made our captor clutch at his handholds.

*

"Fog's lifting," Jeep said, quietly, after we'd been travelling for an hour. He nodded to the east, our starboard side. I saw the light, then. Merry Island lighthouse, not far from Sechelt and Halfmoon Bay. We were a hell of a stretch north of Spanish Banks.

Hans was taking notice, too. Staring around at the scatter of shore lights showing. Sechelt was a sizeable patch among several to the east. Vancouver Island was an equal distance to our left. Balenas Light with its ten-second flash interval and Entrance Island Light marking the approach to Nanaimo harbor were clear.

"Very well, Mr. Sutter. Exactly where is this anchorage you are taking us to?" Hans demanded.

"To which I am taking you. Never end on a preposition, Hans. It's ugly English."

"I see. You are playing games with me. I suspect we are nowhere near the Spanish Banks anchorage. Am I right?"

Jeep looked at me and mouthed "Do something."

I twitched my hand, next to Jeep's shoulder and stood. My left shoulder felt like a lump of molten lead. I said, "You get the brass spitoon, Hans. We are thirty miles away."

"But the fog is leaving, as your partner said. So I need none of you any longer." He raised the Browning.

I nudged Jeep with my knee and he twitched the steering wheel hard right, then hard left. *Miranda* swerved. Hans scrabbled to keep his aim and I tackled him, diving right over the aft cockpit windshield.

I pulled him out of the forward cockpit and we struggled across the *Miranda's* crowned engine hatch, between the two cockpits. I concentrated on his gun hand, forcing his aim high.

He fired twice. Hot ejected casings burned my cheek, then rattled on deck and over the side.

My left hand was matched to his right and my left shoulder was the one with the gunshot furrow plowed through it. It felt as if someone was driving a white hot poker through the wound with a sledge hammer.

I got my right free and hit him. I couldn't get much power into the right cross since I was sprawled across the hatch with no place to anchor my weight. But it seemed to slow him up a little and his nose streamed blood.

The bastard was powerful. And doing his damnedest to strangle me. At the same time he was trying to pistol whip me.

Jeep did creative things with the wheel, keeping him off balance. Keeping me off balance too. But I had better sea legs. I broke his choke-hold, flipped over and got a wrist lock on him. I cranked the wrist lock, hard. He heaved up in a wrestler's bridge, nearly shoving me overside. But he couldn't break my hold.

I found some purchase with my knees and smashed his gun-hand wrist across the edge of a bronze air scoop. His gun flew high over the aft cockpit windshield landing with a clatter on the floor grating of the aft cockpit. He gasped in pain, his wrist broken. But that didn't stop him.

Hans elbowed me in the solar plexus, knocking the wind out of me. Struggling for my breath, I watched as he pulled a long-bladed knife from somewhere. Some kind of commando knife with brass knuckles built into the handle. He slashed at me, left handed.

I dodged back.

His right was useless. So was my left. I pounded him with three hard rights to the head. He seemed to have a thick skull. Or his rage and adrenaline overcame any physical damage. I'd pounded his face into jelly and he still kept coming. He was covered in blood. So was I but it was mostly his blood.

We tumbled into the forward cockpit and I was forced to fend off his knife with my right, my only effective weapon.

We staggered like one-armed drunken wrestlers teetering back and forth. I held his knife at arm's length with my right, wondering if I could make my left hook work. My shoulder said no.

I swung hard, anyway, catching him a terrible blow in the ribs beneath the heart.

He gave a sobbing grunt that matched the explosion in my shoulder. My vision wobbled as I nearly passed out with the pain. Hans was in no better shape and we leaned on each other, gathering ourselves. At last I caught my breath.

He kneed me and I folded in agony.

Hans braced on his knees, straddling me, chest heaving, his face twisted, tasting his moment of triumph.

Raising his knife for a killing stroke.

In that nightmare moment I saw Tats holding the Browning, aiming two handed, her wrists braced on the windshield frame.

"No Tats! You'll hit me," I yelled. The gun barked with a thunderous crack.

Hans staggered.

I slammed his knee with both feet, dislodging him. His howl of pain ended with a burble of sea water as he went over the side.

"Stop the engine and turn her one-eighty," I shouted, gesturing a half-circle with my hand.

"What? You gonna pick that bastard up?" Jeep shouted.

"Just *do* it."

Jeep slowed *Miranda's* engine and we lurched into a wallowing turn.

"Tats, give me the gun." I crawled into the aft cockpit.

She ignored me.

Jeep grinned. "You're kinda out of shape, Hank. You need more time on the mat with me."

"Yeah? You try it with a bullet hole in your shoulder. See what great shape you're in," I said. Smart-assed cousin.

"Tats, give me the damned gun."

She passed it over, reluctantly.

I readied a life-ring and we searched the black waters of the gulf, crossing back and forth over our track and using our searchlight. Jeep was upset that I didn't intend to leave the guy. But it didn't matter. We couldn't find him. After searching for half an hour I threw the life ring in, watching its beacon light bob in the swell. If he was out there, he might see that. It was a small sop to my conscience.

At last I said, "How much time since we talked to Cam?"

"Hour an' thirty minutes," Jeep said.

"He'll have the *Solange* out around Spanish Banks and be wondering what the hell happened to us. Let's not keep him waiting."

I switched on the VHF. "*Miranda* calling the *Solange Picard*," I said.

"Go ahead, the *Penguin*," Cam's voice said.

"Yeah, Cam. She's here and so is Jeep. I gather you are looking for us."

"You gather right, Hank. We're just off the can buoy."

"Head south to the lightship. We should meet you a few
miles south of the North Arm jetty so keep a sharp eye out for us."

"Roger that. Not every day a steam engineer gets to play captain but will you please tell me what in hell was all that with the phony call signs? And when did berthing tugs start meeting ships out at the Sand Heads Lightship?"

"Never did, far as I know. I'll explain the rest later. You have any trouble getting away from the dock?"

"No…but we do have a problem. Corporal Nunn is aboard."

"Say again? I think I misheard that."

"Jimmy's got him locked in the mess room. I figured you'd want to deal with him yourself."

"Thanks a lot, Cam."

"See you soon. *Solange Picard* clear."

Sure. He'd see me on visiting days at the B.C. Pen. At this rate I was going to spend the rest of my life behind bars.

I slumped into the aft cockpit seat again, beside Tats.

"You scared the hell out of me with that gun," I said.

It was the wrong thing to say. She pushed away from me when I tried to gather her in a hug.

"That was frightening," she said. From the quiver in her voice, I realized she was crying.

"Hey. No need for tears. We won. We're all safe."

"You didn't think I was competent to shoot -- and he nearly killed you."

"You're a good pistol shot?"

"Good enough. I tried to hit his shoulder on the side he held his knife. To just knock him down. But a Browning is a man's gun. The butt is too big and awkward for me."

"...You know guns?" I was jaw-dropped and staring.

Jeep said, "I was busy steering back and forth tryin' to keep him off balance and I couldn't let go of the wheel to grab the gun. So Tats got it. I sure as hell didn't think she could ventilate the bastard like that."

"Well I'll be damned," I said

Tats let me gather her then. "I think I killed him," she said, voice quivering, staring at me with tear-filled eyes. "But if I didn't shoot..."

"I'd be dead. So thank you, my love."

"Yes," she said. Then after a pause, "We owe each other."

Jeep put the engine in gear and pushed the throttle forward all the way, putting an end to our conversation.

I held Tats close, wondering where in hell a Hungarian ballerina would get to know a large military pistol by its first name.

CHAPTER

22

expected some kind of explosion from Corporal Nunn but it didn't happen. He remained seated, calmly ignoring me as I entered the mess room.

Jimmy Lee locked the door behind me. I might have been entering the cage of some ferocious beast that had, unaccountably, fallen asleep. My bloody appearance upset his act.

He put his newspaper aside. "The hell happened to you? Looks like you been dragged through the mill, ass backwards," Nunn said.

"Nice to know you care. Had a little altercation with the leader of the killers."

"Yeah? What's he look like?"

"Don't know. We lost him."

He stared hard at me, as if his prolonged glare might elicit an explanation. When it didn't he shrugged and picked up his newspaper again.

Nunn had removed his perennial sports jacket and tie and folded them neatly on the seat cushion beside him. The first thing to meet my eye was his long-barreled service pistol in an upside-down, tooled leather shoulder holster. I suspected displaying that had been his intention. He'd also rolled up his sleeves, showing off his brawny forearms. Jimmy Lee had provided a large insulated coffee urn and a selection of reading material.

He sipped his coffee and gave me the Really-Seriously-Pissed-Off-Cop stare. "You know how long I've been stuck here?"

"No."

"Well, never mind that. You'll do a little stir time of your own, soon enough. You know what you got hanging over your head?" His eyes were pale blue, and chilling.

"Charges, I assume."

He snorted. "Charges! This screw-up has gone all the way to Ottawa. I just got a rocket from the Commissioner about you and your shenanigans."

"At least he knows your name, then."

"Don't get fucking smart with me, Sutter. You are in deep shit."

"Why was Ottawa interested?"

"Your little chum, Picard, is a political animal. I guess you knew that?"

"Yes."

"Well Henri A. Picard, Junior, has aspirations for a post with the current crop of Diefenbaker Conservatives running this godforsaken country. And guess what? He's on the short list for an appointment. They listen to him."

"So you got a what? A letter? A cable?"

"Telex. I'm ordered to pick you up in no uncertain terms. They are well aware that we know each other since you've turned up in my reports. You've cooked your goose properly, this time. You got any idea what Picard's fancy goddamned speedboat is worth?"

"Something less than my girl's life," I said.

He grunted. Touché.

"What time did they send the Telex?"

"That's police business."

"Could be critical. What time?"

He stared hard at me, then shrugged. "Two P.M. local time. Close of their business day in Ottawa. Why critical?"

"Did you answer?"

"How the hell could I answer? I came aboard this bucket looking for you right after I got it and that crazy Chinese cook--"

"Canadian. Jimmy is Canadian, not Chinese."

"Yeah? Whatever, then. He was real polite. Sat me down and got me coffee and sandwiches and allowed as how you should be along real soon. And then he locked the bloody door. Next thing I know, the boat is leaving the dock. Fortunately for him, it's a steel door. I've been stuck aboard this rust bucket since two-thirty this afternoon. And that's one more reason my goose is on the fucking barbecue, right beside yours."

Nunn was a complete landlubber, obviously. With any sea experience he'd have known there have to be two or more ways out of any crew space aboard a ship. In the case of our mess room, there are six. A door to the galley. Locked. And one to the inside wheelhouse companionway. Also locked. The four other ways out are two-foot diameter portlights (with inch-thick glass) in hinged bronze frames that open inwards with only a wing-nut to lock them. Nunn could have crawled out through any of them. It seemed like a shame to tell him that now.

"Good," I said.

Nunn flushed. "Good, huh? Know how I've been spending my time?" His voice rising. "Thinking up every possible charge I could hang around your neck. So far, I'm up to fifty-three and counting."

"I meant good that you didn't answer. I've got a proposition to offer you. If it works, you come out of it a hero."

Nunn slumped, his fire spent, or re-charging. "The fuck you mean, hero?" he growled.

"You know we saved Tatiana Kovacs and got the people who murdered her brother and Jake Feldman today?"

"McRae said something about it. Four guys. Delta Police holding 'em?"

"Five guys. Including the joker McRae's got in the secure ward at Vancouver General. We lost one--"

"What happened to him?" he interrupted.

"After he got kicked in the nuts, which caused him to go for a swim off the houseboat;s sun deck, we thought he'd made it across the channel to some little mud-pie islands --"

"Who kicked him in the nuts?"

"Tatiana."

"Figures. Tough little bird."

He had no idea. "Anyway, he doubled back and sneaked aboard the Miranda. When Jeep and Tats and I left to bring the boat back to town, he crawled out of a locker and held us at gunpoint. We had a little tussle and he went over the side. We couldn't find him."

"Jesus. Add manslaughter to those charges."

"Did McRae tell you the two guys running this caper were ex-Gestapo?"

"No." That gave him pause. His expression changed from contemptuous and sneering to close attention. His eyes were appraising, suddenly.

"Go on." Nunn said, tersely. McRae had said Nunn was a vet. His reaction seemed to confirm that.

I told him the story, from the point when we'd stolen the Miranda, leaving nothing out.

At the end of it he stared at me for a long moment. "Jesus. She heard all that?"

"They spoke in German and they didn't realize Tats is fluent in that language."

"But why did they go after her brother? And Feldman?"

"Feldman was Nazi-hunting for Wiesenthal's organization. Sandy was doing the leg work and he got too close. Spooked Heinrich Beyer, their shipping company connection, and Beyer reported to the boss in Ladner."

"You got a name for this boss?"

"Hans something. Tats probably knows. He was the guy who drowned."

"Went over the side in your wrestling match?"

"Right. Anyway, their operation was at the stage where it couldn't be stopped and they couldn't risk blowing it. So they murdered Sandy. Then they realized there was a paper trail to Sandy's investigation. So they forced Feldman to open his document safe, cleaned it out, and shot him.

"They made a try for Irene Bradshaw, Feldman's secretary. That didn't work out too well when their hit man had an accident with a coal truck and hospitalized himself."

Nunn snorted. "I heard about that," he said, with a trace of a grin.

"But the punk had already shot Beyer that morning. They'd decided Beyer was unreliable. Scared of his own shadow."

"Jesus." Nunn said. "Here I was looking at the next war and the Reds and all the time the last war was still going on all around us,"

"You could say that."

"So that's why Kovacs was snooping around shipping companies and longshore union halls? Looking for the route?"

"And he found it," I said. "Beyer and Son have two modern freezer ships running out of South America under charter. One of them, the *Dolores Olivera*, arrives here around eight this evening."

"That's less than an hour from now. Too late to get a warrant to stop the ship."

"Right."

Nunn stared off into space for a long moment. McRae was right about him. Obnoxious, maybe, but not dumb. "And this is why you've hijacked the tug? You've got some scheme up your sleeve?"

"Hijacked is rather strong language, corporal. I am the master of this ship. If I judge it necessary, I can take the vessel to sea at any time. Legally. Junior Picard may own the *Solange Picard*, and he can fire me if he doesn't like what I do, but he does not run this ship."

"Splitting hairs, aren't you? I think you've already been fired. You and half the crew. But I haven't been officially notified of that. So what is your scheme?"

"The *Dolores Olivera* will be under an outside pilot from Brotchie Ledge, off Victoria, inbound. She'll pick up a river pilot off the Sand Heads Lightship at about eight P.M. and proceed up river to New Westminster."

"Two pilots?"

"If you want to dock in New Westminster. River pilotage is a specialty."

"You know the time they're coming? How?"

"Tats heard them discussing the time. The guy I tangled with told us the same thing."

"This ship is considerably bigger than your tug. Right?"

"Ten thousand tons to our sixteen hundred. I looked her up. The *Olivera* has a pair of 4,000 horsepower Sulzer diesels. So for power, we're not so much of a missmatch."

"Everybody needs a pilot in the river? What about you?"

"Doesn't apply to local shipping. In fact most of the pilots on the coast are ex-towboat skippers."

"So what's the drill?"

"They'll stop to pick up the pilot within a mile of the lightship. The channel is bouyed and tricky. They'll run at maybe half speed and they'll choose a time near high water to give them good depth in the channel. High water is at 8:46 P.M."

"They're going to put these Nazis ashore in New West?"

"No. They can't risk a customs inspection. But the passage through the Gulf Islands and up river is like a sieve when it comes to landing people or stuff. It's simply impossible to watch a ship, all the way in from Juan de Fuca Strait."

"Tell me about it. So where do you figure?"

"That's the part we can't be sure of. If I were doing it, I'd drop them right after we picked up the pilot and before the ship was moving at any serious speed. That would explain the location of their safe house, too."

"How would they do it? How many guys are they bringing in?"

"Five. A fair sized outboard would do just fine."

"There's more to this than what you've told me so far. Spit it out, Sutter."

A tap on the door interrupted us and Jeep poked his head in. He seemed disappointed to find no blood on the deck. "Cam wants somebody to take over the wheel. He wants to be in the engine room when things start happening."

"It's Dunc's watch, isn't it?" The chief engineer and the skipper usually work the six-to-twelve watch.

"Cam says Dunc's a case of nerves. Gettin' old, I guess."

"More likely he's got some Picard shares. Where are we?"

"Couple of miles past the North Arm Jetty."

"Take it for now, Jeep. We'll be up to the wheelhouse in a few minutes. Oh, by the way, you're officially mate. Gus will have to give up his day-man job and take a watch as straight deckie."

"Gotcha, skipper. Uh, we?" he gestured at Nunn and I.

I nodded in answer. Jeep's forehead, when he's puzzled, looks like a plowed field.

"How's Tats doing?"

"Eaten two triple-decker sandwiches an' used all the hot water on the ship. Now she's in your room doin' something creative with the stuff in your closet." He grinned and moved to close the mess room door again.

"Leave that, Jeep," I said.

Nunn gave me a nod of acknowledgement. "Now tell me how in hell you plan to stop these buggers," he said.

"Well, it's like this, corporal. It seems you were investigating the same things Sandor Kovacs was. You might even make a case that Sandy was an informant. And in pursuit of your investigation you commandeered the *Solange Picard*--"

"I what!?" he bellowed, half rising in his seat.

I said. "Let's say this is the river channel." I made a channel out of Jimmy Lee's cutlery. "And this is the Dolores Olivera, going up river." I plunked down a mahogany cruet holder. "And this is us, following them in the channel." A capsized salt shaker represented the *Solange*. "Clear, so far?"

"Yeah? So what?"

"So what if we did this?" I moved the salt shaker.

Nunn's eyes widened. "Shit! You could actually do that?"

"You bet."

"What would happen?"

"This," I said, moving my pieces again.

Nunn stared at the crude table-top model for a long time. "And high water is at 8:46 P.M.?"

"Now you're thinking, corporal."

His face was not quite impassive. His eyes gave him away. Thoughtful. I guess the plan didn't look improbable to a non-sailor. I, on the other hand, was only too aware of the million ways it could blow up in all our faces.

I waited for his reaction. When it seemed to be stalled I said, "You could make sergeant for this. Maybe get back to Ottawa and B section." God help me, I should have been a used car salesman.

He digested my pitch for a long moment. "And if it goes wrong?"

"You win either way. Just lock us all up and leave it to the courts."

"Not that simple, as you well know," he said.

He was right. He could still come out looking like an asshole, considering that he'd allowed himself to be hijacked along with the tug. And especially after some judge listened to Tatiana's story. Not to mention the stories of Chung Chuck and the rest of the people involved. I was willing to put money on it that fifty of Nunn's fifty-three charges were for crimes against property. Those don't hold up too well when lives are in the balance.

But the possibility of him scoring a major success from his position here, exiled in the boondocks -- maybe making sergeant in the notoriously promotion-stingy force -- seemed to sway him.

He took a deep breath and said, "One thing you'd better know. Picard has got some toady in Immigration looking at Tatiana Kovacs' landed immigrant status."

"For Christ's sake, why?"

"Association with criminal elements. Way I get it, they could deport her."

"Over my dead body," I said.

"Yeah. Exactly." He paused, locking stares with me. "All right, Sutter. I'll go along with this. But it bloody well better work or you and your lady friend are history."

Yes. It had better work. Nunn's one-upmanship was getting on my nerves.

The squawk-box on the bulkhead squealed and Jeep's voice said, "Need you topside, skipper. Like now."

*

Tooey was on the wheel and Jeep was hanging out the open port-side wheelhouse window, looking just like a towboat mate, as Nunn and I entered. "Got her on the radar," Jeep said. "She's about five miles south of the lightship. And we are five miles north of it."

"Did you plot her?"

"Yeah. Bugger's doing eighteen knots. Got a little speed edge on us."

"Only two knots. He's got to stop to pick up his pilot. You see the pilot boat yet?"

"Nope. Most likely masked by the jetty."

"Could be. I don't want to be into the channel ahead of the ship. And kill the navigation lights. We don't need to advertise."

"The hell you plannin' to do?" Jeep wondered.

"All in good time, Jeep. Where's Tats?"

"I am right here," she said from behind me. "I was outside, looking at things." She gestured towards the port bridge wing. Her wrap-around plaid skirt had survived but not the black leotards. The rest of her outlandish outfit had been pirated from my closet including a drastically modified white dress shirt that would never be the same again. My Cowichan Indian sweater, which she wore like a cape with the sleeves tied across her chest, dragged on the deck.

"What things?" It was pitch dark and a fine mist of rain had replaced the fog.

Junior's *Miranda* surged back and forth in our wake. She didn't tow well on a short line at this speed but I hadn't wanted to just cut her loose and let her drift.

"There is a boat following us," Tats said.

I stepped to the outer rail of the bridge and stared aft. I couldn't see a thing. "Show me," I said. She tucked herself under my arm and pointed.

At last I saw the faint phosphorous white of somebody's bow wave. They were about a mile astern and keeping pace with us. I switched on the big carbon-arc bridge searchlight and swung it around. And found varnished woodwork and a gleaming black hull. A Scott Payne pattern RCAF crash boat -- ex-crash boat -- acquired from war surplus by the Vancouver Harbor Police.

The police responded with their own light. The fine rain made the searchlight beams look like dueling light swords.

I led Tats to the door to go inside but she tugged at my elbow, holding me back. "They will put you in jail for taking the *Miranda*?"

"We can't worry about that now."

"How did you charm that awful secret policeman? I was sure he would be furious after being locked up for so long."

"He is furious. But that won't do him any good and he knows it. If he goes along with me, he stands a chance of looking good in the end."

"And you have a plan?"

I nodded. My God. Tats had no idea what we were attempting. I was about to launch into an explanation when she said, "Ah! My monster is a chess player?"

"Not a good one. Why?"

"I will teach. You will be grand master in no time."

"That was a compliment?"

She kissed me. And I forgot about explaining.

As we stepped back into the wheelhouse, I said, "Okay, my love. When things start happening, I want you here in the wheelhouse. And if I tell you to scrunch down, that means flat on the deck. Okay?"

"Yes sir! captain sir!"

"Don't get all smart-assed on me, Tats. This could be dangerous."

"Mmm? It will be exciting?"

"I hope not. Jeep, don't you have a hunting rifle aboard?"

"Yeah. Thirty-ought-six Winchester with a four power scope."

"Anybody else got anything?"

"Cam's got a shotgun, I think. Tooey? You still got your thirty-thirty?" Jeep asked.

"Yup," Tooey said.

"No handguns," Jeep added. "The Delta cops got your magnum." He lowered his voice, casting a wary eye in Nunn's direction. "But there's the canon that gestapo guy dropped."

Nunn didn't seem to notice.

"Collect everything aboard that will shoot and all the shells anybody has. Okay?"

"Gotcha." He vanished down the companionway.

"You planning on a fire fight with these guys?" Nunn asked.

"God no. But we might need to encourage them to keep their heads down if they do shoot at us."

"Looks like they're slowing now," Tooey said.

He was right. The *Dolores Olivera* was visible as a gray smudge in the deep black around her. Red and green navigation lights, and a masthead light, were visible -- meaning she was steering straight for us. That wouldn't last for long. They'd have us on their radar, if they bothered to look. Maybe they'd be too preoccupied. Jeep arrived again with an armload of weaponry, stacking three rifles and a shotgun in a corner.

"Rig the steam hose, Jeep."

"What? You gonna steam-clean the bastards?"

"Could be useful." I nodded in the direction of the following police launch. Sometimes Jeep was quick on the uptake. Sometimes. "Right," he said, after too long a silence, "Guess we got a little grease on deck, back aft." He left again.

"Okay, Tooey, relax and get yourself a coffee. I'll take her from here," I said.

We were less than a mile from the *Dolores Olivera* and the lightship now. I rang up "stand-by" and, when I got the answer on the indicator, "slow ahead." The *Solange* slowed her bustling progress and eased forward in near silence. Ahead I could hear the grumble of the pilot boat's engine as the pilot boarded the slowly drifting ship. I put the wheel over and circled behind the *Dolores Olivera*, into the shadow she made from the lightship's flashing beacon.

The pilot launch pulled away.

Jeep was back, giving me a thumbs up sign. "Done," he said. Then, "Hey. They ain't pullin' the ladder."

The vertical rope ladder with wooden steps was rigged over the ship's side, fifty feet forward of the stern. A floodlight rigged high on a cargo derrick had illuminated it while the pilot was boarding. The floodlight went out but as we swung in behind the ship on her starboard side, I could see the ladder still in place. Unusual. Normally a crew would lift that ladder, the moment the pilot stepped on deck.

Unless it would be used for something else.

The ladder was well aft of the usual midships location.

Then it hit me why they'd placed it there. It was just past the start of the aft curve of the hull which put it out of sight from the bridge and the two pilots aboard.

The *Dolores Olivera* slowly gathered way in the channel. Her deck lights flashed on, suddenly, illuminating a high, white, midships deckhouse. A loudhailer sounded from her bridge. "*Vessel astern of me, keep clear. You are interfering with my navigation.*" The deck lights went out.

Nearly simultaneously, another bull-horn sounded off astern of us. "*Solange Picard, this is the Vancouver Police boat. Heave to and stand by for boarding. Your ship is under arrest.*"

23

I said, "Goddamn! Everybody wants in on the act. I don't have time for bullshit on bullhorns." Holding position in the wake of the *Dolores Olivera* was giving me a workout on the wheel.

"Hadn't we better say something?" Nunn wondered.

"Okay corporal. You get on the blower and tell them to back off. This is a government operation."

"Jesus, Sutter. I can't do that!"

"Sure you can. Here." I handed him the loudhailer microphone. "You push the button to talk."

Nunn sweated out his decision. At last he raised the mike. "This is Corporal Nunn of the RCMP speaking. Stand clear of this vessel or I will not be responsible for damage or injury to you or your vessel. This is a federal security operation."

The police boat seemed to check. Then Junior Picard's voice boomed out. *"Sutter, this is theft. And I don't believe that was Corporal Nunn speaking. He told me he intended to arrest you. We are boarding you now."*

Nunn said, "See what you mean. The guy's an idiot." Then on the loudhailer, *"Board at your own risk, Mr. Picard."*

"You want me to steam the sucker?"

"Better not, Jeep. We might drown him."

"A guy could hope. Here they come," Jeep said.

The police launch nosed up to the Solange's starboard side aft, where she was relatively low in the water, and away from the *Dolores Olivera*. I had the *Solange's* bow almost abreast of the boarding ladder. "Jeep, go aft and warn them we are turning hard to port. Right now."

Jeep trotted down the boat deck aft of the wheelhouse and I heard an exchange of shouts. I didn't have time to see what was happening back where Picard was trying to play Bluebeard, the pirate boarder. The *Dolores Olivera* was making about nine knots and gathering speed.

I matched our speed with hers, having Cam increase revs a few at a time, talking to him on the squawk box. I could see several heads above the *Olivera's* bridge rail, watching us. A searchlight came on. A big carbon arc, trying to blind us. Several more heads were gathered at the top of the boarding ladder.

"Turning now!" I shouted and put the wheel hard over.

The *Solange's* massive rubber bow bumpers smacked into the side of the *Dolores Olivera* with a sound like a semi with all eighteen wheels locked. I rang the telegraph to full ahead, three times, quickly. Telling Cam to goose it.

The surge of power was incredible. I knew Cam had screwed down the safety valve stops for this but I'd never felt anything like it from the tug. I couldn't imagine what her boiler pressure must be. But something over six thousand shaft horsepower shoved the stern of the *Dolores Olivera* sideways with the thrust of our two twelve-foot diameter, four-bladed screws mounted in *Kort* nozzles.

Within minutes, the *Olivera* was at a sharp angle to the run of the channel.

Her skipper tried frantically to counter with his rudder. Then reversed his engines, boiling up brown river-bottom mud in a huge, evil-smelling whirlpool. But the *Dolores Olivera* was a motor ship. That whirlpool would do little more than fill his engine cooling water intakes with mud. The ship had the momentum of ten thousand tons in motion at ten knots and no way she could stop or correct her course in time to save herself.

Just under a hundred yards south of the center of the main channel, she grounded, driving solidly into a bed of river-bottom mud.

I looked at the wheelhouse chronometer. It was eight fifty P.M. Four minutes into the ebb tide. The *Dolores Olivera* wasn't going anywhere for an absolute minimum of twelve hours. And maybe not even then, without a dredge and a tug something like our size to pull her free.

The engine room squawk box buzzed. "Yeah, Cam," I said.

"Can you get us the hell out of here?" he said. "I'm silting up my condenser sea water intakes like crazy."

"Okay, Cam. He's hard aground now. You can back off to revs for dead slow. Will that help?"

"Long as it's not for too long."

"Jeep, what's happening with Junior?"

"Him an' one cop made it over the rail. They're standin' by the towin' winch, scratchin' their butts and trying to figure out what to do next. The police boat is hangin' off astern with the other cop."

"Yeah, that's the big question. What happens next."

"You ain't plannin' to board that sucker?" Jeep asked, nodding towards the ship.

"Be asking for trouble. We don't know if the crew is involved, or just the officers, or what. They could be armed." I turned to Nunn. "Could you call in a cutter?"

"No. Be the same problem we talked about before. They'd want a warrant."

"Unless they shoot at us," I said.

"That'd be probable cause in spades," he agreed.

I stared at our prize. Four hundred feet of steel ship with maybe twenty feet of freeboard at her lowest point. And getting higher out of the water by the minute as the tide dropped. Except that she was hard aground forward but not aft. Her stern was settling as the tide dropped, while the bow rose. If her crew had opened her hatches, as they normally would to prepare for cargo handling, the *Dolores Olivera* could sink right here in the channel. If she put her stern under. More damned complications than I could keep track of.

Then I had an idea. "Cam, give me steam on the anchor winch."

"You got it, skipper." He came back on the squawk box. Moments later, a wisp of steam vapor hissed from the winch's mechanism.

"You gonna drop the hook?" Jeep asked, surprised.

"I just want the option," I said. "We might have to stay here a while and Cam says he's silting up his intakes. Go down and heave her up a notch, so the claw is loose."

"Right." Jeep trotted down the steep for'd companionway, not even holding onto the handrails. He crossed the hatch cover and the narrow patch of deck between the hatch coaming and the massive anchor winch. He cracked steam to the hoisting engine. Then banged at the devil's claw with the bar we used for that. But he didn't remove the claw. "She's hangin' on the brake, skipper," he shouted. I gestured him back to the wheelhouse.

"Corporal, you want to get on the hailer and order them to offload those five guys? Tell 'em the alternative is to have their ship arrested and impounded."

"Dicey legal position," Nunn said.

"What else is new?"

He took the hailer microphone from me. "*Motor vessel Dolores Olivera, this is the Royal Canadian Mounted Police. You are ordered to deliver five men aboard your vessel to our custody aboard this ship.*" He turned to me. "Quick, what are the names?"

Tats said, "Give me the microphone."

Nunn handed it over like a hot potato. She said "*The names are Lajos Kun, Victor Liepa, Jurgen Hauser, Dieter Shintz and Kurt Faber.*" She handed it back to Nunn.

An argument broke out on deck, near the top of the boarding ladder, and another on the bridge of the *Dolores Olivera*.

After several long moments, their loudhailer came on again. "*This is the captain espeaking. I have no persons of such names aboard. I do not unnerstan' you are doing. You have put my ship agroun' in a dangerous position.*"

I grabbed the microphone. "*You understand your ship is impounded? You are under arrest? We can explain in any language you like. Comprende usted detencion, senor capitan?*" After a pause, he said, "*Si. Es muy claro. Momento, por favor.*" He sounded miserable.

The row on the bridge of the *Olivera* got louder then, with much machine-gun Spanish and arm-waving. Then somebody descended from the bridge and walked aft to the group at the ladder. The discussion there was quiet.

"Jeep?"

"Uh?"

"Could you take out that damned searchlight? If anybody is using a searchlight I'd just as soon it was us."

"Piece of cake," he said.

"Okay, get up on top of the wheelhouse and get a bead on the thing. So you can hit it if I holler. You can cover us if there's any shooting from the ship."

"You got it, skipper."

The ship's loudhailer clicked on again. "We will comply with your request, officer." The captain's Spanish accent was miraculously improved.

"Request, my ass," Nunn said.

A man climbed over the Olivera's rail and started down the rope pilot's ladder, a seaman's duffle bag slung across his shoulders. A second man started down at once. All five men were on the ladder before the first reached our bow.

Nunn went forward, pistol in hand, to meet them.

The five scrambled across our bow fenders. One man moved with the uncertainty of age and two of the others helped him aboard the tug.

Then I saw a gleam of dark metal. "Nunn! Look out!" I yelled. "Jeep! Shoot the light."

Jeep's hunting rifle barked and the searchlight flared and went out.

Then I saw Junior. He was on the for'd companionway to the bridge, looking around in surprise. At the same moment, a burst of fire from a burp gun rattled off the metal shell of the starboard bridge wing, just over his head.

"Oh God!" Junior cried out. He was frozen on the steps, halfway up.

I dove out of the wheelhouse side door and ran in a stoop for the head of the companionway. Junior's eyes were the size of saucers and he stared in panic, not recognizing me.

Another burst of fire took out four of the wheelhouse windows, which were half-inch armored glass.

I grabbed Junior by his shirt-front and heaved.

No use. His grip was frozen to the handrail. "Let go of the goddamned rails, Junior," I yelled.

"Oh God, oh God," he said, clutching the rails like some giant leech.

I leaned out to him and gave him a good smack across the face. That seemed to break his funk and I managed to dislodge him and drag him onto the deck beside me.

I heard Jeep dropping from the top of the wheelhouse to the bridge wing. Suddenly our port-side searchlight came to life as he trained it on our bow.

Our oversized anchor winch handled anchors not just for the tug but of a size to hold any ship we might be towing. The mechanism completely filled the deck forward of our salvage gear hatch. The five men who'd boarded us hid beyond the winch. I couldn't see Nunn.

Somebody on our side was firing at them from the main deck under the starboard bridge wing. The Vancouver Police Boat cop.

A burst of fire ricocheted between the steel deckhouse and the bulwark, striking a shower of sparks. A faint cry sounded from where the cop had been firing.

One of the men ahead of the winch shouted. "Tug boat captain. Back your vessel away from the ship and turn into the river channel. We are taking over your ship."

"The fuck you gonna do, Hank?" Jeep asked. "Looks like four of 'em got those grease guns."

"Don't know. How much reach you got on the steam hose?"

"Plenty. Where d'ya want it?"

"Right up for'd here. Can you do that quickly?"

"Watch me." He vanished aft along the boat deck behind the wheelhouse, shouting for Gus and Axel.

A head popped up beyond the winch and somebody fired at it from the wheelhouse. Tooey, I thought. That drew a fusillade of return fire, taking out the rest of the wheelhouse glass and punching large dings in the thin upper deckhouse plating. I dragged a limp Junior behind me and crawled back to the port-side wheelhouse door, propping him up so I could trundle him into the wheelhouse without standing up. "Stay flat on the floor," I said.

"Yes, yes. Oh God, oh God."

"Tats! What the hell are you doing?" She was at one of the glassless windows.

"Shooting. What do you think?"

"Give me the damned gun and get down. You think I went through all this to have you killed now?"

"What? I am prize livestock?"

"I just don't want you dead livestock."

She handed over the Browning. The gun was hot. "I hit one of them," she said.

"You sure?"

"Of course I am sure. He is going nowhere. There are maybe five rounds left in the magazine."

"Okay. Stay on the deck. This is going to get nasty."

"That wasn't nasty?"

"Holy Mary, mother of God, have mercy and protect us," Junior babbled. My sentiments exactly. Junior didn't seem to remember his rosary too well but I didn't think God would mind.

A deafening clatter of gunfire and ricochets spanged off the plating and made us all duck. "Tug boat captain. You will come down on deck. We will take over the ship. If you do not, we will shoot your police officer."

Shit. They had Nunn. "Give me something white," I said. Tats squirmed and ripped something beneath the Cowichan sweater-cum-cape. I caught a flash of breast as she handed me what remained of my best white dress shirt.

The squawk box from the mess room buzzed and Jeep's voice said, "Ready on deck, Hank." He didn't expect an answer.

I stood and waved the white rag from one of the broken wheelhouse windows. I shouted down to the Nazis, "You will have to come to the wheelhouse. If I leave the wheel and come to the for'd deck we will go aground."

"Very well. Throw your weapons down."

"Give 'em the shotgun and the rifle, Tats." I rang up "stop" on the telegraph and the *Solange* drifted away from the *Dolores Olivera*, carried slowly downstream by the river current.

Tats threw out Tooey's Winchester carbine and an ancient single-shot twenty two. She clutched the shotgun to her chest, refusing to part with it.

No time to argue with her. Two of the bastards were heading for the companionway. Each cradled an Uzi.

Where the hell were Jeep and Axel?

The first of the Nazis was at the top of the stair and his partner was just starting onto it. Too late, the climbers realized their mistake in not covering each other. The steam hose made a hellish roar but it didn't drown out the shrieks of the singed Nazis. They collapsed onto the for'd deck, writhing in pain.

Jeep and Axel maneuvered their steam hose from behind a slab of steel plate that I recognized as deck plating from the engine room. They'd converged on the companionway, right beneath the two men climbing the stair.

Jeep stepped over the pair, kicking their weapons away, and turned his hose on the men using the winch as cover. There should have been three men sheltering forward of the winch but only one was firing. The guy was an expert with the Uzi. He fired tight five-round bursts, rattling them off Jeep's piece of deck plate with sparks enough for a fireworks show. Jeep couldn't get close enough for a direct shot at him with live steam but he could do something about his shooting.

The whole fore deck vanished in a steam cloud. The machine gunner stopped shooting, unwilling to waste ammunition with no targets in sight. An Uzi can blow away a thirty-round magazine in a single burst. How much ammo could they have? I didn't have time to think about the irony of Nazi war criminals packing Israeli-made weapons. I slid down the companionway, heading for the winch controls. "Keep smokin' 'em, Jeep," I yelled.

"You got it!" He shouted.

I slid on my belly through the dank fog of condensing steam towards the gunman, keeping the hatch coaming between myself and him. But at the end of my crawl only a corner of the winch was between us. I felt for the brake wheel.

Got it.

The tricky part was next. I had to crawl beneath the drum and chain sprocket to reach the claw. If Jeep's steam blew away I'd be lying helpless at the gunman's feet.

The claw was hinged above the chain. I reached to lift it clear -- carefully, silently, I hoped. But the men huddled ahead of the winch were excited and shouting to each other. With any luck, they wouldn't hear me. And Jeep was letting off noisy bursts of steam. Now!

The claw jammed! I hammered at it with my fist, timing my efforts to match Jeep's bursts of steam, numb to the bruising cuts to my knuckles.

The claw fell clear with a clatter.

I skidded backwards, fast. And fifteen hundred pounds of navy-pattern anchor hung free in the hawse pipe, held only by the brake.

My steam screen faded. From my prone vantage point, suddenly the knees and boots of the gunman were less than five feet from me.

The man doing the shooting straddled the anchor chain where it led down into the hawse pipe. He swiveled like a rattler, looking for prey, bracing the Uzi on the chain sprocket.

I prayed he wouldn't look down.

Nunn was against the rail, face down on deck. The guy Tats had hit lay in a pool of blood on the port side, with an older man who didn't seem to be armed.

I grabbed the brake wheel and wrenched it free.

A sudden growl of heavy chain, links as big as a man's head, started slowly. Then the anchor fell in a rush.

The gunman howled. His weapon clattered to the deck. Nunn shouted, "Stop the chain! You're making mince meat out of him!"

I cranked the brake on but it wasn't necessary. We were in shallow water and the anchor had already bottomed. The chain stopped of its own accord. Not soon enough for the gunman, humped over, clutching at his groin.

The steam cleared. Nunn collected two Uzis and his own revolver, gesturing the surviving Nazis to move aft. But the man Tats had hit was bleeding profusely and I bent over him, using my white flag shirt to make a crude compression bandage.

And Tatiana was there beside me, holding the muzzle of Cam's Remington Bushmaster twelve gauge against the forehead of the older man cowering against the bulwark. The man who had to be Lajos Kun. They exchanged rapid-fire Hungarian and I didn't need to be a linguist to read the fury she hurled at him.

"Tats! You can't shoot him--" I yelled.

"Yes I can," she said. Not looking at me. She braced and snugged the shotgun's butt tight to her shoulder.

Jesus! I lunged and slapped the gun's barrel aside as the shot blasted the night. Pellets ricochetted around the for'd bulwark, missing Lajos Kun by a fraction of an inch. His right ear and cheek were blackened, powder-burned.

"Sutter! Take that Goddamned gun away from her before she kills somebody," Nunn yelled from across the ship.

"An accident," I said, waving the gun above my head to show Nunn I was in control of things.

Tatiana uncoiled like a steel spring, falling on the terrified Kun, tearing at him, screaming and sobbing and swearing in Hungarian by turns.

Lajos Kun pissed himself.

She was a wildcat running on adrenaline with strength no woman could possibly have. I picked her up bodily. It was like grabbing a bundle of animated razor wire.

I sat her on the hatch cover twenty feet from Kun. "Calm down, God-dammit! Now stay there."

She nodded but her glare never left Kun. She was shaking.

"I've got things I have to do. You can help by translating for Corporal Nunn while he questions these bastards."

I handed Nunn the shotgun. "It was an accident. She slipped and the gun went off," I said.

"If you say so," Nunn said. Lajos Kun was seated on deck, one hand clutching his blasted ear. He reached with the other hand, imploring Nunn. "Officer? A moment, please?" he said.

I said, "Jeep, give me a hand." I turned away from Nunn and the Hungarian. The man didn't seem to be injured.

In a few moments we had the four Nazi casualties stretched out on the hatch cover. Jeep and I both had Class A industrial first aid tickets but I'd never seen anything like those steam burns. Jimmy Lee provided some of the answer to treating them. He produced a bucket of warm, salty water and began soaking them with it.

The most dangerous injury was to the man Tats had hit with the Browning. The nine millimeter slug was the variety fired by the Stirling sub-machine guns we'd found at the houseboat, a kind of metric magnum load. Brownings are the only handgun strong enough to fire the stuff safely. The slug had smashed ribs and punctured a lung, tumbled, mushroomed and left a ghastly exit wound. I made pneumo patches to stop the burble of blood and air he was losing and gave him a shot of morphine from the aid kit. A fraction to the right and she'd have shot him dead. We had to get him to a hospital soon if he was going to survive. He gave a choked cough, then, and I thought he'd stopped breathing. I moved to pull a blanket over him. But suddenly his rasping breathing began again. With any luck Nunn and his colleagues wouldn't be able to match his wounds to the gun Tats had been using.

"I am lousy shot tonight," Tats said from her perch on the corner of the hatch. "That gun kicks like hell." She massaged her wrists.

I said. "You took that joker out before he could wound or kill anyone. That's good shooting where I come from."

"He is dead?"

"No, but he might not make it."

"I am not sorry. Such scum don't...don't deserve..." She ran out of words, then. She was shaking and it had nothing to do with the night chill. Sorry would come later.

"Best if you don't admit that you're the one that shot him. The law gets sticky, even when it's self defense. Where in hell did you learn to shoot large military pistols?"

"On my uncle's target range. I am better with a Mauser."

"With a--?"

"Hank, give me a hand," Jeep hollered.

And I turned away to help him make a splint and a dressing for the cop from the police boat. His wrist was probably broken and he had a painful bullet crease from wrist to elbow to complicate things. His partner was aboard now, glaring around, confused. After all, this had started as a simple case of boat theft.

The *Solange* checked to her anchor, head to the current a few hundred yards from the *Dolores Olivera*. The ship wasn't going to sink after all but she was down by the stern and listing twenty degrees. A nice little salvage problem.

Tats slid off the hatch to stand, leaning against the deckhouse, arms folded in a posture of frustrated anger, holding my Indian sweater tight around her shoulders. She ignored my encouraging smile.

Junior poked his head out of a glassless wheelhouse window. "Is it over?" he quivered.

"Except for the bandages," I said.

"Er, bandages?"

"You aren't injured, are you?"

"Ah, no. I don't believe so."

"Good. Get us some coffee with a splash of brandy in it while we patch these guys up."

"Uh, coffee? Yes, of course."

When he'd gone, I said to Jeep, "We'll have to pick up the hook and move over to Steveston docks. That guy that Tats winged needs a hospital fast."

"She the one that got him?"

"Yeah. Why?"

"'Cause he don't need no hospital. He needs an undertaker," Jeep said.

"Jesus. He's dead?"

"As a doornail."

"Don't tell her that. She's already pretty shook up."

"You got it, skipper."

"We need some press out here. Make a good headline, don't you think?"

"Thought you didn't like those guys."

"Well Jeep, there are times for exceptions and I think this is one of them."

I called the two major newspapers and six radio news rooms plus the TV news people. Some of them didn't seem enthusiastic, at first. The middle of the Fraser River, in the middle of the night, isn't the easiest place to get to. But the hint of a major shoot-out and a rescued damsel in distress lured them. "What's she look like?" A newsie from a notoriously rednecked TV station demanded.

"Gorgeous," I said.

"Yeah? What's she wearing?"

"What the hell do you think she's wearing? She's just been through a fucking war."

"We'll meet you at the Steveston docks in half an hour." Chauvinist bastard.

"I am not gorgeous," Tats protested. "I am exhausted." Thank God. She was speaking to me again.

"I should have told them `dangerous' instead," I said.

She almost smiled. "Do not scold, please. I'm not proud of myself."

I knew how she felt, facing the killer of her parents. My consuming rage, when I'd damned near killed the jug-eared hit-man stalking Irene Bradshaw had left me with the same bitter residue of self-knowledge. Neither of us were the kind who took prisoners.

I said, "That Hungarian joker, Kun? He seemed to have a lot to say. What was that about?"

She looked away, taking a deep breath. "He tried to bargain with me," she said.

I should have pursued that but Junior appeared, juggling a tray of coffee mugs which he deposited on a locker-top beside Tats. "Er, Sutter...," he began, handing me a cup.

But Tats cut him off. "Oh Mister Picard! Thank you so much for everything you did for me."

"Thing...I did?"

"Loaning the *Miranda* to Hank. Without her, I would be dead. And then allowing the tug to be used by Corporal Nunn to catch these terrible people."

"I, ah..."

"The TV news people are coming with cameras and everything." Damn, she was a sly one. She knew how to push Junior's buttons. And mine, dammit.

"They are?" Junior brightened at the prospect, smoothed his droopy, smudged moustache.

"And I want to tell them that you made it all possible."

Junior looked like his mental processes had hit a brick wall. "I, ah...am happy to have been of service, Miss Kovacs. We cannot do enough to stamp out international criminal activities. Canada must take a leading part--"

"Junior," I said. "Save the press statement until they get here."

"Yes, of course," Junior said.

Pompous little bastard seemed to think he'd been in charge of everything from the beginning. But he'd undoubtedly get his senate appointment, or be made a parliamentary secretary, on the strength of his "heroic" part in Tats' rescue.

But Junior wasn't finished with me yet. "Er, Sutter, I wanted you to know that our firm, that is Picard and Son Navigation and Salvage, has had a change of management."

"Changed...?"

"My family and I have accepted an offer for a substantial block of shares from a Vancouver company. In fact a controlling interest. We intended to announce this at the November stockholder's meeting but our buyers asked that the change be made as quickly as possible. I have agreed that they will take full control at the end of this month."

I felt as if I'd been pole-axed. "What company? Another towing outfit?"

"No, I believe not. They have extensive marine holdings, however, and will appoint their own general manager shortly. They made an unusual request, specifically that the *Solange Picard's* status, and that of her crew, remain unchanged for the present. Therefore I have rescinded yours and Sawchuck's firings."

He walked away from me, puffed up with the fact that he'd dropped a zinger on me. And he still hadn't answered my question. What company?

"You look unwell, Hank," Tats said.

"Little shit just pulled the rug out from under me. As long as he was going to scrap the *Solange*, I had a chance of persuading his stockholders to sell her to me at some figure above her scrap price. Now I don't know what I'm dealing with."

"How much is your ship worth?"

"Depends on who is buying and selling. To build and equip a new ship like her would run fifteen million, minimum. But the demand for big steam pots isn't great. Taking age and the lack of bidders into account, maybe four million. Scrap yards would bid about a quarter million."

"You will find a way," she said, with total confidence and the damnedest Cheshire cat grin.

"Yeah?"

Jeep shouted, "Outboard comin' alongside. Tooey, go take their lines, 'fore they drown themselves."

"Come. The reporters are coming aboard," Tats said.

"Oh, shit. You can't let them interview you half naked like that."

"Why not? It isn't cold," she said, adjusting my Cowichan sweater down another scandalous notch.

C | H | A | P | T | E | R

24

Epilogue - August 1958

About sixty people gathered around Ella Feldman's pool on a Saturday afternoon late in August. The *Solange Picard's* crew, with wives and girl-friends, were a noisy mob. Only someone who knew them would realize they were a little subdued. Mick O'Conner and Dunc McAdams main-tained a semblance of quiet dignity but that could be blamed on age. Both had retired in November, leaving me in formal command of the ship with Cam as chief engineer. At the moment O'Conner was dipping into the non-alcoholic punch bowl, its only customer. Dunc dozed in a deck chair. The rest of them were getting blitzed.

Things had changed around the city. In June the unfinished second narrows bridge had collapsed, dropping span after span into the harbor like fallen dominos. And taking the lives of nineteen members of the Iron-workers Union. One had been Cam's younger brother.

The Sandheads Lightship broke free of her moorings and was driven ashore in a storm, the week after we rescued Tatiana. It hadn't been re-placed yet. I'm not sure we could have managed Tats' rescue without it. I guess God was paying attention part of the time.

I was unwinding after a long, rough, salvage job towing a broken-down Greek freighter in from the Gulf of Alaska. The Open Form Lloyds contract had been risky. No solution, no pay. But we'd been successful and the job had brought my fledgling company its first serious earnings. The shock of several weeks in the brutally frigid Gulf of Alaska right after three weeks in the sunny Caribbean was bad enough but then I'd gotten the shock of my life.

Tats had promised to explain herself, but with Tatiana, explanations were always "later." Today I was damned if I'd let her escape.

Chung Chuck had turned up, to everyone's surprise. He sat with Jimmy Lee, both sipping tea. Either Jimmy was bending Chung's ear about the restaurant business or Chung was holding forth on the finer points of potato growing. It seemed to be an animated conversation.

Hilda Brunning, without boyfriend David, sat with Jeanie Halford, my new office manager. Hilda would be starting work with us shortly.

Tats was in and out of the water like a seal and had lost the top of her bikini three times, so far. Keeping her clothed was about as difficult as keeping her fed, I was learning.

"Tats! Don't get sunburned. We can't give our audience roasted swans," Gowan shouted.

"We should open with Cleopatra. Then I can look like a Nubian," she said.

"Cleo was a Macedonian and whiter than you," Gowan said.

"Your backers came through, I gather," I said, putting an arm around a dripping Tats.

"Yes indeed," Gowan said. "And we have an anonymous donor who has been most generous. We will have thirty-five dancers and a full orchestra for our opening season."

"You don't know who your supporter is? Surely you've got some idea?"

"I don't know and I don't care to speculate. Anonymity was *the* condition of his support," Gowan said.

"How did he tell you that?"

"Not directly. The arrangement was made through a lawyer's office. He made other conditions, as well. Tats must continue as prima ballerina. No fear on that score. And he insists that she get three months off every summer. I think the chap must be smitten with her."

"Got my blessing," I said. "As long as he stays anonymous."

"Ooh. My monster is jealous," Tats said. "Must be feeding time." She dragged me away from Gowan and over to the buffet table to load up a platter of salad and cheeses and hot little sausages wrapped in pastry and stuffed mushroom caps. I went to take it from her, but with her mouth full, she said, "This is mine. Get your own."

Clara closed in on us. "Oh, there you are. Here, let me hold your plate, dear, while you put this on," she said, handing Tats the top of her suit. "I fished it out of the pool."

"Thanks," Tats mumbled, still chewing, and tucked the dripping garment into my pocket. I swatted at her wet backside and missed.

Clara looked dismayed but that didn't last. She shrugged and went off with the latin-looking band leader who'd brought her a drink.

Eventually I persuaded Tats to get decent. The wet top was dripping down my leg.

Ella Feldman shouted over the uproar, "I'm going to make a speech. Everybody please settle down and shut up."

"She's kidding, isn't she?" Jeep wondered.

"Hey, it's her party. She's entitled," I said.

Ella finally got the rowdy bunch assembled in some sort of order. She took the band leader's microphone and tapped it.

"This working? Oh, good. I won't spoil the party with a long speech but I need to say a few things. First of all, Senator Picard responded to my invitation. He was unable to attend but he has sent a most gracious telegram of congratulations to all who participated in last October's perilous rescue of Tatiana and the solution of Sandy's and my husband's murders.

The telegram is long so I will leave it on the lectern for all who wish to read it. "Senator Picard informs us that the five men being brought into Canada by the smuggling gang have been returned to the jurisdictions of their war crimes convictions."

Tats said. "They shot Kun in Budapest last week."

"Shh."

Ella continued. "As most of you know, my corporation, Seaford Maritime Enterprises, acquired a controlling interest in Picard and Son, Salvage and General Towing, at the beginning of November last year. The company has been renamed SME-Picard Navigation with new directors and financing so this is essentially a merger. I'm happy to tell you that business has been good since."

"Yeah, since she fired Junior," Jeep rumbled.

"Rumors have been flying, so to clarify things, I will explain the deal Hank and I have reached. First, I persuaded Mr. Picard that it would be in his interests to turn the *Solange Picard* over to me, as sole owner."

"How'd ya do that, Ella? Thumbscrews?"

I think it was Jeep.

"I offered him a better price than the Singapore scrap yards. But not as much as he wanted. And no, I didn't blackmail him." Her grin had a devilish twinkle that belied her words.

"Anyway, after several weeks of negotiations, Hank's and my lawyers have thrashed out a lease-back contract. Hank will take title to the *Solange Picard* and will operate as an associate company. SME-Picard's will provide any tugs or equipment he needs, under charter, to meet an overload of business. In return, SME-Picard's will be able to call on Hank and his ship, should they undertake any salvage jobs.

"Hank wore out a lot of shoe leather looking for finances to meet the guarantees required but I understand he has now solved that problem and the last legal hurdles were cleared early this week.

"So I am now in a position to offer the crew of the *Solange Picard* a choice. Up until this week, you have been on SME-Picard's payroll and I've been billing Hank for you. You may continue on it, in which case we will fit you in with our crews. Or you may go with Hank's new company. In either case, seniority, pensions and other benefits will continue unbroken. Can I have a show of hands, please? Who wishes to go with SME-Picard Navigation?"

Nobody moved.

"Those wishing to go with Sutter Salvage and Navigation?"

"Yay!" The hands shot up.

"I see. I believe Hank has pirated Jeanie Halford from me. Is that right, Jeanie?"

"He got me, Ella," Jeanie shouted, happily, from the back of the pack.

"Doesn't sound like there was much resistance there," Ella said, to general laughter. "But you've got yourself a hell of a manager, Hank.

"One last thing," Ella said. "Hank will share some office and dock space with us. Hank, your wharfage bill will be in the mail." That got a titter. "I thought I'd better get this said while you were all still more or less upright. That's all for now. Hank? You want to say something?"

"No."

But Tats pushed me so that I stumbled over Jeep's feet and into Ella's hands. She stuck the mike in mine.

"Just…thanks to all the people who did things for us at the right moment last October. You all know who you are. Oh, and a special thanks to my crew who found themselves at risk without being asked. And nobody quit or even filed a grievance. That's it. End of speech."

I gave the mike back to Ella who said, "If you've got questions, just ask me. Oh, I almost forgot. Your cars are all stuck behind some road building machinery that somehow got parked blocking my driveway." (Groans) "So taxis will be standing by to take anyone home, later tonight. Have fun."

She gave the microphone back to the band leader. The band started on something Latin.

"Time for your tango lesson, monster," Tats said.

"Not unless you get dressed," I said.

"You don't like me this way?"

"Love you this way. That's the damned trouble. Doing a tango in this condition could be dangerous."

"Oh? You need to cool off?" And she shoved me into the pool. That seemed to be a popular move and several more dressed and semi-dressed people landed in the water beside me. Soon a conga line was threshing around in the shallow end.

I crawled out and made my way to the row of changing rooms, along the back side of the pool, where I tried to change in spite of Tats, who had different ideas about what the little changing rooms were for. Eventually I made it into a tee-shirt and a pair of cut-offs, the only clothes I owned that were dry. Tats rummaged in my carryall bag and fished out a skirt. She shimmied into it, keeping her treacherous bikini top more or less on.

As we passed the end cubicle on our way back to the pool deck, I swear I heard Jeep's voice and a feminine giggle. I looked around. Neither Jeep nor Irene Bradshaw were in sight on the pool deck. I spotted McRae and Nunn, late arrivals, at the buffet table. Nunn had a tall drink in hand.

"Do you have to talk to them?" Tats pouted. "After I got dressed so you would dance with me?"

That was "dressed?" Ye Gods!

"Nice party," McRae said.

"Ella throws a good one," I said.

"Should be more handy road-building machinery around. Keep all you drunks off the road."

"Devious lady, that Ella."

"We got four guys going to trial in September. Guess the prosecutor's office has been in touch with you?"

"They have. They're going for first degree murder, I gather. The whole gang could hang."

"Naw. Too many bleedin' hearts around, these days," McRae said. "Immigration is giving the ex Gestapo types a hard look. Be a waste of time to try 'em here when they've both got death sentences waiting for them at home. The local talent?" McRae snorted. "The poor chaps all had terrible childhoods. Got beat up at school. Shit like that. Pock marks, they might stretch, but if they do it'll probably be the last hanging before Ottawa does away with capital punishment. Speaking of him, are you going to tell me what you did to the bastard's ears? The MO wants to know as well."

"Why nothing. What was wrong with his ears?"

"Damned near doesn't have any left. That's what," McRae said.

I turned to Nunn. "Heard you got a commendation along with your stripe, sergeant," I said.

"I did, thanks to you, Sutter." He gave me a grudging half smile.

"It was a joint effort. We needed each other to get the thing done. They didn't recall you to Ottawa?"

"Not yet," he said. "Still have a few loose ends of the case to tie up, out here on the coast."

"Oh? Like what?"

"Like their finances. They had less than ten thousand in cash. Not much for an operation like that. With the South American end of the thing, it looks like it was going to be a regular pipeline for itinerant Nazis."

"I heard there was a second ship under charter through the same shipping outfit. That check out?"

"We're still looking at it. The latinos aren't very helpful. Guess they'd just as soon be rid of the bastards. But that Hungarian joker claimed they had their funds in a bag of about two pounds of rare diamonds. Says Miss Kovacs stole them from him."

"You searched her aboard the tug, didn't you?"

"Uh, yes." Nunn colored. "She certainly had no place to hide anything, I have to admit. Maybe he was just blowing smoke."

Time to change the subject before I got in the glue. "But you got back to `B' division?"

"Not at liberty to say."

"Congratulations." I turned to McRae. "Sergeant, I hear you were commended as well."

"You ain't gonna tell me about his ears, huh?"

"Nope."

"Never mind. We got some wild yarn from the coal truck driver. He thinks you're a homicidal maniac."

"They didn't give you the commendation?"

"Yeah, they did. I hear Picard dropped his charges about you swiping his speedboat and hijacking the tug. How'd you manage that?"

"Oh, well, it seems Junior had the *Miranda* listed as a company vessel. Utility runabout or something. So he could charge off his expenses against taxes. Revenue Canada was a mite curious about that and to make all his tax scams stick, he had to claim the boat wasn't his personal property. That Ella's new company now owns it. Which, strictly speaking, is true. The newspapers made Picard such a hero he had to drop the rest of his charges or risk blowing his shiny new image. To hear him tell it, he masterminded Tats' rescue from the beginning."

"I heard the police boat detachment sent him a bill for their time and gas," McRae said. "Speaking of masterminding, you considered the department's offer?"

"Very kind of them but no, I don't want to be a cop again. I've got a new company to run."

Tats tugged at my arm. "Tango time, monster." She moved to drag me off.

"Did you get my tickets, Miss Kovacs?" Nunn asked.

"Yes. See me before you go," she said, over her shoulder as she steered me away.

"What tickets?" I demanded. We slid into our version of the tango. People gathered to watch us and it wasn't because of my dancing, though I suppose a guy in cut-offs dancing a tango with a barefoot lady wearing a split skirt and a perilous bikini top was some kind of spectacle.

"For the ballet," she said. "Our opening season. Sergeant Nunn asked for tickets to all our performances."

"Free tickets?"

"Of course. I can have a hundred if I want them."

"Little unusual, isn't it?"

"Why? Jeep asked for tickets as well. Vancouver is a, mm, sophisticated city for dancing."

"Jeep? Oh come on! Jeep?"

"He is bringing Irene Bradshaw. I got them backstage passes, too."

I had to admit that Irene had been a great civilizing influence on my cousin. Jeep usually kept his shoelaces tied these days and there were rumors he'd been seen wearing a tie. I said, "What in hell does an educated girl like Irene see in cousin Jeep?"

"What I see in you. Animal."

"What do you know about the benefactor who's dropping all this money on Gowan?"

"Nothing. Not a thing," she said. Turning away from me and then spinning back, under my arm. Flashing a lot of thigh. Did she own any skirts that weren't split to the hip?

"Methinks she doth protest too much," I said, leaning over her. Tangos are good for inquisitions.

"What funny English. I can't look in your eyes and dance at the same time."

"Shakespeare. You can't look me in the eye, woman, because you know something."

"There. The music has stopped. Come and get me a drink."

So I got her a double Black Russian, her favorite. And another plate of sandwiches. And cornered her in Ella's garden gazebo, a safe distance from the pool.

"This deal of Gowan's sounds suspiciously like your deal with me, Miss Kovacs. You promised to explain everything and I've been in town all week, waiting for you to talk."

"Ooh. My monster growls."

"We've had this conversation before," I said. "So stop clowning and tell me where the money came from."

A million dollars in financial guarantees had turned up, out of the blue, on Monday of last week, allowing my deal with SME-Picard to be finalized. I'd refused to accept it without knowing the source, so three days later, over breakfast at Blossom's, Tats had confessed. She would be my silent partner. No silence. No deal. I'd made her promise to explain, without a lawyer being in the room, and by God now was the time.

"It was an accident." She sipped at her drink, watching me over the brim of her glass.

"What was?"

"You remember that last day aboard the Solange, when you had subdued the fascists?"

"I'll never forget it."

"And you stopped me from killing Lajos Kun?"

I'd told so many people the same thing I'd told Nunn about that frightening incident, that she'd slipped and the shotgun had gone off accidentally, that I'd come almost to believe it myself. I knew better.

"You'd be in jail for the rest of your life. I couldn't believe you'd chuck your career and let that happen."

She gave me a smoldering look. "You saved his life. And maybe mine. I would have killed him and to hell with police and judges. He knew it. He tried to bargain."

"Bargain for what?"

"His life."

"For what? What was the rest of the bargain?"

"He had a bag of diamonds and emeralds. It is a compact way to carry a lot of money."

"You traded his life for diamonds?"

"Not exactly. After you took my gun away you remember I tried to scratch his eyes out?"

"Yeah. Damned near did it, too."

"I got his diamonds then."

"In a trade?"

"I just took them. His life wasn't mine to trade. The communists in Budapest had things to settle with him, too. But you pulled me away from him so I guess I traded him a few months. I didn't get to cut his throat right then." I stared at her.

"Cut his throat? With what, for God's sake?"

"Scissors. I got them from Jimmy Lee when I was trying to make your shirt into a blouse. They were in the pocket of my Indian sweater. They are lousy knife."

"Thank God! And you took his diamonds? How much were they worth?"

"A lot."

"Jesus Christ almighty! How much?!"

"Shh. Keep your voice down. The diamonds are what they call Argyle Pinks. From Australia. Very rare. One eleven carat stone sold for three hundred thousand dollars. That's all I will tell you."

"Jesus!...How many?"

She wouldn't answer me. I stared into those dark, mysterious eyes and wondered if I knew this woman I loved, or if I ever would know her. I thanked God she hadn't succeeded in killing Lajos Kun. "And you're going to keep them?" I asked.

"Why not? Kun sent thousands to the death camps. Think of me as, mm, proxy of all those people. If the police found the diamonds, the government would take."

"How...? I mean...where did you put them? I didn't see anything."

"At first I hid in your baggy sweater. Then in the box beside the hatch, where Junior put the coffee tray. They were in a chamois leather bag."

"You sold some? How in hell did you manage it?"

"I took a few to a, mm, dealer? in the city."

"Dealer? You trusted some shady character? A guy who could lay hands on more than a million bucks in cash?"

"I don't trust, but he wants more at this price and he will keep his mouth shut."

My God. My love had a streak of peasant merchant in her a yard wide. "Does anyone know?"

"Lajos Kun has very bad English but he tried to, mm, bribe Sergeant Nunn. And buy his freedom with diamonds he didn't any more have. He tells Nunn I stole them. But he doesn't know about policemen who do not take bribes. Sergeant Nunn was there when you pulled me away from choking that bastard. He saw no more than you."

"And whatever else Nunn may be, he isn't crooked. Did he question you?"

"Yes. I showed him I had no place to hide anything."

"Is that why Nunn was so flustered?"

"Maybe. Canadian men are funny that way," she said, looking at me as if I were an especially peculiar example.

"What way?"

"Never mind. So Nunn didn't believe him."

"You think...Jesus, Tats."

"You think Sergeant Nunn doesn't believe me?"

"No more than I believe. Your diamond-selling expedition in East Vancouver is the biggest crock of shit I've heard in years."

"Crock of...? That means you don't believe?" Injured innocence, writ large.

"Tats! You asked me to be your detective. Right? Did you think I was some kind of idiot?"

She sighed. "No. You are too clever for me. I didn't sell them myself. I had help."

"Who?"

"Ella Feldman sold them in New York for me, as part of Mr. Feldman's estate. You mustn't let her know I told you."

"I won't. Just pray Nunn doesn't get wind of that. Snooping into whatever you are doing is his hobby. If he finds out about our deal he'll be onto you like a bloodhound."

"Why would he? I don't spend any money I can't explain and my bank account still has only fifty-three dollars."

"Why don't you just retire? We could buy a villa on the Riviera. Live happily ever after?"

298 | EUGENE JAMES |

"Who is this `we'? I am business woman and we are talking about a trust fund, not spending money. You will make our company work. Just as Donal Gowan must make a success of his ballet company."

I stared at her, blankly. This was a pragmatic, hard-headed Tatiana I'd never met. Or maybe I had and hadn't recognized the signs. For instance the day she'd shot two people and tried for a third.

"And now Nunn is a member of the ballet public."

"Yes." She watched me from beneath downcast lashes. Not contrite, exactly, but worried about my reaction. Or lack of it. I was too numb to react.

"What happens if he finds out you are the mysterious admirer of Miss Kovacs, the famous ballerina? And then puts that together with my new silent partner?"

"I don't know. Possibly I will need your help."

"Aha! That's why you are keeping me around? To keep you out of jail?"

"Why else?" she said, laughing, all sweet innocence. "But I do everything through lawyers and numbered companies. Even the lawyers don't know who I am so Sergeant Nunn will have a long search."

"The guy's a career flatfoot. About as cultured as a clam. Why do you think he's taken a sudden interest in the ballet?"

"I think maybe he is silent admirer. After he watched me in Don Quixote, he told Donal he thought I was `pretty good'."

"Nunn did?"

"Donal was upset at his choice of words."

"I can't imagine why. You just couldn't resist negotiating yourself a holiday clause?" I grinned.

She thawed a little with my smile, relieved. "Mmm? You think I should ask for more time?"

"You'd never get away with it. Tats, you are an enigma," I said.

"Sexy, too?" She closed in on me, dropping the bikini top. Stepping out of the skirt.

"God, yes."

"I am Magyar. That is enough mystery."

"The Magyar cipher. Until Nunn figures you out."

"Until then." She kissed me.

ISBN 142515116-7

9 781425 151164